DESTINY'S CHOICE

The Raymouth Saga / Book 3

J R Clemons

VERSION 1

ISBN 979-8-9876839-4-1 *(paperback)*

ISBN 979-8-9876839-5-8 *(ebook)*

A man will come to change the fate of the clans and the king-
doms.
He will come from an unimaginable distance and live his life
in the life of another.
The clans will rise with him and a daughter.
He will be a warrior, a hero, and a legend.
Good will flow from him for a thousand years.

Prophecy of the Ancients

HIGH KINGDOM

Blue and White Mountain Clans

CRAG
D'ZOO

LEDEN GRUBI

CASTLE

TEARDROP
KINGDOM

SHAH TRECERE

RAYMOUTH

PORT

PRIMA TRECERE

CAPITAL
CITY

CRESCENT

RESSETT

OTT

BLOUNTSMYTH

WEIRSHEM

TALLON

OTOK

TRADE ROUTE

BELLOWS

NATAS
KINGDOM

COUNCIL
OF
JUSTICE

CHAPTER 1

'VENTURE

"Petri," Prince Merryk yelled as he walked into the stable. From the far end of the row of stalls, a sandy-haired young man replied, "Here, Your Highness. What can I do for you?"

"It is a beautiful summer's day. I was thinking it might be a good day for an adventure," Merryk answered.

A couple of small heads popped out from behind a pile of hay. "I like 'ventures," Maizie said.

"Me too," JoJo echoed.

"Perhaps Goliath would like to take the wagon this morning to see Ali and the new construction."

"I am sure he would. Just give me a few minutes," Petri answered.

"You two," Merryk said, directing his attention to the small waifs. "Go tell Jane. She and anyone who wants, can come with us. I will ask Nelly to pack us a lunch. But hurry! Maverick and Goliath wait for no one."

Captain Yonn was forced to step out of the way as two young ruffians scurried out of the barn. "What is all the commotion?"

"Ven—," was all he heard as the two fled.

"They are coming with us. I need to check on the construction of the homes for Ali's family and the new winter stables," Merryk replied. "And Tara wants to verify the two hundred horses for shipment to Masterroff."

"Speaking of Masterroff, the swordmaster confirmed they have the relay system working between here and the Capital City. Masterroff's last report came to the Chancellor in a day."

"Good. Did he say if he got a message to Bowen?"

"The swordmaster and Chancellor Goldblatt thought Masterroff could get a message to Bowen with the least attention. The last time the sword-master showed up was with Father Bernard. They were concerned his going to the castle again would attract attention and put extra pressure on Bowen."

"We need to protect Bowen. As a member of the king's personal guard, he is our best connection to the king. I feel better knowing we have some way of getting information. Now Bowen or Masterroff can let us know of events in time so we may respond."

"Respond. To what?" Tara asked as she and Yvette entered the stable.

"Nothing specific. We just expanded the relay system to allow for messengers to come from the Capital City," Merryk answered. "Now let's get this adventure started."

It took Petri less time to get the wagon and the four Clydesdales ready than Jane needed to gather the children and lunches. However, with minimal delay, the wagon was loaded with the children. Maizie had taken the spot in the center of the front seat between Jane and Petri. JoJo and John sat with their legs hanging over the back of the wagon. Soon, the entire group headed out of the main castle gate into the village.

The village was bustling with the mid-summer market. Fresh vegetables, early fruits, milk and cheese, and a wide assortment of necessities like saddles and blankets were all on sale. People from all around had come to the village. Blue-and-White Mountain Clansmen mixed freely with the locals. The whole place seemed very happy and secure.

"I cannot believe this village, just a few months ago, was completely abandoned and marked for destruction," Tara said.

"I remember coming down this road with no one around. The quiet was as frightening as the Army of Justice outside," Yvette said.

"It was unnerving to go out the gates to face the five thousand Judges," Yonn added. "Our horses and the wind were the only sounds after the drums stopped."

"The space on the other side of war always seems better," Merryk said. Changing the subject, "I have been told the engineers are making good progress on the houses and the stables. They also finished the bridges across the river."

After the group exited the gate in the old wall, everything seemed to open up. All the destruction from the breached dams had been masked by a burst of spring greenery. Only occasional logs sticking out of the soggy ground gave any indication of the spring's events.

"I can never cross this plain without thinking about the two hundred and fifty men we never found. This is their burial site," Prince Merryk said, as he looked pensively across the grass.

"You did what you had to do," Tara said, reaching out to touch Merryk's arm. "If you had not acted, none of us would be here and the children would be without a home."

After crossing a new bridge, it was only five minutes to the construction site. The engineers had made quick work of the new stables for the breeding stock and new homes for the wranglers. Already the main stable's external frame and roof were in place. The homes, Merryk's priority, already had their siding.

Ali and several of his sons stood at the edge of the road to greet their guests.

"Great Prince and Missy Princess, your presence honors us," Ali said as he and his sons bowed respectfully.

"It is our honor to visit you," Tara replied in conformity with Ali's custom.

"Prince Merryk! Prince Merryk! Can we go play with Ali's children?" an insistent Maizie asked.

"If it's all right with Jane and Yvette, but do not go far. We cannot stay too long," Merryk answered. At his words, the children bolted from the back of the wagon like cats escaping from a box. Everyone went in a different direction.

"I hope we can find them when we are ready to leave," Yvette said. "I will go and speak with Sarai." Yvette moved a short distance, then returned to the prince. "Your Highness, what do you think about asking Sarai to bring her children to the school, two or three days a week? We could work on their reading and numbers."

"An excellent idea, but ultimately, Ali and Sarai must decide what they think is best. Also, you may find they have already taught their children numbers beyond ours. Ali's people are mathematicians of great fame. They invented the number zero."

Yvette looked puzzled by his answer.

"Not important," Merryk said, shaking his head. "Yvette, you are in charge of the school. Do what you think best. From my point of view, the more educated people are, the better."

"Thank you, Your Highness."

"Ali, we would like to see the herds and the new construction," Tara said.

"Yes, Missy Princess. If you and the Great Prince will follow me." Ali and his sons mounted their horses and moved beyond the construction to the herds. "As you instructed, we have moved all the breeding stock away from the general herd. We have kept each breed separate. The new stables and the corrals will make this easier," Ali said. "We have selected two hundred horses for transfer to the port. They can leave tomorrow if that is your will."

"Where is Raj?" Tara asked.

Ali's eyes scanned the grass field. "There," he said, pointing to the stallion in a group of mares.

"Tara placed her fingers to her lips and produced a loud high-pitched whistle. The stallion raised his head to locate the sound. Then, with an effortless stride, he erased the distance to come to Tara.

"I see you still remember how to call him," Ali said.

"It was the first thing you taught me," Tara said with pride.

Tara handed Bella's reins to Merryk and jumped to the ground to greet the horse. She wrapped her arms around his neck, and he turned his head to clasp her in a hug with his neck. "How are you adjusting to your new home?" Tara asked.

The horse bobbed his head up and down

"He loves to run in the big open fields," Ali said. "But I will be happy when I can get him inside at night. We hear wolves. With all the young foals, they would be easy prey. I am afraid he will seek to defend the herd and be injured."

"Captain Yonn, ask the clansmen who are their best at hunting wolves," Prince Merryk instructed. "And until we destroy the wolves and get the stables done, send extra men out here at night to help Ali and his sons protect the herd."

"Thank you, Great Prince. We appreciate your support," Ali said.

———

As Yvette expected, it took some time to gather the children back into the wagon, but ultimately, all were in their places.

"Ali, I am going to send a wagon for your family. This will make it easier for your children to come to school. It will be for your use as you see fit.

I assume you will find appropriate horses to pull it," Prince Merryk said with a smile.

"Thank you, Great Prince. Yes, we can find the right horses." Ali's face beamed as he bowed his head. "May your journey be safe and please return often."

Chapter 2

SUMMONS

The two golden eagles, who claimed the floodplain as home, were making their first flights of the day. From the top of the tower, Merryk had watched their aerie grow in a large fir tree on the ridge top. *Perhaps this year I will see some young. It is going to be hot today. The morning air is already warming.*

A rider, hastily crossing the gap in the trees at the bottom of the plain, caught Merryk's eye. *It is unusual for the morning courier to be here so early.* The rider disappeared into the forest road. Merryk moved to the other side of the tower to watch for his exit.

The clansman wasted no time after entering the gate and went directly to the guards. Merryk caught the words, 'important and urgent.'

By the time the courier had reached the back door of the old castle, Merryk was there to greet him.

"Your Highness, I have an urgent message for you and Chancellor Goldblatt from Monsieur Masterroff."

"Thank you," Merryk said as he accepted the note. "Smallfolks," the prince called, and without waiting for a reply, continued. "Find Chancellor Goldblatt and have him join me in the study."

"Yes, Your Highness," Smallfolks answered from just outside of view. *How does he do that? He is always there when I need him.*

———— ❈ ————

Chancellor Goldblatt was waiting by the time Prince Merryk reached the study. "What do we have?" he asked.

"Some kind of summons, and a letter from Masterroff. You read his letter and I will review the summons," Merryk replied.

Both men took a few moments to read the parchments. As they did, Captain Yonn entered the room. "Good," the prince said. "I'm glad you're here."

The prince began. "This is a formal summons to the king's court this coming Friday, midmorning, to hear the petition of the Duke of Ressett to the king for the restoration of personal property currently being sold unlawfully by Masterroff. In addition, it says, Masterroff is selling illegally seized horses belonging to the duke. He is demanding an immediate return of the horses and a full accounting for any sold. It also asked that any other seized property be returned to their rightful owners. He makes the last petition as an act of a noble person for the greater good. Chancellor Bates signed it."

Goldblatt continued, "Masterroff says the duke has been attempting to rally other nobles to support his position. It pleased Masterroff to learn they hated him less than the duke. Ressett was, however, successful in getting Chancellor Bates to support his petition, and Masterroff's sources say he has the support of Prince Merreg, although in the background. This is a clever ploy. There are two petitions in one. The first is about horses, and the second hidden one is about ships. If they convince the king to give preference to the duke's claim, they may also get the ships back for King Natas and the Council."

"It's a good thing we have Masterroff to represent us," Prince Merryk said

"Unfortunately, Masterroff's brilliance does not extend to arguing before a group of people. It was the only thing he struggled with in school. Also, he does not understand the legal aspects of war, as I would," Chancellor Goldblatt said.

"What are you suggesting?" Merryk asked.

"An adverse ruling would require you to give up all you have gained. Refusing would be an act of rebellion against an order from the king. I need to represent you before the tribunal."

"How are you going to do that? It is already Wednesday," Captain Yonn said.

"Masterroff sent this message yesterday. He used the new relay system. I think the duke is counting on our inability to know what is happening until it is too late," Prince Merryk said. "Chancellor, I agree there is no better person than you to defend our claims. If you could make the evening tide, you should arrive on Friday morning. You would need to ride at the pace of the couriers. Do you think you can do it, or should I go?" Prince Merryk asked.

"Flushing you out of the Teardrop may be the reason for this action. Your safety would be compromised by going. No, you cannot go. I will make the journey." Goldblatt stood immediately and began picking books from the shelves. "Excuse me, I need to gather a few things." Looking over his shoulder as he left the room, "I just hope I do not fall off the horse," Chancellor Goldblatt said with a brave smile.

Merryk turned to Yonn. "Go to the stables and pick the softest saddle you can find and send the swordmaster with him. I am not the only person others wish dead."

———⊰❧⊱———

"It is barely midmorning. Where are the Chancellor and the swordmaster going in such a hurry?" Princess Tara asked as she joined Merryk on the back wall of the castle.

"They need to catch the evening tide," Merryk answered.

"The evening tide! They will need to ride like the wind."

"Our future depends on it," Merryk said. Merryk took a few moments to explain to Tara the letter and the summons. "One of us needed to be there, either the Chancellor or myself."

"Why did you not go?" Tara asked.

"Goldblatt thought it might be a trap to get me out of the Teardrop."

"This is exactly the kind of plot father would plan. But the petition, in and of itself, is also a trap. The only thing better for them than the return of the property would be to drive a wedge between you and the king. It would assure Prince Merreg would be king."

"Prince Merreg will be king. I do not want any conflict between him or my father. The Chancellor's representation is our best defense."

Changing the subject, Prince Merryk said, "Now, have you seen the progress made in the dams? With the extra manpower, we should be done in a little more than a week."

Seven hours later, a road-worn Chancellor Goldblatt and swordmaster arrived in Newport. "We need to go directly to the docks," the swordmaster said.

At the first dock, the *Trident* sat at loose slip; a single gangplank connected it to the land.

"The tide is turning. It is now or never," Admiral Bellows shouted from the wheel deck to the two travelers. "All hands prepare to depart!"

The Chancellor had barely touched the deck when the "Drop sails" command rang out. The wind caught the sheets with a snap and the *Trident* moved into the evening sunset.

"How did you know to expect us?" Goldblatt asked the Admiral.

"Masterroff and I share a love of veal and fine red wine. He sent me a note explaining the situation. He said he needed help. Only two choices made sense, you or the prince. Either would need a ship, and if you did not come this evening, it would not matter. You were the wisest choice, but it was even money if the prince would have tried to spare you the ride. Also, I thought the whole thing might be a trap, and if so, you are the most expendable."

"Thank you for reminding me, but you are right. In the end, I convinced him his safety was the most important," Goldblatt said.

"I should have known he would listen to reason. I continue to learn about our prince."

"As do we all."

CHAPTER 3

DUKE VS. PRINCE

"The corridors are crowded today," the swordmaster said, as he and Goldblatt made their way to the throne room. The swordmaster stopped in an alcove and removed from his bag a deep blue cloak with gold trim, the mark of the king's personal guard. "Queen Amanda had this made for me. I thought it might be useful."

"We may need it. They have shut the doors and appear to be turning people away," Goldblatt said.

Two regular army men stood at the door. Approaching, the swordmaster said, "My instructions are to escort this man to the king."

"Prince Merreg has instructed us not to allow any to enter."

"My instructions are from the king. Step aside," the swordmaster said with the voice of command. The men at the door recognized the tone, if not the authority, and opened the door to allow them to enter.

The room was packed with people. Almost all wore garments indicative of their noble birth. There was an empty square directly in front of King Michael and Queen Amanda. The air held a tinge of electricity, like the feeling before lightning strikes.

"Everyone knows this is important," Goldblatt said under his breath to the swordmaster. "I will take it from here, thank you."

Chancellor Bates opened, "Your Majesty, the matter before the court is a petition by the Duke of Ressett, seeking restitution from Monsieur Masterroff. Both parties are present."

"Your Majesty, I am only an agent," Masterroff said. "My principal should be the one to speak to these claims. We received notice of this hearing on Monday afternoon, not nearly enough time for him to attend or to give me instructions."

"People work on the king's time. The notice was properly given, and you are here. I think Monsieur Masterroff, you are stalling," Chancellor Bates said with sarcasm.

"But I am just an agent," Masterroff inserted. "Fairness would dictate a delay."

Chancellor Bates did not like being opposed. He started to comment when a voice broke across the room.

"Excuse me, Your Majesty, I am sorry to be late. The tides were favorable, but the streets are more congested than I remember."

The Lord Chamberlain dropped his steel-tipped staff to the marble floor and announced, "His Excellency, Chancellor Geoffrey Goldblatt."

Bates looked at Ressett. Ressett looked at Prince Merreg. They had expected only Masterroff.

"You mean ex-chancellor," Bates said, feeling intimidated by his famous predecessor.

"No, I am the Chancellor for his Royal Highness Prince Merryk Raymouth, the rightful owner of all the property subject to this petition." Turning to the king and queen, "Your Majesties, your son, and Princess Tarareese send their best wishes and apologize for not being able to be present."

"Perfectly understandable," King Michael said with a warm smile. "Well, everyone seems to be here now. Duke, proceed."

The Duke of Ressett took a deep breath and moved to the center of the open square to begin. "The facts are quite simple, and the solution is very clear. Earlier this year, a long-term business associate, King Natas, contacted me. He needed three hundred horses for a short period. As a favor, I loaned him the horses. I did not know what he intended, but we have exchanged breeding stock before, so this did not seem unusual.

"You can understand my surprise to hear the horses had been seized by Prince Merryk as part of his unexplained victory over the Army of Justice. I was even more astonished to hear Monsieur Masterroff, as agent for the prince, was selling the horses to my customers at an increased price.

"As further injustice, the prince did not seize everyone's property, only some. Prince Merryk seized ships owned by King Natas and the Council of Justice but allowed independent merchant ships to go. In fact, he even paid them to deliver his stolen goods."

A murmur rippled through the crowd.

"If the prince recognizes the independent nature of the ships, he should also accept the independent nature of my horses. They were in the Teardrop as beasts of burden, not unlike the ships."

A few heads bobbed in acknowledgment of the argument.

"Not only was I treated unfairly, but the prince's right to seize property at all is in question. The Council of Justice has the right and the duty under the Faith to discipline those who transgress. Surely, we cannot have the church's property seized when they were doing their duty.

"The solution is as clear as the facts, restitution for my horses and for all others who have been similarly harmed. As a member of nobility, I make this request for the greater good."

Pleased with his presentation, Ressett looked first at Chancellor Bates, then bowed to the king and stepped aside.

"You said the facts are clear," Goldblatt stated. "But I, for one, am confused by your description. If I may ask a few questions, Your Majesty?"

King Michael nodded his head.

"Duke, you are a noble, but you are also a man of business. You are in the business of breeding and selling horses. How long have you been engaged in this endeavor?"

"My family has been breeding horses for over four hundred years."

"How long have you been a friend of King Natas?"

"I did not say we were friends. We are long-term business associates."

"How much did you charge King Natas for the use of the independent beasts of burden?"

"Nothing, it was a favor."

"The fact then, as an experienced businessman, you loaned for three or four months, without charging, three hundred horses to an associate who is not your friend. If this is normal, who else have you loaned hundreds of horses to?"

"No one. As a practice, it would not be prudent."

"If I told you three thousand horses were seized, of which you say three hundred are yours, how do you know the horses being sold by Monsieur Masterroff belong to you? Are they branded?"

"No, but they must be mine or you have mine. Either way, I want them back. They were seized illegally."

"You keep saying that. Do you have any firsthand knowledge of why the Council of Justice invaded the Teardrop Kingdom, a part of the High Kingdom?"

"Not firsthand, but they would not have acted without justification."

"If they had no justification, would the invasion be an act of war?"

The duke paused and his face tightened. Clearly, he knew where this question would lead. "I am sure the Council was justified," he said with confidence.

"Very interesting. Because the Council itself is uncertain. In the words of the new Provost, *the incursion may not have been justified*. Your Majesty has talked with Father Bernard, who at the time of the invasion was the secretary to the Provost. He identified the actions as being done for the benefit of King Natas to gain part of the High Kingdom—a disguised act of war.

"The attack on the Teardrop Kingdom was an 'act of war' and the rules award to the victor, the spoils. Prince Merryk was not obligated to release the independent merchant ships, but realized they had not transferred soldiers, horses, or arms. He was merciful. That mercy cannot now be used against him.

"The ships of King Natas and the Council transported men, weapons, and horses to the Teardrop to effect the invasion. The seizure was justified, as was the seizure of arms and horses, the tools of war."

The duke's face turned red with anger.

"If your Majesty will allow, I have only two more questions." The king nodded.

"Duke, did you know King Natas was going to use the horses to support the invasion of the Teardrop Kingdom?"

"Absolutely not."

"My last question. Either you knew King Natas' intent and gave him the horses to support an act against the kingdom, or you are a fool of a businessman because no one would loan three hundred horses without payment. Which is it? Are you a conspirator of treason against the throne or a fool?"

The duke's eyes now burned with rage and hatred. A swell of whispers ran through the crowd at the mention of treason.

Before anyone could speak, Prince Merreg interrupted. "Father, this has gone too far. The duke is from a noble house. His word is entitled to belief and support. We cannot allow it to be questioned by a mere chancellor. Even if the duke knew of King Natas's purpose, it would not mean he was engaged in treason."

Goldblatt interjected, "Your Majesty, the young prince does not mean to imply he supports actions against the kingdom. I am sure he remembers the unfortunate history of the duke's father and Great King Mikael."

"I remember the history well, and I will be the judge of what is too far," King Michael said, looking directly at his son.

"Enough arguments. In this matter, I agree with the duke." Ressett looked at Chancellor Bates with a smile. Masterroff looked at Goldblatt, his face filled with apprehension. "As he said at the beginning of this hearing, *the facts are clear and so is the solution*. Based upon the evidence presented, including the sworn testimony of Secretary Bernard, the invasion of the Teardrop was an unjustified 'act of war.' Once Prince Merryk defeated the aggressor, the spoils of war were his to do with as he saw fit.

"Duke of Ressett, I want to believe you are not foolish enough to repeat the errors of your father. But it is also hard for me to believe you would loan three hundred horses, without charge, to an associate, whom you do not consider a friend, and not at least ask why he needed them. If you did, then you are not the businessman we all thought." The king stared at the duke for an uncomfortable moment, then took a breath, looked around the room. "That is all for today."

With the last pronouncement, the Lord Chamberlain banged his staff. The king and the queen stood, and everyone bowed as they left the room.

As Chancellor Goldblatt picked up his satchel, Masterroff came to him. "I was afraid you would not receive my message, or you would come too late. The only thing I could think of was to stall."

"Admiral Bellows said you now owe him a dinner of veal and red wine and..." Chancellor Goldblatt's sentence was cut short as rough hands grabbed his shoulder and spun him around to face Prince Merreg.

"You need to be careful, old man," Merreg said with a snarl.

Before he could say more, the swordmaster physically placed himself between the prince and the Chancellor. "You need to be careful, young man," the swordmaster said.

The two men locked eyes. A physical confrontation was averted only when an aide to the prince interrupted. "Your Highness, the king wishes to see you immediately. He is waiting just outside."

"This is not over," the prince said.

"It never is," the swordmaster replied.

Chapter 4

After

Prince Merreg found his father waiting in the corridor room, a long narrow room with doors on each end, designed to hurry the king in and out of the throne room. As the prince entered the room, King Michael turned to Queen Amanda. "You should go on ahead. I want to talk to Merreg. I will not be long."

"As you wish," Queen Amanda said.

When the door shut behind her, King Michael began, "Why do you insist on such reckless speeches? I warned you before when you took the position of the Provost over your brother. Today, you disregarded the warning and did so in front of the full chamber of nobility. Your statement of support for the duke could be interpreted as a conflict with me. Chancellor Goldblatt attempted to save you from your blunder. You were supporting what may have been treason. Only a fool would believe the duke loaned the horses without asking why. But your statement of support made you that fool.

"Raymouths stick together. They never take a position against the family. I could understand your blunder if there were a good reason. But you heard exactly what Father Bernard said. You know it was an invasion of a part of our territory.

"Also, your comments strengthen the duke's position with some of the other nobles. We hold the throne, but we cannot allow opposition groups to gain too much strength, or our hold will be weakened."

"I was just trying to let everyone know I supported the nobility. I will always give them the extra credence," Prince Merreg said.

"Sometimes you need to slap them down so they do not believe they have independence. You must be jealous of your power. The king holds all the power. Others have power only because the king allows it," King Michael said. "Do you understand?"

"Yes, but Merryk seems to be gathering power for himself."

"Merryk is one of us, a Raymouth. Next year is the selection, and for you to be seen as a viable candidate, you need to show caution in your speech. You need to talk to me before you speak. I want to see the markings of discretion and balance in your thoughts," King Michael said.

There was a knock at the door. "Enter," the king said.

"Excuse me, Your Majesty. I was looking for Prince Merreg," Chancellor Bates said.

"We are through, and I need to find the queen," King Michael said as he turned to leave the room.

Bates and Prince Merreg watched as the king left.

"What was that about?" Chancellor Bates asked.

"He admonished me for speaking against my brother, again," Merreg said. "And I am to be more discreet with my opinions. I do not know how long I can endure this dawdling old man. He even had a veiled threat about things I needed to do to make myself a viable candidate at selection. As though there is any doubt he will select me as his successor. Merryk is a momentary celebrity. He will fade in the next few months."

"In all honesty, today's hearing will strengthen Merryk's position. The duke, however, wanted you to know he appreciated your support. He and the other nobles heard what you said. He recognized you would have made a different decision," Bates said.

"At least someone appreciates me. This has been a frustrating morning. I think I will see if I can find someone or many someones to distract me," Prince Merreg said with a sly smile.

———— ✦ ————

Chancellor Bates left the meeting with Prince Merreg and scurried out of the castle to the Pipe and Pint, a selective gentlemen's club just a short distance from the castle's gates.

As he entered the front door into an enclosed foyer, a butler greeted him. Bates asked, "Is anyone expecting me?"

"Yes, the Duke of Ressett said you might stop by and asked if you would join him in the small library."

The clientele of the Pipe and Pint was exclusively nobility, wealthy merchants, and a select group of government officials and military officers. It was known for its selection of wines and absolute discretion. Beyond the foyer was a large meeting parlor with overstuffed chairs and a fireplace for a casual visit. For more privacy, well-appointed rooms lie on the upper floors. The small library was one such room.

The butler escorted Chancellor Bates up the winding stairs to the double doors of the room. Opening the doors, the butler announced, "Your Grace, Chancellor Bates."

"Bates, I was wondering how long it would take you to get here. Please come in. Would you like some wine or sherry?"

"Sherry, please," Bates replied. The butler immediately went to the decanter and poured a glass. After delivering it to the chancellor, he discreetly left the room.

"Not the morning I had expected," Bates said in a defensive tone. "I should have challenged Goldblatt more directly."

"And what, be chopped up like stew meat? Do not flatter yourself, chancellor. You will never be a match for the wit and skill of Chancellor

Goldblatt. He is dangerous with just an argument, but when bolstered with facts, he is unstoppable." The duke's tone was bitter and harsh. "I feel fortunate to be walking freely. My only salvation was he focused on saving the prince's property and not on my incarceration. I should never have listened to you. *We can persuade the king and get the horses and the ships,* you said."

"I had no reason to believe Goldblatt would appear. Everyone knows Masterroff can suck money out of your pocket from across town, but freezes with large audiences," Bates said.

"How did Goldblatt find out about the hearing?"

"I do not know. We served the notice after lunch on Monday. It is a two-day voyage each way to get to the Teardrop port and another three days to send the message to and from the castle. It should have taken at least a week."

"Except, Chancellor Goldblatt was here in two and a half days," the duke said, shaking his head from side to side. "Rehashing this will not make any difference. The question is, what do we do now?"

"I could ask the prince to talk with the king about at least getting your horses back," Bates suggested.

"You really are dense. King Michael nearly sent me to the dungeon, and he publicly shut down his own son. The prince cannot approach the king, especially on my behalf."

"I guess you are right. Prince Merreg met with the king after the hearing. The king told the prince there were several things he needed to do to make himself a viable candidate for succession. I fear the king may rethink his selection of Prince Merreg," Bates said.

"Really? You just figured that out? I can lose a few horses, but I cannot lose the opportunity to make my daughter queen. Prince Merryk is an unknown. With his current advisors, manipulating him will be difficult, if not impossible."

"We both know Prince Merryk is an imbecile. His advisors are directing his every move. They are making him into a hero by keeping him away from everyone's sight, even the king's."

"Speaking of sight, where is Prince Merreg?" the duke asked.

"Finding comfort somewhere."

"Everyone sees how he lives. He is his own worst enemy. I am concerned he will reveal his true nature to the king before the selection."

The carriage ride back to Ressett Manor was not as pleasant as the duke had hoped. The wheels found every pothole, constantly shaking the duke back into a review of the recent events.

King Natas attacked Prince Merryk and lost spectacularly. So much so, the young prince is becoming a legend. I foolishly allowed Chancellor Bates to convince me to petition the king for my horses, and oh yes, add a request for Natas' ships. Masterroff cannot defend the seizures, but then Goldblatt appears. I lost the argument spectacularly. So much so, I barely got out of the castle without being charged with treason.

Most of the time, when things go wrong, I have made mistakes. The only mistakes I have made are not charging for the horses and picking the wrong prince. But no rational person would have picked Prince Merryk. He is an imbecile.

What am I going to do? I cannot give King Michael any direct reason to believe I am involved in treason, even if I am.

I have avoided direct contact with Natas. Now I have little choice. We share too much in common. Neither of us can afford to have Prince Merryk become king. As king of the High Kingdom, I cannot imagine the pressure Merryk would put on King Natas.

If Merryk became king, I would have little chance of getting Katalynn to be queen. It would be another half-century before we could restore our family's rightful place. That is just too long to wait.

I will need to take the risk of contact. We should meet in person, rather than putting things in writing. I will send my courier with the message to avoid discovery. Something simple like:

> King Natas,
> I propose we meet to discuss our outstanding issues. You pick
> the time and the place. My courier will wait for your reply.
> The Duke of Ressett

One last thing, I need to create some alternatives.

Chapter 5

Horse Sense

The longer days and warmer nights caused an eruption of color in the Teardrop. The water-soaked plain had continued to dry. The road from the front gate of the castle wound like a ribbon against the floral patterns of the multicolored wildflowers. There was no silence from dawn to dusk, just the incessant hum of bees. "Tara is right, Maverick, this is going to be a great year for honey and wax," Merryk said as he sat on his horse at the gate in the old Roman wall. "I remember being here, facing soldiers. Now it's flowers. I like flowers better. What about you?"

The black stallion nodded his head in vigorous agreement.

"Talking to your horse again," Captain Yonn said, as he rode to join the prince.

"As I told you long ago, you should talk to your horse. You might learn something."

"I told you my horse did not think about much."

"I know, Yonn. Now you have more and more on your mind. You have been preoccupied with invasions, navies, and maintaining order throughout the Teardrop. Your horse would tell you to stop and think about yourself and those who are important to you. You'll always have your duties, but you deserve more."

"I see Yvette talked to Tara, and she talked to you. Before you begin again, I know there is no reason for me not to ask Yvette to marry me, other than the biggest one."

Merryk interrupted. "You don't love her?"

"Of course, I love her. We live in a kingdom full of available women, and the only one I want to be with is Yvette. But I have no title. I am from the barn. Yvette's family will never accept me as the man to marry their daughter."

"I see. You are going to ask her family to marry you. I bet her mother is beautiful, but who knows about her father?" Merryk's face filled with an oversized grin.

"I know what you mean. In the real world, nobles would shun her for marrying a commoner. Our children would be outcasts, neither noble nor commoner." Captain Yonn's tone was serious and his voice tight with frustration.

"Are you planning on marrying Yvette and moving back to the Capital City or to Natas' Kingdom?"

"No."

"In the Teardrop Kingdom, you are Yonn, Captain of the Guard, responsible for the safety and security of the entire population. You command hundreds of men, secure our borders, collect our taxes and act as the personal protector of the prince and princess. You are an important man. Your importance rises from merit, not from blood. No one gave you a title at birth. You have earned the respect of the people. So, unless you're going to leave your position and move, I think you are worthy to ask Yvette to marry you. If she demands a title, then she is not the woman you and I believe she is."

"Every time you explain it, things seem fine, but then I begin to think. She deserves better."

"Why don't you give her the choice? Let her decide if you are good enough. Do not decide for her by not asking. What do you think, Maverick? Good advice?

The horse bobbed his head up and down again in affirmation.

"Have I forgotten anything?" the prince asked the horse.

This time Maverick slowly shook his head 'no.'

Yonn looked at the great black stallion. "You are one to be giving advice. How are things going between you and Bella?"

The horse stopped short and shook his head briskly from side to side.

"What is that supposed to mean?" Yonn asked.

"He doesn't want to talk about it."

CHAPTER 6

XAVIER

Merryk and Tara retreated from the hot sun to the cool air of the new library.

"I like this place," Tara said. "It seems to have the right balance of temperature and light. It is good for reading all day long."

"I am pleased with the progress you and the Chancellor have made in getting it organized," Merryk said.

"Your categorization system made it easy."

"All you had to do was read all the books and decide which group they go in. I can imagine how easy it was to do, with only a few hundred books," Merryk said jokingly.

"I have to admit, I am only reading enough to get the book into the right major category. We will need to come back later and put them in the subgroups."

"Excuse me, Your Highness, we have visitors," Smallfolks said. "They are from the new Provost."

"They must be the ones sent to investigate the charges against us," Tara said.

"Father Xavier, welcome," Prince Merryk said as he greeted the three men standing near the doors.

"Prince Merryk and Princess Tarareese, how nice to see you again," Father Xavier said with a slight bow. "I cannot believe it has been almost a year. Please, allow me to introduce Deacons John and Abel. They are here to assist me."

Both men bowed politely.

"I could ask what brings you this time, but I already have a good idea," Prince Merryk said.

"We had weapons with us at the port, but your men refused to allow us to carry them," Deacon Abel said with a tone of disapproval.

"I hope my husband's men made it clear you were welcome to travel, but not your weapons. Deacon, excuse our sensitivity. The last time armed priests came, they were instructed to burn us at the stake. The prince does not believe weapons of war are needed to pursue the ways of the Faith," Tara said.

"We will have plenty of time to talk about philosophy during your stay," Merryk said. "My guess is you want to see Father Bernard. We have been working on the rectory, but I don't know if it is ready for guests. In any event, you can always stay with us in the castle."

"Father Bernard is here?" Father Xavier said in surprise.

"Yes, he has been with us since mid-May," Prince Merryk replied. "We are making improvements to the church and the rectory. It had fallen into disrepair. We are very pleased to have him as the pastor for the Teardrop."

"No one at the Council knew where Father Bernard had gone. We were worried about his safety," Father Xavier said. "I cannot tell you how pleased I am to know he is here."

"Father Bernard was our instructor," Deacon John said. "We have missed him deeply."

"My guess is he will be pleased to see you," Tara said. "If you are available, please join us for dinner. Father Bernard, Chancellor Goldblatt, and Prince Merryk often have conversations which are as filling as the meal."

"You know, our mission is one of seriousness," Deacon Abel said. "It is not a social event."

"Deacon, all interactions between people are social. They can be serious or not, but they are always social. We can create barriers to communication, or we can be open to discussion. I prefer openness. In the end, the truth will be revealed. Why not make the process of discovery more pleasant?" Prince Merryk said with a smile.

"Forgive my young associate," Father Xavier said. "This is his first inquiry, and he is determined to do it well."

"Everyone would be disappointed if it were otherwise. Now, go find Father Bernard and plan on dinner with us."

Prince Merryk set aside significant time during the next weeks for the visiting priests. He suggested Father Xavier outline what needed to be reviewed and then let the deacons gather the information.

As the hot days of summer followed, they could find Father Xavier sitting in a chair in the shade as Father Bernard directed the workmen on the rectory and the church. "We have known each other almost all of our lives," Father Bernard said to Prince Merryk. "He was a senior teacher when I first came to the Council. My skills carried me away from him, but we have always maintained contact, even if it was just a cup of tea once a week. It is good to have him here."

The two deacons quickly showed why they had been selected. Both were meticulous and thorough in their reviews.

"Princess Tarareese, I have heard you are working on a library. Might I see it?" Deacon Abel asked.

"Of course."

"The first thing Prince Merryk did was to establish an index system to record the books," Tara said as she escorted the deacon into the large room. "The system is based on three criteria: title, author, and subject. Title and author are filed alphabetically, but the subject is based on a system Prince Merryk designed."

"Very interesting," Deacon Abel said as his eyes swept the shelves of books. "The organization of knowledge has always fascinated me."

"You should talk with the prince. I do not always understand him, but he can explain the purpose of each of the groupings. Our current problem is Chancellor Goldblatt, Prince Merryk, and I are good with the koine Greek, but all struggle with the classical."

"I had not expected to be having this discussion," Deacon Abel said as his face lit up with excitement. "I have always had a natural aptitude for classical Greek."

"I know you have much to do, but if you could help with even a few of the classical books, we would appreciate it," Tara said.

"I would be happy to review at least a few," Deacon Abel said.

"It is time for a reading lesson. Why not come with me to see the children? We can return to the library later," Tara said.

"I wanted to see the children, orphans, I think. They are mentioned in my notes."

"They are not orphans. They are the wards of the prince. I also believe they were the initial cause of animosity between Father Aubry and Prince Merryk."

"I would like to hear that story," Deacon Abel said.

"Good evening, everyone," Prince Merryk said as he and Tara entered the main dining room. The normally sparsely occupied table was now filled with Yvette and Yonn, the Chancellor, and the four clergymen. This gathering had become a daily event during the preceding weeks.

"I hope everyone had a good day," Tara said as she sat down.

"Most certainly," Father Xavier replied. "But it was also bittersweet. I cannot believe the time has gone by so quickly. It has been four weeks. Now, we must return to the Council."

"Does this mean you have finished your inquiry?" Chancellor Goldblatt asked.

"We finished our inquiry the first week," Deacon Abel said. "Ever since, we have been enjoying the Teardrop, its people, and your hospitality."

"You spent most of your free time in the library, categorizing books. I would not consider that enjoyable," Yvette said with a smile.

"I know you prefer to teach children, which I would not consider en-joyable at all. It was my pleasure to help. I just wish I had more time," Abel added.

"Yes, our investigations were quickly completed, after Father Bernard offered his insight into the actual reasons for the incursion. I am afraid history will view this as a most unfortunate event," Father Xavier said. "The most radical idea we discovered is your attempt to educate all men, women, and children."

"Only an educated population can grow a country. Education and skills, coupled with new opportunity and a safe environment, make for long-term success," Prince Merryk said.

"I know Father Bernard will be sad to see you go. He had grown tired of arguing with only the prince and me," Chancellor Goldblatt said.

"How much intellectual stimulus is one man expected to handle?" Father Bernard replied, playfully mocking the Chancellor.

"I know you must return with your report, but I want you to know we have built the rectory big enough to handle everyone. We need a permanent curator for the library. I know Father Bernard would like to have a younger priest to assist with the ministry. Father Xavier, you've been connected to Tara and my life since the very beginning. It would be our honor to have you retire and stay with us in the Teardrop."

"Absolutely," Father Bernard said. "I could think of nothing better than having you review my sermons."

"You have given us much to consider. I am nearing the end of my full-time commitment to the Council. A quiet place away from the drama would be nice," Father Xavier said.

"Who said anything about *no drama?*" Yvette exclaimed. "I did not agree to such a thing."

Everyone broke into laughter.

CHAPTER 7

HITS

A cloud of dread cloaked the otherwise sunny day for Admiral Burat as he made his way into the castle. King Natas' current chancellor greeted the admiral just outside the doors to the audience hall.

"I hope you have good news for him. I certainly do not," the chancellor said.

"I was just pleased to see you rather than Colonel Lamaze," Burat replied.

"Do not get comfortable. Lamaze is already inside."

"It may come down to who has the worst news."

"Mine is terrible," the chancellor said.

"Worse than two sunk ships?"

"It could be close, but delaying will not make it any better. We should go in."

The large ornate doors swung open, and the two men entered. The distance between the door and the throne was only about thirty feet. By their appearance, both looked like it was the longest walk they had ever taken.

"My two favorite people. I know you have good news for me," King Natas said.

"I do not," Burat said. His mind raced. *Might as well go out with my honor.* "I took the R.S. *Cleaver* and four other warships to disrupt or capture the merchant ships we had lost. We discovered two of our ships, under Merryk's flag, at the end of the peninsula on their way to the Capital City. They were traveling together, which is not unusual. Three of our ships moved to intercept. The two merchant ships did not run. Initially, I thought they were going to surrender. Just as we got near, signals flew from the deck, shot into the open sky. Within moments, we saw an answer on the horizon."

"We pursued the attack, intending to board. Suddenly, the sides of the ships dropped and trebuchets with fire balls came into view. They had modified the merchant ships to carry the larger weapons. They were floating attack platforms. Two of our ships were immediately hit and began to burn. The third ship went to their assistance, hoping to either put out the fire or rescue the men."

"When I looked away from the battle, I saw additional warships were closing from the east and two more from the west. We had lost the initiative and were not prepared for an attack of this intensity. We saved as many men as we could and then retreated. The two warships were a complete loss. The rigging of the third was severely damaged. As we cleared the horizon, I saw eight ships. If we had stayed, we would have lost them all."

King Natas clapped his hands. "Another remarkable defeat! You never cease to disappoint me, admiral. How long will it take to repair the rigging on the third ship?"

"They estimate three weeks."

"Well, chancellor, it will be hard to beat the admiral. What do you have? Have you ordered the new ships for spring?"

"I am afraid we will not have new ships by spring, Your Majesty. Masterroff and Prince Merryk have contracted with the shipbuilders for all ships until this time next year. By the time we gathered the money for payment, the builders were already committed."

"How many ships are they building?"

"Four. All merchant ships," the chancellor replied. "Masterroff has also completed contracts for the fall and spring horse sales. Our estimated income will fall by nearly half, even if we can get them delivered. Salt orders are down only by twenty-five percent, but Prince Merryk has driven down the price by twenty-five percent, so the net impact is close to a fifty percent loss.

"We have received six demands for compensation from horse customers who had to purchase horses from Masterroff at higher prices. They are demanding we repay their losses before they purchase any additional animals.

"We have sent representatives to the eastern kingdoms seeking new business. They are reporting a general animosity toward any of your products. Everyone is blaming you for the destruction of the Army of Justice. Even the priests at the Council of Justice are not interested in buying horses or salt from us.

"Furthermore, we are still having difficulty finding independent merchant ships to carry our products. Everywhere we go, people are talking about Prince Merryk.

The chancellor took a deep breath and then continued. "In addition, your general in the south sent word the army has run into stiff resistance. They may be forced to retreat unless they receive reinforcements. They are also running out of supplies. A significant amount of what they need is from outside the kingdom. With the merchant ships reluctant to deliver to us, it is hard to get supplies. Unfortunately, you may have no choice but to withdraw.

"Regarding our search for a groom for the Princess Mandaline, we are continuing our search, but the larger kingdoms simply said, 'No.' The smaller ones want to wait until next year before continuing the discussion.

"I am sorry to provide this information, but you must know the truth."

The king sat in his chair without comment. The gap of silence was so great, the two men standing in front of him began to sweat. Both knew silence from the king was never a good thing.

"Colonel Lamaze, which of these men has the saddest story?" King Natas asked.

The colonel cast his eyes at both for a long moment. "Losing ships in battle happens all the time; we can eventually replace them. The economic impacts seem extreme. They are the greater threat. The chancellor's is the saddest story."

"I agree. Chancellor, you and I will talk later. Right now, leave us. I want to talk to Admiral Burat."

The chancellor bowed politely and scurried from the room, leaving the admiral alone.

"Admiral Burat, I want to meet a ship from the High Kingdom in a place half-way between here and the Capital City. It needs to be discreet. Is there such a place?"

"Yes, Your Majesty. There is a small island just north of the major trade routes called 'Otok'. It has a harbor on the southern end, but a sheltered bay on the north where two ships could meet with no one knowing."

CHAPTER 8

LETTERS

A week after Chancellor Goldblatt returned from the Capital City, a familiar figure knocked on his door. "Willem, my goodness, it has been forever. How have you been?" Chancellor Goldblatt said as he left his desk to greet the road-weary letter carrier.

"Amazingly busy," Willem replied. "I was concerned the new fast pony connection between Newport and the castle would mean I was not needed, but the opposite has happened. After the battle, I received bundles of letters from ordinary people. I guess relatives wanted to know if people were all right. Also, everyone outside the Teardrop wants to know the details of the fighting. The cobbler in the little village near the old Southbridge told me he got a letter from a sister-in-law saying she thought he was dead. He found it funny because it was the only time she had written him in over twenty years."

Chancellor Goldblatt chuckled. "People seem to like disasters and wars, especially if they do not have to be in them."

"So true. The pony courier said I could drop this bundle off so I could say hello. I also have mail for Nelly and one of the new stable lads."

"Well, it is good to see you. Remember, you can stop anytime, even if you do not have mail. Now go to the kitchen. I know Smallfolks and Nelly will want to visit. Thank you."

Chancellor Goldblatt looked at the bundle of notes. Following his normal practice, he sorted them into piles. One pile for important and another for informational. Three letters made the important stack. There was a note addressed to him from Masterroff, and two letters directed to Prince Merryk. One parchment letter bore the seal of the House of Ressett, and the other the House of Crescent. In addition, there were three other letters of interest from lesser noble houses. *It is interesting to receive so many first-time letters from noble houses.* Goldblatt thought.

Goldblatt tore the seal from Masterroff's note. *Good, he secured the building of four new ships, which will be available next spring. I will need to ask Captain Slater to find new captains.* Goldblatt chuckled as he read the letter. Evidently, a few days after Masterroff had confirmed the purchase, an agent for King Natas attempted to acquire ships, only to find the builder committed until late next year. *King Natas is having difficulty replacing his ships. This will only make him more likely to seek alternatives. I need to get the other letters to the prince.*

Goldblatt found the prince and princess at the dining table finishing a midmorning breakfast. "You two are off to a late start," Goldblatt said.

"The princess detained me this morning," Merryk said, seeking to shift the blame to her.

"If you are expecting me to apologize, forget it. Someone must think about future generations of Raymouths," Tara said with a glint in her eyes.

Merryk smiled and reached out to touch Tara's arm. "Well, there is no worry about that."

The Chancellor, needing the conversation to shift, interrupted, "We received some interesting letters this morning. Five from noble houses, including one from Ressett, and another from Crescent."

Prince Merryk took the letters from the Chancellor and handed some to Tara. "Why don't you read these, and I will read the others."

Merryk broke the seal on the Ressett note. "This is interesting. The duke wants to apologize for the misunderstanding over the horses."

"There was no misunderstanding," Tara inserted.

"The duke believes our family histories slanted our views. He is offering to come to the Teardrop with his daughter, Katalynn, for a visit, *to restore mutual trust between our families.*"

"The duke wants to be on the right side of the king and the prince," Goldblatt said. "The loss in front of the other nobles has weakened him. He is smart enough to know he cannot be at odds with either of the king's sons."

"And he wants us to meet his daughter," Tara said with a smile. "Perhaps the duke thinks she and I will have a connection from our contacts so many years ago."

"Or perhaps, if we don't like the thorn, we might like the flower," Merryk added. Merryk turned his attention to the second note from the House of Crescent. Before opening the note, he asked Goldblatt, "Tell me about the House of Crescent."

"The history of Crescent is the exact opposite of the House of Ressett. During the great rebellion, the noble houses had to take sides. The first to pledge loyalty and provide men was the House of Crescent. The Duke of Crescent's forces came from the east against Ressett, and the Great King Mikael came from the west. The two forces converged at Ressett Manor, crushing the rebellion. The bulk of the land stripped from Ressett was given to the Duke of Crescent. The current Duke of Ressett has openly accused the Duke of Crescent of stealing his land. An interesting fact, the wives of both men were sisters."

"Why did you say *were*? Tara asked.

"Another source of conflict between the two families, Ressett's wife died in an accident. She is said to have fallen down the stairs. The Crescent family has always believed it was not an accident."

Merryk read the letter aloud: *The Duke and Duchess of Crescent, and their daughter, wish Prince Merryk and Princess Tarareese congratulations on their spectacular victory. If you ever have time, we would be most honored to welcome you to our home.*

"A very practical and political letter," Tara said. "They want you to know they are loyal to the family."

"They should've sent a letter to my father. Loyalty to him is important," Merryk said.

"Loyalty is a perpetual issue. It runs from generation to generation. They are laying the groundwork for the next generation," Goldblatt said.

Tara put the three letters of the lesser houses in the center of the table. "Each of these is a form of the Crescent letter with congratulations and expressing the support of their entire family."

"You both know I dislike taking credit for the victory when it was based on luck," Merryk said. "It seems false to accept the congratulations."

"The victory was more than luck. It was leadership and courage. It was what you have done *with* the victory. You made the Teardrop important. You took what you called luck and converted it into opportunity for all the people." Tara's voice was filled with conviction and pride.

"It never hurts to have noble friends. I will prepare appropriate replies for each," Chancellor Goldblatt offered.

"Thank you. I still have difficulty with the obligations of nobility," Merryk said.

"We can always help you," Tara said.

Tara found Goldblatt sitting in the afternoon shade on the terrace bench, just outside his study. The warm air of August gently stroked the leaves in the overhanging trees and broke the sunbeams into small flashes of light.

"I thought I might find you here. May I join you?" Tara asked.

"Please do," the Chancellor replied. "I do not enjoy this bench nearly often enough. This is a restful place to think."

"I wanted to ask you about the letters. It seemed to me each had a double purpose. The first and obvious was congratulations, and the second to remind the prince each house had a daughter of marriageable age."

"Yes, the most significant thing is the noble houses are viewing Prince Merryk as a potential ruler. When the prince first came to the Teardrop, the general opinion was he was an imbecile. The letters show the noble houses are now accepting him," Goldblatt stated.

"I think it is interesting they will accept him without proof that he is not an imbecile."

"People are drawn to power, like a moth to the flame. If Merryk has power, he is worth pursuing. It will please the king that the prince is being accepted. It would make his selection easier."

"Am I correct in assuming the letters show a feeling Merryk might need an Inland wife?"

"Absolutely. Merryk may not be paying attention to the rules of succession, but others are. I did not see any purpose in pointing it out. He has been so adamant about not wanting to be king."

"Do any of the families who sent the letters have daughters we should put on the list?"

"Yes, Lady Crescent would be a natural choice for selection. She would strengthen the centuries old alliance between the two houses. The three lesser houses are looking for some way to enhance their status, but they do not strengthen the throne. The one most interesting was the apology from the Duke of Ressett."

"Surely his was not an overture like the others."

"I believe it was. More subtle, but a queen from the House of Ressett would end any question of loyalty to the crown. It would cure the rift between the houses. This would be an excellent match for either brother. The duke would gain much influence, and if he still believes Merryk can be manipulated, he will think even more."

"So, you would put both of the daughters of Crescent and Ressett on the list?"

"Yes, and do not forget Lady Zoo."

"Oolada?"

"Lady Zoo would strengthen the support from the Blue-and-White Mountain Clans, making the entire kingdom stronger. Gaspar has been a great friend and ally to Prince Merryk. The prince knows and likes Oolada. The negative is some view the clans as inferior to the other noble houses. They would object."

"I know Oolada so well. I am surprised she did not come to mind immediately."

Tara stood and moved toward the door, then stopped. "We need to keep this list going. Add others if you think they are appropriate. Of one thing I am now certain, we are not the only ones who see Prince Merryk as king."

Chapter 9

STORM CLOUDS

The thick wooden doors, which sheltered the council chamber in the winter, were folded back to the sides of the balcony, revealing a panoramic view of the Valley of Zoo. On the right, looking south, was the sawtooth range of Blue-and-White Mountains. To the left, another set of mountains rolled more gently toward the rising sun. Helga knew that beyond the deep forest to the south, the land eventually ran into the sea. This morning her eyes were focused past the forest to a rock sitting within a vast blue ocean.

Gaspar had awakened two hours earlier; about the time the sun first tinted the horizon with the light of a new day. He chuckled to himself. *Everyone thinks Jamaal is unique in getting up so early, but nobody ever asks where he got it.* Normally, Gaspar would walk around the Great Square, check on the guards at the gate, and then return to find Helga making the morning tea. This morning he returned, but Helga was not there.

Years of life and love had taught Gaspar to know where to look for Helga. "I thought I would find you here," Gaspar said as he came up behind Helga on the balcony. "What is going on this morning that has you gazing south?"

"There was a rumble in the earth this morning. It woke me. I came here to see." Her eyes shifted and became distant. "I saw three storm clouds lying on the horizon. One to the west was black with anger and bolts of lightning. The other two were smaller, but distinct, a young cloud and an old cloud. The old cloud churned with a long-held darkness. The young cloud is filled with thin clouds, which seem to be constantly changing. All three were moving together to form a bigger storm. They were meeting today, in the shadow of a gray stone, near an island which is green on one side and brown on the other. When they join, a great danger will arise."

Helga's eyes seemed to flicker, and then refocused. "Who is the target of their danger? Prince Merryk?" Gaspar asked.

"Yes and no," Helga said. "Prince Merryk is not the focus, but the reason. I also feel we are in as much danger as the prince. The storm will be big enough to shake the foundation. This woke me."

"The dark cloud from the west could be King Natas, but who could be the others? When will the storm strike?"

"You know I do not know who the other two are, but they are near. The storm will strike soon. I know it is weeks, not months. We must prepare, but I do not know how." Her voice showed her frustration. "I am sorry I cannot help more. I just know this is important." Tears pooled in Helga's eyes and then rolled down her cheeks. Gaspar reached out to wrap his arms around Helga and pull her to his chest. She burrowed her head into his shoulder and softly sobbed.

"This must be extremely important to upset you so much. It is time for Jamaal to return to the Teardrop. We will have him share the vision with the prince."

"Oolada must go with him. She must see Prince Merryk," Helga said firmly. "The storm will touch her. I feel it."

Five hundred miles to the southwest, the island of Otok lay just north of the traditional trade routes. For centuries, the island had been a refuge in times of storms. It was a curious place. The south side sat in the center of the warm ocean currents and winds. This created an abundance of water and resilient tropical vegetation. A small harbor provided food, fresh water, and rum for those who strayed into its bay. Enough visitors came to allow for the survival of the few people who lived there, but not so many as to destroy the local beauty. A large range of mountains shielded the north side of the island. They captured all the warm waters on the south side, leaving only mist to fall on the northern. The result was a brown and desolate wasteland.

The Royal Ship *Cleaver* skirted the west side of the island, carefully avoiding any ships headed into the south harbor. Shortly before noon, it eased into a sheltered bay on the north side. High stone walls on three sides shielded the ship from the winds and from unwelcome eyes.

Within an hour, a second ship appeared on the horizon. This ship bore the flag of the High Kingdom and a second flag of the Outland Prince.

"Our guests are here. Notify the king and prepare the rowboat." Admiral Burat commanded.

King Natas, Colonel Lamaze, and two Royal Dragoons boarded a rowboat to go to a small beach exposed by the retreating tide. A similar craft with Prince Merreg, the duke, and two Royal Guards joined them from the prince's ship.

"Good afternoon, Prince Merreg and Duke of Ressett," Natas said as the men stepped onto the sand.

"Good afternoon, King Natas. It is nice to meet you," Prince Merreg said, extending his hand in greeting.

Natas accepted his hand and nodded in acknowledgment.

"It is good to see you again, Your Grace," King Natas said as he shook the duke's hand.

"None of us can afford to be away from our duties for long, so we must be more direct than normal." King Natas said. Turning to the guards and Colonel Lamaze, "If you would take a short walk so that we might talk."

In moments, the three men were alone.

The duke began. "I suggested this council so that we might meet each other and speak openly, without concern our discussion would be overheard, or our correspondence intercepted." Turning to Prince Merreg, "I believe we all have a common adversary, your brother."

"Prince Merryk has caused significant financial and military loss to me," King Natas said. "He has disrupted the duke's marriage plans between you and his daughter. Merryk's false claims of victory have made him a rising challenger to your becoming king."

"Prince Merryk is no challenge to my becoming king. He is being propped up by his advisors," Merreg snapped.

"Do not delude yourself. Your brother looks more like the next king every day. If you do not recognize the threat, you will end up like your uncle, taking care of the army and serving Merryk," Natas said sternly.

Merreg bristled with anger.

"Nothing is gained by lying to you, My Prince. As hard as it is to hear, I believe King Natas is speaking the truth," the duke added.

Prince Merreg gathered himself. "What are we to do? You used an entire army and failed to kill him. I know it was not the first attempt. Everything you have done to destroy him only seems to strengthen him. As king, I could curtail his influence immediately. We just need to wait and let my father select me."

"You need to listen," King Natas said firmly. "If I were your father, Prince Merryk would be my choice. I might like you better, but he looks the best suited to protect the kingdom. Merryk is the safe choice, the legendary victor over the Army of Justice."

"My father will not choose Merryk," Merreg countered.

"Your father already selected Merryk over me, and in doing so, reprimanded you in front of the entire court," the duke said. "You do not demean a man, like your father did you, if you were going to make him king. I need to remind you, he would not let you discuss my marriage proposal, even though my daughter was your choice."

"I did not even get a polite reply to the offer of my daughter, Mandaline. King Michael treats you like a child," Natas said. "He is amplifying your shortcomings and glorifying Merryk. You will not be his choice."

Prince Merreg's face became pensive. "Merryk will be hard to kill. You know that better than any. We do not expect him to leave the Teardrop any time soon. My father is protecting his economic interests, so beating him commercially will be difficult. I had hoped to let his fame burn out before the selection."

"So, your plan is to hope Merryk does something wrong, or hope King Michael will pick you," King Natas said. "Perhaps your father is right. You are not suited to be king if this is how you plan to solve our problem."

"All right, what do you suggest we do?" Merreg said with a snippy tone of irritation.

"Do not give your father the opportunity to choose. Under your law, if your father were to die before the selection, you would be king. Your only requirement would be to have an Inland, and an Outland Queen. I have offered my daughter and I believe the duke is still offering his. In addition, I will send a group of assassins from the east. One of them will kill the king. You will have no way of knowing they were there. You just need to put the king in a place for the assassins to reach him and remove his security. No one will ever know. Kings make enemies all the time. I know," King Natas said.

"What do you want in exchange?" Merreg asked.

"Marry my daughter, return all my ships and horses, and help me isolate and destroy your brother," King Natas said.

"What do you want, duke?"

"I want you to marry my daughter and let me be your advisor."

"Why cannot you do this without my help?"

"The security around your father is significant. We could try, but we cannot assure success. If we fail, it will just make it harder the next time.

When we succeed, we would not want you to hunt for the assassins," Natas said.

Merreg restated the proposition. "Basically, you are asking me to get out of the way and let you kill my father, then be sure no meaningful search occurs for his murderers."

"Yes. In the simplest terms, if you let us, we will ensure you are king," Natas said.

"When would you do this?" Merreg asked.

"I will let you know when to expect the assassins. I will communicate with the duke by sending him information about the delivery of a black stallion. By the first of November, we will be relatives," King Natas said. "And you will be king."

Chapter 10

Warning

"Where has the summer gone?" Gaspar asked Helga as the two stood on the balcony, looking across the horizon. The summer's shadows stretched themselves into long stripes as the sunset moved south.

"Before long, the shadows will reach across the valley. Another season is running away," Helga said.

"I think all of my seasons are running with them." Gaspar stretched his hands over his head. "Soon I will be as stiff as the mountains."

"Stop. You will watch the rise and fall of many more seasons. You may slow down, but that will allow you to watch what you have taken for granted."

"Will you stay with me to point out the things I miss?"

"It will always be my pleasure to point out what the Walt misses."

"I sometimes think you take too much pleasure in your task."

"Or there are just too many opportunities."

The playful banter between the two was interrupted as Jamaal and Oolada entered the council chamber. "Good. The two of you are here just in time to save me," Gaspar exclaimed.

"From what?" Oolada asked.

"Himself," Helga replied with a chuckle.

Gaspar shrugged off the exchange. "We should sit." Gaspar motioned to the chairs on the balcony. "Helga has had another vision."

Turning to face the two young people, Helga began. "It differs from the last. It touches both Prince Merryk and us directly. A group of three have gathered to create a large storm. The target of the storm is unclear, but it is somewhere south. I feel the prince's victory set this in motion."

"Prince Merryk defeated the Council's army, and we have received no word of another gathering. Chancellor Goldblatt's sources would have alerted us," Jamaal said.

"This is part of the confusion. I see armies in battle, but I cannot see the uniforms or flags of those battling." Helga continued, "Whatever is going to happen will be soon, weeks, not months."

"I need you to go see Prince Merryk and Chancellor Goldblatt. Find out if they have discovered anything which would match Helga's vision. Go over Ledin Grubi; it is the shortest path. Be sure the path is clearly marked, in case others need to use it later," Gaspar directed. "We should move as many of our men as possible from the castle south to the port. It will place them in a position to move west if needed, and if not, they can come home this fall. Double the horses and men on the relay path. We need to be able to communicate quickly with the prince."

"We must notify the other clans sooner rather than later," Jamaal said. "Many would have sent men last time, but did not have the opportunity. I suggest you call a council meeting, even if I am gone."

"I agree. I will send messengers," Gaspar replied.

"What can I do to help?" Oolada asked.

"You can go with Jamaal. Stay close to the princess and the contessa," Helga answered. "They will need you."

"I do not understand."

"You will."

"Send information as you receive it. This will also give us time to plan and will train the men in the relay system." Gaspar added, "And I am not as patient as I once was."

Oolada waited outside the council doors for Helga to exit. "This is going to be extremely hard. You know that last time I did not want to come home. Just thinking about seeing Prince Merryk has upset me."

"The threads of fate have bound you to the people in the Teardrop. You cannot stop their pull any more than you can stop how you feel. You need to prepare yourself to love the prince even if you see no sign of how he feels in return. He is a man of great honor. He will do nothing to break his vow to the princess. Remember how he kept his promise to not touch her, even though we all thought it was foolish?"

"He would not be who he is if he acted differently. Just being near him *must* be enough."

Helga wrapped her arms around the tearful Oolada. "We must get you prepared to leave. Jamaal will want to make an early start. Trust that everything will work out as it should."

"How was your journey?" Prince Merryk asked.

"I had forgotten how rough the trail is over Leden Grubi," Jamaal said. "It took over five days; two just to get from the southern road."

"We were marking the path as we went, which slowed us a little," Oolada said.

"I, for one, would not want to make that journey again, even if we took our time," Yvette added. "My mind refuses to remember parts and what I do, all seems black and white."

"It was the moonlight," Tara chided. "I remember it was a grand adventure."

Looking around the table, Prince Merryk smiled. "We are always happy to have you join us. However, my guess is this is more than a social visit."

"Yes, Helga had another vision. This one affects both you and the clans." Jamaal described the vision to Prince Merryk, Chancellor Goldblatt, Captain Yonn, and the ladies.

"Three meeting at sea," Goldblatt replied. "The only thing we have heard was Prince Merreg told his father he was going to review the naval forces near the Inland Passage, and he would be gone for about six days. The information came from Masterroff's weekly report, and the timing would be about right."

"Who are the others?" Captain Yonn asked.

"An easy guess would be my father," Tara said.

"It may not matter who the third is. If Merreg and King Natas are in direct contact, it can only mean trouble for my father," Merryk said.

"We should warn the king," Captain Yonn said.

Goldblatt injected, "We do not have concrete information to incriminate Prince Merreg. If we accuse Prince Merreg and we are wrong, we will lose all credibility."

"A parent never wants to believe their child would mean them harm. Without clear proof, the king will reject any claim," Tara said.

"Perhaps there is a way to protect my father without making any assertion against my brother. Yonn, the swordmaster's friend, Bowen, could be placed on heightened alert. He might get the help of some of the army and Royal Guards pushed aside by Prince Merreg."

"Yes, that would work. We just need to give him some notice," Yonn said.

"Helga said weeks, not months. So, it is soon," Oolada added.

"We have the best chance of protecting the king if we can be as specific as possible," Merryk said.

"Helga's visions have always been accurate, but their timing is less certain," Jamaal said.

"Currently, we have the vision and Prince Merreg's trip. We need something more to tie them together. We have no information about King Natas' movements," Goldblatt said.

Prince Merryk turned to Jamaal. "You and I should go to Newport to talk with Admiral Bellows. If we could determine where the meeting occurred, we may get additional insights."

Merryk looked back to Yonn. "We need to be ready to send the swordmaster to deliver the message to Bowen. He needs to come with us."

"Remind him to stay away from Prince Merreg," Goldblatt added. "The prince and he almost came to blows last time."

The next morning broke blue and clear. "It is going to be hot today," Tara said as she watched Merryk prepare Maverick for the trip to Newport. "It is good you will travel under the cover of trees for most of your journey. I assume you will camp along the road."

"With fifty men, it makes little sense to do it any other way. Where I spend the night is not what is bothering you."

"I never enjoy being away from you," Tara said, as she reached up to wrap her arms around Merryk's neck.

"I don't like being away from you, but this is a quick trip. You will be safe. Yonn is leaving all the guardsmen."

"It is not my safety which concerns me."

"I'll be fine. This will give you, Yvette, and Oolada the time to complain about the men, without having to hide your comments."

"It will also give you time to talk with Yonn again."

"This is a decision Yonn must make. It does not matter that you and I believe things will be fine. The proposal must be right for him and Yvette. But if it comes up…"

Before he could continue, Tara squeezed his neck one more time. "I knew you would not give up."

"If it comes up," Merryk said with a shake of his head.

Tara released Merryk and went to the stallion. "Maverick, will you take care of him?"

The stallion nodded his head.

CHAPTER 11

MATTERS OF MARRIAGE

Tara, Oolada, and Yvette stood on the top of the main gate to watch the procession of warriors cross the floodplain.

"The castle is going to seem empty without your clansmen," Yvette said. "They became a part of our daily activities. I do not know what Nelly will do without fifty extras to cook for."

"My guess, we will have a new dessert for dinner," Tara chuckled. "Her energy is boundless. She is a mother to us all."

"Helga is like that. We focus on her gift of vision, but the actual gift is her support for the clan and my grandfather."

"Why have the two not married?" Yvette asked.

"Yvette is consumed with why people marry," Tara added.

"They are tied together in a special way. I know they love each other, but my grandfather needed time after my grandmother died."

"Did anyone ever challenge Helga for her hand?" Tara asked.

"No, just like breaking a suitor's nose, no man wants a woman who knows his thoughts."

"Most of the time, you do not need to be a seer to know a man's thoughts," giggled Yvette.

Oolada continued. "Time passed, and the two grew to be responsible for the clans. Who they are to everyone else has kept them from marrying. But I think in the quiet moments, they are more married than anyone I have ever met. It is hard to explain, but marriage would not make any difference."

"Well, it would make a difference to me," a frustrated Yvette said as she looked across the valley. "I just want to know he truly loves me. He says he does, but…"

Tara reached out to console her friend. "I know he loves you, but he is worried he is unworthy. In a strange man sort of way, he is telling you he loves you so much, he wants you to have better, even if it means losing you."

"*Strange man* indeed, that really summarizes it. Why not let me decide if he is worthy? Helga was afraid I would let my past stop me from loving. Now it is my stupid title. I would be happy as Queen of the Barn if I could be with Yonn."

"*Queen of the Barn*? I have known you almost all your life, and you have never been a fan of the barn."

"Well, it would have to be a really nice barn," Yvette added in her defense.

Tara turned her attention to Oolada, who had laughed with the pair through their exchange. "What about you, Oolada? Do you have a sheep-herder or a really nice barn in your future?"

"As a girl, the only thing I hoped to be was a warrior. When my suitor came, no one explained I was supposed to lose if I wanted him. You both know I dislike losing. I broke his nose and his sword. Since then, no one else has come. It is just like Helga."

"What kind of man would you choose?" Tara asked. "Perhaps someone like Merryk?"

"You and I know there are no men like Merryk. But if you mean strong, gentle, courageous, sensitive, and extremely intelligent, then someone like him would be fine."

"If that man were available, would you fight for him?"

Tara's questions were too close for Oolada. Her face turned a bright red. "Yes, but I would be sure to lose."

The three laughed out loud.

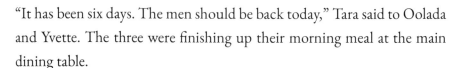

"It has been six days. The men should be back today," Tara said to Oolada and Yvette. The three were finishing up their morning meal at the main dining table.

"It seemed to go quickly," Oolada added. "I have enjoyed my time with you. Every time I visit, I find it harder to leave. I wonder if they have discovered anything by talking to the admiral."

"If there is a place at sea that matches Helga's description, the admiral will know it. We will have our answer soon enough. We should get our day started," Tara said.

As if on cue, Smallfolks appeared at the door. "Excuse me, but the contessa has visitors and a letter."

"Visitors for me?" a perplexed Yvette said.

"They asked that I give you this letter. They said it was from your father. I have them waiting by the door, if that is all right."

"Yes, Smallfolks. Just give us a minute and we will come down," Princess Tara replied.

Yvette looked at the parchment with her father's seal. "I dislike the look of this."

"It is the outside of an envelope. What is there not to like?" Tara said.

"In her last letter, mother said father was concerned. I just hope it is not bad news, or he has not done something stupid."

"Open it. You cannot face an enemy before you see them. You may be worried about nothing," Oolada offered.

Yvette's hand trembled as she broke the seal. "I cannot read it."

She handed it to Tara. Tara looked down and read the letter out loud:

My dearest Yvette,

Your mother and I were deeply concerned about the events which have transpired within the Teardrop Kingdom. When we allowed you to go, we never thought it would be to the front row of a war.

I appreciate your version of the events, but King Natas has assured us they are false, a hoax perpetrated on you. The people around you have embroiled themselves in a conflict which will not end soon.

My patience with your sheepherder is over. It is time for you to take your position as the mistress of your own house. Perhaps I have been too lenient on you in the past. Now this must stop.

I am sending this letter with the son of the Earl of Witman and his Bannermen. With my blessing, I have instructed them to return you home; forcefully if necessary.

I have entered into a contract of marriage for you to marry the Earl of Witman. The contract has been ratified by the Council of Justice and must be honored by all.

The earl is a man of sensible age who can control your wilder tendencies. The wedding will occur as soon as you return.

I do not expect that you will like this situation, but as your father, I must do what is best for you. You will not see it now, but this is best for your future and safety.

Your loving Father

Yvette began to sob and shake uncontrollably.

"What are you going to do?" Tara asked. "A ratified contract of marriage cannot be broken. I know."

"I need to talk with Yonn. I cannot just leave."

"You need to ask for time before you respond," Oolada said. "This will give you a chance to talk with Yonn and Prince Merryk. If there is a solution, the prince will find it."

"That sounds reasonable. We should tell the men from the earl you need time before responding," Tara said. "Besides, we cannot just leave them by the front door."

"We will be with you, Yvette. No one is going to force you to leave until you are ready," Oolada said.

Baron Lawrence Witman was the oldest son of the Earl of Witman. He was twenty-four years old and unmarried. With sandy colored hair and bright eyes, he might have been considered handsome. However, his presence was permeated with a sense of entitlement and arrogance.

Princess Tara greeted the guests. "Good morning. I am Princess Tara-reese, wife of Prince Merryk Raymouth, and this is the Lady Zoo of the Blue-and-White Mountain Clans."

Baron Witman rudely interrupted and looked at Yvette. "You must be the Contessa Yvette. Your family said you were striking with auburn hair; at least they did not lie about that."

"I am not sure I like your tone," Princess Tara said. "My husband will be back this evening. He will decide when you may speak with the contessa. Until then, there is lodging in the village. Good day."

"No. I am here to collect the contessa and return her to become my father's third wife. I do not wish to stay in this godforsaken hole one moment more than necessary." Baron Witman stepped past Tara and moved to address Yvette directly. "Go gather your personal effects. I will give you half an hour, then we are leaving with or without your clothing."

"You are collecting nothing," Oolada said, stepping into the baron's path.

Witman laughed at Oolada. "Men, remove this person."

The two Bannerman moved forward to Oolada. Reaching her first was a mistake. Oolada grabbed the first man and twisted the man's arm to lock it into a stick, then used him as a blunt force weapon to pummel the second. Within moments, both were lying on the floor holding different injured parts of their bodies. "Tara, please open the door."

Merryk, Yonn, and Jamaal rode into the courtyard to find a carriage driver and four guards. Three extra horses were being held, showing there were three more riders. Four Teardrop guardsmen bracketed the group.

"What's going on?" the prince asked.

"These men came to gather the contessa. A marriage contract binds her to their lord, the Earl of Witman," the senior guardsman replied.

Before they could explain any more, the front doors of the Great Hall sprang open and through the breach, two Bannermen came tumbling into the courtyard. Merryk heard noises from within the hall. Then another man, more finely dressed, rolled headfirst out the door, and fell in a puff of dust in the yard.

Oolada and the other women walked out the door. Oolada held a broadsword, which she tossed at the feet of the lord. "I think this is yours. Before you draw it again, you should learn how to use it."

A reasonable man would attempt to rise with some dignity. Witman, however, stood cursing.

"What is going on here? Explain yourself." Prince Merryk's tone was firm and measured.

"I am here to collect the contessa for my father. Everything was fine until that bitch," pointing to Oolada, "interfered."

There was a flash in Merryk's eyes. He crossed the two strides between himself and the baron. With an open hand, he slapped the man, knocking him to the ground. Then he reached down, grabbed him by the collar, and lifted him to eye level. The shorter man dangled in Merryk's grip.

"If you ever say anything disrespectful to Lady Zoo again, I will personally break your neck."

Merryk held the man until Jamaal intervened, "Your Highness, the man cannot breathe."

Merryk released him, allowing him to crumple to the ground.

A look of surprise crossed Witman's face, but equally the faces of Yonn, Jamaal, and the women. No one had ever seen Merryk angry.

Merryk walked to the women. "Are you all right?" The normal tone of concern and control returned.

"We are fine," Tara said as she wrapped her arms around Merryk's side.

"We have a legitimate claim which deserves to be heard," Witman shouted from the back of his horse.

Merryk turned to face the young man. "You may present your claim tomorrow midmorning. Captain Yonn, send your guards to see our guests find accommodations and provide them with security, so they do not violate any of our rules."

As the carriage rolled out of the castle yard, Oolada went to Merryk. She did not remember ever standing directly in front of him. It required her to look up, way up to his deep blue eyes. For a moment, she was lost. Then, regaining her composure, "Thank you, but we were not in any real danger."

"One of these days, you and I are going to have a discussion about what you consider *real danger*. Armed men entering my home, uninvited, and confronting everyone I care for—danger gets no more real than that for me. You should expect my protection. You are to be respected because you are a woman. In addition, you are Lady Zoo. You are entitled to respect because of your position and, more so, because you earned it. I will allow no one to insult you. Please forgive me for failing to protect you." Prince Merryk bowed his head and then moved up the steps into the hall.

Merryk's words and his eyes froze Oolada in place. She felt her face blush. Jamaal moved to her side. "Oolada, are you really unharmed?"

"Yes," she replied with a smile. "The men in the hall did not touch me."

CHAPTER 12

YES OR NO

The midday sun streamed into the Great Hall. Tiny particles of dust meandered through the air, catching the light. Prince Merryk led the group back inside the door. Turning to Captain Yonn, "When this is over, I want to know how armed men entered the hall without being escorted by guardsmen."

When Merryk stopped, Tara and Yvette talked simultaneously. Each attempted to describe the events, both asking Oolada for confirmation. After several minutes, Prince Merryk raised his hands over his head. "Stop! I am hot, and tired, and hungry. Before we have any more discussion, I am going to clean up and ask Nelly for food. In three quarters of an hour, I want everyone in the dining room. Smallfolks, send someone to get Father Bernard."

A quiet voice from the edge of the room responded, "Yes, My Prince."

"Yonn and Yvette, before we struggle to find a way out of the situation, we need to know what you really want. I need a *yes or no* answer. I will not disrupt international law unless you are committed to each other."

"Of course, we are committed," Yvette said.

Merryk raised his hand again. "Don't tell me. Talk to each other. Three quarters of an hour in the dining room. *Yes or no.*"

The group disbanded, leaving Yonn and Yvette alone. Yonn moved to one table and sat down. Yvette followed. Before Yvette could speak, Yonn began, "Perhaps this is best, a man of equal station and acceptable to your family. It will be hard initially, but in the long run, best for you."

"Best for me!" Yvette nearly yelled. "Best for me! Why not let me have some input on what is best for me? You are just like my father, making my decisions. I am going to be absolutely clear. What is best for me is *you*. I do not want a title, in a remote castle, as the third wife of some fat bellied earl. I want to have no title and be with the courageous young captain who stole my heart with his first mischievous smile. I want you. I thought you wanted me. If you do not love me, I will go to the Earl of Witman. Merryk's right. Now is the time to choose."

"Did you know your nose scrunches up when you are angry?"

Yvette's hand smashed into Yonn's shoulder as hard as she could. "Stop it! You must be serious. Do you want me as your wife?"

Yonn grabbed both of Yvette's arms in his hands and looked directly into her eyes. "There is nothing in the entire world I want more. I wanted you as my wife from the first moment I saw you. But do you realize what it would mean? You would lose everything you know, all your friends and family. I will never be worthy in their minds."

"First, the only real friend I have is Tara. I will not lose her. Second, my family pretty much gave me away at age twelve. Not seeing them will not be unusual. Finally, I like it in the Teardrop. I have people who listen to my opinions and rely on me for support. Most of all, I have you to argue with, laugh, and love. Yonn, I love you. I want to be your wife. That is all the title I need."

"I love you, Yvette. There is nothing in the world I want more than for you to be my wife." Yonn gave Yvette a gentle kiss, then dropped out of his seat to kneel on the floor. "Yvette D'Campin, would you do me the great honor of marrying me?"

Yvette jumped from her chair to encircle Yonn's neck, almost causing the two to tumble onto the floor. "Absolutely!"

———— ❧ ————

Yvette and Yonn entered the dining room, hand in hand.

"The decision looks like it was simple," Tara said.

"Yes, but now we must figure out how to make it work." Merryk pulled his chair closer to the table. "Chancellor, any suggestions?"

"Father Bernard will be here in a moment, but I am certain he is going to tell us the marriage contract is binding, unless one party is dead or mentally unstable. You and Tara know this better than most."

"Yes, that is exactly what I am going to say," Father Bernard said as he entered the room. "Smallfolks told me the details on the way over. Yonn and Yvette, I have seen the two of you since I arrived. I have been hoping you would be my first wedding, but now, I am not sure that is possible under the circumstances."

"Prince Merryk, could you just refuse to honor the contract?" Yvette pleaded.

"Perhaps, but the question is, would that do more harm for everyone else? It would solve your problem, but it would put me at odds with the Council, just as our relationship is being restored. The church has real value to the people of the Teardrop. As long as it does not meddle in politics, the church helps everyone. It is present in births, deaths, and weddings, all the major events in people's lives. The priests provide counseling to the people, help with education, and assistance for the poor. People need something to believe in bigger than men. The church helps with all these things."

Father Bernard shook his head. "My Prince, you never cease to amaze me. I could not express the role of the church any better. To reject the contract would be to deny the authority of the church over all the other things you described."

"This is all my fault. If I had simply asked Yvette sooner, she would be my wife," Yonn said in a voice filled with tension.

"The law is clear," Goldblatt reiterated. "The contract must be honored, unless one party is dead or mentally unsound."

"Does the law say that, or does it say a party must be competent to marry, meaning not dead or mentally impaired?" Prince Merryk asked.

"But that is the definition of competence," Father Bernard added.

"It also means, for example, if Yonn had married Yvette, then she would not be competent to marry another. She would already be a wife," Prince Merryk said.

"Clearly, a married woman cannot be the subject of a marriage contract to another man." Father Bernard added, "But the contract is signed and ratified, and she is not married."

"Gentlemen," directing his comments to Goldblatt and Father Bernard, the prince continued, "when must the person be competent, at the time of the contract, or the time of the wedding?"

"At the time of the wedding," both answered.

"If Yonn and Yvette were married, the contract would be void," Goldblatt said.

Father Bernard placed his hand on his chin in contemplation. "We have been told of the contract, but Prince Merryk, have they given you any tangible evidence?"

Shaking his head, no. "I assume Baron Witman will do so tomorrow."

"Right now, neither of us has any actual evidence of the contract. However, Yvette cannot choose a husband without the permission of her family," Bernard said.

"Father Bernard, do women have the ability to know right from wrong? Do they have the ability to choose or reject their personal salvation?"

"Your Highness knows the answer to both questions. A woman has free will just as a man."

"But not in terms of property and person," Goldblatt interrupted. "The senior male member of her family controls her decision to protect the family's property rights."

"Property is not a matter of Faith, but only a matter of the law of inheritance. If I am correct, the church does not care about how property and titles are passed," Merryk said.

"It gets mingled, but you are right, the Faith does not care about either," Father Bernard said.

"Since the evidence of a marriage contract has not been provided to Father Bernard or me, neither of us would be ignoring a ratified contract. I believe we are free to act. If Yonn were to renounce any claims for property which would arise from the marriage, then the family should have no concern about property rights. Yvette, as a woman with free will, could choose to marry Yonn. She might be violating the wishes of her father, but the marriage would still be valid. When the contract is presented, Yvette would be incompetent because she is already married, Merryk concluded. Only, of course, if Father Bernard agrees."

Everyone's eyes shifted to look at Father Bernard. "Most ingenious. I believe the reasoning is sound. There will be a breach of contract for your father, but given he did not know of the wedding, it would be a simple mistake of fact. The problem is my schedule is very crowded." Bernard paused. "I think, however, I might squeeze you in this afternoon, but only if you promise not to do something silly, like the prince and princess, and not consummate your marriage."

A major sigh of relief rose from the room. "We promise, absolutely," Yvette said earnestly.

CHAPTER 13

THE BARON

The firstborn son of the Earl of Witman appeared promptly mid-morning. Smallfolks and a guard escorted him and his two men into the audience hall. Smallfolks motioned for the baron to be seated at the table in front of the raised dais. His demeanor had changed markedly from the previous day. He now moved to his chair with caution. He stood promptly as Captain Yonn entered the room and in a loud voice announced, "Their Royal Highnesses, Prince Merryk Raymouth and Princess Tarareese, Jamaal ZooWalter, the Lady Zoo, Chancellor Goldblatt, Father Bernard, and my wife, Contessa Yvette.

A look of confusion crossed the face of the young man as he watched the group find their places to sit. Everyone sat, except Yvette. She moved to hold the hand of Captain Yonn, who stood to the side of the dais. When all were seated, Prince Merryk nodded to Baron Witman.

Reaching into his leather portfolio, the baron retrieved a stack of documents. "I have been sent by my father, the Earl of Witman, and the Count D'Campin, to collect Contessa Yvette D'Campin to fulfill a marriage contract ratified by the Council of Justice. He handed the documents to Captain Yonn, who delivered them to Chancellor Goldblatt.

Before sitting down, the young lord added, "Also, I would like to apologize to Your Highness, Prince Merryk. I did not know who you were.

My actions were unacceptable. I should have waited to present my petition directly to you."

"Yesterday, you showed complete disrespect," Tara said. "I believe you owe Lady Zoo an apology for ordering your men to remove her."

The young lord was unaccustomed to being reprimanded by anyone, much less a woman. However, the one thing his father had taught him was to be respectful of people with superior titles, especially if they were powerful. "Yes, Your Highness." Turning to Lady Zoo. "Please forgive me. I did not know you were a lady."

"In this kingdom, every woman is a lady," Prince Merryk inserted. "It would serve you well to remember. They deserve respect regardless of their station. Is that clear?"

"Yes, Your Highness. I will remember." His hand went to the bruises on his neck.

"Chancellor, what has the baron given us?"

"These are copies of the ratified contract for Yvette D'Campin to marry the Earl of Witman. Everything appears to be in order." Goldblatt handed the contract to Father Bernard.

Bernard quickly scanned the document, then nodded to the prince. "Everything is in order, other than Yvette D'Campin does not have the legal capacity to marry. She is already married to Captain Yonn."

"But she cannot be married. Her father has agreed she is to marry the earl. Her father is the one to tell her who she may marry and what is best for her."

"Facts are often different in person than they appear from afar. Even well-intended parents can be wrong in their assumptions. The count assumed she was still unmarried," Tara said.

Father Bernard handed a copy of the marriage certificate to Witman. "A married woman cannot be the subject of a new marriage contract. This agreement is void."

Witman quickly reviewed the document. "This is dated yesterday. This is an outrage. The Council will not accept a sham marriage."

"Perhaps you do not recognize Father Bernard. Most recently, he was the Secretary to the Provost, a position which he held for over twenty years. I am confident the Council will confirm his interpretation. You cannot collect another man's wife for marriage. Your petition is denied," Merryk said with authority.

"There will be repercussions," the baron said with false bravado.

"You do not fully understand to whom you are speaking." Jamaal said. "You are in the Teardrop Kingdom, and the man you are addressing is Prince Merryk Raymouth, who defeated the Army of Justice. There are no repercussions you or your father can threaten which will intimidate the prince."

The sudden realization of the truth caused the color to drain from Baron Witman's face. His voice cracked, and he stuttered, "I ... I am sorry, Your Highness. No disrespect was intended. I was so focused on my task, I forgot myself. Please forgive my impertinence. I hope my actions will not permanently taint the relationship between our country and yours. Please forgive me."

Prince Merryk raised his eyebrows as he looked sternly at the baron. His voice was level and firm. "I assume this will be the end of this matter."

Witman nodded in agreement.

Prince Merryk continued, "We were all quick yesterday, and I am sure we are past everything today. Now, enjoy the rest of your visit, which I assume will be short. We are concluded."

"What happened in there?" Oolada asked Jamaal. "Why did the young lord suddenly cower before Prince Merryk? He looked like the prince's words would cut him."

"Power, and fear of power. We know Prince Merryk. We have traveled, hunted, and fought with him. To us, he is just our prince, but the last events have changed how the rest of the world sees him. My guess is yesterday, the baron did not know who grabbed him. Only this morning did he discover he had offended *the* Prince Merryk, a famous conqueror of armies and navies, and an economic force."

"But Prince Merryk does not want the people to treat him differently. He does not want to act like a royal."

"Which, strangely, makes him the most royal man I have ever met."

CHAPTER 14

UPDATE

With the issue of the earl resolved, Merryk asked the group to join him again in the dining room. "With all the excitement, we have not shared the results of our trip. We met with Admiral Bellows. After hearing the length of Prince Merreg's absence, he produced a chart of the waters within a three-day radius of the Capital City. Initially, there were several alternatives, including actually visiting the Inland Passage."

"However, when he heard Helga's description," Jamaal said. "He immediately identified an island called Otok. It lies just north of the trade route between Natas' Kingdom and the Inland Passage and is an equal sailing distance from Natas and the Capital City, both a little over two days. It also has mountains which keep one side from getting rain, while the other side is drenched."

"Our initial guess was King Natas and Prince Merreg were part of Helga's vision. Now we have at least circumstantial evidence, but not enough to go to the king," Chancellor Goldblatt said. "We do not know if King Natas was really there."

"I've been thinking about Helga's comment about the storm rocking the foundation. Kingdoms live and die upon the strength of their king. I cannot think of anything, except an attack on the king, that would shake all the kingdom. I don't understand why my brother, who will be the next king, would want to join an effort to harm our father." Merryk asked.

"If you are a spoiled child," Tara said. "there are two possibilities. You are being stopped from something you want, or you are not getting what you want fast enough."

"He's not becoming king fast enough?" a puzzled Merryk asked. "Selection will be next year."

"But he would not be the actual king for many more years," Goldblatt added.

"It is not the first time in history a son has wanted to seize control before his father is dead," Jamaal added. "Even the clans have stories."

"If that is the reason, why now? I understand King Natas. He is under great economic pressure. King Michael rejected Natas' request for the return of his ships. Could he believe that Merreg, as king, would reverse the decision?" Prince Merryk asked.

"Not without risking a civil war," Jamaal said. "The clans will not support a reversal of your victory."

"I concur," Goldblatt added. "The decision would be extremely unpopular with the people. The nobles hold no love for King Natas, so unless they would gain, they would also object."

"But my father does not care if the High Kingdom goes into a civil war, particularly if he controls the new king," Tara said.

"We are forgetting the third person," Merryk said. "If Merreg and Natas had a noble to provide support and split the loyalties of the noble houses, it might provide enough cover for Merreg to survive the objections."

"Now you see why pledges of loyalty to all members of the royal family are so important," Goldblatt said.

"The Duke of Ressett attempted to get horses back for my father. They have a long-term business relationship and I believe the Ressetts may be part of a larger family tree. His apology to Merryk may have been an attempt to hide his involvement."

"What would he gain?" Jamaal asked. "Economic advantage?"

"Yes, and he has a daughter," Oolada spoke for the first time. "If she became queen, his financial leverage would be significant. In addition, a male heir, his grandson, might end up on the throne. This would reposition his family in the line of kings. Old men often focus on the future, more than the young. Also, he is in the unique position of not needing to take any action until he sees the outcome of the others' efforts."

Merryk's face broke into a broad smile as he looked at Oolada. "Gaspar told me you were as good with interpersonal issues as you are with the sword. Although circumstantial, I believe we have our three clouds and the target, the king. Now, when will they make their move and how?"

"We need something more concrete to tell Bowen. If they increase security too soon, it could let the others know we are aware of the plot. Hard as it is, we must wait for something more," Goldblatt said.

"Oolada and I need to return home in the morning," Jamaal said. "The Walt has called the Council meeting for the full moon. I need to be there. We have moved all the clansmen to Newport. Now we have one-hundred fifty warriors who can be shifted toward the Capital City or held in reserve to protect the Teardrop."

"Jamaal, my instincts say we are not the target. There have been multiple direct attacks, and all have failed. I think they are going to attack the root of our power, my father. Without his support, they would drive us back into the mountains."

"I agree with the prince. The king is the target," Goldblatt stated. "We need to position ourselves to support the king."

"I left the swordmaster at Newport so he can go quickly when needed," Yonn said.

"Very well. I could say I hope we are wrong, but in truth, I believe something will happen," Prince Merryk said. "Now all we can do is stay vigilant and wait."

"Tara said I could find you here," Oolada said, as she exited the door to the top of the old tower. "What a beautiful night. The moon is so bright."

"It is still a week to full, but it fills the night," Prince Merryk replied.

"Today, you said they might push you into the mountains. Would that be so bad?"

"No, not bad at all."

"You would love the mountains. They are so quiet, with clean air and beautiful sunsets."

"I would love them." Prince Merryk again smiled broadly at Oolada. "Unfortunately, to speak like Helga, I do not believe that is my destiny."

"I have never heard you speak of destiny before."

"Probably because everything about me is improbable. Sometimes I believe I should not be here at all—not this person, not this time."

"But your presence has made things safer and fuller."

"There is much about me that cannot be shared. I do not deserve the faith you have in me."

"I cannot imagine any world where I would not have faith in you."

"That is very kind. I believe I have started things which I cannot stop. I fought the Army of Justice to save those around me. I would have surrendered, but the general would not allow it. Now my father is in danger from his own son. I tried to save a few, but now, many may die."

"You can only do what you think is right at the time. You deal with what follows, again by choosing what seems to be best, at that time."

Merryk looked at Oolada, shaking his head slightly. "My mother used to say a similar thing. She would say doing the right thing may not be easy, but it's always the right thing. Thank you for reminding me."

Oolada continued to look directly into Merryk's eyes. "Regardless of what happens, I want you to know I will always be here to support you in whatever way you need."

"Thank you. Even though I think fighting alongside of me in Newport and defending the castle in my absence might be enough."

"But we were in no real danger."

Merryk laughed. "There you go again. I wonder what you consider real danger, but I pray the two of us never find out."

Tara carried a candle lamp as she moved down the hall to the Chancellor's study. Knocking on the door, she asked, "Chancellor, do you have a minute?"

Chancellor Goldblatt sat in his overstuffed chair. Several candles burned around him to provide light as he read. "Of course, Your Highness. Where are the prince and Lady Zoo?"

"Both are on the top of the old tower. I sent Oolada to say goodbye to Merryk."

"You know Oolada is infatuated with the prince?"

"Yes, I wanted her to have a few moments alone with him."

Chancellor Goldblatt frowned and looked critically at Tara. "Why would you want that?"

"We did not talk about the other issue today. For Prince Merreg to be king, he must have two wives. The Duke of Ressett and my father both have daughters. Two pieces that are required for Merreg to assume the throne."

"You are right. We skirted the obvious path we are on. If Merreg attempts to overthrow the king and fails, Merryk will be the Crown Prince. If his attempt is successful, Jamaal is right. There will be a revolt. Only one man can rightfully claim to lead that revolt, Prince Merryk."

"Both circumstances mean Merryk must be ready to fulfill the requirements of the king, whether or not he wants it. We must be ready to help him, even if it means I must share him." Tara's voice was heavy with resignation.

"I perceive there is something you want," Goldblatt stated.

"Several noble families made us aware they have daughters. We have our list. My question, is there a way to see if Gaspar wants Oolada formally on our list? Today, she showed a different side. She is far more thoughtful than just a warrior," Tara said.

"I noticed that too. Her comments were well thought out and insightful. The questions are: How do we make this inquiry without binding the prince to a commitment? Can we do this without his permission? And finally, why do you think Oolada would be an excellent choice?" the Chancellor asked.

"She is just like Merryk. Neither wants to be anything except themselves. Merryk does not want to be king, and my guess is Oolada has never thought of being queen. Another woman from a noble family would have thought about nothing else her entire life. I know."

Goldblatt thought for a second and then answered. "I will send a private note asking for Gaspar's suggestion about whom to consider. This would allow him to include Oolada without us being committed. He can also give suggestions without including Oolada. I can ask the note to be kept confidential, a preparation to help the prince."

"Very well," Tara replied. She sat for a moment, looking at one candle. Finally, she let out a deep breath. "All my life, I wanted to be a queen. Now, when it is in sight, a big part of me wishes to just stay where we are. But I can see fate pushing Merryk. We must help him when the time comes, even if it is not our desire."

CHAPTER 15

STONE & WIND

Colonel Lamaze stood on the wheel deck of the freighter as it turned into the harbor. *There are places in the world I do not want to go. This is at the top of my list.* The colonel's eyes scanned the odd collection of vessels attached to the dock. All lacked any markings, no flags of affiliation, even their names were covered with black cloth. He and Lieutenant Jordan had removed their military garb, substituting plain sailor clothing to help them blend in, though the fact they were clean set them apart.

Turning to the ship's captain, Lamaze directed. "Remember, no one goes ashore. Stay alert. In this port, they can attack you as you lay at anchor."

The captain acknowledged the instructions.

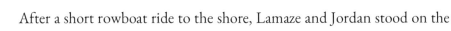

After a short rowboat ride to the shore, Lamaze and Jordan stood on the dock. "Do we know where to go?" Jordan asked.

"If we stay put, I think they will find us," Lamaze replied.

Within five minutes, a group of six ragged men stomped down the dock to greet them. "What'cha business here?" the black-toothed leader snarled.

"None of yours, unless you can take us to see Stone and Wind."

"Why shud I?"

Lamaze stepped up to look the man directly in the eye. "Because if you do not, Stone will tie you to a stake in the tide pool for the crabs."

"No reas'n tuh get nasty. Jus' ask'n."

Clearly Lamaze spoke his language. "Now!"

Lamaze and Jordan followed the leader through a series of narrow alleys which snaked their way from the dock. Everywhere they looked, an assortment of filthy men and women lay in doorways. All seemed to be recovering from the previous night or a week of cheap rum and debauchery. The air was filled with the smell of human excrement.

"This place is disgusting," Jordan whispered to Lamaze.

"Ignore how it looks and smells. Every corner is deadly. Stay alert."

After a few minutes, the alley opened into a broader road which meandered up a small hill to a large white house. The house was immaculate, in stark contrast to the squalor of the shantytown below.

"I gotcha to the gate. Not allowed beyond," black tooth said.

Lamaze dropped a gold coin in the man's hand. "For your trouble."

An eight-foot-high, iron-spiked fence surrounded the house.

"What do we do now?" Jordan asked.

"Knock on the door."

The gate was unguarded. Lamaze unlatched it and walked to the front door.

A neatly dressed butler answered the bang of the doorknocker.

"Please tell Stone and Wind their old friend, Colonel Lamaze, brings greetings from King Natas."

Without a word, the butler motioned for them to enter a well-appointed parlor. Within minutes, their host arrived.

Stone is a man who looks like his name, Jordan thought. *The only one I have ever seen who is as tall as Prince Merryk, but the prince was not as heavy.*

"Good afternoon, my old friend," Stone said as he pounded Colonel Lamaze on the back. "Who is your associate?"

Lamaze smiled back at Stone. "This is Lieutenant Jordan."

"Jordan," Stone said as he extended his hand.

"Monsieur Stone," Jordan said, accepting the hand.

Stone clamped down on Jordan's hand and squeezed hard. A toothy grin appeared. His eyes narrowed and sparkled as he watched the lieutenant wince at the unexpected pain.

"Stop playing with our guests!" a bright red-haired, green-eyed woman shouted as she flowed into the room. She was wearing a flowered caftan with slits on both sides from the hip down and a gaping neckline.

"Just having some fun. Not gonna' hurt him, much," Stone replied, smiling; finally releasing the lieutenant's hand.

"Colonel Lamaze, I am amazed your master allowed you off the leash long enough to visit us," Wind said.

"How kind of you to notice," Lamaze replied, his eyes locked on her, the way a mongoose would watch a snake.

The woman walked over to Lieutenant Jordan. Reaching down, she gently took the hand Stone had crushed and raised it up to examine. She exaggerated the motion in a way to allow her ample breasts to almost fall from the front of the caftan. Her eyes were on Jordan's eyes, not his hand. "Where did you find this innocent one?" her voice had a deep, sultry Franc accent.

"He is not innocent. He just has good manners," Lamaze replied.

"Too bad," the woman said as she dropped Jordan's hand and stepped back to Lamaze. "Sit." The words were not a request, but an order. "The last time, you did not have the courtesy to come. You just sent a letter."

"And some gold," Lamaze added.

"Oh yes, gold," Wind answered. "Even so, two of our men never returned."

Jordan watched the exchange with fascination. Stone grabbed a jug of rum and slumped into an oversized chair. All the discussion was with the woman, Wind.

"I am here today," Lamaze replied. "And I bring the opportunity for much more gold."

"Much more gold," Wind parroted Lamaze's words. "Which means much more risk. What task does your devil of a king want done now? Certainly not another attempt to kill young Prince Merryk. I heard an army failed last time."

"This task is easier than killing Prince Merryk."

"The first time you did not want to pay for me to kill him." Wind's face changed from an otherwise pleasant expression to a vicious snarl.

"This is a bigger project. We do not need your special skill. King Natas wants you to lead about two hundred men to back up the new king of the High Kingdom."

"I was unaware the old king had died," she replied.

"He has not, yet," Lamaze said.

"Killing a king is very high risk and would carry very high payment." Wind's eyes were now fixed on Lamaze. "What did you have in mind?"

"His son, Prince Merreg, will remove his guard, so there will be little risk. Afterwards, the prince will need protection until he solidifies his position as king."

For the first time in the discussion, Stone spoke. "What is it with everyone in that family having the same name: Merryk, Merreg? We should kill them all, just for that."

"Yes, we should kill them all." Wind said to placate Stone. Refocusing on the colonel, "How much gold and when?"

A different group of ragged men escorted Lamaze and Jordan back to the dock. The two did not speak until they were on the rowboat, headed back to their ship. "A most unpleasant place. I would be all right never returning," Lieutenant Jordan said. "What a strange relationship between Stone and Wind. Do you know how they came together?"

"Not exactly, but the two were made for each other. Stone is big and enjoys hurting people, as you have seen. Wind is a skilled assassin. She is a master with small blades. They say no one is better. She is more polished than Stone, but she has the same taste for watching people suffer. She got her name by striking like the wind, and then disappearing without a trace. She is extremely smart and will kill anyone for gold. Stone is the brawn, and Wind is the brains; together they formed the Black Hats."

"I cannot say I am pleased to be working with them," Lieutenant Jordan said.

"We are not working with them. We are using them as a tool. The same way we would a pack of hunting dogs. But remember, hunting dogs can turn on you, even if you feed them."

CHAPTER 16

ANNOUNCEMENTS

The end of September was uncommonly warm. The days were bright, but the nights reflected the chill of the winter to come. As if following an unpublished timetable, many of the deciduous trees had begun to change colors.

Captain Yonn found Maizie sitting on top of the fence with Maverick standing beside her. Both were watching the prince. "What is he doing?" Yonn asked.

"*Speer'ment*," Maizie said with certainty. Maverick nodded his head in agreement. "He made a new thing that is light and tough. Now he is going to shoot arrows at it."

Prince Merrick had placed a square of metal against the pile of hay and was walking back to where Yonn had joined Maizie.

On the ground in front of Maizie was a bow and a quiver of arrows. "Good afternoon, Your Highness. What are you working on?" Yonn asked.

"An experiment." Both Maizie and Maverick nodded at Merryk's confirmation of their statement.

"Have you ever noticed how heavy armor is? A full set of plate is almost forty pounds. I have created some alternative armor which is lighter and more flexible. I want to see if it gives the same protection."

"Plate always gives the best protection," Yonn said.

"True, but wearing it all day in battle will tire even the strongest man." Merryk picked up the longbow and grabbed an arrow.

"Do you want me to do that for you?" Yonn asked. "I would not want you to miss the barn."

"Thank you for the vote of confidence, but I think I can at least hit the side of the barn." Merryk released the arrow, which rang true, hitting the metal squarely in the center. The arrow fell harmlessly to the ground. "Excellent! The arrow may leave a mark, but otherwise perfect."

Merryk moved closer to inspect the target. "Yonn, walk with me. I have been thinking. You and Yvette have not had a proper honeymoon. I want you to take the next couple of weeks off."

"I cannot possibly leave now, just as things are becoming critical."

"I want you to have a honeymoon, but I also need the new Commander of the Guard to be near our troops. They are in Newport, and that is where you need to be. I think nothing will happen in the next few weeks, but if it does, all of our responses will need to pass through the port. Besides, Yvette has not seen the ocean since she arrived. The beaches are beautiful to walk on at sunset."

"Your Highness, I sincerely appreciate the elevation of my rank, but I promised Goldblatt I would never leave your side," Yonn said, struggling with the concept of leaving.

"You made that promise before we faced armies, and when we had only a few men. Now I am behind almost four hundred, which you command. With our relay system, we can talk in less than eight hours. It will do you no good to object. Tara and Yvette are already packing. You will take a carriage and stop along the way. I also had the harbormaster find a small inn just outside the port. You will be close, but you will have some privacy."

"Thank you, Your Highness. I do not know what to say."

"Say you will try to enjoy yourself." Merryk picked up the square and returned to Maizie and Maverick. "Maizie, please take Maverick back to the stables."

"Maverick, be sure she gets there." The horse nodded and then let out a small whinny. "I will not forget to tell him," Merryk replied.

"Tell me what?" Yonn asked.

"Maverick wants to congratulate you and Yvette on your marriage and thank you for giving him hope."

A puzzled Yonn looked at the horse. "Hope?"

"Yes, Maverick is encouraged by your being with Yvette. It gives him hope for Bella."

"Why?" Yonn asked.

"Because he has the same problem with Bella that you had with Yvette. No pedigree."

The first of October brought a change in the weather. A heavily overcast morning sent a steady rain to pound on the housetops. A chilly wind blew in from the south, tumbling the clouds in waves like an upside-down ocean.

For the first time in the season, fires were lit throughout the castle. Merryk started one in his room to knock off the morning chill.

"Oh, it is cold this morning," Tara said, as she slipped onto the sofa beside Merryk.

"How can you be cold in a huge robe?" Merryk asked as he put his arm around her. "You got a letter this morning." Merryk handed the parchment to Tara.

"Who is it from?" Tara asked as she broke open the seal. After reading the note, she turned to Merryk. "It is from my mother, and I think it is a warning."

Merryk took the note and read.

My dearest Tarareese,

I could not wait to tell you the exciting news. Your sister is to be married soon. Father concluded the arrangements on a trip the first of September. He has been very secretive to keep the groom a surprise. We have been told to prepare for the wedding on the first of November. We are to leave the last week of October for Mandy's ceremony.

You know how Mandy hates sea voyages, but father assured her the trip would take only five nights at sea. She is understandably very nervous. I think more about who the groom may be than the length of the trip.

Father has assured us where we are going has furs if Mandy needs them. We have so little time; we are struggling to get the dress prepared. I know you appreciate the need to prepare in advance.

Under different circumstances, I would invite you to the wedding, but I fear the current conflict will not end. I know you share my fears and apprehension about an unknown groom. Although the groom is a secret, father believes the groom will be a good fit. It is my belief he would have been appropriate for you.

We will keep you in our prayers. Love always.

Queen Stephanie.

"Your sister is to marry, but what makes you think it is a warning?"

"Mother carefully drafted the note. At first glance, it looks like a simple announcement. However, my mother never calls me Tarareese unless I am in trouble. And she never signs my letters with anything other than 'mother'. The letter contains critical facts. Father had a meeting on the first of September and the groom is five days away, the exact distance to the Capital City. They are preparing for the wedding where the weather will be cold. Additional facts stand out, a warning the conflict will not end, and the groom would have been suitable for me. Prince Merreg was father's first choice for me."

"I think we may have our timeframe," Merryk said. "Dress. We need to speak with the Chancellor."

Chancellor Goldblatt was still in his robe when he joined the prince and princess in the study. After reading the letter, he asked, "Are you sure this is from your mother?"

"Absolutely. I would know her handwriting anywhere, and she never calls me Tarareese unless I am in trouble.

"The timing of your father's trip matches Helga's vision and Merreg's absence from the Capital City. The wedding on the first of November, and their departure the week before, suggests something must occur by then. The next two to three weeks would be the timeframe," the Chancellor concluded.

"We need to get the information and warning to Bowen," Prince Merryk said.

"I agree," the Chancellor replied. "We know when, but we still do not know how."

The prince turned as he stood on his way to find the courier. "Some warning is better than none."

Chancellor Bates received the nondescript note from a valet. *Please meet me at the PnP at noon.* The only person who would send such a note was the duke.

Entering the front door of the Pipe and Pint, the butler again greeted Chancellor Bates.

"I believe the duke is waiting to see me."

"Yes, this way, please.

The butler escorted the chancellor into the general meeting room. After greeting several other members on his way, he came to the table with the Duke of Ressett.

"I am glad you could make it. I have selected some light fare for our lunch," the duke said. "Help yourself to the wine."

"Thank you. This is an interesting place to meet."

"On the contrary, a public meeting is precisely what we need."

In a quiet voice, which only the two could hear, Chancellor Bates said, "I assume you have some information for me."

"Yes, our mutual friend has acquired the black stallion for Prince Merreg. The horse will arrive in the middle of the month. I assume you want to put him in the large stable, the one that holds two hundred."

"Two hundred?" the chancellor questioned.

"My associate wants to be sure there are no conflicting allegiances which would interfere with our transaction," the duke said.

"I understand," Bates replied. "Nothing will interfere. The prince is looking forward to getting the horse."

CHAPTER 17

DARK OF NIGHT

The sea had a light chop. The moonlight illuminated the thin clouds drifting toward the shore. Two ships, cloaked in black, glided quietly into an abandoned dock on the far side of the Capital City port. The only sound was the lapping of waves on the sides of the ships.

Lieutenant Jordan stood with a High Kingdom officer he had only met earlier in the evening, watching the two ships as they approached. Jordan felt a knotting of his stomach. *I really do not want to see these people again.* Within a quarter of an hour, the first ship docked.

The first person off the ship was a tall, burly man who wasted no time in approaching the lieutenant. "Jordan, good to see you," Stone said.

"I am sure you will forgive me if I do not shake your hand," Jordan replied.

Stone laughed. "Lamaze said you were smart. Now where are you going to put us?" Stone's big grin could not hide the evil sparkle in his eyes.

"Prince Merreg has arranged lodging for your men. We have separate apartments for you and your lady."

"How far away from the men will we be?" Jordan had not seen Wind approach.

"Less than a quarter mile. This officer will direct your men, and I will guide you."

Wind turned to Stone. "Go with the men. See they are settled, then join me. Be sure everyone knows our presence is to be hidden, for now. I will go with Lieutenant Jordan."

With no discussion, Stone complied, moving to gather his men.

"I thought Lamaze would come himself," Wind said.

"Unfortunately, he is recognized in the Capital City. I can move without attracting attention."

"I assume you have information for me."

"Yes," Jordan replied. "Midmorning, Chancellor Bates will meet with you at the apartments. He will bring the current schedules for the king and Prince Merreg for the next two weeks. Also, he will have the guard schedules. After you review the information, Chancellor Bates will arrange a time for you and Monsieur Stone to meet with Prince Merreg privately. They wish to keep your presence a secret as long as possible."

"There are many questions which need to be answered. Be sure the prince knows I will need to meet with him sooner rather than later."

The military barracks, like the dock, were in a seldom used portion of the port. They had cleared it out for the visitors. Apartments for Stone and Wind were just a few blocks away and had been completely refurbished.

Chancellor Bates arrived at the apartments right on time. "I hope you find the accommodations sufficient."

"Yes," Mademoiselle Wind replied. "They are quite nice, but we are not here to enjoy your hospitality. We have a job to do. Do you have the schedules?"

"Of course." Chancellor Bates began to interpret the documents for Wind.

"I can read," she said bluntly. "When will we meet with Prince Merreg?"

"I will need to check with the prince, but soon."

A knife flashed into Wind's hand, stopping just a hair's breadth from the chancellor's throat. "I do not have the time, and certainly not the patience, for lackeys. You will go tell your master I want to meet with him this afternoon. If he cannot come to me. I will come to him. Understood?"

Any blood the chancellor had in his face immediately fled, and his eyes became large orbs. He nodded, with a small bob, his understanding.

A note arrived within an hour of the chancellor's departure, confirming the meeting later in the day. The prince arrived, with the chancellor in tow, near the appointed time. A little late, but nothing unusual for a royal.

Stone greeted him at the door. "Please come in, Your Highness. I am Stone and allow me to introduce Mademoiselle Wind."

Wind was dressed in fashionable clothing with her hair appropriately styled. She would have blended into any gathering of polite society, other than her bright red hair and beauty would have attracted much attention.

"Mademoiselle Wind, I must say, I am surprised by your appearance. Chancellor Bates' description of this morning had me expecting someone else," Prince Merreg said with a gracious smile.

"I can be whatever you need, my prince," Wind said as she bowed. The motion was slow and intentional, allowing the prince an excellent view of her cleavage. She watched the prince's eyes sweep across the rounded curves. A small smile appeared. She had learned much about the prince.

The prince took her hand and led her to the sofa. "The chancellor says you have questions. Shall we sit?"

Wind did not waste any time on small talk. "Next Tuesday, the king is going to open the annual cattle show in the center of town. He will pass through several streets, but also, he will walk through the crowd in the square. When a person is surrounded by many people, it is hard, if not impossible, to protect them. Will you be with him?"

"I can be."

"Fine. Use your personal guard to protect the king and you. This will make removing his protection easier and justified," Wind suggested. "Are your men to be trusted, or should we eliminate them at the same time?"

"I will assure those closest to the king do not interfere," Prince Merreg said. "They will step aside to leave the king unprotected."

"Very well. If there are any changes to the schedule or route, I must know at once. The chancellor loves to deliver messages to me. I am sure he would bring them promptly," she said with a sadistic sneer.

"Agreed," Merreg replied.

"After the attack, some of our men will escort you back to the castle for protection. We will move the rest to just outside the castle."

"That is unnecessary. All my men are loyal."

"But are the men who they command? Trust me, an attack on a king challenges everyone's loyalties. We do not want your new position stolen by a zealot."

Stone spoke. "I hope you are not squeamish. We will defend you and stop resistance, but not gently. If you worry about blood, you should stay away."

A tightlipped smile crossed Prince Merreg's face, and his nose flared. "There is something special about the look in a man's eyes as he dies. I must admit, I like the smell of fresh blood," adding, "as long as it does not soil the carpet." His face brightened at the thought, and he laughed. Stone and Wind joined in the laughter.

"You may be the only royal I ever like," Stone said with a grin.

CHAPTER 18

NOW!

"Get Prince Merreg, *now*!" Wind was not pleased, and all who crossed her path were in peril. "*Now*!" she shouted again. She was wearing a brown wig and a plain household dress. She tossed the wicker basket she had been carrying to the ground.

"What happened?" Stone asked as he charged into the room. "The king had a second ring of protection. The prince's men allowed the king to drift away, as promised. The king was alone, but when I moved through the crowd to reach him, a wall of men blocked me."

"Yes, I estimate at least thirty extra guards, all without uniforms. They were mixed in the crowd. How could the prince not have known they were there?" Wind tore the brown wig off her head and threw it at the wall. "I dislike surprises."

She seemed to quiet herself for a moment. Her external demeanor seemed to calm. Her voice became steady. "Prince Merreg can get through any ring of protection. *Now,* I think the prince must prove he really likes the smell of fresh blood."

Oolada found Gaspar and Jamaal in the Great Square, talking with the men near the stables. "Grandfather, Helga needs you *now*."

Gaspar stood immediately to follow. Years of experience told him Helga never said *now* unless it was urgent. "Did she say about what?"

"No, only to get you *now*," Oolada repeated.

Gaspar, Jamaal, and Oolada rushed to the Council Chamber. Helga was looking south through the open window, waiting for them.

"Helga, what is it?" Gaspar asked.

"Start and stop. I cannot describe it any better. The events we were waiting for started; then stopped. Now the clouds are churning, boiling like a pot of hot water, mixing in a great darkness, a great evil. Another force has been added—one filled with death and blood."

"There is a fourth?" Jamaal asked.

"Yes." Helga said. "Gaspar, we need to go *now*. This force may be delayed, but it will not be stopped. We are needed. If we delay, it may be too late."

CHAPTER 19

MESSENGER

G aspar's instructions to double the men and horses required more rotation of guards than before. Yarron used it as an excuse to feel the air away from the sea. All the relay stations were discreetly hidden off the road. People could move up and down the path without knowing of their presence.

Yarron and six men had just arrived at the station where the road from the Capital City joined the road north to the mountains, and south to Newport. Before they turned to enter the trees, a lone rider struggled his way out of the road from the capital. He was slumped over the neck of his horse. Yarron saw the horse was covered in a lather from running hard for a long time.

"Sir, what is the problem?" Yarron asked.

"Quick, get off the road. They are right behind me," the man said. As he spoke, Yarron saw the blood-soaked arm and the uniform of the King's Guard.

"Off the road," Yarron ordered without question.

Seconds later, a gang of four men entered the road from the same direction as the first. Yarron knew the look of hunters.

"Sir, you must get these letters to Prince Merryk and Gaspar ZooWalt. The king's life depends upon it," the wounded man whispered, as he frantically pushed the parchments into Yarron's hand.

Yarron looked at his warriors. "We need to stop these men." The clansmen divided themselves into two groups: one went to block the road toward the port, and the other to cover a retreat of the four men. Although given the choice, the four were not wise enough to surrender.

Yarron returned to the King's Guard. "What happened?"

"Get the letters to the prince and the Walt. Prince Merreg stabbed his own father in the back. They have trapped the king in the castle. Prince Merryk must come. Get the letters—," the guard's voice quivered and ended.

───────※───────

It was near midnight when the rider charged into the courtyard. "I have an urgent message for the prince," he yelled to wake anyone who would listen.

Smallfolks knocked on Prince Merryk's door. "Your Highness, there is an urgent message from the Capital City."

Prince Merryk opened the door to accept the note. After skimming it, he said to Smallfolks, "Have the Chancellor meet us in the study immediately."

───────※───────

Within the hour of Helga's warning, the entire fortress sprang into action. Riders left to alert the other clans, horses moved in and out of the Great Square, and supplies and weapons were being checked for a second time.

Gaspar and Jamaal reviewed the last details for the trip south. "Everything appears ready," Jamaal said. "We should have everyone start out after the late morning meal. It may be the last hot one for a while."

"The other clans will meet us in three days on the hills just outside the Capital City. We can gather without attracting attention until we are ready," Gaspar said. "Oolada already left. She took men south to Leden Grubi."

"Good," Jamaal said. "The prince and I agreed if there was trouble, he would cross over Leden Grubi to the south road."

Gaspar nodded. "Oolada will turn east along the path until they find the prince. I pray the weather holds."

"We will all need prayers during our journey," Helga said as she entered the room. Uncharacteristically, she was dressed in soft deer hide pants and carrying a warm travel cloak.

"What do you think you are doing? War is no place for a woman," Gaspar said. "You are too important to risk."

"For whom? You, or the clan," a feisty Helga replied.

"I will not lie. I could not survive your loss."

"Then do not lose me. You are not packed and now you must hurry if you want to eat," Helga scolded.

Gaspar took a deep breath. He had lost this battle before.

It was just after dawn the next morning, when the relay rider with the message from the Capital City reached the first columns of Zoo warriors moving south.

"This message was also sent to Prince Merryk," Gaspar said. "The prince will go over Leden Grubi as planned. Oolada will be in the right place."

CHAPTER 20

GOODBYE

Somehow, in the time it took Smallfolks to wake the Chancellor and for him to join Merryk and Tara, Nelly produced hot tea and sweet cakes. She entered the study just as the Chancellor finished reading the messenger's note.

"This is most disturbing. I did not think Prince Merreg was capable of such treachery," Goldblatt said, shaking his head in disgust. "The depth of the hatred his uncle must have instilled in him is unbelievable."

"Again, we have many unanswered questions," Merryk said.

"I assume the red splotches on the note are the messenger's blood." Tara said. "His death alone confirms the message. Prince Merreg tried to kill his own father, the king."

"The messenger said the king was wounded. How severely we cannot know. The note from Bowen says they are trapped inside the castle, but we do not know by whom or how many," the Chancellor said.

"Two notes, both asked for help. One came to us and the other went to the Walt. I will respond," Merryk said. "I will leave soon after dawn and go over Ledin Grubi as I promised Jamaal.. It is the quickest way. The only concern is winter already stalks the mountains, but the sky is clear now."

"What do you mean 'I'? You will not be going alone. We will go together," Tara said.

"No, Tara, it could be treacherous to cross the mountains this time of year and I do not know what dangers lie on the other side."

"If you will not be let me go, then wait until Yonn gets here. Send for him at once."

"Unfortunately, we do not have time. Waiting would add at least two days, and I need to leave Yonn to direct the forces here if we are attacked in my absence. No, I must go alone." Merryk insisted.

"Your Highness, going alone is not prudent. Too many things can happen to a single person," the Chancellor said. "In addition, when you finally get to the Capital City, you will need the princess to navigate the issues of royalty."

"I am going. I have traveled over the pass before, and I can do it again. You will not leave me here alone." Tara's words were tinted with tearful eyes.

"Against my better judgment, all right. But we need to pack warm and light."

Having won, and before Merryk could change his mind, Tara left to pack.

"Chancellor Goldblatt, there are several things I need you to take care of in my absence."

"Yes, Your Highness, what can I do?"

"First, get a letter off to Commander Yonn; explain to him why I did not wait. Tell him he is in command of all the forces in the Teardrop. I want him to stay in Newport in the event we are attacked. He should coordinate his activities with Admiral Bellows. I would suggest he send Yvette home. Hopefully, he'll have better luck with his wife than I did with mine. Yvette can take responsibility for the castle. I need you to help them through this period. I wish you could be with me. You are right about needing help when I get to the Capital City, and Tara will be invaluable. There is something different about this event than the others. I am concerned I may not be back as quickly as I hope. I want you to know how much you mean to me. I would not have survived without your guidance."

"Your Highness needs to do what is necessary for the sake of your family and for the good of our kingdom," Chancellor Goldblatt said. "Do not worry about me or the people here. We will take care of ourselves until you return. You, of course, will be greatly missed, but if you can stop this terrible attack on your father, it will benefit all."

Prince Merryk returned to his room to find Smallfolks laying out clothing. "Warm and light, that is what you said. I oiled the black travel coat. It is good for rain and snow and, of course, any kind of wind. I have not oiled your grandfather's sword, but I can do that while you eat."

"Everything is fine, Smallfolks. You don't need to worry about the sword." Merryk sensed more than clothing was weighing on the small man's heart. "Smallfolks, I would like to say I will be back soon, but we both know what I am facing. Even if we save my father, I do not know when I can return."

Smallfolk's eyes stared at the floor in front of him. "This is not the first time a Raymouth has left our castle. Fate seems to let them stay for a while and then takes them away. They are always meant for bigger things."

"Smallfolks, this is a big enough place for me, but my father is wounded and trapped in his own castle. I must go."

"I understand." Tears now welled up in Smallfolks' eyes. "I am old, and I may not see you again."

"Don't talk like that. You will be here as long as the castle. I'm sorry I cannot leave the coat and sword for you to care for, but..."

Smallfolks interrupted with a brave smile, "I know, you need both. Your grandfather told me you would need them. I did not understand at the time, but I do now."

Smallfolks could not continue. He broke down into large sobs, tears flowing freely down his cheeks. "I am sorry, My Prince, but I will miss you so very much. You gave these last years of my life meaning. I will never know how to thank you, and I will always be your servant."

Merryk wrapped his arms around the little man and let him cry.

Tara came into the room quietly to see Merryk's arms wrapped around Smallfolks. As soon as Smallfolks realized she had entered the room, he let go of Merryk and turned his back to wipe his eyes. Without facing her, Smallfolks asked, "Princess Tara, is there anything I can get for your journey?"

"No thank you, Smallfolks," Tara replied with a soft voice. "I think I have everything."

Turning to leave, Smallfolks grabbed the things on the bed. "Very well. Your things will be waiting for you in the stable, My Prince."

Tara looked at Merryk. His eyes glistened with moisture. "Hard?"

"Hard," Merryk replied.

The early morning light grew behind the hills to the east. The stars were gracefully leaving, blinking out one by one. Merryk and Tara, with saddle-bags in hand, moved to the stable. Before they could leave the castle hall, Nelly caught them.

"I have been looking for you," Merryk said. "You disappeared before we could talk."

"I have been baking your favorites for the road." A touch of flour tinted her dark hair, just as it had the first time Merryk saw her.

Tara reached out to give Nelly a hug. "Thank you so much, Nelly. You are always here to support us."

Nelly was looking down, trying not to make eye contact with the prince.

"Nelly, don't tell Smallfolks or the Chancellor, but I know you are the heart of the castle. Without you, this place would just be a pile of rocks."

"You exaggerate, My Prince. And here you go, getting me all flustered. Now, you have a long journey, but hurry back to us."

"I will be back as soon as I can, but I don't know when."

"I understand." Nelly's voice cracked as she spoke.

"My goodness," Tara exclaimed. "I did not expect so many of you to be up so early this morning."

Ali was holding Bella's reins. "Good morning, Missy Princess. I have prepared Bella for your journey. She is strong enough to carry you through the great distance. Remember to remind her to rely on the strength of the stallion to lead her."

"Thank you, Ali. Take good care of the herds. Your advice is excellent for more than Bella." Tara looked at Merryk as she spoke.

Ali turned to Merryk. "My Prince, if the journey were flat and long, I would suggest you take the great horse, Raj, but this journey will require more than speed." Looking at Maverick, he continued. "The one that bears you is strong, brave, and loyal. He will carry you to success." Ali then bowed formally. "May the High God of all men protect you on your journey, My Prince."

"Thank you, Ali."

Petri held Maverick's bridle. He and Jane had brought Maizie to the stable. Jane stood by Maizie, who was wrapped in a blanket and sitting at the edge of the corral fence. Merryk placed his saddle bag on Maverick and went to say goodbye. "Maizie, why are you up so early?" he said in a cheerful voice.

"I came to say goodbye. Everybody is sad, but you do not need sad people. You need people who can give you big hugs and tell you to be safe. You know, the kind of thing you did with me before the big battle."

"Yes, Maizie, that is exactly what I need. I'm going to leave Yonn and Yvette in charge while I'm gone. Yvette is going to need a lot of help."

Maizie took a quick breath, then let it out in a sigh. "I know, with Smallfolks," she said with resignation. "He really is not that bad. He is really sad now, but I know just what to do. I will do something he says is 'really dangerous,' but is not really, and he will say 'I cannot take my eyes off you for a moment.' And then he will be too busy watching me to be sad about you."

"Exactly. I could not have thought of a better plan." Merryk took the little one in his arms and gave her a big hug. "Don't get big too fast. I want to recognize you when I get back." Merryk sat Maizie back down. Then he reached out to say goodbye to Jane, touching her gently on the cheek. "Be safe and take care of everyone for me."

Prince Merryk went to take the reins from Petri's hand. "Petri, when the time is right, you have my permission to ask Jane to marry you. But only when she is ready. You can only hope she will be foolish enough to say yes." Merryk looked back over his shoulder at Jane, whose face was gleaming with joy. Shaking Petri's hand, he mounted Maverick.

"This will not get easier," Prince Merryk said to Tara. "Goodbye, everyone. I pray to return soon."

Nelly, Smallfolks, and the Chancellor joined the others to watch the prince and princess leave. There were a few more waves and some additional tears as Merryk and Tara moved out of the rear gate, over the bridge, to take the path to the east.

When Merryk and Tara were no longer visible, Maizie broke into tears.

"What is wrong, little one?" Nelly asked as she picked up the child.

"Prince Merryk is not coming back."

"Why would you say such a thing?"

"He going to the Capital City. There are many people there. When they learn how great he is, they will not let him come home."

Chapter 21

LEDEN GRUBI

The morning light continued to grow on the hills surrounding the Teardrop. A chill air lay like a thick blanket on the ground, making the dewdrops cling to the leaves in near ice. Merryk and Tara rode in silence into the forest leading to the eastern ridge. The recently fallen leaves muffled the sound of the horse's hooves. The quiet of the forest reflected their silence.

Merryk was lost in introspection. *It has been less than four years since I arrived in the Teardrop. Arrive is maybe not the right word, more like dropped in. I did not know when I was or where I was. Now, it seems like all I have ever known.*

The path abruptly broke into the open as they reached the crest, allowing a view backwards. Merryk stopped and turned to look.

"It certainly is beautiful this time of morning," Tara spoke for the first time since they had left the gate. "When I first came, I thought it was a godforsaken place. Now, all I see is home."

"I was thinking much the same thing," Merryk replied. "I think it is the people who make a place home, not the place itself. The Teardrop is beautiful and has a lot of special people. Yes, it is home."

Merryk looked back one more time. The top of the old tower could still be seen on the horizon. The first smoke of the day had begun to rise from the village. His last sight, as he turned Maverick, was the sparkle of water in the lake rising behind the new dam.

"We need to keep moving. This is going to be a long day," Merryk said.

"How far to Leden Grubi?" Tara asked.

"I'm not sure. I was half asleep when we made the reverse trip. It is my hope we will make it to the tree line on the other side of the peaks by dark. We only have about ten or eleven hours, plus an hour of dusk."

"I hope Jamaal and Oolada marked the trail well. We cannot afford to get lost on the way."

Merryk pointed to a fresh mark on the side of a tree as they passed. "So far, they're doing a good job. Also, I believe Helga will have warned them. And Jamaal said, at the first sign of trouble, they would send someone back on the path to guide us."

"Not that I do not have faith in you, but a guide would not hurt," Tara said. "It would also be all right if the sun warmed this air." Tara tugged her long fur coat closer.

"It will warm up this afternoon but, as the sun fades, the temperature will drop quickly. I just hope the sky stays clear. We can travel in the cold, but if it snows..." Merryk let the balance of his statement speak for itself.

"It may be cold, but I am here with you. I cannot think of anywhere else I would rather be. I could not have borne being left behind."

"You just didn't want me to have all the fun," Merryk said.

"Ten hours from now, you can tell me about all the fun," a sassy Tara snapped back.

Oolada and a half-dozen men left Crag d'Zoo half a day after Helga called the clans to muster—a full two days before Merryk received the message from the Capital City. They had stopped in the evenings along the way but maintained a steady pace during the days. Two hours after noon on the third day, the group came to the tree line on the east side of Leden Grubi.

"We will make camp here for the night. With luck, the prince will make it over the summit and be here by nightfall." Oolada instructed. "The sky is clear and the path bare. I will ride ahead to see if I can locate him. If I do not find him in a couple of hours, I will turn back."

"You want one of us to go with you?" a clansman asked.

"No, there is nothing ahead but a steep climb. No reason for anyone else to go. I will be back by dark. Everyone rest. Tomorrow, we move to the Capital City."

Tara and Merryk rode along what turned out to be a well-marked path. They stopped at midday for a brief rest and enjoyed Nelly's baked treats. In less than an hour, they were moving again. "This is a truly beautiful ride, if we could stop and enjoy it," Tara said.

"We were so tired the last time. I know I just wanted to stay on Maverick and not fall. I'm not sure I raised my head any more than necessary to follow Jamaal. Maybe we can come back sometime."

"That sounds nice, but on a warm summer's day. I think the temperature is already falling."

"The sky is still blue and clear, but it feels like it's getting colder. We must be getting near the pass."

Merryk's suspicion was borne out. Turning the next bend, they hit the tree line. Behind them lay the forest and ahead of them the bare rocks of Leden Grubi.

"Now we have a choice," Merryk said as they stopped to allow the horses to rest. "There are about three hours of light, plus one hour of dusk, and a near full moon. The sky is still clear. The safe thing to do is to stop here and wait until tomorrow, but we would lose half a day or more. My guess is from tree line to tree line, is about five hours. Remember, at least two of those are walking at the top."

"We do not know how your father is doing or who has him trapped in the castle. Helga and Gaspar will know of the attack. They will send help for us and help for the king. You must be there, and you must lead them. You are my prince and my husband. There is no one who I trust or love more. If I were not here, you would not hesitate. No, we ride and let the moon be our guide."

"The princess has decided. Is that all right with you, Maverick?"

The stallion nodded his head and let out a whinny. Bella answered back. "We are all in agreement. Ride it is."

⁕

I know better. I should have turned back an hour ago, but now I can see the summit. From there I can see half the back side. If Merryk is on the mountain, I will know. Oolada stopped for a moment. *I have been walking for an hour. I will go just a bit further. Your love for this man is going to get you killed.*

A particularly bitter wind smacked into Oolada's face as she broke the summit. Not a gust, but a sustained blow. "Oh no!" Oolada said out loud. The setting sun was being covered by fast-moving, low clouds. It would hasten the dusk, but more significant, the clouds would drop snow as they climbed the mountains.

I must turn back, but I cannot until I see if the prince is there. Oolada's eyes scanned the path rising between the two volcanoes. *Yes, there are two riders and three horses. They have started the walking portion of the climb about three quarters of an hour from the top. They are going to get caught in the wind and snow.* Without hesitation, Oolada moved down the mountain to join them.

Merryk was well aware of the rows of clouds descending on the mountains. The stiff, consistent wind had lashed them for most of the last hour. The sunlight had flickered on and off with the passing clouds. Now more off than on.

"Tara, we are in trouble. The clouds behind us are coming fast. They will probably bring snow or ice. We must get to the crest and hope that on the other side we can find shelter. The challenge now will be the loss of light."

Tara looked out from under her hood of fur. "It is so cold. Perhaps moving quickly will warm us. Go!"

Tiny ice crystals pinged off the leather of Merryk's coat. *Smallfolks was right about this being good for all kinds of weather. One more reason to thank him.* Merryk kept his head down, looking for sharp rocks in the path. *I can't afford to have the horses bruise a shin.*

"Merryk! Merryk!" a voice rose from over the roar of the wind.

Merryk turned to look at Tara. She was plodding along behind him, head down. Again, "Merryk, Merryk!" This time it was stronger and in front of him. Soon, a shadow appeared through the ice and snow; one person leading a horse.

Merryk waved and moved toward the shadow. "Oolada, what are you doing here?"

"Freezing to death like you, unless we get out of this wind."

Tara joined the other two, throwing her arms around their new travel companion.

"There are caves on the face of the mountain. I will lead the way," Oolada said.

"Tara, follow Oolada. Maverick and I will bring the pack horse," urged Merryk.

Merryk watched Oolada carefully pick a path toward the cliff face. Soon, the vertical columns of rocks appeared in the blowing ice and snow. Oolada went along the face, then stopped and disappeared into a hole in the wall. Tara pulled Bella forward until they, too, disappeared.

"I'm not a fan of caves, Maverick, but anything is better than this wind."

Maverick nodded in agreement.

CHAPTER 22

THE CAVE

The opening to the cave was relatively narrow, just wide enough for the horses to walk through. "Goliath would not make this, Maverick," Merryk said. Merryk's first impression was no wind, although the wind passing the opening made a sound like blowing over the top of an empty bottle. The second impression was one of pitch blackness. The latter made Merryk and Maverick stop. "We can't see anything," Merryk said, speaking for himself and Maverick.

Oolada answered, "Walk straight toward my voice. The floor is reasonably flat with no big rocks. I have a fire starter. It will give us a few minutes of light, but we do not have any wood for a fire."

In fulfillment of her promise, a small flame flickered, then flashed to illuminate the interior of the cave. Tara and Oolada stood with their horses near the center of a large cavern. The interior sides and roof were all made of pentagonal stones which were characteristic of the Palisades.

"I have something which may help," Merryk said, producing a teardrop shaped candle about the size of his fist. "It's beeswax. It will not produce heat but will give us light for a short time."

Tara moved to Merryk's side. "We are out of the wind, but not the cold. The moisture from my breath is sticking to my gloves."

"We need to get the horses settled while we have light," Merryk said. "They will do better if they can stand next to each other."

Oolada replied, "So will we. We will need to share our body warmth, or we will freeze."

"Anything with warmth is fine with me," Tara said, as she shivered uncontrollably. "What do we need to do?"

"Oolada, help Tara prepare a place to sleep. I will finish with the horses."

Merryk set the small candle on a rock pedestal high enough to cast light over both sides of the cave. Once freed of the burdens of the saddles and supplies, Merryk led Maverick, the mares, and the packhorse to one side of the cave, away from the opening.

"Keep everyone as warm as possible. We will get out of here and off the mountain at first light." Merryk promised as much to himself as the stallion.

The women wasted no time collecting the accumulation of furs and extra blankets to make a sleeping pad. Both were tightly buried within when Merryk finished. "Hurry," Tara said. "Join us."

Merryk removed his leather riding coat and spread it over the women. With the removal of the heavy covering, he shivered.

"Stop delaying. Get undressed before you freeze," Tara ordered.

Within the hour, the small candle flickered and went out, throwing the cave back into darkness. The only thing which remained constant was the roar of the wind.

When Merryk joined the women, all three were shivering. Lying down allowed his body to relax enough to drift toward sleep. *I hope I'm just falling asleep and not freezing.*

The next time Merryk woke, it was still dark, and the wind still roared. *I'm not shivering, and neither are the women. We may make it.*

Several hours later, Merryk woke again to the darkness and the wind. Now he felt warm. *The shared body heat is working. Under different circumstances, spending the night with two beautiful, naked women would be a lifetime dream. Now I have a lifetime to thank for it.*

⁂

A small sliver of light slid through the entry passage into the cave. Maverick's sounds caused Merryk to stir. A dim gray light filled the cave. The sound of the wind was gone. *It's morning. Maverick and I want off this mountain.* Sliding quickly out of the sleeping pile, he made every effort to not wake either woman. *It is one thing to be naked with Tara, but Oolada!* Merryk dressed as quickly as possible, even though he needed little encouragement to get dressed. *It is still freezing!*

Merryk bundled up as best he could and moved to the opening. The sun was not fully up, but enough to cast bright light on the tops of the twin volcano peaks. *I was afraid we would wake up to snow on the ground, but the wind swept the mountain clean. There are a few patches of ice and snow, but no accumulation.*

"You need this," Oolada said, handing Merryk his coat. "It will do you no good to survive the night and die in the day. Tara is getting dressed."

"Thank you." Merryk said. "Without you, we would not have survived. I am sorry I put you in a position of peril, and I apologize for the sleeping arrangements."

Merryk's comment confused Oolada. "Warriors do whatever is necessary to survive."

"But you are not just a warrior, you are Lady Zoo," Merryk said. "In any event, I am glad we are all alive this morning. We should go."

As Oolada watched Merryk turn toward the cave, she could not help but smile. Speaking quietly to herself, "He really thinks of me as a woman."

In the morning light, they saw how close they had come to the summit. Just ten minutes of climbing and they started down the other side. Another three quarters of an hour walking and they could ride. Not long after, they met two clansmen who came looking for Oolada.

"The storm blew in so quickly, we were afraid it caught you in the open," one said.

"I found the prince and princess. We went to one of the caves. Everything turned out fine." Oolada offered no additional details.

The second clansman offered, "We left the others with the fire and breakfast at the tree line. We also have food and water for the horses."

"That sounds wonderful," Tara answered. "I will not miss this mountain."

CHAPTER 23

THE ROAD

True to their word, a warm fire and food awaited the three as they entered the camp.

"Take the horses and rub them down quickly. We need to leave in no more than two hours." Oolada instructed.

"The three of you riding off the mountain," the oldest clansman shook his head from side to side. "Cave or not, surviving what we saw from below is unbelievable. How did you find each other? You could have passed within feet of each other and never known the other was even there. This is going to be a story to share around our fires for years to come."

"Not much of a story," Oolada said. "It was cold. We found a place to stay warm and then came down the mountain the next day." Dismissing the entire discussion, Oolada changed subjects. "How far are we from the south road?"

"Three hours," the clansman replied.

"We will be ready to go in two hours," Merryk said. "We could use the warm food and a bit of rest."

It was early afternoon when the group reached the main south road. Twenty Zoo clansmen awaited their arrival. "Your Highness, Princess Tarareese and Lady Zoo, Jamaal ZooWalter has instructed us to guide you to the meeting point behind the Capital City. It is an eight-to-nine-hour ride. Would you like to rest before we proceed?"

"You are being awful formal, Zurah. I have known you all my life. What is going on?" Oolada asked.

"Lady Zoo, these are momentous times, not to be taken lightly. Never in my lifetime has the clan mustered to the defense of the king, and to be given the honor of protecting the prince. Yes, formal."

Merryk intervened before Oolada said something she would regret. "Zurah, we are pleased to be guided by you and your men. We are hardy travelers and do not shy from an eight-hour ride. Shall we?"

The group spread out until Merryk rode next to Oolada. "A little while ago, Tara and I would sit with Yvette and Yonn at the dinner table. I asked to have places put two to a side so we could look at each other as we ate. But every time I came in, the staff had me at the head of the table. I started to get angry, but Tara explained my placement was not for my benefit, it was for theirs. I did not need the formality, but those who supported me did. Does that help you understand Zurah better?"

"He needs the formality to remind him of the importance of his task," Oolada replied.

"Exactly. we don't need it, but he does. We just need to be who we are and respect their need for formality. Understand?"

"Yes," Oolada replied. "Even though I do not think it will be my worry."

"You never know, Lady Zoo."

When darkness fell, Zurah's men lit torches to light the way. Although the road was clear and straight, it seemed strange to ride under torchlight. Merryk noticed all the men were warriors with modified body armor, part chain-link and part light plate. All were as intent on their mission as Zurah.

Whenever the group stopped, sentinels were posted and scouts sent out ahead. Gaspar had trained them well.

It was three hours before midnight when Merryk, Tara, and Oolada crossed off the road and over a small ridge to see the army of the clan. On the plain below, hundreds of tents were placed in orderly circles around the Council's hut. They had crossed two rows of sentinels as they came from the road, at least two they had seen.

Gaspar ZooWalt and Helga stood beside the center hut as they arrived. "Welcome, My Prince," Gaspar said in greeting. "You have had a long day. Please come in."

"Gaspar, it's good to see you. I have many questions," Merryk responded. "First, can someone take care of our horses?"

"Absolutely. Do you remember Arras Gorg?"

"Yes, but you've grown at least a foot," Merryk said as he shook the young man's hand. "Do you remember my horse, Maverick?"

The young man's eyes widened. "Yes, Your Highness, I remember him, but does he remember me?"

"Maverick, do you remember Arras?"

The stallion nodded.

"Arras, keep the horses together. They depend on each other. Extra oats and curry time. And Maverick. No tricks."

Helga greeted Tara and Oolada. "You two had an adventure."

"I see what Oolada means. It is unnerving to know you have seen everything which has happened," Tara said.

"It can make conversations move quicker," Helga chuckled with a smile. "The two of you seem to work well together."

"We do get along well," Tara said. "Look, Gaspar and Merryk are going inside. We should follow."

"Tara, the Blue-and-White Mountain Clans are a male-dominated group. We can go in and listen, but unless they ask, we should not speak. If a man's woman speaks in council without permission, it lessens the strength of her man."

"I understand. My mother would never speak without my father's permission. In her case, she would later pay physically," Tara said. "I know Merryk does not think this way, but I will honor the tradition of the clan. Merryk needs all the support he can get."

Gaspar led Merryk into the tent. "Everyone, this is Prince Merryk Raymouth, firstborn son of the Inland Queen. Your Highness, we are the heads of all the clans. This is the Council of Walters. We have gathered our forces to aid and support your efforts to save your father."

"First, thank you for being here. I truly appreciate the sacrifice all of you have made to travel so far. Now, tell me what we know. Do we know anything about my father's condition?"

"The last word out of the castle said the king was gravely injured. Each morning, we look at the castle standard to see if the king still lives. Each day his flag flies, he lives," Arron Gorg added.

Jamaal Zoo Walter spoke. "We know his own son, Prince Merreg, stabbed him in the back. Men loyal to the king, from the Royal Guard and army, protected the king and got him back into the castle. We now believe only those loyal to the king are with him. Those officers loyal to Prince Merreg have been falling from the castle walls like pinecones. Prince Merreg is outside the wall with the bulk of the king's army, and approximately two hundred mercenaries who are protecting him in a manor house near the front gate. The prince's forces are in position to keep anyone from leaving the castle."

"We cannot tell how much of the regular army is loyal to Prince Merreg, or if it is just his officers. There are about four thousand outside the castle," Gaspar added.

"How many do we have?" Merryk asked.

Arron Gorg Walter replied, "Four thousand at sunset with more arriving hourly. By morning, we will have over five thousand."

"I dislike the idea of the clans fighting other members of the High Kingdom. Even if we win, it seems like a loss," Merryk said.

"We will win. We have distributed all the armor you gained from the Army of Justice to the whole of the clan. Better fighters and better armor—we will win," Arron said with confidence.

"Unfortunately, whether the king's flag flies in the morning or not, we cannot allow a man like Prince Merreg to become king by killing his own father," Gaspar said. "We must bring Prince Merreg to justice."

"I agree," Merryk said as he looked at Tara in the back of the room. "At the end of the day, the law requires he and I must resolve this."

"You have our total support," Arron said. All the other Walters nodded in agreement.

"Thank you. If you would all excuse me, I could use some rest. Until tomorrow."

"Yes, Your Highness," the Walters said as they stood to leave.

Gaspar, Jamaal, Helga, and Tara remained in their places. Only after the Walters left did Oolada enter the tent.

"Everyone responded as predicted," Helga said.

"We have a superior force, of that I am confident. But fighting other members of the kingdom just doesn't seem right," Merryk said again.

"Even if we can neutralize the regular army, the mercenaries will fight. Tomorrow there will be bloodshed," Jamaal said.

"Perhaps with some rest, we can see another way," Oolada suggested.

"We should all get some rest," Gaspar added.

Merryk stopped before exiting. "Gaspar, after I get something to eat, I would like to review the battle plans."

"Yes, Your Highness."

Helga caught Tara's arm as she followed Merryk out. "Have you told him?"

"Until now, I was not sure. I did not want to raise his hopes."

"It would give him a purpose to fight and a reason to be safe."

"He already has a purpose to fight, and the knowledge might make him cautious. Being cautious could get him killed. Also, he would insist I go somewhere safe, away from him. That I cannot bear."

"He will need your support and skills in the next few days."

"What should I do?" Tara's voice filled with concern.

"Only you can decide. I have no vision to guide you. But you will know when the time is right."

CHAPTER 24

DAWN

Despite his exhaustion, Merryk could not will himself to relax. A gentle wind ruffled the canvas of his tent; nothing compared to the sounds of the previous evening. Still, it kept him awake. After hours of restlessness, Merryk finally gave up. He rolled carefully away from Tara so as not to wake her. *Tara has slept this entire journey. Anytime she can stop, she can sleep. I wish I had that skill.*

Throwing on his leather coat over his clothes, he stepped from the tent. Immediately, six sentinels snapped to attention. *Gaspar has guards outside my tent. I should not be surprised.*

"Good morning. I'm going for a short walk. Stay here with the princess."

"We will leave men to watch the princess, but the Walt will remove our skin if we leave you alone."

Merryk chuckled. "I believe he would. All right."

The sky was still dark, studded with stars, but a whisper of light already grew in the east. The plain holding the forces sloped from north to south. They organized the camp in traditional clan fashion—concentric circles with the Council tent in the middle. Merryk's tent was in the first circle near the center, with the Walt and the other Walters. The well-ordered camp was silent, other than the occasional sounds of the ever-present guards.

Merryk walked toward the back of the camp. *Perhaps I can get a view.*

After several rows, he stopped to look back. *There is something special about the time before dawn, especially before a battle.*

"It is so still," Jamaal said as he joined Merryk. "I thought you might like a cup of hot cider."

"Yes, thank you," Merryk said as he accepted the cup. "I agree about the stillness. It's the anticipation of the battle to come. The quiet personal moment before the anxiety kicks in."

"Soon the stillness will be displaced as the camp fills with fires, food, and fear. Why are you up so early?"

"I was trying to think of a way not to risk so many men's lives."

"My prince, we are here for you, but also for the king. Your brother attacked his own father. Gaspar was right, a man like that cannot be allowed to become king."

"All I want is a way to ensure my father's safety without the loss of life."

"I think you know, sometimes we can only stop people with force. This is one of those times. Prince Merreg is the one who put this in motion; now, he must be stopped."

"I know you're right, but death seems to follow me around lately."

"The Council sent the Army of Justice to its demise, not you. Prince Merreg attacked your father, not you. You are a man who does not shy away from difficult tasks. We know you will do what is necessary. That is why we follow you."

"Thank you again, Jamaal." Merryk placed his hand on Jamaal's shoulder. "Now I think we should get ready. We meet Gaspar at dawn."

By the time Merryk returned to his tent, Tara was already up and dressed.

"Where have you been? Helga will be here in a few minutes with your breakfast. You need to get ready."

Merryk reached out to grab Tara with a big hug.

"Stop! Let go. You need to hurry."

"Tara, calm down. I have plenty of time; particularly time for me to hold you in my arms."

Tara now crumbled into Merryk's chest. Tears flowed down her cheeks. "I am afraid."

"Only the insane are not afraid, but you and I cannot let others see our fear. The one thing I know about leadership is there is a time to show courage even if you don't feel it. This is one of those times. We must be strong so those around us can be strong. We must lead with certainty."

Tara now pushed away from Merryk and wiped the tears from her face. "I have a cloak of royal colors for you. I was thinking it would show the regular army they were fighting one of their own."

Merryk's face brightened. "Tara, you are brilliant." Merryk gave Tara another big hug and a kiss. "Did Goldblatt send one of my royal flags?"

"Yes. I have given it to Gaspar."

"Have I told you I love you often enough?"

"You are acting foolishly. Are you all right?"

"Yes, very much so."

An hour later, just before the first full light of day, the battle horns of the Blue-and-White Mountain Clans sounded. Made from the horns of mountain sheep, they generated a deep resounding call to arms.

Merryk exited his tent in his new armor and the deep royal blue cloak of the Family Raymouth. Arras held Maverick and Bella by the reins. Both horses looked well fed and rested. Maverick wore a shiny steel chest plate, a head guard, and the royal Raymouth blue.

They had given Princess Tarareese lightweight plate armor and a royal blue cape. Bella wore colors to match Tara.

Gaspar ZooWalt and Jamaal ZooWalter, both in armor and mail, rode in to join Merryk and Tara. The clans had modified heavy plate armor received from the Army of Justice into a combination of mail and plate, better suited to mounted combat. The other Walters joined.

The last two riders to join the group were Helga and Lady Zoo. Helga wore her normal brown cloak. She would be near, but not in the combat. Lady Zoo was different. She wore the same lightweight armor given to Princess Tara. However, the only colors she wore were those of the Clan Zoo in the sash which circled her waist. The two handles of the short knives Merryk had given her rose at her shoulders. A regular sword hung at one side and a bow with a quiver lay on the other.

Merryk thought. *If she feels fear, no one will ever know.*

Merryk rode to Gaspar's side. "Gaspar, how will I ever repay you for your support?"

"You are the son of our king. We owe you our support."

"No, your personal support. The first day we met, I said I hoped you would be my friend, as you were to my grandfather. You have been that and more. How can I repay that friendship?"

"You could marry Oolada and make us relatives," Gaspar said half seriously.

"Oh, but if I could. However, a man can have only one wife."

Gaspar simply nodded and moved forward to allow Merryk to return to Tara's side. Under his breath, he whispered, "Except the king, who must have two."

An hour later, the entire army was assembled on the hillside immediately north of the castle wall and the main gate. The city of the capital lay between the castle and the port. They built the castle to protect the port, but today, it was not the port which was the target.

Gaspar stopped the group of leaders. "This is as far as the women go," he said in a gruff voice.

Merryk turned to say goodbye to Tara and Helga. Tara immediately objected. "I want to be closer to you."

"No, this will be close enough."

Oolada rode forward to be with her grandfather. "Oolada, this is as far as you go," Gaspar said.

"But grandfather, I want to fight at your and the prince's side," Oolada said in surprise.

"You are to stay here with Helga and Princess Tarareese. There will be no argument." Gaspar's voice showed his determination. "Jamaal's men will stay with you."

Twenty of Jamaal's best warriors broke from the main group to surround the three women.

"Grandfather, let these men go with you. I can protect the princess and Helga."

"No," was his only reply.

Prince Merryk rode to Oolada. "I am pleased you are staying with Tara and Helga. I can think of no one else I would choose."

A tearful Oolada turned to Helga. "I should be with the prince and grandfather. I do not understand why I must stay here."

Helga looked at Oolada with eyes only a person who raised a child could muster. "Everything is as it must be. Please trust. You are too important to risk."

As Merryk on Maverick moved away, Bella and Oolada's roan mare both attempted to follow.

"Even our horses know where we should be," Tara said.

Chapter 25

FIELD OF BATTLE

Prince Merreg's army had its first sign of trouble when the clan's battle horns rang to announce the dawn. Castle Raymouth was designed for defense, but not from outside its walls. Roughly four thousand men were hastily organized in clusters, rather than orderly ranks. The army was positioned with the castle wall and moat at their backs. They would hold the ground or be swept into the waters.

Gaspar ZooWalt surveyed the field of battle. "The poor bastards are ill prepared and poorly commanded. They have not replaced the loss of the Lord Commander."

"I think Prince Merreg's purge of officers based on loyalty reduced the experience of command," Merryk added.

Prince Merryk looked at the field and the array of men in front of him. "Gaspar, we cannot move as planned. They cannot defend themselves. Arron GorgWalter was right. We will win, but it will be a slaughter. We would kill fellow countrymen. I must give them another choice."

"There is a significant risk in what you propose," Gaspar replied.

There was the sound of a horn from inside the castle.

Being wakened at any time made Prince Merreg angry. Being awakened at dawn made him furious. Crawling over an unknown woman in his bed, he charged to the door. "What is the meaning of this?" he bellowed.

"An army is on the hillside," a guard declared.

"An army. There are no armies, except mine."

"Evidently not. At least five thousand armor-clad cavalry are on the hillside, just beyond the gate," An equally irritated Wind said, "I dislike surprises," as she came down the hall tightly gripping the front of her robe.

"Do we know who they are and what they want?" Merreg asked.

Stone ran his hand through his unruly hair. "Not yet, but you can bet it is about the king."

Simultaneously, with the sound of the horn from the castle, a large royal blue flag with the king's crest unfurled over the tower.

A single clan horn answered, and another identical royal flag, only with the addition of the insignia of the Inland Prince, opened at the head of the columns of clansmen.

Prince Merryk, wearing his royal blue colored cloak, rode out on Maverick. Gaspar ZooWalt rode to his right and Jamaal ZooWalter held the royal flag on his left.

A murmur of surprise and confusion swept through Prince Merreg's army. Merreg's officers attempted to silence the chatter, but Prince Merryk was famous. Every man knew he had defeated the Army of Justice, and he was flying the king's flag.

Prince Merreg, with Stone and Wind, watched Merryk move forward. "Unbelievable! It is my little brother. How did he get here so fast and with so many? My uncle said the Blue-and-White Mountain Clans were few and not a threat because they could never agree on anything."

"Looks like your uncle was wrong, and he is dead at the hand of your 'little brother,' I believe," a sarcastic Stone snipped.

"They did not pay us to fight an army, only to protect you. We cannot do that against both armies. Your men are confused about who they follow," Wind said emphatically.

"There is no confusion. They will follow me. I am their commander."

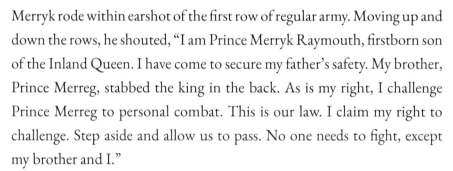

Merryk rode within earshot of the first row of regular army. Moving up and down the rows, he shouted, "I am Prince Merryk Raymouth, firstborn son of the Inland Queen. I have come to secure my father's safety. My brother, Prince Merreg, stabbed the king in the back. As is my right, I challenge Prince Merreg to personal combat. This is our law. I claim my right to challenge. Step aside and allow us to pass. No one needs to fight, except my brother and I."

Merryk repeated his message several times to the rows of troops. When he finished, he returned to the center of the clan formation. Again, he moved forward. This time, three rows of cavalry formed on either side of him. Like the tip of an arrow, he moved into the ranks of the regular army. Merryk took a deep breath. *I hope this works.*

Soon he learned his words were effective. The army parted to allow him to move toward the gate.

"I think he made his first mistake. We cannot beat an army, but we can kill one man," Wind said. "When he gets close, he will face our men. We will fight and Stone can be your champion."

⚘

"I cannot see him anymore," a concerned Tara said as she scanned for Merryk in the crowd of warriors.

Oolada looked at Zurah, the commander of their guards. "Your instructions were to stay with us. Tarareese and I are going to move closer."

"I am sure that is not what the Walt meant," Zurah replied.

"Follow us, and you can ask him yourself," Oolada replied. Turning to the group of men, she continued. "Half of you stay here with Helga, the other half come with Princess Tarareese and me." Without waiting for debate, the two women rode into the middle of the wedge of warriors, moving behind the prince and the Walt.

⚘

Although there were a few struggles between the ordinary soldiers and officers loyal to Merreg, the rows of regular army parted completely. However, in front of the gate, the group of two hundred black-dressed mercenaries stood their ground.

"They will fight," Jamaal said.

"We should fight them on foot. There is no room for the horses to maneuver," Arron GorgWalter said as he dismounted.

"Agreed," Merryk said. "Someone hold my horse."

After handing the reins to a clansman, Merryk turned to face the gate. From out of nowhere, three bolts from crossbows struck Merryk's chest. The force of the arrows knocked him to the ground. The prince did not move. The army let out a collective sigh.

An archer to the left of Jamaal dropped the arbalist on the left. Jamaal grabbed his bow and hit the second. The third struggled to get his bolt in place for a second shot. There was the sound of a blade turning through the air with the characteristic swish, which stopped abruptly when the blade caught the third archer directly in the eye slot of his helmet. Everyone turned to look back to see who had thrown the blade. To everyone's relief, Prince Merryk had risen to one knee as he threw. He now rose completely. When he fully stood, they could see the three shafts extending from his chest. With a wave of his hands, he swiped the three shafts away. Seeing Prince Merryk stand and knocking off the shafts brought a loud cheer from all around.

"Gaspar, use the archers!" Merryk yelled.

The Blue-and-White Mountain Clans had some of the finest archers in the world. Mercenaries dropped across the front of their ranks. They would all have been killed, but a burly man raised a white flag and walked into the center of the fray. "I am Prince Merreg's champion. I will fight in his place," Stone yelled.

CHAPTER 26

CHAMPIONS

Stone grabbed an old-style helmet with a strip of metal over the nose and his favorite weapons—two battle axes. Each ax was about two feet long, extending his already significant reach.

"Do not wear that helmet, it will block your vision," Wind yelled to Stone.

Stone simply laughed. "I will not need to see to kill this fool."

Gaspar watched as Stone prepared. Turning to Prince Merryk, he said "You do not need to fight anyone, except Merreg. This man is a professional killer."

"I need two axes," Merryk said as he dropped his blue cloak. Merryk looked over to see Oolada. "You dropped the first archer?"

"Yes," she nodded. Oolada and Tara had made their way to the sides of Gaspar and Jamaal.

Gaspar looked back at his granddaughter. "I am glad you disobeyed me. They caught us by surprise with the crossbows."

Arron GorgWalter handed Merryk two battle axes, both of good weight and length.

Stone had never lost a fight, not even as a child. He was always big, strong, and willing to cheat. This made him supremely confident. His weapons of choice—axes—which frightened his opponents and gave him the advantage of reach. A clearing broke between the two groups. Stone entered the gap, swinging his axes in broad circles, each stroke followed with a swish. The evil grin of a killer lay upon his face. His nose flared as he thought of the blood to come.

Stone's face changed when Prince Merryk came forward. *I expected a snot-nosed royal child, not this man. But it does not matter. He will die anyway.*

The prince now held two axes. With both men in the clearing, comparison was possible. The prince was at least as tall as Stone, if not taller. *He is too skinny to swing an ax. Any man can pick up an ax, but how many really know how to use it.* Stone laughed as he thought about Merryk's ignorance. *He thinks he is being honorable by using my weapons of choice. Fool.*

The first exchange between the two wiped any smile off the Stone's face. Merryk caught Stone's circular motion and matched it with a clash of metal.

Merryk's eyes narrowed as he focused on the defensive moves the sword-master had taught him. *Circle for circle. Most people who use an ax do so to frighten their opponent. Most of the time, it is fear which defeats them, not the warrior.*

Stone quickly learned he did not have the advantage of reach when Merryk's ax cut across his chest in a broken circle move. The pain of the cut sent Stone into a rage. He doubled his axes in both hands and flailed at Merryk as though he held a sword.

Merryk remembered his training as a Marine. **Fear and anger kill. Breathe, plan, execute**. He stepped back and let Stone swing wildly.

From the side of the circle, Wind paid careful attention to the battle. She saw what Stone had not yet realized. He was losing. She knew Prince Merreg would only become king if Stone won. *How Merryk dies is not as important as his death.* She moved around the edge of the clearing, toward the space near Merryk's back.

Oolada watched the battle with the same intensity as Wind. *Merryk is doing well, but one slip and it is over.* A flash of red hair caught her eye. The spot of red moved around toward the back of Merryk.

Merryk accepted a glancing blow to his side in exchange for a punch of his ax directly into the thin metal over Stone's nose. The metal crumpled inward. *One more such blow and he will not be able to see.*

Wind saw the blow. *One more stroke like that and Stone will die. It is now or never.* Wind stepped from the crowd, pulling her short knives, and moving to strike Merryk in the back. Her efforts came up short as opposing steel blocked both blades. *What happened?*

Oolada stepped in between Merryk and Wind to block each of her strokes. "I am at your back!" Oolada shouted to Merryk.

Merryk swept one glance backward, just enough to locate Oolada, and then continued to focus on Stone.

If Stone was confident, Wind operated with certainty. *I am the best in the world,* she said to herself as she unleased a volley of alternative slashes with each blade. To her amazement, each stroke was matched—stroke for stroke. Pausing for an instant, she looked at her opponent. A young woman, with her hair in a tight bun, wielded two long shaft knives. Her face showed no sign of fear. She had killed before, and she fought for a purpose. The question now reached Wind's mind. *Which of us has the greater purpose?*

Prince Merryk continued to match Stone's circle of strokes. Stone had never had to fight this long. His extra bulk and excessive wine drained him. One more time, Merryk took a light stroke to hit the bridge piece of the helmet. It folded completely. Stone was blind. He bellowed like a bull and began swinging wildly.

Wind heard Stone's cry and tried to break through Oolada to reach Merryk. Oolada did not break. Her blade caught Wind on the left side and slid into her heart. She crumpled. Her last words, "stupid helmet."

Merryk moved behind the flailing Stone. His next strokes buried both axes in the sides of Stone's neck. With the fall of Stone and Wind, the remaining mercenaries fled the field of battle, running into the city.

"This was real danger," Oolada said as she smiled at Merryk.

Merryk wrapped his arm around Oolada. "Yes, I think it was."

Tara rushed forward to Merryk and Oolada, grabbed both, and pulled them into a group hug. "The two of you were amazing. I have seen nothing like it," Tara exclaimed. "Oolada, I can never thank you enough for saving Merryk's life again."

CHAPTER 27

BROTHER

Gaspar joined the group. "This is not over. One remains."

"Yes. I need some water. Where is my brother?" Prince Merryk asked.

"But you are wounded," a worried Tara said.

"Nevertheless, where is my brother?" Merryk asked again.

In answer to his question, a voice called. "I understand you came to see me, little brother." Prince Merreg stood alone in front of the massive gate to the castle.

Merryk took a large swig of water, then dumped the rest over his head.

"Maverick, I need my sword," Merryk yelled.

The young man who held Maverick's reins was pushed forward by the horse he was supposed to control. "Thank you," Merryk said as he patted Maverick on the neck. Maverick made a couple of low snorts.

"Yes, I will be careful," Merryk replied.

Oolada stepped forward and handed her knife to Merryk. "We have not retrieved yours. This one is light, but swift."

Prince Merreg yelled again, "Come on, little brother, I have other things to do today."

"Remember, your uncle trained him. He will not fight fair," Jamaal said quietly to Merryk.

Merryk drew his grandfather's sword from its scabbard. For the first time, he heard a distinctive tone, like a deep hum.

The two men faced each other in an open space just outside the gates. A large circle of spectators had formed around the area. More looked from the top of the castle wall. There was an unusual quiet in the crowd.

Merryk thought. *I have never met my brother. He looks much like the Lord Commander, shorter, but with muscular arms. It is unfortunate to meet this way.*

"Finally! I thought you were going to send the woman to fight for you." Prince Merreg taunted.

"That would've been unfair. I wanted you to have a chance," Merryk replied.

"All right, I will kill her later." Prince Merreg struck first with a series of double handed strikes, alternating between high and low.

Merryk parried each blow, but stepped backwards at the assault.

Prince Merreg laughed. "Still afraid of shiny swords, I see. Just like when you were a child." Prince Merreg swung his blade. This time a quick blow toward Merryk's middle. Again, Merryk blocked the blows, but stepped backwards.

"What is Merryk doing?" Tara asked. "Each time Prince Merreg attacks, Merryk retreats."

"Merryk is measuring Prince Merreg, the way a teacher tests his students," Oolada replied.

The next set of blows started high, then quickly dropped low. Again, Merryk blocked each strike, but retreated.

"You need to stop running, little brother. I should have known you might be able to stand up straight, but still have no courage. You are still the skinny bastard who fell and cried to his mommy. And they said you were a hero." Prince Merreg's voice dripped with contempt.

Prince Merreg channeled his contempt into the next flurry. Merryk blocked each stroke but did not retreat.

"I see someone wasted time trying to teach you to use the blade. Our uncle, the Lord Commander, taught me. He was the finest teacher. Now, I grow bored. Stand still and die quickly."

Prince Merreg garnered a quick set of strokes and a deep strike to the middle of Merryk's stomach. The tip of Prince Merreg's blade slid off the side of Merryk's armor. Prince Merreg laughed. But Merryk did not retreat. Instead of blocking the next blows, he matched them with a counterstroke and a step forward. Each movement of the blade forced Prince Merreg backwards. He now retreated. A look of concern replaced the smirk on his face.

"I think I had a better swordmaster than our uncle," Merryk said.

Seriousness now filled Prince Merreg's face as he attacked again with more strokes to Merryk's middle. Merryk's response was a furious display of counter strikes and attacks, which forced Prince Merreg backwards so quickly he almost stumbled.

"Why did you attack our father?" Merryk asked.

"The bastard was never a father to me. If I had not had our uncle, no one would have taught me." Prince Merreg snapped.

"You might have been better off without his kind of guidance." Merryk added, "You might have been a better man."

Prince Merreg did not like being criticized by anyone. Merryk's words hit particularly close to the frail ego of Prince Merreg. Mustering all the strength he had, he lurched at Merryk with the thrust of his sword. Merryk sidestepped his brother and hit him on the backside with the flat of his sword as he passed. "Surrender now."

"Never," Prince Merreg shouted, as he turned and charged again.

Merryk did not move from his position, but drove his brother's sword away with a massive downward stroke. Then, reversing his blade, caught Prince Merreg under the chest plate of his armor. Only his brother's chain mail kept the stroke from being a complete kill, but the force dropped Prince Merreg to his knees.

Merryk stepped behind his brother. For the first time, Prince Merreg's face reflected his fear. He knew he was going to die. Merryk drew Oolada's knife from its sheath and placed the tip at the base of his brother's neck. With a single push, he drove the blade into Merreg's heart—a gladiator's kill. "You should not have tried to kill our father."

Chapter 28

VICTORY

"There is no joy in death, but there is in victory," some historical military commander said. Merryk knew why he thought of this obscure quotation. *I'm sad my brother had to die, but I'm grateful to have won.*

A cheer rose from the surrounding crowd. Tara, Oolada, Jamaal, and Gaspar all ran to congratulate him. "I need water again," Merryk asked. After downing half a skin of water, Merryk began. "First, can someone please take care of the body of my brother? He is a member of the royal family and needs to be treated with respect."

Gaspar nodded in acknowledgement.

Merryk then turned and looked back at the castle gates. "Why are these gates not open?" Merryk shouted. "In the name of my father, the king, I order you to open the gates."

There was a loud clack, like the lifting of metal bars, and the gate crept open. The first person out of the gate was an exhausted-looking member of the Royal Guard. "Your Highness, I am Bowen of the King's Guard. I cannot tell you how happy we were to see you on the hillside this morning. We did not know if our message got out and we feared no one would come.

"How is the king?" Merryk asked.

"I am afraid his condition is grave. Your mother has stayed by his side these many days."

"I want to go to him right away, but first I need to deal with a few things."

"Arron GorgWalter, my guess is a hundred or more mercenaries escaped into the city. Find them, remove their weapons, and confine them."

"If they resist?" Arron asked.

"Then collect their bodies for the sharks," Oolada inserted.

"I agree. They do not deserve to be treated with the respect of soldiers, and include the bodies from the front of the castle."

"Bowen, the king's army stands outside the gate. They parted to let us pass, but I do not know which of their officers can be trusted. Do you have someone loyal to the king who can help?"

"Yes, Your Highness. Several high-ranking officers were with us in the king's defense. I will send one immediately."

"Where are the army's barracks?"

"Just outside the castle to the east. Only a limited number were inside the castle," Bowen answered.

"Gaspar, we need to get the king's army back to their barracks and their weapons into the armory. Send men to see they are settled, but remind them these are our countrymen, so do so gently."

"Then have the other Walters secure the castle. Anyone inside may leave, but no one may enter without approval."

"Yes, Your Highness."

"Now, Bowen, I want to see my father."

The smell of human excrement, sweat, and, most of all, fear filled the castle interior. Merryk and his group followed Bowen across the castle grounds toward a large building in the center.

"Your father is in his quarters. I am sure you know the way," Bowen said.

"It would just be quicker if you led," Prince Merryk said. *I hadn't thought about everyone assuming I would know my way around. I need to get maps right away.*

Immediately, Merryk was glad he had asked Bowen to lead. The building was massive. They entered two great doors into a long corridor which looked like it led to the throne room. Bowen went halfway down the corridor and up a large circular stairwell to the second floor, then down several wide halls to a sitting room outside double doors to the king's bed chamber. The further they moved into the castle, the darker and danker it became. Guards were stationed in multiple places along the walls. *They all look like they have been at their stations for a long time. The windows are closed, probably in anticipation of an attack.*

"Open the windows. We need to get some light and air in here," Merryk commanded.

As light streamed into the rooms, what had been dark and gray grew color and texture. At the double doors, Bowen stopped. The guards outside the door did not move. "This is Prince Merryk," Bowen said. "He is here to see his father. He has defeated his brother and broken the siege."

Two emotions washed across the faces of the men. The first was relief, and the second was caution. Merryk thought. *They have protected the king since the attack. They are wise not to fail now.*

One of the older guards smiled. "You are the spitting image of your grandfather. Never thought I would see you again, Prince Merryk. Welcome home."

"Thank you for protecting my father. Now if I may?"

The man stepped aside so Merryk and the others could enter.

The king's bedroom was, as expected, large. An ornate bed sat in the center of the wall facing the door. On the wall to the right was a fireplace, almost as big as the one in the Great Hall of the Teardrop. Multiple windows dominated the opposing wall. The drapes were partially open, allowing some light to enter the room, but in all, it was quite dim.

Merryk's mother, Queen Amanda, sat in a chair at the head of the bed. Several other women were nearby, most likely ladies to the queen. A man who wore the medallion of a doctor stood with two assistants in the corner, and an unusually old man in a floor-length robe, holding a long staff, stood near the foot of the bed.

"Mother," Merryk said. *It seems awkward to call her that, but I don't know what else to call her.*

"My son," the queen said, as she stood to give Merryk a hug.

Tara followed Merryk and gave Queen Amanda a hug. Merryk stepped to the head of the bed to see the king. *It has been just over a year. This is not the man I spoke to in the Teardrop.*

The king was whitish gray. No real color touched his face. He was emaciated. His cheeks and eyes sunk into his head. His breath was shallow and labored.

Merryk looked back at Helga. Her lips were tight; she shook her head slightly from side to side.

"Father, you're safe. I came with the Blue-and-White Mountain Clans to break the siege."

"Merryk?" the king's voice was very weak.

"Yes, I am here." Merryk gently took the king's hand.

"Thank you. I knew you would come. We have much to discuss."

"Father, let me introduce Gaspar Zoo, Walt of the Blue-and-White Mountain Clans. I do not know if you have met before." Merryk motioned to the man standing at the end of the bed.

"Thank you for supporting my son." The king coughed.

"It was our honor, Your Majesty." Gaspar added a bow.

Oolada caught Tara's attention, pointing to Merryk's left arm. Blood was dripping from the cuff of the light mail.

"Your Majesty, Prince Merryk has wounds which need attention," Tara said. "With your permission, we will return later."

"Yes, that would be best," Queen Amanda said.

Merryk and the group left the king's room. As soon as the door shut, Tara stated, "Prince Merryk needs a place where he can rest."

The incredibly old man had followed Merryk out the door from the room. "I am Lord Chamberlain. If I may suggest, Prince Merreg's room is near and would have clothing close to the right size for the prince. I can show you."

"Yes, please," Tara said.

Merryk was feeling the strain of the day. "Jamaal and Bowen." Both men stepped forward. "Bowen, your men have protected the king with honor. Your devotion will not be forgotten. Jamaal has fresh men who could relieve them. See that your men are fed and allowed to rest, though I am sure they will want to return to their duties as soon as possible."

Jamaal looked at Merryk with a knowing glance. "It would be an honor to give them a brief rest from their duties, but we expect all will return."

Bowen bowed politely to Prince Merryk. "We greatly appreciate your understanding, Your Highness."

"Now where is this room?" Merryk asked, just as he started to feel a little dizzy.

"This way," the Lord Chamberlain said.

Merryk moved, but stumbled. Before he fell, Tara went to one side, and Oolada to the other. Together, they helped him walk down the hall.

Chapter 29

REST

Prince Merreg's rooms were a smaller version of the king's. The sitting parlor was just outside the double doors that went into the bedroom—a fireplace, windows, and bed.

"Is there anything else?" the Lord Chamberlain asked.

"Yes, please send in the housekeeper. We need hot water. Also, we need accommodations for the Walt and others," Princess Tara directed.

"Yes, Your Highness."

"Helga, could you help me with the prince?" Tara asked.

"Of course. Perhaps Oolada could help us with the armor." Helga replied.

"Under normal circumstances, I don't like being talked about while I sit here, but right now, I am too tired to argue," Prince Merryk said.

"Gaspar, one last thing. I want to know who leaves the castle. Do not stop them, but collect their names."

"Yes, but if you do not mind, why?"

"Something Goldblatt said to me one time, about rats fleeing a ship."

The three women moved Merryk to a chair inside the double doors. With Oolada's help, the armor was removed. Merryk's chest was badly scraped.

"The bolts from the crossbows dented the armor, then with each move you scraped your chest," Helga said. "It looks far worse than it is. You have a couple of deep cuts, which will need to be cleaned and stitched. I will need hot water. Oolada, ask our people to bring food for the prince: broth, bread, and butter."

"Our people?" Oolada questioned. "But what about the castle staff?"

"We are still in unknown territory," Tara answered for Helga. "We do not know who to trust."

Within the hour, Merryk's wounds had been dressed. He sat in clean clothes on the end of the bed as one of the Zoo Clan delivered food and hot cider. After eating, Merryk said, "I would like to see if I can rest for a few minutes before we return to the king."

"Yes, we will give you some time," Tara said.

"Please open the windows more. I need the fresh air," Merryk requested as he stretched out on the bed to rest.

Shutting the door behind her, Tara turned to the housekeeper. "We need to find a place to refresh ourselves."

The housekeeper nodded and led the three women a short distance down the hall to another room.

Oolada was the first to finish. "I am going to explore a little and see if I can get us something to eat."

"Do not be gone long. I have a feeling Merryk is not done for the day," Helga instructed.

"Very well," Oolada answered.

We came from the left last time. I will go right. Oolada stopped. *Something does not feel right.* Oolada quickly retraced her steps to Merryk's room.

"Is everything all right?" she asked the two guards standing at the door.

"Yes, the only person to come in since you left was the doctor sent by Queen Amanda."

"Doctor! Merryk was treated by Helga. He needs no other. When did he get here?"

"Just before you arrived," a confused guard answered.

Oolada opened the bedroom door to see a man standing over Merryk, holding a dagger.

"Wake up! I want you to see me when I kill you," the man said as he shook Merryk with his free hand.

Merryk struggled to awaken. *My eyes feel like lead. What is this and why?*

Merryk fully opened his eyes. "Jarvis?" The ex-tax collector grinned.

There was a swirling sound.

Suddenly, Jarvis' eyes opened wide in surprise, and then he collapsed forward onto Merryk.

Oolada's blade crossed the distance between the door and the intruder's back, just in time to prevent Jarvis from plunging his dagger into the prince's heart.

"Guards!" Oolada yelled.

The commotion attracted the attention of Gaspar, Jamaal, and the other women.

"No one is to enter the prince's room unescorted. I do not care if it is Queen Amanda herself," Oolada was screaming at the two men outside Merryk's door.

"What happened? Is Merryk all right?" Jamaal asked.

"Yes, he is fine. It was an assassin," Oolada said. She was now trembling as she spoke. "One second later and—."

Tara went to Oolada to calm her. "But you were here. Merryk is safe. Yes?" Tara nodded her head as she spoke. "You saved him, again."

Gaspar spoke. "We are all exhausted, but we cannot be careless. Jamaal, double the guards and advise them we are in hostile territory. Many will lose favor because of Prince Merreg's death. No one is to be trusted."

When Tara went to check on the prince, Merryk propped himself up on the bed to drink more cider. The body of Jarvis still lay on the floor.

"I was going to take out the trash, but I haven't had a chance," Merryk said with a broad smile, trying to reassure Tara.

"You may joke, but that was close," Tara said. She sat on the bed next to Merryk. "I had not expected an attack so soon. Few even knew you were in here."

Merryk reached out to take Tara's hand. "Chancellor Goldblatt told me, as a royal, I would never be totally safe. I now know how right he was. Jarvis was a man with a personal grudge. I found him guilty of attempted rape and stripped him of his commission as a tax collector. I destroyed his life, and he wanted revenge. There will be others." Shaking his head slightly. "We must expect it. Now, I am starving."

Gaspar called for his son to walk with him. "Jamaal, we were lucky. Oolada was in the right place, again. Things are going to change quickly. Helga and I saw the king. He will not survive much longer. When that happens, Merryk will not be the prince, he will be the king. Many will demand his attention. He can handle the change, but he will need time. His safety is now of paramount importance.

"Also, I am concerned about Oolada. She, too, must change. She needs to look and act less like a warrior and more like Lady Zoo. Oolada needs to be guarded with the same intensity as the princess."

"She will not like having guards and will demand the reason," Jamaal said.

"You know the requirements to be the king," Gaspar said.

"Yes, but I am not sure Oolada understands the possibilities. She is already deeply devoted to the prince," Jamaal said.

"I believe the prince sees her devotion, but politics will come into play. She can handle herself in combat. Against other noble women, I am not sure. I believe the princess is our ally. We must help Oolada and protect her for her sake, and for the sake of the clan," Gaspar said.

CHAPTER 30

DETAILS

Merryk walked out of the bedroom into the sitting room. Gaspar and Jamaal sat at a small table, talking. "Where are the ladies?" he asked.

"Getting something to eat and a brief rest," Jamaal answered. "Princess Tara delivered your walking stick. She said you might want it near."

"Thank you. What time is it?"

"Mid-afternoon, Your Highness," Gaspar said.

"How are we doing on gathering the mercenaries?" Merryk asked.

"We have met resistance, not only from the mercenaries, but from the locals. They do not understand we are not a conquering force," Gaspar said.

"Has Bowen identified the loyal officers?"

"Yes."

"Have Bowen select several officers and their men to join our efforts in rooting out the mercenaries. If local troops support us, we will not look like invaders."

"Yes, Your Highness, that will work," Gaspar said.

"Also, I'm having difficulty remembering my way around the castle. Please have somebody work with the Lord Chamberlain to get us a map."

"Yes, Your Highness," Gaspar said.

"Is there anything else to report?"

"Only that the Royal Guards ate, rested, and returned to their posts. They now stand at their stations out of respect for the king," Jamaal said.

"Continue to keep your men near, but make it clear the primary responsibility to protect the king is the current Royal Guard. Without their efforts, there would have been no one for us to rescue."

"Understood."

"You asked us to keep track of who left the castle," Gaspar said. "It was mostly ordinary people who went to families in the city. The one exception was Chancellor Bates. He left about an hour ago. His residence is within the walls," Gaspar said.

"Interesting. Let me know when he returns. Now I must go check on my father."

Chancellor Bates scurried out of the main gate after being forced to give his name to the Blue-and-White Mountain clansmen who guarded the gate. He went down the street and turned into his favorite place, the Pipe and Pint.

"There are soldiers everywhere. All seem to be clansmen," Bates said to the butler at the door.

"Yes, sir. Few patrons have come in today. Early this morning, some men who supported Prince Merreg robbed one merchant at sword point. Quite nasty. They not only took his money, but his carriage."

"I dislike the presence of the clan, but I guess it is better than open attacks."

"I agree," the butler replied. "I assume you are here to meet with the Duke of Ressett?"

"Yes, thank you."

"Your grace, Chancellor Bates is here."

"Thank you. Show him in," the duke replied.

Chancellor Bates entered the library where he had met the duke many times. Today, a second man stood by the fireplace holding a glass of sherry.

"Your Eminence, how nice to see you," Bates said as he greeted the High Priest of the Capital City.

"Hello, Bates," the priest replied with none of the respect Bates had shown him. "Get something to drink. I cannot stay long."

The duke had poured a glass for Bates. "What is the condition of the king?"

"He is continuing to hold on, but all who have seen him say it cannot be for long," Bates answered.

"What of the devil worshiper, Prince Merryk?" the priest asked.

"I am sure you know this morning he defeated Prince Merreg."

"How is that possible?" the duke asked.

"I did not see the battle, but I heard there were champions involved. So, my guess is, he had somebody else fight for him. After defeating Prince Merreg, Prince Merryk came to see the king. He brought the Walt of the Clans and their witch," Chancellor Bates said.

"Openly bringing the pagan into the castle. He will destroy all religion, the way he did the Council of Justice. He cannot be king," the disgusted priest said.

"That is why we are here," the duke said. "We all remember Merryk as a boy. He could barely speak his name. I believe he has been bolstered by his advisors, most significantly by ex-Chancellor Goldblatt. But Goldblatt is not here. We have a narrow window of opportunity to get this idiot to give up his kingdom before the king dies, and he becomes the new king."

"I cannot imagine the impact of such a man on the kingdom," the priest said. "The Provost was asked to declare him incompetent, but somehow Goldblatt convinced Father Bernard not to do so."

"This man is harmless, but his advisors will be devastating. This is why King Natas was so against him," Chancellor Bates said.

"I really do not care about what happens to King Natas. His desire to destroy Prince Merryk caused this entire mess," the duke said emphatically.

"What are we going to do?" the High Priest asked.

"We will use his ignorance against him. I will prepare a document which renounces his claim to the throne. I will prepare it in Latin, which we will say is the official language. We will convince him it will streamline the transfer to him if the king dies," Bates said.

"After he signs it, I will take it to the other nobles. Merryk's advisors will object, but it will be the imbecile's word against the three of us. He will have to speak in an open tribunal, which will expose him as a fraud," the duke said. "But whatever we do must be done tonight, before the king dies."

CHAPTER 31

TRAPS

The sitting room outside the king's bedroom had become a place for waiting. All sorts of people found their way into the space: the Royal Guard, who stood watch; the castle staff, housekeepers, even the gardeners; a few clergy and minor officials. All people who personally knew the king.

"I hate to think what this room would have looked like if Merryk would have allowed people into the castle," Gaspar said to Jamaal.

"My men are watching how the Royal Guards react to each person to judge the threat. Anyone trying to move toward the door is stopped immediately."

Their conversation was interrupted as Merryk left the king's room. The linen tunic he wore was a little tighter than he would have liked. It could not hide the bandages Helga had placed around his chest. Merryk was visibly tired. He moved far slower than his normal pace. His eyes had circles forming around them.

"I see you found your walking stick," Gaspar said.

"Tara thought after the incident earlier today, it would be prudent."

"I agree," Gaspar said as he rested his hand on the hilt of his sword.

The three started to return to Merryk's room when a man stepped forward to block the path. "Your Highness, if I might have a moment?"

Jamaal's reaction was swift. He placed himself between the man and the prince. Gaspar's hand tightened on his sword.

"I am sorry. I did not mean to startle you. I am Chancellor Bates. If we could speak?"

"Who are we?" Merryk asked.

"Myself, the Duke of Ressett, and Father Theo, High Priest of the Capital City." The other two men stood just to the side of the hall. Stepping forward, the duke politely bowed his head. Father Theo extended his cross from around his neck for Merryk to kiss. Merryk ignored the offer.

"Step in here." Merryk pointed to a small sitting room with a table and chairs. Gaspar and Jamaal moved forward to join the prince.

"Alone, if possible," the duke said.

Merryk looked at Gaspar. "If I am harmed in any way, kill all three men." A wink of his eye followed the extreme statement.

"As you command, Your Highness," Gaspar replied with a smirk.

Merryk followed the three men into the room and shut the door. Taking one chair, he sat. Rather than speaking, Merryk gestured with the flash of his palms and a shrug of his shoulders, indicating they should proceed.

The duke shook his head slightly at the others. "If I may begin, we are all close friends with your father and are troubled by your brother's attack."

"Unfortunately," Father Theo added, with a solemn voice, "it does not look like your father will survive."

The duke continued. "As your father's closest advisors, we would like to serve you and make his unfortunate passing as easy as possible for both you and the kingdom."

"We have prepared a simple document to transfer power upon the king's death," Chancellor Bates said. "Because this is an official matter, we must write it in Latin." Bates produced a one-page document and a pen.

Merryk glanced at the document and said slowly, "So, if I sign this, I will be king?"

"Yes, Your Highness, this will resolve any issue of who will be the king," the duke said.

"Do all of you think this is the right thing to do?"

The three nodded.

"If I just make a mark, would that be enough?"

"Certainly," Father Theo said. "We will sign after you, as witnesses."

Merryk looked at the document. "All right. Where?"

Bates could not believe their good fortune, pointing to a spot on the paper. Merryk took the pen and made a straight line, starting below the space upward at a steep angle. "Now you," the prince said.

All three quickly signed.

Before Chancellor Bates could pick up the document, Merryk snatched it from the table.

Merryk's tone and pace of speech changed from slow to quick and confident. "Chancellor Bates, I am surprised by your utilization of the verb 'linquo,' which is less formal. It even has a past tense connotation, more like 'to quit or leave.' A document of this nature should have used the more formal Latin, 'abdico,' to abdicate."

The faces of the three men went blank; then all three turned pale. "But how?" Bates started.

Merryk took the pen and completed his initial stroke to convert it into the letter 'V,' the first letter in the word, *Void*. He then drew a line across the entire document.

"Gaspar," Merryk called. Gaspar and Jamaal popped into the room. There would be no escape.

"Duke, I understand your motives. You want to be king."

"You understand nothing," a now defensive duke replied.

"Your father broke trust with my grandfather and led a rebellion. After he was defeated, rather than destroying your house and title, the Great King allowed you to keep half of your holdings. You blame my family for losing your lands, probably more for losing your father. That is the way small boys think. You're motivated by pure hatred and blind ambition."

"Father Theo, I must confess I am interested in what moved you to treason."

"You destroyed the Council of Justice for the sake of devil worship. Such a man cannot be allowed to rule. Your soul be damned," Father Theo snarled as he spoke.

"I am afraid that it will surprise you to learn, the report from the new Provost's investigators concluded the previous Provost acted out of personal reasons and sold the Army of Justice as a mercenary force. Also, there is absolutely no sign of any devil worship. They only used it as a justification for the actions of the army. You have become embroiled in politics rather than focusing on religion. You have lost your way."

Merryk turned to look at Chancellor Bates. Bates was now in full panic. "I was just a middleman between Prince Merreg, the duke and King Natas," he stuttered. "The duke and Natas hired the mercenaries and they, with Father Theo, encouraged Prince Merreg to attack the king."

"Shut up, you fool!" the duke yelled.

"Thank you, chancellor, for your honesty. If I choose your fate, you will live longer than these two."

"Now give me your medallion of office. Duke, your signet ring."

"Never. You cannot take it," the duke said.

"Jamaal, may I have your dagger?"

The duke's eyes locked onto Merryk's. Merryk showed no sign of leniency. "All right, but I will demand it back from the king." Merryk ignored the duke's fake bravado.

"Father Theo, your cross is a symbol of the Council of Justice. I will hold it until the new Provost can appoint a man worthy of it."

"Jamaal, these men are deeply concerned about my father. They need a place where they can pray for his recovery, somewhere quiet, where they can be alone. My guess is there are such places in the dungeon. They can stay there, at least until the king can determine their fate."

Merryk looked at each man. "For your sakes, pray that is my father and not me."

CHAPTER 32

NEW WORLD

Tara and Helga left Merryk's room to join Oolada in the sitting area. They had adjusted the space to add a conference table for discussions. The casual chairs still lined the walls, with a big sofa in front of the fireplace where Oolada stood. "How do his wounds look?"

"He is going to have a few new scars, but everything seems to be healing well," Helga replied.

"I was not sure we would get his bandages changed before he fell asleep," Tara said.

"The past few days would have exhausted anyone," Oolada said, as she joined the others at the table.

"I had a long nap and could still sleep another day." Tara stretched as she spoke.

"Prince Merryk's day was not just long; it was filled with events." As she spoke, Helga picked up the flask of wine and three goblets. "Since he entered the castle, he has experienced an attempted assassination and a coup. I hope for his sake this is not a normal day. Before we get some sleep, we should have a glass of wine. It may be some time before we can sit together." After pouring the wine, Helga continued, "As full as today was, I believe the next few days will be more so. I pray we are prepared, because with the rising of the sun, the world will change."

Oolada inhaled and exhaled quickly. "There you go again. What does that mean? Every day is new, or is it one of your prophecies? *With the rising of the sun, the world will change.* She lowered her voice to exaggerate the last phrase.

The women laughed.

When the laughter ended, Helga looked at Oolada, her face serious. "In this case, both. Tomorrow, the world will change. My vision of the near future is obscure. Many people fading in and out. What I know is the next few days will be filled with peril. Peril specifically for Merryk and for the two of you. You must be very careful. I wish I could see more."

Tara reached out to comfort Helga, who was openly shaken by her vision. "We will be extra careful, and we will stay together."

"And we will watch Merryk," Oolada added.

Tara joined Merryk, and Helga returned to her room for the night. Oolada chose to stay on the sofa. *This is a strange place, and until I know we have everything secure; I am not going too far from the prince and princess.*

The once raging fire slowly burned itself to flickers and coals. The light in the room had faded with the flames. Oolada finally slipped into sleep.

Two hours before dawn, there was a knock on the doors leading into the sitting room. Oolada awoke with a start, grabbed her sword, and went to the door. Outside were the Zoo Guardsmen and the Lord Chamberlain with his long staff. "The prince must come now." The old man's words were measured, but clearly driven by urgency.

Oolada went to the interior doors to wake the prince and princess. "Your Highnesses, the Lord Chamberlain says you must come, now."

Within minutes, Prince Merryk and Princess Tara followed the Lord Chamberlain down the long, dark hall to his father's room. Gaspar and Helga had been advised and followed.

The faces of the Royal Guardsmen outside the king's room were now somber.

Merryk followed the Lord Chamberlain into the room. Queen Amanda was still at the head of the bed. The king's doctors had withdrawn to the side. Queen Amanda motioned for Merryk to come forward to join her. "Michael, Merryk is here."

"My son," the weak voice of the king could barely be heard as he reached out for the hand of the prince.

"I am here," Merryk said, grasping the king's hand.

"There are many things I wanted to tell you. So many things I wish I had done differently." The king coughed.

"None are important," Merryk replied.

"I want you to know I am very proud of you and the man you have become. You will be an excellent king."

As soon as the king finished his sentence, the Lord Chamberlain slammed the long staff into the stone floor, startling everyone. In a voice which belied his age, he announced, "The selection has been made."

Merryk looked back at the king. Queen Amanda reclaimed her husband's hand. The king smiled at his wife and son and then drifted away.

This man is not my father, but I cannot help but feel sadness in his passing. Merryk felt tears forming in his eyes.

Tara recognized Merryk's pain and moved to his side. "Are you all right?"

"I will be," Merryk answered as he wiped the tears away. Taking a deep breath to fill his lungs helped him strengthen himself, though the expansion of his chest tore at his wounds. Merryk moved around the bed to his mother.

After a few minutes, the Lord Chamberlain said, "We should go out now, Your Majesty."

The sitting area outside the king's room had filled with people—guards, housekeepers, high and low born. As soon as the Lord Chamberlain had cleared the bedroom doors, he again drove his staff to the floor—this time twice. "The king is dead. Long live the king. Long live King Merryk." Two more stabs to the stone followed. The crowd repeated, "Long live the king. Long live King Merryk."

I was not expecting that, Merryk said to himself. Then he realized something else. Everyone in the room was kneeling. *What are they doing?* Merryk turned to Tara, Oolada, Gaspar and Helga. To his surprise, they were kneeling as well. *Oh crap, I am the king!*

Merryk looked to the Lord Chamberlain. The man was on one knee and clearly struggling to stand. "Here, let me help you," Merryk said to the old man. When the man reached his feet, Merryk saw tears running down his face.

"How long have you served the king?"

"With you, I will have served the Family Raymouth for four generations." The sorrow overwhelmed the man, and he began to sob.

Merryk reached out to the man to give him a hug. The Lord Chamberlain stayed for a moment and then broke away. "Thank you, Your Majesty. I will be fine."

I hope I will.

CHAPTER 33

PRACTICAL QUESTIONS

M erryk walked back down the corridor from the king's apartments to his room. Although the light now found its way through the windows, the space still seemed dark. *I am uncertain of the way to go, so everything is darker; not only as I walk through the castle, but forward as a king.*

When Merryk finally made it back to his room, he excused himself to retreat to his bedroom.

"I think he just needs a minute," Tara said to those who had returned with him.

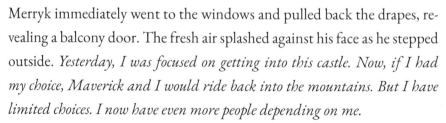

Merryk immediately went to the windows and pulled back the drapes, revealing a balcony door. The fresh air splashed against his face as he stepped outside. *Yesterday, I was focused on getting into this castle. Now, if I had my choice, Maverick and I would ride back into the mountains. But I have limited choices. I now have even more people depending on me.*

Merryk looked at the interior of the castle yard for the first time. He was on the second floor of a large central building, probably the original fortification. Centuries of building had created an outer wall which prevented any view of the outside world.

From Merryk's balcony, the space appeared reasonably organized. *This place is enormous. Most of the support buildings are within the outer wall. At some time, the entire city must've been within the walls. Attention has been paid to open spaces and gardens, but other than looking straight up, nothing of the sky. I bet they have a tower with a view. I need to find that soon.*

You are putting off accepting your responsibility. You are exactly what you did not want to be, king. But, like it or not, you are now the king. I already miss the Teardrop. Merryk felt tears welling in his eyes. *You're not a crier. You must be exhausted and feeling overwhelmed. Men have been kings for centuries. If one man can do it, so can you. Good talk. Great confidence!*

Merryk shook his head and returned to his room. *Cold water on the face will help. Remember how you eat an elephant. One bite at a time.*

Merryk exited the bedroom to be greeted by a sitting room full of people, half of which he had never met. They all bowed as he entered. "All right, who are all these people?" Merryk asked harshly.

Tara, as much as anything to soften his tone, replied, "This is Jamas, the king's head butler, and Eleanor, the head housekeeper. Together, they manage the castle staff. The others are various members of the staff who have direct contact with the king and the queen."

Both Jamas and Eleanor stepped forward and bowed politely. The rest of the staff bowed again.

"Speaking for the entire staff," Jamas said, "we are very sorry for the loss of your father. Many have known King Michael most of their lives. All will share your sorrow. I know you have much on your mind, but there are several pressing matters. First, we cannot find Chancellor Bates. He handles your schedule. We have requests from nobles and diplomats for audiences, and the plans for your father's funeral. We do not know how to proceed."

Merryk took a deep breath to calm his response. "I have relieved Chancellor Bates of all duties. He currently resides in the dungeon. Make a list of all those who wish audiences, and advise them I need a few days, then we will schedule later. I assume all will say it is critical, but do not be swayed."

"Yes, Your Majesty." Jamas looked pleased with his answer.

"Eleanor," Queen Tara said, "I need you to be sure Queen Amanda has everything she needs. She is your priority. Please ask that one of her ladies come to me to provide input on the funeral. All normal household questions can be directed to me. You and I will set a time to meet each day. Today, it will be midmorning."

"Yes, Your Majesty." Eleanor's face reflected her relief.

Jamas stepped forward again. "Your Majesty, the head chef is particularly distraught. He does not know what to prepare for you. He remembers when you were a small boy you liked sweet cakes, but now?"

"Well, I may be bigger, but I do like an occasional sweet cake, but not every day. How about we do this one meal at a time? Right now, I would like breakfast: ham or bacon, fried eggs, hot bread, honey, and butter. Also, several other people will join me."

Jamas smiled. "Immediately, Your Majesty." A slender man with a white hat gripped tightly in his hand quickly bowed and left the room.

"Is there anything else which needs immediate attention?" Merryk asked.

"No, Your Majesty," Jamas replied, "other than, may I suggest, you take breakfast in the dining hall."

CHAPTER 34

CHANCELLOR

Merryk and Tara, with the core group of Gaspar, Oolada, Helga, and Jamaal, followed the new map to the dining hall. An extremely long table sat in the middle of an elongated room. The table could have accommodated at least fifty people. Merryk thought. *Is everything in this place going to be oversized?* Slender windows ran from floor-to-ceiling on one side of the room; two fireplaces, both with warm fires, were equally spaced on the opposing wall.

The day was overcast, suppressing the light and the mood. The filtered gray permeated everything with its somberness.

They had placed settings for the group at the far end of the table. As soon as everyone was seated, a group of servers began offering breakfast.

After everyone had finished, Gaspar said, "Your Majesty, when you are ready, there are several things we should discuss."

"Now would be as good a time as any," Merryk replied.

Gaspar started. "The castle is secure. Today, we need to evaluate the army's officers. If that threat is removed, we can send the clansmen home. If we could do this before winter hits, everyone will be happy."

Jamaal added, "Ex-Chancellor Bates will not shut up. He keeps saying King Natas is due to arrive in the Capital City in three days."

The Lord Chamberlain appeared from the side door. "Excuse me, Your Majesty, but you and the Walt have a visitor."

"I hoped to delay all audiences," King Merryk replied.

"I believe you will want this visitor," the old man replied. "Chancellor Goldblatt."

"Goldblatt! Absolutely, please send him in," Merryk replied with a broad smile.

Merryk rose from his chair to meet Goldblatt halfway down the table. "I am so glad to see you. But how did you get here?"

"I arrived yesterday midmorning on Captain Slater's ship. With all the commotion in the streets, I could not get to the castle until this morning. I spent last night with Masterroff. The only way I could get into the castle this morning was to ask for the Walt."

"Have you had breakfast? Please come join us," Merryk said.

"No, thank you. One never goes hungry at Masterroff's."

Merryk picked up the previous conversation. "Jamaal was saying Chancellor Bates says King Natas is coming in three days."

Queen Tara added, "This matches the information my mother gave about Mandy's wedding and their attending."

"King Natas has been out at sea and will not have known of the current turn of events," Gaspar said. "He might just sail into our hands."

"He will not enter the harbor if he thinks there is any danger," Jamaal added.

"If I had Admiral Bellows, I would let Natas sail close and then block any retreat," Merryk said.

"Admiral Bellows and your fleet lay just two hours due west of the harbor—over the horizon and out of sight. Captain Slater is ready to convey any messages to the admiral," Goldblatt said. "The admiral wanted to support you or offer a hasty exit, if needed."

"I need the admiral. I hope he will take his old position and gain control of the king's navy," Merryk replied.

"You mean your navy," Tara said to remind Merryk of his new position.

"We should see what other information about Natas' visit we can gain from Bates. Jamaal and I could question him," Goldblatt said. "I would also suggest we have Admiral Bellows come ashore immediately. He can gain control of the entire navy and plan a surprise for King Natas and then return to the fleet before Natas arrives."

Merryk looked at Gaspar, who nodded in agreement. "He will also give us more information about the army's officers."

"How is Arron GorgWalter doing in collecting the mercenaries?" Merryk asked.

"Very well, with the help of the regular army," Jamaal answered. "He also found two ships docked on a deserted pier which look like the mercenaries' transportation. We confined those who have surrendered in one; the other, we are using for the bodies."

"We should get the bodies into the sea this evening before they attract rodents," Oolada suggested.

"Agreed," Merryk said.

Turning his attention to the Chancellor. "Chancellor Goldblatt, the last time the king asked you to be his chancellor, you declined. Is that still your answer?" Merryk asked with a broad smile.

"I believe I would like to reconsider," Goldblatt replied with a grin.

"Very well. You may have the job. I just hope you will not take too long to learn it." Everyone laughed.

"Gaspar, we should gather the Council of Walters. I need to apprise them of the current circumstances," Merryk said. "I also need to know if they require anything."

"Yes, Your Majesty. I will arrange it at once."

CHAPTER 35

NEWS

Gaspar and Merryk had just finished their meeting with the Council of Walters.

"Your Majesty, the Walters appreciate your taking the time to include them in your decisions. Letting them know you want to get them home before winter was very important."

"How can I not want people to be with their families? I'm just thankful we had so few casualties. I will never forget the clan's willingness to come to my father's aid."

"They came to your aid, King Merryk."

"You know how hard it is for me to have that title. You know I never wanted to be king. But circumstances just kept pushing."

"Helga would say it is your fate. She has told me many times I will do what fate wants, even if it was not my desire."

"I still like to believe I have free will."

"Do not tell that to a woman. She will go out of her way to show you your error."

Both men laughed.

Chancellor Goldblatt was waiting when they entered Merryk's apartments.

"I have news from the discussion with Bates. Jamaal was right. The man is a virtual magpie. Once he started talking, he could not stop. Besides a full signed confession implicating the prince, the duke, and the High Priest, he described the duke and the prince's relationship with King Natas. The summary is all of this started with Natas, and his plan to gain control of the High Kingdom. Princess Tarareese's marriage to Prince Merreg was the first step in their plan. When that was prevented, King Natas tried everything he could to get the plan back on track."

"Natas is coming in two days to marry his younger daughter to Prince Merreg as the Outland Queen. Bates also believes it was the duke's plan to marry his daughter as the Inland Queen. The two men then could exert influence over Prince Merreg."

"Currently, Natas has a man in the Capital City named Lieutenant Jordan. He met the mercenaries when they arrived. We need to find him. Bates believes Natas' Royal Marines will arrive in the next couple of nights. They are to support Prince Merreg after the mercenaries leave. Unless we find Jordan, he will attempt to wave off the marines."

"How long until Admiral Bellows is here?" Merryk asked.

"He should be here with the tide in the next couple of hours," Gaspar replied. "If I had my guess, they will dock the marines in the same place they did the mercenaries. We can be ready."

"Very well. Let us see if we can find Jordan in the next few hours," Merryk said. "In any event, we need to be prepared to greet the marines."

Merryk had a few minutes before dinner. Stepping out of his room, two guards immediately followed him. "I suppose you were instructed not to leave me alone, under penalty of death by the Walt or the princess."

"Both, Your Majesty," the guard replied.

Merryk laughed. "I must get used to this. Where is the princess's room?"

The guard politely corrected Merryk. "The Queen's quarters are this way."

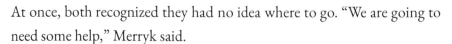

Merryk entered Tara's rooms. Oolada stood looking out the window.

"Not much of a view," Merryk said cheerfully.

"Certainly not the mountains," Oolada replied.

"Where is Tara?"

"She is taking a nap. I think she is still tired from the journey."

Merryk looked around for a moment and then started toward the door. "I am going to see if I can find some place with a view. Would you like to join me and my guards?" Merryk added.

"If you would not mind me and my guards joining you." Oolada said with a tone of resignation.

"You have guards too?"

Oolada nodded. "This place is so safe, everyone has guards."

Merryk laughed. "I have my walking stick."

"And I have my knife," Oolada said, pointing to the blade strapped to her thigh.

"Shall we?"

At once, both recognized they had no idea where to go. "We are going to need some help," Merryk said.

The first person they encountered was the Lord Chamberlain. He was moving some books down the hall.

"Lord Chamberlain, why are you carrying books? Get one of the younger men to do it," Merryk said.

"I am fine, Your Majesty. How can I be of service?"

"Is there a place where we could get a better view of the city and surroundings?" Merryk asked.

The Lord Chamberlain thought for a moment. "When I was a younger man, I would go to the top of the old turret on the south end of this building. It had a magnificent view of sunsets. I do not believe anybody has been up there in years."

"Sounds like just the place," Oolada said.

"How do we get there?" Merryk asked.

The Lord Chamberlain's directions were perfect—up one floor, to the end of the corridor, then up to the top. "He was right about no one coming up here," Merryk said as the dust sprang from the sides of the oak door as it opened. Merryk handed his walking stick to Oolada, grabbed the torch, and started up the circular stairs.

The climb reminded Merryk of the tower in the Teardrop, except it was three floors of steps rather than two. The top door was rusty and required Merryk to force it with his shoulder. The door broke open to reveal the view.

The sun was just touching the horizon in the west. An entire array of red and white clouds flitted over its surface. The Capital City and the main port lay to the south. The city was a large warren of streets and alleys, filled with people scurrying home for the evening. The port beyond was a forest of ships' masts rising in bundles around the docks. A broad river delta lay to the west; its glasslike surface reflecting the ever-changing clouds. Everything was tinted by a light red to match the sun's glow. To the north, beyond the hillside, they could see the tips of snowcapped mountains, now in red and gray. The east revealed rolling hills and grasslands, slowly sinking into the gray of dusk.

Merryk, Oolada, and their four guards all stood in silence as they absorbed the sunset.

"The Lord Chamberlain did not give this view justice with just *magnificent.* I really do not know how to describe it." Oolada said.

"I think I just found my favorite place in the castle," Merryk answered.

A light breeze floated across the top of the tower, reminding everyone it would soon bring winter with rain and snow.

"It could get cold up here," Oolada said.

"But not as cold as Ledin Grubi," Merryk said with a smile.

"Nothing is as cold as Ledin Grubi," Oolada replied with a chuckle.

The sun continued to fall as the group stood in silence.

Finally, Merryk pointed toward the door. "I think we need to get ready for dinner."

"Yes, but I am glad we found this place. It reminds me of home," Oolada said.

"Me too."

Chapter 36

BREAKFAST

Goldblatt found King Merryk sitting alone at the end of the dining table. "Chancellor, I was just about to have breakfast. Would you like to join me?"

"Of course, Your Majesty. Where is Queen Tarareese?" Goldblatt asked.

"She is sleeping in this morning, still exhausted from the trek here." Merryk handed Goldblatt a plate of eggs.

A frustrated steward immediately appeared to serve them properly.

"I'm having difficulty with all these people. I know they are just doing their jobs, but I can pass you an egg."

Goldblatt laughed. "This is something you will get used to. I have a report from Admiral Bellows and Arron GorgWalter. I told you last night Masterroff helped us find Lieutenant Jordan, who was hiding in the back of a tavern called 'Sally's.' With little encouragement, he gave us the details regarding the arrival of the marines. He helped bring them ashore. We now have them successfully locked up, with no casualties on our part."

"Did Bellows seize the ships?"

"Yes, two more of King Natas' warships have joined your fleet."

"Excellent news." Merryk replied.

"Also, Admiral Bellows and Captain Bowen have prepared a list of loyal officers for both the army and the navy. On the list are men who were junior

officers during my time with Great King Mikael. I can say with reasonable
certainty, you now have control of the military.

"Again, excellent news."

"Admiral Bellows also wanted you to know he pulled all the fleet out of
the Teardrop, other than one warship. He did not want to get them trapped
there by the weather," Chancellor said.

"After we receive our guest tomorrow, we can bring them into port."

"Yes, Your Majesty," Goldblatt said.

"Admiral Bellows has proven himself a capable commander and a loyal
friend. I am considering appointing him as commander of both the army
and the navy, at least until we can groom more senior officers in the army."

"An excellent suggestion. It will be seen as a vote of confidence, and a
reward for his support."

"With the military under control, I think we could tell Gaspar it is all
right for the clansmen to return home. Winter cannot be far away, and they
must travel north."

"Might I suggest he start with half until we meet with the nobles? It is
still possible we could face resistance."

"You think the nobles are going to be a problem?"

"Potentially, yes," Goldblatt said. "Unfortunately, they all remember
Merryk, the boy. They know they sent you away to keep you from being
declared incompetent. Now, that boy is their king. Yes, they have doubts."

"We must have the opposite of the meeting we had with Father Aubry.
Now we need to show my competence," Merryk said.

"They need to see King Merryk, who saved the kingdom and defeated
the Army of Justice, who is more than a warrior but a decisive leader."

"Sounds easy," Merryk said with a grin. "We should do it."

"May I suggest we invite all the nobles to the castle the day after tomorrow? But before then, you should meet with the Duke of Crescent. If you
remember, he sent you a letter of congratulations. The Crescent family is
as old as the Raymouths. They have always supported the throne and are

deeply respected by most of the noble families. If we reassure him of your competence, it will make the meeting with the others go more smoothly."

"Certainly. Arrange a meeting as soon as possible."

"Which brings me to the next issue, the Duke of Ressett. Have you decided what you are going to do?"

"Not completely, but I will by the time we meet the nobles," Merryk answered.

Goldblatt fidgeted in his chair. "There is one last thing, but you will not like it."

"The last time you were this uncomfortable was when you told me I was incompetent," Merryk said.

"I said *thought to be incompetent,*" Goldblatt said defensively. "You are aware there are requirements to be king. Specifically, you must have two queens: one from within the kingdom and one from without."

"Surely everyone can see the only thing that comes out of this requirement is pain and bloodshed."

"What everyone will see is the requirement gave the kingdom a prince exactly when he was needed. A prince to save the kingdom from the evil of another," Goldblatt said.

"Will they not also see there would not have been the need if the requirement had not created the conflict between brothers—first between my father and the Lord Commander; then between Prince Merreg and myself. It is a savage rule, one which turns brothers against each other and demeans the women who are queen."

"Women who recognize the importance of selecting the strongest possible heir for the benefit of the kingdom," Goldblatt replied.

"I will not have two wives," Merryk said emphatically.

"If that is the case, the man you have locked up in the dungeon has a genuine claim to the throne."

"He will not be king." Merryk stood from his chair and walked to the window. "Who would be next in line?"

"You cannot think like that. You are the king. I have met many men who wish to rule. None have ever had your skills as a natural leader or were as rational and compassionate. Our kingdom will thrive under your leadership. You must be king," Goldblatt insisted.

"I cannot be the first prince to become king without a second wife. What is the protocol?"

"Technically, you have a year to find a wife, but the sooner you decide, the better."

"For whom is it better? I like having only one wife." Merryk's tone was firm. "As king, why can't I just change the rule?"

"You can. But you are not fully the king until they crown you, and they cannot crown you unless you have two wives," Goldblatt explained.

"I do not want two wives. Do I have to decide now?"

"No, but you need to be ready for the meeting with the nobles. They will quickly go from concerns about your competence to pushing their daughters. And every royal family has a daughter."

Merryk placed the palms of his hands over his eyes and rubbed his temples, hoping to ward off a growing headache.

CHAPTER 37

RIDE

Merryk finally awakened Tara. "I want to go for a ride. It is almost noon."

"It is so cold this morning." Tara continued to resist Merryk's prodding. "Why cannot we just walk around the castle grounds? I want to talk with you."

"You can talk with me from the back of a horse. Now come on."

"I am not sure which of the two of you was the happiest to see the other, you or Maverick," Tara said, teasing Merryk as they finally rode out the east gate of the castle.

Merryk reached down to rub Maverick's neck one more time. "We can't help it if we like each other."

Maverick bobbed his head up and down in agreement.

"You can't tell me you haven't missed Bella."

"Of course, but so much is going on. So many things." Tara let her statement drop.

The day was perfect for early November. The air had a deep chill. Only remnants of leaves hung on the deciduous trees. Just outside the east gate was the military barracks. As the two passed through, a contingent of a dozen Zoo Clansmen fell in behind. It took about five minutes to leave behind the clutter of houses near the castle wall.

Soon the horizon opened to a set of gently rolling grass hills. The sky was a light blue, not the deep warm blue of summer, but clear and crisp.

"What a beautiful day," Merryk said as he stopped to look at the scenery. His breath created little puffs of condensation as he spoke.

"It is a chilly day," Tara said, tugging again on her fur.

"You and I know this isn't freezing." Merryk's face was filled with a smile. "This is the first time in days I feel like I can breathe. You are right, there are so many things happening."

"But you are handling them all marvelously. I knew you were excellent with organization, but your attention to detail is impressive. And before you object, I want you to know that would be my opinion, even if you were not my husband. I am sorry I have not been more help." Tara reached out to catch Merryk's hand.

"Well, I need you to be rested for the next two days. Tomorrow your father and mother arrive. Then on Saturday, we have the gathering of nobles. How are you feeling about seeing your parents?"

"I am excited to see my mother. I have missed her the most. My little sister will blame me for losing her groom. Perhaps we should save one of those rooms in the dungeon for her. I can already hear her complaining about my ruining her life." Tara shook her head from side to side and laughed.

"She can't possibly be that bad," Merryk said.

"Wait to judge." Tara continued to hold Merryk's hand.

"What about your father?" Merryk's tone was serious.

"I will never forgive him. You must make him suffer for what he did." Tara's hand tightened on Merryk's.

"Admiral Bellows has a plan. Unless things change radically, we will capture him. Then I will face the tough decision of what to do with him. Executing him would destabilize the southern continent, which would not be good for your people, although it would be just for all those who died because of his actions." Merryk's brow furrowed as he spoke.

"You have clearly given this much thought. I trust you will do the right thing. Now, enough with talk about my father. I have some news for you."

Tara's face lit up as she spoke. "Remember when you made me promise if ever I had news, I would tell you at once." Tara stopped to let Merryk think about what she had just said.

Merryk's face did not change. "I don't know what you're talking about. You promise me things all the time."

Tara could not believe her ears. Her mouth fell open in surprise. "How could you not know what I mean?"

Merryk's face now cracked into a broad smile. "You mean we're going to have a baby." Joy covered his face.

"Yes," Tara screamed in frustration and happiness.

Merryk moved closer and swept Tara off Bella onto Maverick in front of him. Holding her tightly, he said, "Now your need for sleep makes more sense. This is more exciting than becoming king."

"I hope so." Tara wrapped her arms tightly around Merryk's neck.

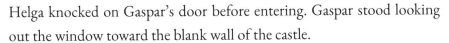

Helga knocked on Gaspar's door before entering. Gaspar stood looking out the window toward the blank wall of the castle.

"I do not believe you are really looking at a wall," Helga said as she moved to his side.

"Chancellor Goldblatt said King Merryk has secured the army and the navy. We can start planning to return our people home. He also said the king had requested a meeting of the nobles in two days. I think the time is right to raise the issue of Oolada. But I do not know if I should go directly to the king or discuss it with the Chancellor."

Helga looked directly into Gaspar's eyes. "Neither."

Gaspar shook his head in disbelief.

"I know you believe Merryk is the one and you hope Oolada is the daughter of the clan in the prophecy. However, things are still changing. Merryk does not want to have two wives. Everything we know about him says he may give up the kingship rather than comply with rules he does not support."

"That is preposterous. No man would give up being king."

"Except the man who should truly be king. He is a man driven by principles. He only fights when it is necessary. He gains wealth and then shares it freely. Right now, he would give up being king if it would make him violate his principles. There is also something else. I do not believe you need to do or say anything, because fate is already in charge."

Gaspar looked confused.

"When Merryk was attacked, Oolada was going in the opposite direction. She told me something did not feel right. I believe they are already tied together. Feeling another person's peril is most unusual. It is only present between people with intense connections, like a parent and a child, or a husband and wife. If I am right, you need not do anything."

Gaspar did not like Helga's advice. "But Merryk is going to meet with all the nobles. They will quickly conclude Merryk needs an Inland Queen."

"Gaspar, if you press, Merryk might choose Oolada, but it would be because of obligation. Oolada would be queen, but she would never have love. If you wait, fate may give her both.

Lady Ressett paced back-and-forth in the stable, waiting for King Merryk and Queen Tara to return. She had pulled her long black hair into several braids. Her green eyes showed signs of worry and sleeplessness. *There is no assurance the king will speak with me. but I must try. I am afraid my father has gone too far this time.*

"My lady, this really is not the place for you to wait," a worried stable hand pleaded.

"I will wait." Defiance and resolve filled her voice.

The sound of horse's hooves on the stone surface heralded the arrival of the king. Although she had prepared a speech in her mind, nothing prepared her to see the new king. A large, powerful black stallion came down the row. The man who rode it was a match in size and strength. He wore a long black leather coat. His beard was impeccably trimmed, and his bright blue eyes sparkled. For a moment, all she could do was stare. Only the appearance of a woman with blonde hair on a magnificent white mare broke the spell. As they dismounted, she thought. *They are both extremely tall and beautiful.*

King Merryk was giving instructions to a young stable hand. Queen Tara talked with her mount as the horse was being attended by the staff.

"Your Majesties. Your Majesties, may I speak with you for a moment?" Katalynn pleaded.

A Royal Guard stepped between Katalynn and the king. "The king is not available now. You need to schedule a meeting with the Chancellor."

"Your Majesties," Katalynn yelled over the guard. "Queen Tara, I am Katalynn. We met when I was a child."

Katalynn's voice reached Tara. "Merryk, I think this is the Duke of Ressett's daughter."

"Allow her through," Merryk commanded.

"Thank you, Your Majesty. My father is the Duke of Ressett. Two days ago, he joined Father Theo, the High Priest, for lunch at a local club. They left in my father's carriage for the castle just after noon. The driver sat outside until midnight. My father never returned. The driver overheard my father saying he was going to see the king. I have heard nothing for two days. I was hoping you knew something. It is not like him to disappear for days at a time. The people at the Cathedral also said the High Priest is missing. With all the soldiers in the street and the turmoil, I am worried."

Tara stepped forward. "Katalynn, I remember you. Your father and your mother came to visit us."

"Lady Ressett, there is no easy way to say this. Your father is unharmed, but currently confined in the dungeon. Chancellor Bates, the High Priest, and your father are charged with treason and conspiracy to kill King Michael."

Merryk's words hit like a hammer.

"There must be some mistake. The people who are saying this are lying. My father would never do such a thing."

Merryk raised his hand to stop her. "I am saying it. I witnessed their treason. There is no doubt."

Katalynn went silent for a moment. "Forgive me, Your Majesty. I do not know what to say. Could I at least see him?"

"Yes. Guards, take Lady Ressett to see her father. Stay with her so she comes to no harm."

CHAPTER 38

THE PLAN

In the absence of a storm, the weather in the Capital City port followed a time-tested pattern. The days started with low morning clouds or fog, which burned off as the day progressed, a light onshore wind in the morning, and an offshore breeze in the evening. Today was no different. The morning gray sky showed breaks of blue as the day passed.

"When do you think they will arrive?" Merryk asked Admiral Bellows.

"Burat may be on the wrong side, but he is an excellent sailor. He will reach the dock near high tide—midday."

"Good morning, Your Majesty. You are up early," Admiral Burat said as he approached Queen Stephanie, who stood alone near midships.

"I am afraid I will never become accustomed to sea travel. Five nights and I still have trouble sleeping."

"My guess is many things are weighing on you."

A swell caught the RS *Cleaver*, causing the ship to shake like a dog shaking off water. "I hope I will not need to add foul weather to the list."

"No, My Queen. As you can see from the morning sky, nothing but small clouds and a light roll of the sea. Under normal circumstances, I would say it is a beautiful morning."

Queen Stephanie smiled.

"Do you have a schedule of events?"

"No, and I am sure that is part of my concern. I do not know what awaits us, or who." Stephanie's voice reflected a growing fear. Quietly, she spoke to the admiral. "I am frightened."

"I will not leave you. You have no reason to fear," Burat responded, allowing his hand to touch the queen's for a moment.

"We will always have fear," Stephanie replied. "But knowing you are near is comforting. Please, be cautious. Now I need to get Mandy ready. She is almost frantic with anticipation."

"Very well, Your Majesty." The admiral bowed politely as the queen moved away.

By midday, the morning gray had completely burned away. The onshore winds carried the RS *Cleaver* neatly around the small peninsula to reveal the Capital City of the High Kingdom. Gentle waves covered the sea, and the sound of seagulls rose around the ship.

King Natas and Colonel Lamaze stood together near the bow.

"Will we have a signal from Lieutenant Jordan?" the king asked.

"Yes, he said he would send the pilot boat," Lamaze replied. "I have been watching our approach, and I have seen no warships. Everything appears to be just commercial vessels moving in and out of port."

"Admiral Burat has been on the bridge most of the morning. He is constantly scanning the horizon. I am sure he would change course at the first sign of trouble. No, this is going to be a good day," King Natas said with confidence.

"Father, it is so big. I do not know what I expected," Mandy said as she excitedly joined him at the rail.

"The Capital City is appropriate for the High Kingdom—a big city for a big kingdom— and you will be its queen," King Natas said.

Within half an hour, the RS *Cleaver* moved into a more confined channel leading to the docks. "There is the pilot boat," Lamaze announced.

A large rowboat, flying the flag of Natas' Kingdom, waited a short distance ahead.

"Greetings from the new king of the High Kingdom. Please follow me to your berth."

The pilot boat moved efficiently past the other docks to a large central berth. Flags of the High Kingdom flew on the surrounding buildings and fluttered in the gentle wind. An honor guard of Royal Guards and army personnel lined both sides of the dock to the pier. A group of officials had gathered to await the arrival of King Natas. "Your betrothed will be there." Natas pointed for Mandy.

Queen Stephanie moved the short distance behind Mandy and the king. Admiral Burat moved to her side. Stephanie turned briefly to look at Burat. Her face was carefully controlled, but her eyes showed fear.

Burat responded by nodding ever so slightly.

Sailors scrambled to secure lines to the front and the rear of the ship. They extended a large gangplank from the dock to the ship. Four Royal Dragoons in red cloaks were the first off the ship, followed by King Natas, with Queen Stephanie walking at his side. Mandy, Colonel Lamaze, and Admiral Burat followed. Another set of Dragoons brought up the rear.

The path from the *Cleaver* to the officials was not long, but Natas made it a procession, a victory march.

The sound of slapping water on the side of a ship caught Admiral Burat's attention. He twisted his head to look back. Her sister ships—the

Broadsword and the *Trident*—now bracketed the *Cleaver*. *This was a trap!* Rather than raising an alarm, he moved closer to the queen.

Reaching the end, Natas stopped. "We meet again, Prince Merreg, or should it be King Merreg?"

Merryk turned to face Natas. "It would be better to say King Merryk."

In an instant, a bristle of sword points surrounded Natas and his family. Admiral Burat placed his body to shield Queen Stephanie.

"There is no reason for bloodshed," King Merryk said. "Surrender and order your men to stand down."

Natas looked bewildered. Uncertain what to do, his eyes searched the surroundings.

"There is no need to look for your marines or mercenaries. Those who are alive are secure, and Prince Merreg will not come to your aid. Surrender, now," Merryk said again.

"What if I do not?" Natas snapped in reply.

"Surrender can be done with dignity, or defeat can be humiliating."

King Natas thought for an instant and then commanded, "Stand down."

Merryk's men quickly disarmed Natas' Dragoons.

King Merryk looked at King Natas and shook his head. "I never expect answers from you, or at least honest ones. But I have been unable to understand why you didn't stop trying to kill me. Now you have forced me to become king. I told you in the beginning I did not want to be king."

"Everyone wants to be king," Natas replied.

"I didn't and now I have little choice."

"You cannot possibly understand. You do not have the true bloodline of kings. You are unworthy," Natas returned to his normal smug tone.

"Well, this unworthy bloodline has defeated your worthy one at every turn. I have a place for you in the tower, where you can think about how unworthy I am, and think about the price you're going to pay for your actions. And when I am ready, we will discuss the terms of surrender."

Tara and Oolada observed the exchange from behind Merryk's left shoulder. Now Tara stepped forward to face her father. "My father's men have surrendered, but he has not given up his dagger."

King Natas snarled at his daughter. Reaching for his belt, he said, "You have been my biggest disappointment. You are a traitor to your blood."

"I hope you will not think the same of your grandchild," Tara said as she placed her hand on her stomach.

King Natas' eyes went wide with rage. "Never!" he bellowed as he tore his dagger from the belt and plunged it into Tara's belly.

For an instant, Oolada and Colonel Lamaze both froze in disbelief. Lamaze took the moment to drop to his knee to retrieve a blade from his boot. Without thinking, he surged at King Merryk. He did not fool Oolada. She stepped into his path, blocking the dagger down and away with her left hand. The knife in her right hand struck upward, just under Lamaze's rib cage, driving it to the hilt. Lamaze crumpled to the ground.

Merryk could not believe what had happened. Merryk's hand tightened on his walking stick. There was a click as the walking stick came apart. Merryk moved directly toward King Natas. At the appearance of the long shiny blade, Natas held his arms wide apart, allowing his dagger to fall. "I surrender," he said with a smirk.

Merryk's blade flashed toward Natas' neck, stopping just short of breaking the skin.

"I surrender," Natas said again, this time with a full smile.

Merryk looked directly into Natas' eyes. There was no sign of remorse. "Hell no! You bastard!" Merryk shouted as his blade slid effortlessly across Natas' throat. As the blood surged from his neck, Merryk turned his blade and plunged the tip through Natas' heart.

———————— ❦ ————————

Oolada kneeled next to Queen Stephanie, who held Tara in her arms. Tears ran down her face. The front of Tara's gown was soaked in blood. Oolada yelled, "We need to get her to the castle!" Merryk picked Tara up in his arms and ran toward the carriages. Oolada and Queen Stephanie followed.

The guards prevented Admiral Burat from staying with Queen Stephanie. Burat ran to Gaspar. "Walt, I beg you. Please let me stay with Queen Stephanie."

"No," Gaspar said. He followed the others, then stopped. "Guards, bring the Admiral and the princess with me."

Chapter 39

TARA

I hate waiting. Someone you love is injured and all you can do is wait. Which is worse, modern hospitals with large-faced clocks and cruel slow-moving second hands, or today, with no way to measure time other than the passing of the sun on the windowsill?

This day could not have gone worse. What kind of father would stab his own child? I've never had a child, but I have been captured by the thought twice. How precious; how special. How could he?

I should've protected her, but on the list of threats, this one was at the bottom. It happened in an instant. What father would?

He surrendered, and I killed him anyway. Sometimes evil just needs to die. My anger will destabilize another kingdom. Yes, I was angry. I would do it again. Tara's mother said he would not stop. Now, he will. I am not sorry he is dead.

Tara was so happy; so excited. I hope she will be fine. This is when I wish I had the big modern hospital, with the cruel second hands and the blood transfusions, drugs, and surgeons.

Oolada saved my life again. I didn't see Lamaze. She did. How many times has she saved my life? She probably blames herself for not saving both of us.

If they didn't do such a good job of dusting, I could mark the time on the windowsill. It must've been at least thirty minutes, or is it ten?

"Has Your Majesty had anything to eat since breakfast?" a concerned Jamas asked.

"No, Jamas. But I'm all right for now."

"I am going to get you some tea and biscuits, just in case you change your mind."

"Thank you."

The sitting room outside Merryk's bedroom reminded him of his father's, except this time he was in it. Helga said she would let him know when he could come in.

Gaspar came across the room to where Merryk sat. "Have you heard anything?"

"Nothing."

"If there is anything that can be done, Helga will do it. She has saved many warriors from battle injuries."

"Thank you, but Tara is also carrying our child. My guess is saving both is making everything more difficult. I have not seen Oolada for some time. Do you know where she went?"

"My guess is somewhere to be alone. That is what she does in times of stress."

"Gaspar, she saved my life again. But I fear she will blame herself for not stopping Natas. Tara and Oolada have a special bond."

"No one could have stopped that maniac. I must tell you; I am not sorry you killed him."

"I did it in anger. He deserved to die, but it should've been an act of reason, not one of anger."

"He is dead. The world is better off. Reason or anger, the result is correct." Gaspar spoke his words with certainty. He placed his hand on Merryk's shoulder. "My young king, I have killed many men. At night, before I sleep, I ask myself if they deserved to die. If I can answer that question 'yes,' then I sleep well."

The inner door to the bedroom opened. Helga looked out, motioning for Merryk to come. Human communication is so much more than words. The look on Helga's face explained everything before her words. "She has lost a great deal of blood and we cannot stop the bleeding. The stab wound was severe; it triggered a miscarriage. She is fighting both shocks at the same time."

Tara's mother sat on one side of the bed, gently wiping Tara's forehead with a damp cloth. As Merryk moved to the other side of the bed, he thought. *This is the second time this week I have seen people so pale.*

Merryk kissed the back of Tara's hand. Tara opened her eyes. "This is not how we planned our day. I thought Mandy was going to cause all the difficulty, not me." Her voice was weak, but clear.

"You're not being difficult."

"What of my father?"

"He will never hurt anyone again."

"Good. They say I lost another baby. I am so sorry."

"Don't worry, we will try again."

Tara looked directly into Merryk's eyes. "You are not a good liar." Tara paused for a moment and then took a deep breath. "I want you to give Bella to Oolada. She is a wonderful woman. She would make an excellent queen."

"Don't talk like that. I don't need another queen. We will get through this together."

"You must promise me, you will do whatever is necessary to remain king. It is your fate. Promise me."

A ripple of pain caught Tara's breath.

"I promise. Don't talk, just rest," Merryk softly whispered.

He looked across at Queen Stephanie. Her eyes were red and flooded with tears. She was struggling to control her sobs. Tears blurred Merryk's vision as he tightened his grip on Tara's hand and waited.

Chapter 40

TOWER

Merryk walked past everyone in the outer sitting room. *I don't feel like being consoled. I just want to be alone.* Going out the doors into the hall, his guards started to follow.

"You will stay here."

"But, Your Majesty, we were told to accompany you."

Merryk snapped. "The last time I looked I was king! You will stay here."

"Yes, Your Majesty," a startled guard responded.

Merryk grabbed a torch from the wall and started down the corridor toward the south end of the building. Up one floor, then to the end, until he came to the tower stairs. *The Lord Chamberlain said no one ever came here. This is exactly what I need.* The door to the top of the tower swung open, allowing a rush of brisk air to hit his face. He stepped out to look at the approaching sunset.

"I am sorry, King Merryk. I did not believe anyone would come here," Oolada said from the edge of the tower. "I will leave."

"No, Oolada, you can stay. This is your spot, too."

"There is only one reason you would be here rather than with Tara," Oolada said, her voice shaking.

As Merryk moved closer to Oolada, he saw she had been crying. "She did not survive the attack." Now his eyes stung with tears.

"I am sorry I failed to protect her." Tears flowed from Oolada, and she sobbed.

Merryk reached out to pull her close. "You could not stop him. I was there and I couldn't stop him. Who would believe a father would personally attack his own daughter? There was much evil in King Natas. Now at least he's gone."

Oolada's head buried in Merryk's chest as she continued to sob and cry. After a few moments, she pushed herself away to stand by the edge of the tower.

Merryk followed to stand by her side. Looking north to the mountains, he said, "I wish I could take Maverick and ride into the mountains, away from all this, away from the responsibility and pain."

"You are the king; you can do whatever you want. But Helga would say you cannot run away from your fate. It will find you and bring you to where you need to be."

"Fate. Tara said much the same thing. You know, I never wanted to be king. I was happy in the Teardrop with the children, honey, and maple syrup. I really don't belong here in this place or in this time."

"Your presence here and now saved the kingdom. I am the one who does not belong here. I need to go back to the mountains, away from all of this."

"And what would Helga say about that?" Merryk tried to smile.

"You do not understand. I do not fit in anywhere. I am not Oolada, the warrior, or Lady Zoo. Tara and Yvette are the only women who have ever treated me as an equal. They talked to me. We laughed and gossiped together. At Crag d'Zoo, the women stay away from me. They do not view me as a woman. The men of the clan recognize my skill, but to them, I am a warrior, never a woman. Tara was my only true friend. Without her to guide me, I cannot survive here. I fear nothing in battle, but a room of noble women strikes terror in my heart."

"We are both where we don't belong, but here we are. Helga's fate has a sick sense of humor. Are you sure we can't just run away?"

"The kingdom would drop into chaos if you just left. The petty nobles would rip each other and the kingdom apart. This place only works with a strong king to lead it; someone exactly like you. You must do what you do not want. It is the right thing."

"I may have told you this before, but my mother used to say, *the right thing may not be easy, but it's always the right thing.* It might be easy for you to run away from the castle and the crag, but you cannot run away from yourself. Your task is to find Lady Zoo in Oolada."

"And you need to find King Merryk in Merryk."

"I don't know if it's possible."

"What would Tara want us to do?" Oolada asked.

"She would want us to embrace our responsibilities and not run."

"I do not know how to do that," again a tearful Oolada said.

"Neither do I. Maybe we could if we try together."

Chapter 41

NOBLES

"You do not have to do this," Chancellor Goldblatt said to King Merryk. "Everyone will understand your delay. You just lost your wife and your father."

Merryk sat at the end of the dining room table. His breakfast sat untouched.

Gaspar was across the table from Goldblatt. "My heart agrees with Goldblatt, but my head says the delay will only allow doubt to grow. Is it your grief or is it your weakness which drives the delay? This will become the only question. You need to remove all doubts now. Most have never seen you. They are filled with questions." Gaspar advised.

"My sorrow must be personal. For the king, his people come first. Gaspar is right. I cannot allow doubt to linger, much less give it a reason to grow. I will meet with the Duke of Crescent and then the nobles as a group. I also want to talk with Admiral Bellows before I meet with the nobles."

"Yes, Your Majesty," Goldblatt said as he left the table to make the arrangements.

"If this meeting goes well, the balance of your warriors can head home."

Gaspar nodded in agreement. "Yes. They are ready and it has started to snow. Jamaal said there is a group of men, mostly unmarried, who would like to stay as part of your personal guard, at least for a while."

"Ask Jamaal to speak with Bowen. We need his agreement. I would like Zoo warriors near, but I want to be sure their presence is not viewed as my lack of faith in the Royal Guards. Have him present it as a way to help Bowen until he can restore his ranks."

Gaspar's face showed his approval. "My King, you never stop surprising me. Your understanding of people is amazing."

"Nothing so grand. I just asked myself how I would feel if others came to do my job without an explanation. Now, if you'll excuse me, I need to go get ready."

It is the little things that make me miss Tara. I have no idea what to wear, and she would have known. "Jamas, I need your help. What should the king wear to meet nobles?"

"Your Majesty, allow me to introduce the Duke of Crescent," Goldblatt said as he escorted a stately gray-haired man into the room adjacent to the throne room.

King Merryk rose to greet the duke. "Your Grace, thank you for meeting with me so early."

The duke bowed politely. "This is my pleasure, Your Majesty. If you will forgive my surprise, you are nothing like I had envisioned. Now I feel quite foolish. I was uncertain if I would recognize you, but you are the very image of Great King Mikael, though younger, of course."

"Several people have told me the same thing."

"I believe you are taller," the duke said. "I am pleased we finally meet. Let me start by offering my condolences for the losses of your father and your wife."

"Thank you. The last few days have been emotionally challenging, not only for me, but for the kingdom. All are struggling with the loss of the king and an unknown man to replace him; a man most would not recognize. Add the memories of a less-than-perfect childhood and doubt will grow. You and I know kingdoms will fall faster with doubt than they will with swords."

The duke's face moved to a smile. "You have hit the key concern with your description of the problem, and at the same time, dispelled any concern of your competence. Speaking bluntly, if you were a fool, you would not appreciate the existence of doubt."

"Your Grace, I need your help. I want to be sure I address the concerns of the nobles, hopefully before they can raise them. Also, I need you to know I hold three high-ranking men in the dungeon for treason.

Jamaal, Oolada, and Helga joined the Walters near the center of the throne room. Nobility packed the room. Royal Guards were stationed at the doors. Extra clansmen stood along the sides of the wall for further security. The room vibrated with chatter and a tangible feeling of uncertainty.

Two thrones sat at the head of the room on a multistep dais. Goldblatt explained the custom was three thrones: one for the king and one for each of the queens. With the death of King Michael's first wife, he had removed her throne, leaving only two. Today Tara's throne would sit empty.

The Lord Chamberlain entered from the side door. He moved to the center of the room in front of the king's throne and dropped his staff with a bang. "His Royal Majesty, King Michael Merryk Raymouth."

The people in the room bowed their heads, but many strained at the same time to see for the first time their new king. Merryk moved to the throne, keenly aware of the eyes focused on him. He carried with him his grandfather's sword. *Perhaps some of his strength will bleed into me from his sword. This would have been easier with Tara by my side.* Merryk had spoken as an expert to large groups before, at least in the twenty-first century, but this group questioned his very competence.

"Before I begin, I want to introduce our honored guests, Gaspar Zoo, Walt of the Blue-and-White Mountain Clans, and the other members of the Council of Walters. Only through their support were we able to save our kingdom from the sedition and treachery of my brother.

"I want to reintroduce to you Geoffrey Goldblatt, chancellor to my grandfather and my personal instructor for these past years. He has agreed to accept his former position as Chancellor of the Realm. Finally, Admiral Bellows, previously of my father's navy, who has served me with loyalty and honor. I have appointed him to the position of Lord Commander of our military.

Merryk took a deep breath before continuing. "The throne beside me is empty. My wife, Queen Tarareese, was struck down yesterday by her own father, King Natas. Some advised me to delay this meeting, but I know you wanted to meet me. You have questions and even doubts which must be addressed.

"I have told many it was not my choice to become king, but now that I am, I will assume the responsibilities with all of my ability. Our kingdom will not falter under my reign. Before I go on, I will take a few questions."

"How did you defeat the Army of Justice?" a voice shouted from the crowd.

"The arrogance of its commander defeated The Army of Justice. His hubris and inexperience caused their defeat. I simply took advantage."

The Lord Commander interrupted, "Our king is overly modest. His skill not only defeated a highly trained and well-equipped army but directed the seizing of an entire navy. Two examples of a superior commander."

"What happened to King Natas?" another voice cried.

"King Natas is dead. After he attacked his daughter, I killed him. A death he deserved, but one that I am not proud of. I acted in anger. Justice should flow from thought, not impulse. Which brings me to the next matter. King Natas was part of the conspiracy to overthrow King Michael and place my brother on the throne. My brother wielded the dagger, but King Natas, the Duke of Ressett, ex-Chancellor Bates, and the High Priest, Father Theo, supported and encouraged him.

There were murmurs within the crowd. Merryk ignored them and continued. "We have signed statements from Bates describing each person's involvement. In addition, Bates, Ressett, and Father Theo attempted to trick me into abdicating my position. They believed my reputation for ignorance and submitted a badly written document in Latin. They were so confident in their deception, they signed the document. Chancellor Goldblatt has all these documents for your inspection."

"What are you going to do to my father?" a shaky voice asked.

"Lady Ressett, two generations of treason is enough. My grandfather showed compassion to your family after your grandfather's act of treason. Rather than gratitude, your father chose his own treachery.

"The duke, priest, and ex-chancellor shall learn the hard lesson of treason. There is only one way to commit it, successfully. They failed and now all shall be executed. The House of Ressett and its titles are no more. All lands and property shall revert to the throne. In honor of my wife, who would have counseled mercy, I will hold the manor house and the immediate lands and property sufficient for its support in trust as a dowry for you, Lady Ressett. You may continue to occupy them until you die if you never marry. Also, you may use as an honorary title, Duchess of Ressett. But with your death, no one else shall hold that title again."

The finality of King Merryk's words left the nobles silent.

"Now we are done." King Merryk rose from the throne. The Lord Chamberlain dropped his staff again to the stone floor. As Merryk left the room, his eyes scanned the crowd until he located Oolada, who nodded her head and smiled.

CHAPTER 42

QUEEN STEPHANIE

King Merryk exited the throne room and returned to the room where he had met the Duke of Crescent. He took a deep breath as the door shut behind them. "Well, Chancellor, did I delay a revolt for a couple of days?"

"Of course you did. You gave them a glimpse of their king—honest, skilled, and, when needed, strong. Your handling of Lady Ressett was perfect. A tearful daughter asking for mercy could have turned you into a monster. Now they know you will have compassion."

"I didn't do it to make them like me. I did it because it was the right thing to do. Children do not control the actions of their parents and shouldn't be punished for them."

Gaspar had followed Goldblatt and Merryk into the room. "I agree with the Chancellor. You did well. If I might change the subject. Your Majesty, there is something you might need to know. Yesterday, when I left the docks, Admiral Burat begged me to let him stay with Queen Stephanie. He has not stopped asking about her since."

"Assure him no harm will come to her and let him send a note."

"I am not expressing this well," Gaspar continued. "He begged to stay with her, not as a concern for his sovereign. It is something deeper; more like concern between a man and a woman."

"Interesting. Chancellor, please find the Lord Commander. Gaspar, bring the admiral here. Also, find his sword for me."

"Yes, Your Majesty," Gaspar said as he left the room.

Moments later, the Lord Commander returned with Chancellor Goldblatt. "How can I be of assistance, Your Majesty?"

"Lord Commander, if Admiral Burat gave you his word as an officer and a gentleman, would you believe it?"

Bellows thought for a moment. "I think I would. He always fought with honor. He does not kill needlessly. I have seen him take significant risk to save his men. I believe King Natas has forced most of his battles. Yes, he is a man of honor; nothing like that snake, Lamaze. Why would you ask?"

"In order for Queen Stephanie to hold the throne, she will need to control her military. Having a powerful man at her side might make all the difference. For us, it might mean a chance for peace," Merryk replied.

Queen Stephanie had sequestered herself in her room. She asked to be left alone. Other than a brief visit from Princess Mandy, no one had disturbed her.

Merryk knocked on her door. "Queen Stephanie, it is Merryk. May I come in?"

After a brief delay, Queen Stephanie opened the door to her room.

"Thank you for seeing me. How are you doing?"

The queen looked at Merryk. "I should be the one asking you that question." Tears continued to run down her face. "My guess is the transition from your father to you has not allowed you any personal time to grieve."

Merryk walked toward the window. "Yes, I just met with the nobles to prove I am not a fool. I'm sure you know, people say they are sympathetic, but in truth, they always return to themselves."

"Kings and queens are not ordinary people. If we have sorrow or pain, it must wait until the needs of the kingdom are satisfied, which never happens." Queen Stephanie spoke from experience.

Merryk moved over and sat down on a chair near the queen. "We do not know each other at all. You are my wife's mother and I believe Tara reflected a part of you."

"She was a beautiful daughter. You are kind to say you saw some of me in her. But I think you have something else on your mind."

"Queen Stephanie, Admiral Burat is beside himself with worry. It does not seem like the worry for his monarch. He is begging to see you and to know you are well. Do you want to see him?"

Now Queen Stephanie stood and walked toward the window. "You need to understand, my husband was a brutal man. He was very hard to love, but I knew my duty. For many years, I did everything I could to make him happy. But duty alone can be very lonely. Please do not think badly of me, but I would like nothing better than to see the admiral."

"I've already sent for him. He will be here in a few minutes. Now I must ask you something else. With the death of your husband, can you hold your kingdom together?"

"Exactly as we just said, the needs of the kingdom over the person. If I could show to the nobles I control the military, yes, I could and can hold the throne. My husband constantly removed anyone who looked like a threat. It will take time for opposition to rise. If I use that time and can remove some of his repression, I can gain loyalty and maintain the throne."

"An answer exactly as I would have expected from Tara's mother." Merryk smiled. "She was so much your daughter."

"Thank you again, but why are you asking? Would this not be an opportunity for you?"

Merryk paused for a second. "I have no interest in expanding the High Kingdom. I want to expand our trading partners, but not our territory. Chaos on the southern continent would not help this goal. I need you to have a viable, stable, and hopefully, non-hostile kingdom. It would be best to have a partner, but some steps take time. My question bluntly is, would Admiral Burat help you secure the military?"

"My daughter said you were special. I thought she was speaking like a woman in love. I now see she was describing something more. Yes, with Admiral Burat at my side, I can secure the military."

There was another knock at the door. "Your Majesty, we have the admiral."

"Please send him in. Untied," Merryk answered.

Admiral Burat entered the room with his hands unbound. He rushed quickly to Queen Stephanie's side. "Are you all right?"

Stephanie ignored the decorum and wrapped her arms tightly around him. Tears again flowed from her eyes.

Merryk gave them a few moments and then said. "Admiral Burat, Queen Stephanie has explained your relationship. I will leave you alone in just a moment, but first there are several things. Initially, Queen Stephanie and you can leave whenever you want. In fact, I believe you should leave as soon as possible. Not that you are under any threat here, but word of King Natas' death will spread quickly. You must get back to secure your kingdom. Second, I do not want to be an enemy with your kingdom. I want a peace treaty signed between us with no taxes on imported goods for either kingdom. Also, I ask your navy to join ours to guarantee the safety of each other's vessels and strive to protect other trading vessels in the open waters. I will release the three vessels you came with, along with your marines and their weapons."

"Why would you not just take this opportunity to seize our kingdom?" Burat asked.

"Neither of us needs more land. We need more places to sell our products and safe seas to get them there. Stability best achieves these goals." Merryk turned to Queen Stephanie. "Do we have a deal?"

"Yes," she replied. "Yes."

"Finally, admiral, if I give you back your sword, will you promise not to use it against me?"

"I promise." Burat extended his hand to shake Merryk's. A broad smile covered his face. "Thank you."

Merryk turned as he left the room. Looking back, he said, "One last thing. I hope the two of you find happiness."

CHAPTER 43

FUNERAL

S low, but persistent rain began before dawn on the day of the funerals. Merryk's mind wandered as he looked out his window. *Some will say the weather refused to cooperate, but to my mind, it is perfect: cold, gray, and depressing.*

Earlier that morning, before the funerals for King Michael and Queen Tarareese, two other processions had occurred. The first was a group of red-clad Dragoons loading the bodies of King Natas and Colonel Lamaze onto the back of a wagon to transfer them to the RS *Cleaver*. The men, once proud to serve their king, seemed to be at a loss. They plodded through their task as drudgery, not as an honor.

The second group consisted of ordinary gravediggers who moved the box with the body of Prince Merreg to the family plot behind the church. Along the back row, Merreg's grave was dug next to his uncle and two cousins, like another hashmark counting Merryk's impact on the royal family. When they finished, they patted down the muddy ground with their shovels and returned to their daily activities. Just another day.

I never expected so many to line the streets from the castle to the cathedral, especially on a day like this. The people in the streets came to see King Michael for the last time. But they also came out of curiosity about their new king and a now dead queen. It will be a special day filled with sadness for some, excitement, and curiosity for others.

The sound of snare drums set a methodical pace, slow and unstopping as the dripping rain. The King's Royal Guard, men who had served King Michael for much of their lives, were given the honor of leading the procession. Two carriages followed them, each carrying the draped caskets of King Michael and Queen Tarareese. A carriage with Queen Amanda, Queen Stephanie, and Princess Mandy followed them. There had been murmurs about allowing Queen Stephanie to have a place of honor with Queen Amanda. Queen Amanda had silenced the debate with a simple sentence, "We are both grieving losses—me a husband, and she, her daughter."

If I had thought Queen Amanda was weak, this proved me wrong. The tone of her voice alone was enough. Why do men always assume women of powerful men are weak? Tara was certainly strong enough to support me. My guess is Queen Amanda was strong enough to support King Michael.

Merryk on Maverick, with a saddled Bella, rode next. *The presence of Bella seemed essential. Tara loved her horse.* The thought made Merryk's eyes mist. *I am glad it is raining. A king needs to appear strong.*

Merryk glanced over his shoulder, hoping to see Oolada, Gaspar, Helga, and Jamaal riding behind him as they always did. Instead, he was followed by carriages with select high-ranking officials, most notably Chancellor Goldblatt, Lord Commander Bellows, and the Lord Chamberlin.

The coffins entered the cathedral first, followed by King Merryk, Queen Amanda, Queen Stephanie, and the princess. The other members of the party walked behind. Everyone stood as they entered.

Merryk allowed his eyes to sweep the room. *I have never been in this building, but it is everything I would have expected—massive and ornate. Every space is filled today. I am sure they came early to get a place, just as Goldblatt had said. I am glad we had a space saved for Oolada, Helga, Gaspar, and the Council of Walters. Oolada's eyes are red. I hope she is all right.*

When everyone was seated, the ceremony began. *Our priest is very nervous.* With no High Priest, a senior but much younger officiant was chosen to perform the funeral services. *With us, this is about sorrow, but for the young priest, this is an exciting opportunity. From his point of view, this is the most significant thing he has ever done. I am sure he is uncertain about his ability to complete it. It would surprise him to know I feel like that every day. It would have been easier with Tara at my side.*

In hindsight, the return to the castle was a blur. Only Maverick got Merryk back. The complete procession and ceremony took over three hours, mostly in the chilly rain and completely in misery.

Everything concluded in the King's Mausoleum beneath the castle's keep. The only thing that brought Merryk back to the present was the hollow ring of finality as the stone lids of the burial vaults slid into place. *It is real. Tara is gone.*

Merryk followed Queen Amanda and Queen Stephanie up the stairs from the mausoleum.

"This is where I leave you," Queen Stephanie said to Merryk and Queen Amanda. "We want to catch the evening tide."

"I understand," Merryk replied. "I hope you have a safe journey. Please remember we are no longer your adversary. I have spoken with Masterroff. Tell your chancellor he should not have difficulty getting merchant ships. A free flow of trade may help you secure your kingdom."

"Thank you not only for this, but for the opportunity to start a new life for myself and my country."

"If you need assistance, we are here," Merryk said.

Queen Amanda gave Queen Stephanie a hug as she departed.

Jamas, the head butler, stepped forward. "Queen Amanda, your ladies have a dry gown waiting."

"Thank you, Jamas. I would like to change. I will return shortly. Merryk, after you change, try to get something to eat."

Queen Amanda excused herself to change, leaving Merryk to follow Jamas into a side room.

After changing, Merryk slumped down into an overstuffed chair. "Jamas, may I have a glass of brandy?"

"Of course, Your Majesty, but I would suggest you eat something to go with it. I do not believe you have had anything all day."

"Good suggestion," Merryk started to rise from his chair.

"Allow me, Your Majesty," Jamas said as he stepped forward to prepare a small plate for the king.

"I am told the ceremony was very nice," Jamas said.

"Yes, but in truth, I was feeling numb and don't remember it all. Only now is the reality of everything hitting me."

"I want you to know if there is anything I can do to help you, please, do not hesitate to ask."

"Jamas, I am very independent."

"I have noticed," Jamas said. "Did you have a butler or steward in the Teardrop?"

"Yes, a steward and a truly good friend, Smallfolks."

"Your Majesty, I am here only to help you, as I did your father. If I may, I have observed several royal funerals. The reception you are headed into is the worst part; they seem to go on forever. And I do not need to tell you, today, the politics will begin in earnest."

"Another reason not to have too much brandy," Merryk said.

"A clear head is always best, Your Majesty."

CHAPTER 44

RECEPTION

Before Queen Amanda and Merryk could reach the reception line in the ballroom, Chancellor Goldblatt intercepted them. "If I might have a moment with the king, Your Majesty," Goldblatt said to Queen Amanda.

Amanda nodded and moved forward. "King Merryk, you are about to get immersed in the nobility of the High Kingdom. I will help you with the introductions. Queen Amanda will know everyone. I also do not need to remind you—."

Merryk interrupted the Chancellor. "The politics start today."

"Exactly."

Jamas' warning was prophetic. The line of people extending their sympathy seemed to continue forever. *Everyone keeps asking me how I am. It is as though they must say it, but the only people who seem truly interested in the answer are Oolada, Helga, and Queen Amanda. Queen Stephanie was right when she said people only care about themselves and how things affect them. Right now, what they are worried about is the uncertainty of a new and unknown king.*

"The Duke and Duchess of Crescent," Goldblatt announced.

"Your Majesty, on behalf of my entire family, let me extend our condolences for your losses. If I may, I would like to introduce my wife, the Duchess of Crescent, and my daughter, Lady Elizabeth Crescent."

As the duke spoke, both ladies curtsied.

"Your Grace, thank you for your kind words. In a few days, when things stabilize, perhaps I can have dinner with you and your ladies."

"We would be very pleased to join you," the Duke of Crescent replied.

Goldblatt smiled his approval.

Lord Commander Bellows was next in line. "Your Majesty, let me introduce my father, the Grand Duke of Bellweather, and my older brother, Lord Jonathan Bellows."

Merryk could not help but notice the similarities between the three men. *Peas in a pod.* Of course, the Grand Duke was older, but his sons were carbon copies of one other. "Your Grace and Lord Bellows, thank you for coming out on this soggy day."

"Nonsense," replied the Grand Duke. "We Bellows were born for rain and water. Some say we have salt water in our veins. I think they thought it was an insult, but not to us."

Queen Amanda, having experience with the Grand Duke, extended her hand. "Thank you, Your Grace, for coming."

"Queen Amanda, I am so sorry for your loss," the duke said as he moved down the line to accept the Queen's hand.

"Please, do not be offended by my father. He is from a more direct generation," Lord Bellows said to the king. "We are truly saddened by the loss of your father and your wife. We view your loss as ours. Our families have been allies for centuries. This event only strengthens our loyalty. Although, I am concerned about your choice for Lord Commander." An enormous smile spread across his face as he patted his younger brother's back.

"Jonathan. Would you be the namesake of Captain Johnny Bellows?" The king asked.

"Yes, my brother named the poor boy after me."

"A decision I grow to regret daily," the Lord Commander said in mock anger.

"It's good to have a brother to laugh with," the king replied.

"Sincerely, Your Majesty, we are here for you. Anything, please let us know," Lord Bellows said as he shook the king's hand and bowed his head.

"Thank you. I will not hesitate to ask," Merryk answered.

Of all the faces in the line, Merryk finally saw the ones he most wanted to see: Gaspar, Helga, Jamaal and, especially, Oolada.

Gaspar addressed both Queen Amanda and Merryk at the same time. "Your Majesties, on behalf of the Blue-and-White Mountain Clans, please accept our deepest sympathies. I did not know your husband well, Queen Amanda, not nearly as well as I did the Great King Mikael or do King Merryk. I am sure we would have been friends."

"You are gracious to say so, but you and I know King Michael could have been more supportive. I am confident, however, this will change going forward."

Merryk's mind flashed. *Queen Amanda is far more attuned to politics than I would have expected. I need to not make any assumptions about her until I get to know her better.*

"Needless to say, we have total confidence in King Merryk," Gaspar answered. "Your Majesty, please let me introduce Helga, advisor to the clans, my son Jamaal ZooWalter, and my granddaughter Oolada Zoo." Everyone greeted Queen Amanda with appropriate bows.

Merryk turned to Gaspar. "Would you all join me for dinner this evening? I want to talk with you before you leave."

"Most assuredly, Your Majesty. Until this evening," Gaspar said, bowing politely as he moved away.

Oolada gave Merryk a smile and whispered quietly, "Are you all right?"

Merryk nodded.

Oolada reached out and clasped Merryk's hand, just for a moment. "Later."

The next man in line was of a rougher cut than the nobles who came before. The mud from his journey still clung to his boots. In a loud voice, he declared, "I am Sir Timothy, Bannerman for the Earl of Weirshem." Intentionally ignoring King Merryk, he stepped forward to Queen Amanda. "The earl sends his condolences and apologizes for not being here himself. He had a pressing business engagement, which prohibited his coming."

Having completed his assigned task, he turned to leave without the slightest attempt at respect toward either of the monarchs.

"Sir Timothy," King Merryk said in a commanding voice. The power of his voice would have stopped anyone. Knowing it came from the king silenced the room.

Sir Timothy turned to face the king.

"You will remember to bow to Queen Amanda before you step away," Merryk said. "Do we know each other?"

"Yes, I played with your brother and cousins when you were a child."

"Fortunately, we are now men and no longer children. I can see you are good at delivering messages. So, deliver this message for me. Tell the earl his king expects he will come to the castle immediately upon returning from his 'pressing business engagement.' And if he has any difficulties, I am more than willing to ask the Lord Commander to send someone to escort him. Do you need me to repeat the message, or will you remember it?"

The arrogance which had marked Sir Timothy drained from him. He humbly replied, "No, Your Majesty, I can remember."

"Bowen," the king said.

"Yes, Your Majesty," the Royal Guard said as he stepped forward.

"Please see Sir Timothy has something to eat before he returns this evening to the earl."

"You are excused." Merryk's eyes shifted away from Sir Timothy.

This time, Sir Timothy bowed before he departed.

Stepping back to the line, Merryk looked at Queen Amanda. She smiled and nodded her approval.

———— ❈ ————

Oolada looked at Gaspar. "What was that about?"

"A test. And the king passed perfectly," Gaspar replied.

———— ❈ ————

As the reception line continued, Merryk noticed a pattern. "Sorry for your loss, but let me introduce my daughter." *Goldblatt warned me. Every noble family has a daughter.*

After two hours, King Merryk turned to Queen Amanda. In a quiet voice, he asked, "How much longer do you think this will go?"

Queen Amanda hid a slight smile. "How old did you say you were?" she whispered under her breath.

Merryk shook his head. King or not, he knew he had been reprimanded. *It must be a mother thing. My mother could do it with a look. I will stay on this line until I die, or it's time for dinner.* Somehow, the thoughts lifted his spirits.

———— ❈ ————

Across the room, Lady Katalynn, the Duchess of Ressett, stood alone, nursing a glass of wine. Other people in polite society seemed to have decided being near her would adversely affect their standing in the court. Oolada had drifted away from Gaspar and Helga and saw the duchess. *She looks like I feel. I am going to go introduce myself.*

"Hello, my name is Oolada Zoo," she said, extending her hand to Katalynn.

"You clearly are an outsider and do not know to whom you speak. I am Lady Ressett," Katalynn said. "But you can call me Kat. As you can see, I am tarnished by the treason of my father. No prudent person should be near me."

"Well, I am not known for my prudence," Oolada said with a smile, not withdrawing her hand. Oolada's smile was infectious. Katalynn could not help but laugh out loud. Heads turned to bestow disapproval.

Catching herself. "Sorry, I forgot this was a somber event."

"You never know when not to laugh." Lady Elizabeth Crescent said as she joined the two women. "Hello Kat."

"Hello, Beth. How are your mother and my favorite aunt?"

"Mother is your only aunt," Beth replied.

"You two are related?" Oolada asked.

"Please excuse me, Oolada Zoo, meet my cousin, Elizabeth Crescent," Kat replied.

"Please call me Beth. Are you the clan woman who fought the red-haired assassin outside the castle gates?"

Oolada replied cautiously. "I fought with Prince—I mean, King Merryk—against the assassins."

"You must tell us all about it," Kat said.

"And you must tell us all about King Merryk," Beth said.

Nothing happens unobserved around a king. Chancellor Goldblatt watched with curiosity as Lady Ressett, Lady Crescent and Lady Zoo met. Speaking to himself, *Tara's final selections as potential Inland Queen. How interesting.*

Gaspar and Helga also watched from a distance. "I see Oolada has found some new friends," Gaspar said.

"No, Oolada is doing what she always does: face her adversaries directly," Helga said. "Even though she may not see them as that now."

CHAPTER 45

EXECUTION

The morning sky opened to mixed reviews. Sailors would say the bright red at dawn was a warning, but others would look past the patches of red clouds to the breaks of blue—promises of a clear, but cold day.

Merryk stood on the top of the turret at the south end of the building, looking at the rising sun. *Perhaps the red clouds are foreshadowing today's event. I can hear Gaspar telling me not to worry. 'They deserve to die, so sleep well.' The three men to be executed on this day deserved to die. They put in motion the events which killed the king and ultimately, Tara. It should fill me with anger, but all I feel is sadness; sadness for losing Tara, but also sadness for the impact these men had on others. The church is shaken by the loss of the High Priest. The proud House of Ressett is no more, and Lady Katalynn's life is changed forever.*

Although Oolada probably shouldn't be with Lady Katalynn, I love her compassion. She can see beyond the actions of the father and not attribute them to the daughter. Oolada is brave enough to be strong in battle, then thoughtful and considerate of those harmed by the acts of others.

A splash of icy wind in the face encouraged Merryk to shift his position to the other side of the turret. *All this damage runs through me. I ordered the executions. I ordered the destruction of the House of Ressett. I made the choices. I could reverse everything.*

I can also hear Chancellor Goldblatt. 'Treason has only one punish-ment—death. You risk the kingdom if you choose otherwise.' He is right and Queen Amanda is right. Others view compassion without strength as weakness. Weakness destroys kingdoms.

All I can do is hope I can balance compassion with strength. What did my mother say, 'Doing the right thing may not be easy, but it is always the right thing.' Hopefully I am making the right choices.

They directed Merryk to a balcony overlooking a large courtyard. They had placed gallows in the center. People filled the square. *What is it about executions that attract people? I don't think it's a desire to see justice. It's just morbid curiosity. Today it is about seeing the high brought down: the High Priest, the Duke of Ressett and Chancellor Bates. The truth is, they are looking at the arrogant, the proud, and the stupid.*

"Bowen."

"Yes, Your Majesty."

"Please instruct the executioner to hang the chancellor after the others. I promised him he would outlive both."

Oolada escorted Lady Katalynn to the far end of the balcony, away from the king. Katalynn wore a heavy cloak with a hood covering her head and face. Oolada stood by her side, holding her arm. Kat had insisted on attending.

Oolada recalled her discussions with Katalynn from the night before.

"My father was not always the best father. He hit me often, just as he did my mother. A big part of me will not be sorry to have him gone, but another part will miss him. Does that make any sense?"

"Although I can never forgive your father for what he caused," Oolada said. "I can understand how you feel about losing him. I lost both of my parents when I was very young. I never really knew them. My family is now my grandfather, Uncle Jamaal, and Helga. Losing any of them, for any reason, would be unbearable."

The drum's steady beat marked the entry of the convicted into the square. It was the same cadence as the one which rang in Merryk's ears from the funeral procession. *Twice in one week; twice too often.*

There were shouts and insults hurled at the three as they walked to the gallows. The executioner followed Merryk's instruction. He hung the High Priest and the duke first, then Chancellor Bates. After it was done, with no fanfare, the crowd dispersed, leaving only a vacant square. Merryk looked up at the sky. The flush of red was gone. Now it was just cold and empty.

CHAPTER 46

PIPE & PINT

Just before midday, the carriage of Lord Tallon, first son of the Earl of Tallon, stopped at the Pipe and Pint. A young, but heavy man exited the carriage and, with a gasping breath, made his way up the steps to the door.

"Lord Tallon, how nice to see you again," the concierge said in greeting. "We are quite busy today. Executions seem to bring out all our members."

"Understandable when the punished are noble. I was told the Earl of Weirshem would be here."

"Yes, he is upstairs with several other guests. With a wave of the concierge's hand, a butler appeared to guide the rotund lord up the steps to the library.

"Oh good, you made it," a cheerful Earl of Weirshem said, grasping Tallon's outstretched hand with his right and patting him on the back with his left. The earl was a slim man with a long nose and a pointed goatee. "Tallon, grab a glass of wine. I have a toast." The earl raised his glass to the men in the room. "To our friends, the Duke of Ressett, Father Theo, and Chancellor Bates. May their sacrifice not be in vain."

There was a round of "Here! Here!" followed by more wine.

Soon the six men found chairs around a low table in the center of the room: the Earl of Weirshem, Lord Tallon, Sir Timothy, and three others from minor noble houses.

The earl began. "Thank you all for coming on this very sad day. All of us share a common ancestry from Outland Queens and a disgust for all things Raymouth. The Raymouths should be part of our group, but the last four generations have moved further away from their Outland roots."

"This current Raymouth king may be the worst," Lord Tallon said. "To remove any conflicting claims to the throne, he has selectively killed everyone with a drop of Outland blood. He murdered his uncle, cousins, and his own brother. This execution removed the Duke of Ressett, a legitimate successor to the throne."

"It is impossible to believe he is not being directed by Chancellor Goldblatt and Admiral Bellows," the earl added. "His most recent attack on me clearly shows they have coached him."

"More wine," he said to the server standing quietly in the corner.

"It is as though they gave him a list," the earl said with some force.

"Sir Timothy was blatant in his disrespect," one of the minor lords added.

Sir Timothy responded in defense. "Disrespect was the way he called me out in front of the entire court."

"Why were you not present?" Lord Tallon asked the earl.

"It was a dreary day. I did not want to travel in the rain and stand for many hours to pretend to feel sympathy for the dead king. The thought turned my stomach. I chose an enjoyable book and some chianti instead."

"Did you see how they paraded poor Lady Katalynn onto the balcony and forced her to watch her father's execution? They had the clan bitch hold her by the arm," Lord Tallon said with disgust. "Another obvious message. Our families will be targeted if we resist."

The earl continued. "Without his murders, he really has no claim to the throne. We all knew him as a child—a complete imbecile, spilling his soup all over himself. No one can change that much. Only the invading army of Blue-and-White Mountain Clansmen made him king. But they have returned north where they belong."

A silent member of the group spoke for the first time, "He still has the support of the Crescents, the Bellows, and the Blountsmyths, which means the inland blood houses, the military, and the treasury. What can we do?"

"We can wait and watch. The longer he is king, the more opportunities will occur to expose him as incompetent. Even these noble houses cannot support an imbecile on the throne."

The earl inserted, "They have not crowned him yet. To do so, he must have a queen: a queen from inside the kingdom. Who he picks will be telling; if he is even man enough to pick a woman." A chuckle ran through the group.

CHAPTER 47

DEPARTURES

Helga knocked on Gaspar's door and entered. Gaspar was assembling his belongings on the bed. "It is time for dinner. I will take care of your things," Helga said. "If you try, we will need extra horses for the bundles or when we get home, you will have left half behind."

"I know. But it is time to go home. I want to be away from the sea and feel the air of the mountains." With a sigh, Gaspar lowered himself into a chair.

"Oolada came to see me this morning," Helga said.

"And King Merryk came to talk with me this afternoon," Gaspar replied.

"Oolada wants to stay, at least until spring," Helga said with a knowing smile.

"As though he needed it, the king wanted my permission to ask Oolada to stay."

Helga continued, "She said the king needed someone to help him grieve, someone who knew Tara and someone he could talk to."

"The king said the recent events have elevated the status of the clan. If Lady Zoo could stay until spring, as a representative of the clans, it would help the new relationship grow. In addition, he said Oolada was taking Tara's loss hard. She told him, other than you, there were no women in the crag for her to talk with. Is that true?"

"Oolada has always been special to the clan. She is the daughter of a fallen warrior, the granddaughter of the Walt and in her own right, a warrior of fame. The women respect her, but they do not invite her into their circle. I know she often feels alone."

"Why did you not tell me before?" Gaspar asked.

"What would you have done? Order someone to be her friend. No, she has to find her own way."

Gaspar ran his hand through his bristly beard. "I find it interesting; they are both concerned about the other. Once again, I think you were right about letting fate take the lead."

"I told Oolada to ask you for permission to stay."

"And I told the king her staying was a good idea."

Helga and Gaspar both laughed.

"I sometimes think your gift is wearing off on me," Gaspar said.

Helga shook her head. "This did not take a seer. Now, we need to go to dinner. I will get you packed later."

The departure of Gaspar, Helga, Jamaal, and the remaining clan happened with little fanfare. Everyone had met the night before to say goodbye. Gaspar and Jamaal wanted to be moving by dawn. King Merryk, Lady Zoo, and Chancellor Goldblatt waved goodbye from the top of the north gate.

After the goodbyes, Oolada excused herself to settle into her new room. Merryk and Goldblatt went to the dining hall for breakfast.

"It is hard to believe it has been barely two weeks since you arrived at the Capital City," Goldblatt said. "I, for one, hope the events in your life slow down."

"I am not sure that will happen, but a brief lull would be fine. Did we communicate to the Teardrop?"

"Yes, Gaspar sent clansmen, but we should not expect a reply until spring. The snows closed the passes right after your passage over Ledin Grubi and the rough winter seas have arrived."

"Yvette will take the news of Tara's death particularly hard. They were friends most of their lives. I wish the distance was not so great, or the weather had been fairer, so she could have been at Tara's funeral." Sorrow again clouded Merryk's face.

Chancellor Goldblatt tried to change the subject. "The Duke of Crescent talked with me. He is available for dinner tomorrow night. He also said the nobles were impressed by their first meeting with you, but as always, they will continue to be watchful."

"Understandable. I would be foolish to believe they will not be looking for weakness. Tara would have handled them better. I am afraid I did not handle Sir Timothy correctly. I had expected to be challenged, but not at the funeral. His actions were obvious and insulting to Queen Amanda. I had to respond."

"Your response was absolutely appropriate," Goldblatt answered. "Your first response was to his disrespect for Queen Amanda, not yourself. Second, your message to the earl and all others in the room was clear. You are the king and will not tolerate any who do not acknowledge you."

Merryk shifted in his chair. "I have a feeling there is a story surrounding the Earl of Weirshem."

"You know the problems the rule of two queens has caused within your family, but it also ripples throughout all the nobility. Over the years, the nobles have divided themselves into two groups: those whose lineage is from within the kingdom, and those whose lineages are from outside. Over the centuries, the sons, and daughters of the king not selected to the throne married into the other noble houses, but still keep their ties to their respective bloodlines. The houses of Crescent, Blountsmyth, and Bellweather are from the inland bloodline. The House of Ressett, the House of Weirshem, and other minor families hold their legacy to the outland queens. We have seen the power of this tie with King Natas, the old Provost, and the Duke of Ressett. They all quickly joined with your uncle and Prince Merreg. It creates an automatic 'us versus them,' fueling both domestic and international strife. You will need to be aware of these connections when you pick your next queen."

"Not that again. Surely, I have time to decide," an exasperated Merryk said.

"Yes and no," Goldblatt responded. "If you do nothing, opposition will grow. If you act as though you are working on the issue, they will give you some time, but not unlimited time."

"Working on the issue?" Merryk queried. "What does that mean?"

"You need to do things like your dinner with the Duke of Crescent and his family. This will expose you to the duke's daughter, Lady Elizabeth."

"I thought I was thanking him for his support and getting to know him better," Merryk said, shaking his head from side to side.

"You are, but you are also looking for a queen."

"I had a queen." Sadness covered Merryk's face.

Goldblatt could not help but recognize Merryk's pain. "Other than dinner tomorrow night, you have nothing pressing. You need to take some time for yourself and try to rest. I could tell you not to think about anything, but I know you are already thinking about things to be done."

Merryk nodded.

"Do you have any idea where you want to start?"

"Yes, we need to start with the rats."

"Four legged or two?" Goldblatt asked.

"Both."

King Merryk went down the hall to find Oolada's room. Knocking on the door, he said, "Oolada, I am running away. Goldblatt said I can go for at least the afternoon. Do you want to ride with me? I must get out of this castle."

"I will need a few moments to change. I will meet you in the stables," Oolada replied.

Oolada was waiting for Merryk in the stables. "I hope you do not mind, but I had them prepare Bella to go with us. I thought it would be appropriate for our escape."

"The horses need time to grieve, too. Leaving Bella behind would have been cruel." Merryk's words made his eyes water.

Oolada looked at him and shook her head. "Now come on, it is a beautiful day. Tara would want us to enjoy it."

Goldblatt caught Bowen as he went down the hall. "Where is the king?"

"He and Lady Zoo rode out of the castle about an hour ago. My last report said they were headed east. Do not worry, they allowed guards to follow them, even though I believe those two can take care of themselves. They are a remarkable team," Bowen said.

A remarkable team indeed. Goldblatt thought as he turned to walk down the corridor. *Tara saw the connection between the two and even encouraged it. Tara was a remarkable woman, one who loved Merryk and who also understood the need to share him. I hope I can be Merryk's friend and his chancellor. I pray the needs of the realm do not force him into choosing between love and duty.*

Chapter 48

DINNER WITH THE QUEEN

The early dusk of winter settled on the castle as Merryk and Oolada returned to the stables.

"Thank you for riding with me," Merryk said. "Although I'm not sure I was very good company. I just needed to feel the air."

"We both needed the air and a space without all the noise of the castle," Oolada answered.

"I was planning on eating alone, but would you like to join me?"

"If you will excuse me," Oolada replied. "I had promised to have dinner with Lady Katalynn. I thought she might need someone this evening. She may be the only other person in the castle as lonely as the two of us."

"I understand. I scheduled his execution quickly. Justice delayed is justice denied. I wanted this whole situation behind us as soon as possible. Please let her know I have reviewed my decision and could not be merciful. Her father's treason caused the death of both Tara and the king. There could only be one punishment."

Oolada reached out to Merryk's arm. "She expected nothing else. But I think it will comfort her to know you even thought of mercy. Now, I need to go."

"Tomorrow?" Merryk asked.

"Tomorrow," Oolada said as she exited the stables.

———⚙———

Jamas was waiting for Merryk as he entered his rooms. "Did Your Majesty have an enjoyable ride?"

"I'm not sure if it was enjoyable, but it was needed. It felt good to be less confined, if that makes any sense. I'm not sure Lady Zoo and I spoke much on the ride, but we both needed the time."

"Queen Amanda has requested you join her for dinner. She made it quite clear it would be just the two of you."

"Well, Jamas, I'm glad it is just the two of us, but why do you think she was so specific?"

"My guess is she wants time with her son alone or she has something to tell you which she prefers others not hear."

"Jamas, did the king and queen eat dinner alone often?"

"Seldom, Your Majesty. Dinner became more meeting than meal. The only time they ate alone was breakfast."

"Do you believe this is a meeting or a meal?"

"I am uncertain. You are her son, but you are also the king. Everything around you is about politics."

"Even from the queen?"

"Fortunately, yes. In the past year, the only one giving your father sound advice was the queen. Prince Merreg and Chancellor Bates controlled all of those who came to the king. The only independent voice was Queen Amanda.

———⚙———

Queen Amanda was waiting in a small dining room in her apartments. The table was of normal size sufficient to seat six to eight people. Tonight, it was set for two. The place settings were on the long sides of the table, facing each other. Merryk had learned if others joined, the king and queen would have been seated at the head and foot.

I've never really stopped to look at Queen Amanda. She has always been 'your mother' in our encounters. Queen Amanda was an attractive woman. Merryk estimated her age to be in her early forties, about his age in the twenty-first century. She had auburn hair, which she normally wore up, but this evening, it was partially down. *Her hair shows she wants this to be less formal.*

"Good evening," Merryk said as he entered the room.

"I am glad you could join me," Queen Amanda said as she greeted her son with a hug and a kiss on his cheek. "Please, have a glass of wine before we have dinner."

"Thank you," Merryk said to the server as he received his wine.

"Chancellor Goldblatt told me you were overly thankful to those serving you," Amanda said.

"What else did the Chancellor say?" Merryk asked with a chuckle.

"He said you were your own man who thought more about things than anyone he had ever met. You also had good instincts and cared about people. He said you were lightning smart with good common sense and could create loyalty in all around you."

"Those are the things I would have expected my Chancellor to say," Merryk replied, trying to downplay the compliments.

"These are all the characteristics a mother dreams of in a son. Forgive me, but before you left, you showed none of them—not a glimmer. It is as if you look like my son, but somehow you are not my son." Amanda's eyes looked intensely at Merryk.

Is she hoping to see or find some kind of admission? "I'm not sure everyone understands the severity of my injury. Goldblatt did not expect me to live more than a few days. In all honesty, I do not remember any of my childhood. I am sorry to say, other than the contact we have had in the last year, I do not have any memory of you. Once I awakened, I worked on recreating myself. Standing up straight, getting strong, and reading everything I could find. These were my sole motivation. I never wanted to be king. Tara and I would have been happy left alone in the Teardrop."

Queen Amanda's eyes clouded with tears. "I guess I knew. The first time we met, I could not find a spark of recognition in your eyes. I hoped you would have remembered something good about me. Even though it is a blessing you forgot the rest of your childhood. Those memories could have mentally handicapped you with anger."

"I understand some are saying I'm filled with anger and removing all those who tormented me."

"I prefer what others are saying. You have selectively removed anyone who could challenge your right to the throne; killing all who stand in your way."

"If I had to choose, I think I prefer them believing I acted by necessity rather than anger or calculation."

"There is the Merryk Goldblatt spoke of, a man filled with kindness. But Merryk, the king, needs to have the nobles believe he is calculating and intentional. There is 'no fear' in driven by necessity, but in calculating you become formidable. Your childhood image would have made ruling very difficult, but the man who conquers armies and removes opposition is a ruler."

"I guess I never expected my mother to want me to be ruthless rather than kind."

"You need to be thought of as ruthless so that your kindness will not be seen as weakness. How you handled Sir Timothy was a perfect example. I could see your willingness to ignore the insult against yourself, but not against me. All heard your warning to the earl. Honor the king or face the fate of those who opposed you. Others will remember. They will follow you and the kingdom will be stable."

Merryk dropped his eyes to his wineglass. "These are exactly the things Tara would have said. She was raised to be a queen and understood."

"And you are from a long line of kings. It is in your blood. You will master these things the same way you strengthened your body. I can help, but only to a limited degree and never in public."

"I believe women have as much right to express their opinions as men and should be heard."

"That is all well and good, but not for a new king. They would see my public expression as manipulation on my part and weakness on yours. Right now, the rumors say you are still a fool, but controlled by Chancellor Goldblatt and Lord Commander Bellows. Adding your mother to the list would only strengthen their argument that you are weak and unfit to be king. Just like you not having a queen."

Merryk's jaw tightened with anger. "I don't suppose anybody remembers I just buried my queen. I have no desire to replace her immediately."

Queen Amanda's voice was soft and steady. "Merryk, they need a queen. They care little about what you may need. A queen represents a coming heir and the proper succession to the next generation. She represents stability in the throne and stability in the kingdom. People need confidence in a long-term ruler. They need to know they can build their lives in a world of safety: protected by strength and a strong king."

Merryk's face softened. "This is exactly what Queen Stephanie said to me before she left. People care only about themselves."

"When I first became queen, I overheard some of the staff talking about how much easier their lives would be if they were royal. I think the people expect us to be above all the normal human responses, as though something shields us from sorrow and loss. They give a queen some sympathy because she is a woman, but not the king. He must be strong to rule, and emotions are a sign of weakness."

"But I'm a man first and then a king."

"To the people, you are the king. You can be a man only when you have fulfilled your duties as king."

"Which, of course, we both know never happens."

Amanda nodded. "The most important role of your queen is to help you deal with this conflict. The right queen will not only provide an heir to the throne but will also provide a secure place for you to just be a man. That is why, for the sake of the kingdom and yourself, you must be open to finding the right queen."

Queen Amanda tilted her head inquisitively. "Now tell me about Lady Zoo."

"Oolada is a good friend to me and Tara. She saved our lives on multiple occasions. Oolada is taking Tara's death hard. She blames herself for not being able to save her at the docks, even though I told her I was there and failed. Oolada is caught between being Lady Zoo and Oolada Zoo, the warrior. Right now, she is struggling to decide which way to go. Tara had been her guide in the world of the court. Oolada is fearless in battle, but other noble women terrify her."

"Rightly so. For women, there is no more vicious place in all the kingdom than in the battle around the throne. And with an unmarried king, it will be a bloodbath." Queen Amanda's tone was serious.

Merryk could not help but smile. "Certainly, an exaggeration."

Shaking her head, Amanda said, "Men always underestimate how manipulative and ruthless women can be over a man, and when that man is the king, there will be no limits. Perhaps I can help Lady Zoo. I will ask her to assist me with the management of the household. This will give the two of us time to talk."

Merryk took a deep breath. "Thank you. I can only help so much. I know having you talk to her will mean a lot."

Queen Amanda looked directly at Merryk. "You need to understand how serious this will become. Lady Zoo will become a target. You had not passed through the eastern gate with Lady Zoo by more than half an hour before I was notified. Everyone watches everything you do. They will view her as a potential queen and, as a result, a potential threat."

"Oolada does not want to be a queen, any more than I wanted to be king, Merryk said.

Queen Amanda smiled, thinking. *But she may want the man who is king.*

Chapter 49

JUST BREAKFAST

Oolada found Merryk's guards standing at the doors to the old tower. The guards were all clansmen known to her.

"Good morning," Oolada said as she approached. "Is he on the top?"

"Yes, he said we could stay here where it was warm," one guard answered.

"I promise I will not harm him," Oolada said cheerfully as she opened the door to ascend the stairs.

Today, a blanket of thick gray clouds covered the sky. Only the increasing light showed that the sun had risen at all. The mist from the sea had dampened everything. In short, it was cold and gray.

"A perfect November day at the shore," Oolada said as she stepped onto the top of the turret. "I thought I would find you here."

"Am I that predictable?" Merryk replied, turning to greet Oolada.

"Only in the mornings, or perhaps only to me. How was your dinner with the queen?"

"Interesting. Did you know some people consider me calculating and ruthless?"

"Those are two words I would never have applied to you. Thoughtful, but not calculating; never ruthless."

"Queen Amanda thought it was a good thing. It seems, to be a good king, I must have people fear me."

"I would think a good king needs to be respected, not feared," Oolada replied.

"And I will work to gain that respect, if I am given the chance."

Oolada moved closer to touch Merryk's arm. "What has so upset you this morning?"

"You know I did not want to be king. It was not because I wanted to avoid the responsibility, but I was happy in the Teardrop. When I first arrived there, I was injured, and no one expected anything from me. With Goldblatt's help, I gradually worked my way into my duties. Here, I have advisors, but everything I do is being scrutinized. They are looking for mistakes, which I know I will make. I feel like I must fulfill a role I do not want and may not be able to do. I don't feel I can be myself. I must be the king, but by everyone else's standards."

Oolada's voice was soft and reassuring. "Do the two have to be different?" she asked. "You are the king. You can be anything you want."

"In theory, but there are expectations. My childhood was memorable to everyone except me. They saw a different person than I am today, a person very much compromised and weak. Many are looking to see if I validate those memories or if I have changed. Many are betting on me still being an imbecile."

"Then you will prove them wrong. But you will not do it by pretending to be someone you are not. You just need to be the Merryk I know, a kind man of integrity, one worthy of their respect, and one deserving to be king."

"Oolada, I thought there was no sunshine today, but with you here, I can see it. Thank you. Now, enough about me. How is Lady Katalynn doing?"

Oolada removed her hand from Merryk's arm and stepped to look out over the tower wall. "As well as could be expected. Today she is taking her father's body back to bury it in the family plot, next to her grandfather."

"I wish her well," Merryk said. "When she leaves here, will she have anyone to support her?"

"I believe her aunt and cousin—the Duchess of Crescent and Lady Elizabeth—will continue to support her.

"Good. I am having dinner with the Duke of Crescent and his family this evening."

Oolada's voice changed, becoming tense. "I actually have a purpose for coming up here. I have been asked to join Queen Amanda for breakfast this morning. Would you know why?"

"I might have suggested you could help her with some of the household management. Also, I thought she might help you understand the workings of the court."

"I do not need any help, thank you," Oolada said, shaking her head from side to side.

"Really? You are totally comfortable interacting with the court?" Merryk smiled as his voice reflected a tinge of sarcasm.

"All right, maybe I could use a little help. But the queen is so regal. I will seem like a child to her."

"I have an idea. Why not just be yourself?" Merryk's face was now covered with a broad smile.

Oolada obviously recognized Merryk parroting her advice to him. To express her displeasure, she lashed out to strike Merryk on the arm.

"Ouch! Assaulting the king is punishable by death."

"Not if the king deserved it."

"I want you to get to know the queen, and yes, I believe she can help you manage the challenges of the court. She has already been very helpful to me and will be for you, if you will let her."

"I know, but she is intimidating. She is always in control and unshaken by those around her."

"If I didn't know you better, I would say you were afraid of her."

"Well, maybe a little." Oolada shifted her face away from Merryk.

"Would you feel more comfortable if I asked her to spar with you with small blades?"

"Absolutely," Oolada quickly replied. "Those I know how to use."

Merryk reached out to turn Oolada to face him. Gently holding both of her arms, he looked into her eyes. "Think of the queen as your new swordmaster, but with different weapons. You are Lady Zoo, a force to be reckoned with regardless of the weapon. And remember, it's just breakfast."

"Your Majesty, Lady Zoo is here."

"Show her in," Queen Amanda replied.

Eleanor, the head housekeeper, escorted Oolada into the same dining room as the queen and Merryk had used the night before. As Oolada entered the room, the queen looked up. "Good morning, Oolada. May I call you Oolada." Queen Amanda asked.

"Please, Your Majesty. I must admit I find Lady Zoo to be too formal."

"But you are Lady Zoo or Lady Oolada, granddaughter to Gaspar ZooWalt, the leader of the Blue-and-White Mountain Clans—a noble lady from a noble family."

The queen gestured to a chair across the table from where she sat.

As Oolada moved to her place, she took a deep breath. Her face took on the look of defeat.

Queen Amanda immediately noticed the change. "I said something to offend you?"

"No, you just reminded me of how little I understand about the court. I could not get my name out without making a mistake."

The queen smiled. "Who you are is important. Rule number one, everything about the court is based upon rank and power. Controlling what they call you is the first step in this process. You cannot allow people to treat you in any way which does not respect your heritage. Close personal friends and family, in private, may call you by your given name. Other than that, you are always the Lady Zoo. Now, did you eat before you met with Merryk this morning?"

"No," a puzzled Oolada replied. "But how did you know I met with Merryk?"

"Rule number two, everyone knows everything about what you do. Even more so if it touches the king, and you, my dear Oolada, are very close to the king."

"Oh, we are just friends," Oolada responded in defense, even though she could feel her face turning red.

Queen Amanda could not help but chuckle. "I can see why my son is so attracted to you. You are very much alike. But you are not a talented liar. I fear you will expect people to be honest with you." Shaking her head, the queen continued. "Rule number three, people are going to lie to you often, and whenever it serves their purposes. Now, what did Merryk tell you?"

"He said I should think of you as my new swordmaster, but with different weapons."

Again, Queen Amanda chuckled. "An excellent analogy. Court is a form of combat. I am told you are exceptional with the use of blades, and you are fearless. You will need to be fearless if you are to win the king against other ladies in the court."

"Win the king? No, we are just friends. He needs a lady who knows how to be a queen. I assure you that is not me."

"I was mistaken. You do know how to lie, at least to yourself." The queen leaned forward to look directly at Oolada. "Now tell me the truth, Oolada. How long have you been in love with my son?"

CHAPTER 50

CRESCENT

Lady Elizabeth Crescent turned from side to side as she admired her new dress in the full-length mirror. "The color is beautiful, but it shows every bit of lint," Beth said. Her maid picked up a small soft brush to remove the specks from the deep blue surface.

Beth's mother, the Duchess of Crescent, entered the room. "I think you look marvelous," she said. Turning to the maid. "Leave us."

Other than age, the similarities between the two women were striking. Both had auburn hair and deep brown eyes. There was a practiced gracefulness in their movement. They both were the embodiment of elegance.

Beth turned to look at her mother. "I think we both look marvelous."

"Yes, we do," the duchess responded. "Now we must talk." Gesturing toward a sofa, "Father will not tell you this, but tonight could be very important for you and for our family."

"I know we are having dinner with the king."

"It could be much more than dinner," the duchess explained. "We do not know who else has been invited. Father said the Chancellor had not given him any indication of who would be present. Who joins us will be our clue to the purpose of the dinner."

"Purpose?" Beth asked.

"Yes, a small group will show the king has a sincere interest in getting to know everyone. No one knows our young king; other than he is tall, strong, and handsome."

"You forgot his magnificent blue eyes and commanding presence," Beth added with a smile.

Beth's mother ignored her comment. "We are in the first group of noble houses to have dinner with him. Many are concerned about his ability to rule. We will get to judge him up close."

"I understand. You want me to allow father to lead the discussion," Beth replied.

"No, I want you to make yourself memorable to the king. If he is the man your father believes him to be, he will be an excellent king, but he will need an Inland Queen. He will need a wife."

"Mother, the man just buried his wife. The last thing on his mind will be a new one."

"This is about politics. To continue to be king, he must remarry and to avoid unrest, he must do so sooner rather than later. What he wants and what he needs may be very different."

"Are you saying father has been talking with the Chancellor about me as a potential Inland Queen?"

"Not yet, but this may be the first step. If there are several noble families present, be sure the king remembers you."

"Mother, if the king needs a wife, he will most likely pick Lady Zoo. They have fought together and already appear to at least be friends."

"The king would never wed a member of the clans, and certainly not over a choice like you. They are military allies. The only thing polished about Lady Zoo is her blades. She could never be a queen. King Merryk needs to maintain his alliance with the clans. He and Lady Zoo are nothing more than political friends."

"And the king would select me because of politics," Beth stated firmly. "The blending of our two houses would be of great significance. It would end any questioning about his ability to rule. You need to remember, you and father trained me to understand politics. I know what is at stake."

"Would it be such a bad idea?"

"I said you forgot his deep blue eyes." Beth's mind, however, paused. *I only hope he is nothing like his brother.*

———— ❈ ————

"Jamas, do I really need to wear this sash? A plain tunic would be just fine."

"Only if Your Majesty is intent on insulting the duke and duchess, who will arrive in their best attire. For them, this is a dinner of great import."

"In that case, perhaps a crown," Merryk replied sarcastically.

"Now that you are in the right frame of mind, which crown do you want?" Jamas answered, his voice showing no signs of being affected by Merryk's prod.

Merryk laughed. "Thank you, my friend. I am just feeling a bit like a prize bull being shown at the market."

"Your analogy is quite apt. You are the greatest prize in the kingdom." Now Jamas could not control his smile.

Merryk shook his head in resignation.

"Seriously, sire, the Crescents have been loyal to the throne for over four hundred years. Their support is important. Also, I believe you will find the Lady Elizabeth Crescent to be most lovely."

"Do you and Goldblatt meet to ensure your messages are consistent?"

"No, Your Majesty, but we both understand how our kingdom works. We want you to have the very best information. That is our only goal."

"I know, but this dinner seems artificial. I would prefer an informal event around the kitchen table."

Jamas looked a bit puzzled. "I am not sure we have a table in the kitchen. We selected a smaller dining room and a round table. There will be only five of you. For your first official dinner, it should be most manageable."

"Thank you, Jamas. Wish me luck."

"Always, Your Majesty."

The king followed Bowen and four Royal Guards to a new section of the castle, at least a new one to Merryk. It was on the same level as the throne room. The small dining room had windows and doors opening into a small garden. This time of year, the foliage was sparse, but many small trees and trim bushes promised beauty in the spring and the summer. A relatively small circular dining room table sat near one end of the room, flanked by a wall of polished woods and paintings of Merryk's ancestors. The other end of the room held a large fireplace. A sofa and several cushioned chairs circled the brightly burning flames. The room twinkled with the light of a multitude of candles.

The dining room surprised Lady Elizabeth. It was so small. *I had expected at least 15 to 20 people in an intimate gathering with the king. Mother said who attends will be telling. There are only five places on the table. We are three and Chancellor Goldblatt is four. The king would make five. At the least, I will be able to wear this dress again. No one will have seen it.*

"Your Graces and Lady Crescent, it is so nice to see you again," Chancellor Goldblatt said as he extended his hand to the duke. "King Merryk is on his way down. I expect him momentarily. Please have a glass of wine and join me by the fire while we wait."

Everyone accepted the wine. The ladies had found places on the sofa to sit when Bowen announced the king, "His Majesty, King Merryk."

The ladies rose from their seats to greet the king. "Good evening, and welcome to the castle. I am sorry I am running late. I hope you have not been waiting long."

"No, we just arrived ourselves," the duke replied. "Let me introduce my wife and daughter."

Merryk extended his hand to the duke and then, turning to the ladies, said, "Although there is much I do not remember from the reception, I do remember the duchess and Lady Elizabeth." Both ladies smiled and bowed.

As she raised her head for the first time, Beth truly looked at the young king. *Oh my. He is really tall, and his shoulders are so broad. And his blue eyes!* "It is my pleasure to see you again, Your Majesty."

Merryk gestured toward the sofa. "Please, let us sit for a moment before dinner and enjoy our wine." Merryk turned his attention to the duke. "Your Grace, did you travel far to come this evening?"

"Your Majesty, although our holdings are far to the east, this time of year, we stay in a small villa overlooking the sea near the castle."

The duchess interjected, "Many noble families come to the Capital City in the winter for holiday events and stay until early next year. There are many private parties and often a New Year's event at the castle. Although no one is expecting anything in the castle this year."

"Under normal circumstances, I would enjoy a good gathering. I believe it lifts everyone's spirits, especially when the days are so dark. Last year..." Merryk paused for a moment, then continued. "This year, I'm not sure I would be a suitable host."

"It might, as you say, lift everyone's spirits, even yours," Lady Elizabeth said. Her voice was conciliatory.

Shifting the subject away from memories of last year, Chancellor Goldblatt inserted. "I see they are ready for us. Shall we?"

The group sat in their respective places and, after much small talk, Merryk asked, "I hope you don't mind such a small group. I am attempting to work my way slowly into society."

"It is a privilege to have dinner with you and just my family." the duke said. "It gives all of us an opportunity to get to know one another."

Merryk turned to the duchess. "It is my understanding your sister was the Duchess of Ressett."

"Yes, we are Ott's. Our father's lands lie between the estates of Crescent and Ressett at the headwaters of the Ott River. Both dukes came to our father seeking wives. Fortunately for me, I got my husband, who is a true gentleman. My sister, unfortunately, got the Duke of Ressett, who was not only a traitor but also a terrible husband."

"Dear, we do not vent our frustrations with the king," the duke said.

"It's all right," King Merryk said. "I have a reason for asking my question. Lady Katalynn Ressett is your niece. I am concerned the stigma of her father's actions will severely affect her. The estate around the manor will provide a sizable dowry, but she will need emotional support and, perhaps Your Grace, some help with the estate's management."

"Kat is dear to us," Elizabeth said. "She is like a sister to me. I know mother and father feel the same way."

The duke nodded. "Your Majesty, we will not let the young girl flounder."

When the dinner was over, the group again returned to the sofa and chairs by the fireplace. Sitting to have their glasses of sherry, Goldblatt continued a discussion with the duke and duchess. Merryk and Elizabeth stood beside each other, looking into the fire.

"There is something comforting about a sparkling fire," Merryk said.

"I agree, Your Majesty. It makes me think about my childhood and simpler times," Elizabeth said.

"Please, when we are alone, call me Merryk."

"And you may call me Beth."

"The queen says I need to learn to be more formal, but that's not me. I was Merryk long before I became the king."

"Perhaps calling you Your Majesty is just people's way of being polite."

Merryk smiled. "I read about a politician who said a very polite person could tell you to go to hell in a way that would make you look forward to the trip."

Beth laughed out loud. "You are nothing like your brother."

"I really don't know. When I went to the Teardrop Kingdom, I had an accident, a severe blow to my head. The only positive thing about my injury was I forgot all about my childhood. Even my family is a blur. The first time I remember my brother was when we fought outside the castle walls. That was not a long conversation."

"It is just as well. I do not think you would have liked him." Suddenly catching herself, she replied, "Oh, I forgot myself. I did not mean to offend you or the memory of your brother."

"Now look who is being polite. Based upon what I know and between you and me, I do not think I would have liked him, either."

Relieved, Beth smiled. "I hear you have an amazing horse."

"Maverick is his name, and please don't let him hear you say that. He is difficult enough already. He has a mind of his own and never hesitates to share his opinion."

"Perhaps we could go for a ride someday, and you could introduce me," Beth said, being more forward than usual.

"That sounds nice. I will look at my schedule and send word of available dates."

"Soon I hope," Beth answered.

———— ❦ ————

It was only about a thirty-minute carriage ride from the castle's front gate to the Crescent's winter manor. "I thought that went very well," the duke said. "The young king constantly surprises me. His knowledge of our history was telling."

"He may have been coached by the Chancellor," the duchess said, as she covered her lap with a blanket as they bounced along the road.

"Merryk said we could go for a ride soon," Beth added with an enormous smile.

"Merryk?" a surprised duke asked.

"Yes. He said I could call him Merryk when we were alone," Beth responded.

"It is telling that you were asked to call him Merryk. This was a very special dinner indeed. No other noble families joined us. He may be serious about filling his requirements for an Inland Queen." the duchess said.

"The two of you should not get ahead of yourselves." the duke cautioned. "The king is a very charming man, but also a very intelligent one. He will evaluate his alternatives before he chooses. I was, however, impressed by his concern for Katalynn. Few royals would have taken the time to even ask about her. You both need to remember that he will meet with several noble families as he did with us."

"But he met with us first," the duchess replied.

CHAPTER 51

GOLDBLATT & THE QUEEN

Several days passed before Chancellor Goldblatt went to visit Queen Amanda. Lady Zoo was leaving the queen's apartments as Goldblatt arrived.

"Good morning, Chancellor," Oolada said in her cheerful voice.

"Good morning, Lady Zoo. How are you today?"

"Excellent, thank you. I have been working with the queen on several projects around the castle. I was going to ask you, did my grandfather make any arrangements for funds?"

Goldblatt nodded. "Whatever you need will be provided."

"The queen says I need a new wardrobe. My tunic and deerskin pants are not appropriate for the court, at least not all the time."

Goldblatt smiled. "Simply have the dressmaker send the bills to me. I will take care of everything."

"Thank you. Now if you will excuse me, I am late. The king and I are going for a ride." Oolada turned and hastened down the hall.

Goldblatt watched her depart, then knocked on the door to the queen's apartments.

The queen's voice responded immediately. "Come in Chancellor."

Goldblatt opened the door and started to ask how she knew it was him. But before he could speak. The queen said, "I would have known your voice anywhere."

"Good morning, Your Majesty."

The queen sat in a small parlor outside her main suite. Comfortable cushioned chairs and a rather large sofa faced the fireplace, a typical arrangement for all interior rooms in the castle. Various colored pillows and small throws lay upon the furniture. Without question, it was a woman's room.

"Please have a seat. Tea?"

"Yes, thank you," Goldblatt replied.

"I met Lady Zoo as she left. She was on her way to a ride with the king. She also said she needed money for a new wardrobe. Do I see your hand in this?"

"The ride, no; the dresses, absolutely. Oolada is charming. She is so confident in virtually everything, except her relationship with Merryk. You know she is deeply in love with him?"

"I was fairly certain. Queen Tara knew and had already encouraged Oolada to spend time with the king. Tara had made a list of suitable candidates for the Inland Queen even before Merryk was king. He refused to discuss it, but she prepared a list. Tara said we needed to be ready, just in case."

"I wish there had been more time. I think I would have truly liked Tara."

"I know you would have." Goldblatt sipped his tea, then placed it on the table. "I wanted the two of us to review where we are. The dinner with the Crescents went well. The king seemed to connect with Lady Elizabeth. He made a promise to take her riding."

"However," Queen Amanda inserted, "the size of the dinner party, just five, has caused a ripple throughout the other noble houses. There is a rumor marriage contracts are already being prepared. Other noble houses are expecting to be contacted. What you and I saw as easing Merryk into the process has now created a frenzy. I am afraid he must meet with others, and soon. Then there is Oolada."

"What is your impression of Oolada?" Goldblatt asked.

"As I said, Oolada is charming. She loves my son and does not care that he is king. She does not want to be a queen, any more than he wants to be a king. As a married couple, they would be perfect."

"I am detecting a *but*," Goldblatt said.

"But Merryk's greatest weakness is his lack of formality. I worry he will have difficulty ruling unless he claims the mantle of authority. The mantle requires structure. It requires he be separate from all others. He must stand apart, above. He must act like a king. Oolada's advice to him was 'be who you are and not what others expect.' Good advice to everyone, except the king. The problem is he listens to her. A different wife, like Lady Elizabeth, would help him understand how to be separate. A person like her would help him be a better king, but as a wife? I do not know. As his mother, I want him to be happy."

"I want him to be happy and king," Goldblatt said. "You need to spend more time with Merryk. Being himself is more regal than any man I have ever met."

"That may be true, but it will take time for everyone to see what you see in him. In the interim, he needs to be working on getting a wife. Meeting with forty noble families—one by one—will fill a year. He does not have that much time. I am already detecting some impatience." Queen Amanda shook her head. "Do you have any suggestions?"

"Perhaps. Last year, after Tara lost her first child, Merryk held a Christmas celebration to help raise everyone's spirits. During the dinner with the Crescents, the annual New Year's Ball was mentioned. Merryk said he would not be a suitable host this year, but it would allow him the opportunity to meet with a multitude of daughters from the noble houses. He is more likely to attend one evening than fifteen afternoon teas."

"Chancellor, you may have found a solution to two problems: introducing Merryk to a multitude of daughters from the noble houses and the opportunity for Oolada to show she can be a true queen. I have reservations about Oolada, but I still hope she will prevail. There is much about her which reminds me of myself."

Goldblatt scratched his gray beard. "The time is short, only six or seven weeks. Can we arrange it in such a short time?"

"Yes. Particularly with the help of Lady Zoo." The queen smiled. "Also, this will immerse her into running the household. Great training for a queen."

The next morning, Oolada returned to Queen Amanda.

"Oh, I am glad you are here," the queen said. "I was afraid you had not received my message. There is something I need you to do."

"Whatever you wish, Your Majesty," Oolada replied. "Anything I can do to be of help."

"I was hoping you would say that. I need you to organize the Winter Ball."

"Unfortunately, Your Majesty has picked a task I cannot complete. I have never been to a ball. I would not know where to start."

"You are making it overly hard. A ball is just a celebration that gives people a chance to wear new dresses. Do the clans have feasts or celebrations at different times in the year?"

"Yes, we even have a mid-winter feast where we decorate the Great Square with holly and greenery. We serve roast meats and cakes. There are songs and dances. It is the celebration of the end of the longest nights of winter and the promise of the coming spring. It is one of the few times in the year the other women included me in their activities. Ever since I was a child, I looked forward to being part of the decorating group."

"Well, there you have it. You will decorate the ballroom just like you did with your family at the crag. I want you to create the feeling you experienced at home and then share it with everyone here. The staff will do all the work. You just need to give the direction."

"Your Majesty, it will not be grand enough. I am afraid the people of the High Kingdom will find holly with berries and candlelight boring."

"Not if we include musicians for dancing, and did I tell you that everyone gets a new dress? We will include ample food and wine to ensure they have a good time. Now go and look at the ballroom and come back after you have seen it. This year, you will be our inspiration."

"Eleanor, take Lady Zoo to the ballroom immediately. Listen to her ideas and let her know if you can accomplish them in time for the New Year.

"I have a wonderful feeling about this."

Chapter 52

New Council

King Merryk located a wood paneled room on the second floor above the throne room. With the help of Jamas, Merryk furnished it with a large table and a half dozen tall-backed chairs. The room had bright morning light which streamed through windows overlooking a garden. The standard fireplace occupied the wall opposite the windows. A deep carpet on the floor soaked up excess sound, just as a sponge would water.

Chancellor Goldblatt and Monsieur Masterroff entered the room chatting as old friends do. They stopped only when they realized the king had beaten them to the meeting. "I am sorry, Your Majesty, I should have known you would be early," Goldblatt said. "Please allow me to introduce Monsieur Masterroff."

Before Masterroff could greet the king, Merryk left his chair to extend his hand. "It is my pleasure to finally meet you, Monsieur Masterroff. In some ways, I think I have known you forever. I cannot tell you how much I have appreciated your help these past months. Please excuse my delay in not meeting with you sooner."

Masterroff did not know exactly what to say. "Your Majesty, it is my honor to be of assistance. Your understanding of economics and markets has been inspiring."

"I was just a student of Chancellor Goldblatt," Merryk answered.

"I know my old friend Goldblatt and he has no interest in markets. Your concept of managing supply was brilliant. I have many questions."

"If you have questions, then you should invite us all to dinner and you could ask as many as you want," Lord Commander Bellows said as he entered the room and patted his friend Masterroff on the back in greeting.

"Good Morning, Lord Commander," Merryk said. "Now that we are all here, please have a seat. There is tea."

When everyone was settled, Merryk began. "I have asked the three of you here this morning to join me in what I hope will be at least a monthly meeting. I would like to think of the three of you as part of a new council of advisors. As you all know, a kingdom has many moving parts: some economic, some military, and others political. The three of you are the best in each of these fields. Combined, you have the best overview of the kingdom."

"Your Majesty," Masterroff interrupted, "I am just a merchant. I work for myself and you, but I have never worked for the benefit of the kingdom."

"Yet you study the availability of ships, horses, and canvas. You understand how supply and demand affect the price. You know the power of markets. To do so, you must study what is happening throughout the kingdom. It is your understanding of when people are doing well and when they are suffering, which is important to me. This is the information a king needs to direct his attention and support. My guess is you have worked for yourself because no one has ever asked you to work for the kingdom."

"Your Majesty, I must admit, you are the first king to invite me to come to the castle, other than by legal summons," Masterroff said humbly.

"To their great loss, Monsieur Masterroff," Merryk replied sincerely. "I do not want you to stop working for yourself, but I also want you to provide insights which will help the throne's investments in the kingdom. Kings often look at their people as tools to gather money for their purposes. In my opinion, this is backwards. The throne should collect taxes for the benefit of the people. For their defense, of course, but also for roads, bridges, and education. Safe seas and good roads are the best for business and good business helps everyone: merchants, workers, and shopkeepers."

"I could not have said it any better," Masterroff said.

"I need you to carry on with your business interests. Remember my business and your business overlap. I'm counting on you continuing to take care of both. What I want from you is an evaluation of the state of the economy and suggestions where investments would best help the general people," Merryk said.

"Very well, but only if you will allow me to prepare dinner for the group," Masterroff said.

"Veal, I assume," Bellows inserted.

Masterroff nodded.

"Today, I would like your impression of the current market for shipping contracts and horses," Merryk stated.

"The shipping market has been sound. I have encouraged people to do business with the south, specifically Queen Stephanie's kingdom, as you requested. We do not have the large shortage of ships like we did this spring, but we still have more requests than ships."

"When will our new merchant ships be available?" Goldblatt asked.

"Just in time to meet the extra demand," Masterroff replied with a smile. "The market for horses is stable. The current price is lower than at the height, but still is running about twenty percent over the standard historic prices. The shortages caused by the loss of Natas' horses still affect the market. There is also uncertainty about how many horses will come from the old Ressett herds."

"I will have the herd master for the Ressett stock contact you to schedule the quantity and date to release horses." Merryk said. "We should try to reduce the price overall to only ten percent over normal."

"That should be very doable, except I heard a rumor the Earl of Weirshem is offering to sell a hundred horses below the market price," Masterroff said. "This will lower the price."

"Selling below market? Has he done this before?" Merryk asked.

"No, this is unusual. In fact, Weirshem does not have herds large enough to produce so many horses, or at least, never in the past."

"Interesting," Goldblatt said. "Weirshem is known for grain, not horses. His lands abut the property previously held by the Duke of Ressett."

Merryk and Goldblatt exchanged a glance.

"Lord Commander, how are things going with the military?" Merryk asked.

"Excellent, Your Majesty. We have reestablished the normal promotion system. Men of merit are now in the positions they deserved. Stability has returned to our ranks. On the sea, we are having an uptick of incursions by pirates. However, I am confident, with the help from Admiral Burat, we can make this less profitable for the pirates. When they discover we are working together, it will immediately change their activities. On land, we have returned everyone to securing the border as you instructed. Without the provocations of the previous Lord Commander, things have become quiet for the winter."

"Thank you, Lord Commander. I would like you to evaluate your long-term needs for ships. By long-term, I mean in the next two to five years. How many ships and what kind will we need?" Merryk asked. "If we have some forward view, we can do a better job of planning."

"Chancellor Goldblatt, do you have anything to share with the group?" Merryk said, looking to the Chancellor for his report.

"The Earl of Weirshem and Lord Tallon, son of the Earl of Tallon, are grumbling to other Outland families. Nothing more than drunken men pretending courage. They are not a threat to the throne yet. But we must watch them. You do not want it to grow into anything more than the voice of wine."

"We must expect all the houses to have questions," Merryk said. "Some will just ask; others like these two will stew and conspire without facts. They just need a little time to get to know me. I don't want to overreact. Is there anything else?"

"Just one thing," the Lord Commander added. "It follows the previous discussion. This morning, Lady Zoo, with six Royal Guards, left the castle."

"Yes, she is going to visit Lady Katalynn at Ressett Manor."

"I know, but is that wise, Your Majesty?" The Lord Commander asked cautiously. "Lady Zoo is very close to you. Her support for Lady Katalynn, who is the daughter of a traitor, will affect how Lady Zoo and you are viewed."

"Lady Katalynn's only crime is being born to a traitor. She has not engaged in any threat to the throne. I will not have her punished for doing nothing. Lady Zoo agrees with me," Merryk's tone was firm.

"I understand, Your Majesty. In the navy, each man earns his way up regardless of title or birth. My son worked his way up from the deck to command. But the support of Lady Ressett by Lady Zoo gives fuel to the likes of Weirshem and Tallon as proof you have no respect for nobility. If you need time to convince the people of your sincerity, Lady Zoo's actions may erode it."

"Then I will have less time. I will not permit innocent people to be punished for the acts of their fathers." Merryk looked around the room for any additional comments.

"There is one more thing," Masterroff said. "When do you want to have dinner?"

As everyone rose to leave the room, Merryk called out. "Monsieur Masterroff, a moment."

"Yes, Your Majesty."

"I think we should buy all the horses being offered by Weirshem. Buy them through multiple intermediaries, so no one knows of our involvement. At the worst, we will make a small profit and stabilize the market."

"I detect something else in your request," Masterroff said.

Merryk nodded. "Perhaps the horses will shed light on our shadowy earl. Think of this as an opportunity to see his true colors."

———— ❧ ————

The Lord Commander followed Goldblatt out of the council room. "You know they will view his compassion as weakness."

"Have you seen anything in his actions which makes you think he is weak?" Goldblatt responded.

"No, but I have seen him as a commander. Others do not have this experience."

"Then we will advise him, but his sense of fairness will not change. His support for Lady Katalynn is based on principle." Goldblatt shook his head. "King Merryk would risk his throne to support her and Lady Zoo. For now, we need to gain him time so everyone can see him as we do."

Chapter 53

BETH

Mid-morning the next day, Merryk went to the stable. "Good morning, Maverick. How are you today? We are going for a ride this morning."

Maverick shifted his head toward the adjacent stall.

"No, Bella can't come with us this time."

Maverick shook his head. "No, Oolada isn't coming either. She went yesterday to see Lady Katalynn at Ressett Manor."

Maverick made a low grunting sound. "Don't worry, she'll be fine. I sent six Royal Guards with her. It is only for three nights."

Changing the subject, Merryk continued. "Today we're going for a ride with Lady Elizabeth Crescent. She seems very nice."

Maverick shook his head and stomped his front paw.

"I know, I miss Tara too, but I must spend time with other women. It is the whole Inland Queen thing. Everyone keeps telling me it's not about what I want, but about what I need."

Maverick bobbed his head in understanding and then joggled it.

"Yes, Oolada knows I'm riding with someone else."

"Talking with your horse?" a soft female voice asked from behind him.

Merryk turned to see Lady Elizabeth standing in the stable door. She had her auburn hair tied in a tight knot. She wore a waist length tailored coat with a fur collar, soft leather trousers, and knee-high boots. The trousers fitted snugly, accentuating her long legs and rounded hips.

"Good morning," Merryk replied. "And, yes, I am talking with Maverick.

Lady Elizabeth walked to Maverick and patted him firmly on the neck. "Just as everyone said, he is truly magnificent."

"You can't tell him that. He will be impossible to control," Merryk replied.

Beth turned to place her hand on Merryk's arm and looked upward into his eyes. "I cannot imagine anything you could not control," she breathed, letting her gaze linger for an extra moment.

"Well, Maverick may be one."

Maverick responded by bobbing his head in affirmation.

"I see what you mean," Beth said with a chuckle. "Where are we going this morning?"

"I thought we might ride out the north gate, toward the mountains. They are covered with a fresh coat of snow and are sparkling in the morning light."

"Are you always this poetic?"

"I just enjoy beauty," Merryk answered.

"Then we need to be sure you see as much beauty as possible," Beth said with a radiant smile.

<hr />

About two hours later, Merryk and Beth, along with their guard, returned to the stable.

"Could you help me off?" Beth asked Merryk.

"Certainly," Merryk answered, extending his arms to grasp the Lady Elizabeth by the waist. Effortlessly, he lifted her from the horse. Beth turned to Merryk as she dismounted, allowing her arms to reach around

Merryk's neck and bringing her face close to his. When he sat her on the ground, she held on for an extra second.

"Thank you," she said in a breathless voice.

"Excuse me, Your Majesty," Bowen said, interrupting. "There has been an attack at Ressett Manor."

"Is Lady Zoo all right? And Lady Katalynn?" a concerned Merryk asked. "What happened?"

"I am uncertain, but you should talk with them yourself. They arrived less than an hour ago and are in Lady Zoo's quarters." Bowen responded.

"Beth, come with me. You may be needed."

Maverick whinnied as Merryk left the stable. Merryk turned back over his shoulder and replied, "I will send word as soon as I know."

Merryk extended his legs into long strides, requiring Lady Elizabeth and the guards to almost run to keep up. The guards at Oolada's doors opened them as they saw the king approach. Merryk burst into the outer parlor. "Oolada, are you all right?" Merryk went directly to Oolada, gently grasping her arms as his eyes searched her face for any sign of injury.

"I am fine. We were in no real danger," she replied with a smile.

Merryk let out a sigh of relief and reluctantly released Oolada's arms. Merryk turned to face Lady Katalynn. "Are you all right?"

"Yes, thanks to Oolada. but we were in real danger," Kat answered from the sofa.

Beth sat by Kat when she entered the room and placed her arm around Kat's shoulder. "I am glad you are safe, but what happened?" Beth asked.

"Rogger Weirshem, Sir Timothy, and a group of their men came to the manor. The men went to the stables to steal horses, and Rogger and Timothy burst into the manor house. They were drunk. They knocked down Swenson, our butler. They were both yelling for me to come out and play, but that is not what they meant." Kat's eyes now swelled with tears. "I was so afraid."

"Where were the guards?" Merryk's voice was sharp with anger.

"I sent them to their quarters for the evening. There was no reason to believe there was any threat," Oolada said. "They did nothing wrong. When they heard the men breaking into the stables, they responded quickly. They did not know others had broken into the house until later."

Merryk looked back at Oolada, his voice serious. "Are you sure you're all right?"

"Yes, absolutely," Oolada answered, recognizing the anxiety in Merryk's voice.

Kat nodded in concurrence. "But the others are not so lucky. Oolada crushed Rogger's nose and broke Sir Timothy's arm."

"They are both in Bowen's custody," Oolada said. "Their men got away with six horses."

"The horses were my father's prized breeding stock. One was even the son of the great horse, Raj."

"We will get your horses back," Merryk said. "Bowen."

"Yes, Your Majesty."

"See to the injuries of our two intruders, then place them in the same accommodations we used for the Duke of Ressett."

Beth's mind raced through the events of the day. *Merryk said he hoped both Oolada and Kat were all right, but the only one he was truly interested in was Oolada. Someday, perhaps, Merryk will be as concerned about me as Oolada. Mother is wrong. The connection between Oolada and the king is not just political. At least, it is not just political to Merryk. Dissuading him from this attachment is going to require more thought than I had expected. It is a good thing Oolada is so naive.*

Chapter 54

RESPECT

Dawn found Merryk on the top of the tower, looking toward the growing glow of the sun. The crisp air from the sea pushed a layer of broken clouds across the horizon to catch the early light. Merryk's breath billowed into the crisp air; his puffing controlled just like the careful movements of his morning exercises.

The door to the roof creaked open, allowing a bundled Oolada to exit. "I knew you would be here," she said.

"Now you are clairvoyant like Helga, although you haven't seemed to have mastered her ability to be forewarned of trouble." Merryk replied.

"You sound like you are angry with me," Oolada said. "I did not attack myself."

"But you could have been hurt or worse," Merryk replied, his tone serious. "I could not bear to lose you, too."

Oolada moved to Merryk. This time she was the one grasping his arms to look into his face. "Stop it. I was not in any danger. The men were poorly trained, and they were drunk. If anything, I am more responsible for what happened than they. I did not post guards like my grandfather has for years. He would be bellowing at me now about my stupidity. I can hear him. '*Never assume you are safe!*'"

"Unfortunately, good advice," Merryk answered. "How is Lady Katalynn doing? She seemed very upset."

"Her mind focused on what would have happened if I had not been there. She believes she has been stripped of her protection as a noble-woman."

"I will not allow her to be abused by anyone. I will make it clear she has my personal protection. It is hard for me to understand why men would think she was free for the taking, whether noble or not."

"Merryk, you are like my grandfather. Both of you respect women and acknowledge their value. For most men, however, women are only as valu-able as a horse, and sometimes less."

"Perhaps hanging these two will show women's value," Merryk said.

"Merryk, you cannot hang them for this offense. No one was hurt, except them. They were drunk and stupid. If you hang men for this, you will soon have no men left." Oolada's face now flashed a smile.

"You certainly have a low opinion of men," Merryk responded. Now his face reflected Oolada's smile.

"Just some men. You need to hear out the facts and provide a sentence balanced against the crime. My guess is their manhood will be subject to many jokes after their beating. They cannot hide crushed noses and broken arms."

"You're probably right. Now I need some breakfast. Do you want to join me?"

"I should check on Kat and Beth. Beth stayed with us last night. She wanted to be sure everyone was all right. Then I have a meeting with the queen."

Merryk liked breakfast. It was the only meal he could count on being alone. Occasionally, Oolada would join him, but recently she had been going to join Queen Amanda. The staff had grown accustomed to his helping himself and his questions about their lives. He was sure they found it strange that he even asked. He had a customary spot at the head of the massive thirty-foot table. His attempts to make things simple had only been partially successful. The staff still insisted on setting at least five full place settings and cooking for an equal number. Other than a special request, his normal breakfast comprised fried or scrambled eggs, ham or bacon, and hot fresh rolls or breads with butter and honey.

"You're up early, Chancellor," Merryk said as the elder statesman entered the room.

"My preference would have been to sleep, but the Earl of Weirshem had men pounding on my door at dawn."

"I was wondering how long it would be before he arrived," Merryk said as he continued to eat his breakfast. "Are you hungry?"

"I should have something," Goldblatt said as he sat down on the left side of Merryk. "Weirshem is demanding his son and Sir Timothy be released at once. Also, he wants Lady Zoo and her guard punished for attacking them."

"Did he give a reason for them being at the manor in the middle of the night and for taking horses from the stable?"

"Yes, he says he sent the group to pick up the horses he had purchased from the Duke of Ressett."

"Who, conveniently, is dead," Merryk added.

Goldblatt nodded. "What do you want to do?"

"I will be available later this morning in the throne room. I think I have a meeting with an ambassador from the south. Put the earl on the schedule afterwards to present his petition. I will hear him then."

"Are you going to free his son?"

"Not today. We do not have the facts. If crimes were committed, they need to be punished. I cannot determine this without a hearing and evidence."

"This will not make you popular with the outland nobles."

"My first inclination was to hang them. I am sure that would have made me popular. Of one thing I am certain, I will not allow women to be abused by anyone, noble or not."

Rumor of the earl's petition spread. Soon, a reasonable crowd had accumulated. Merryk intentionally prolonged the meeting with the ambassador, leaving the earl pacing in the back of the throne room. Finally, the Lord Chamberlain announced him. "Your Majesty, the Earl of Weirshem."

Weirshem moved in front of the king. "My son is in the dungeon. He must be released at once," he demanded.

"Your Grace, how nice to finally meet you. I assume your pressing business matters are resolved and you are here to extend your respects to Queen Amanda and the throne."

"I am not. I am here to have my son released."

"So, you are not here out of respect for the throne?" The question was more of a statement. Merryk's face was expressionless as his eyes locked onto the earl. An uneasy stillness filled the throne room.

The Earl of Weirshem felt the unwavering stare of the king. After an awkward pause, the earl spoke. "I beg your forgiveness, Your Majesty. I misspoke. I wish to express my respects and deep condolences to you and Queen Amanda for your losses."

"On behalf of my mother, we thank you for your kind words. Now, Your Grace, you have another matter?"

"Yes, Your Majesty, my son is being held unjustly in the dungeon after being brutally attacked by Lady Zoo and her guards, who tried to kill him."

"You may rest assured, if Lady Zoo had intended to kill your son, he would be dead. Unfortunately, neither you nor I can determine if he is unjustly detained. In order to do so, we will need to have a hearing, where evidence can be given by both sides." Turning toward Chancellor Gold-blatt. "Please send notices of a hearing on this matter for next Tuesday."

"But Your Majesty, that is a week away. Certainly, my son can be freed before the trial."

"Both sides will need time to gather witnesses and evidence. Regarding an early release, the initial allegations are an attempt to assault the Duchess of Ressett, and horse theft. Both serious offenses. I will detain Rogger Weirshem until the trial. Don't worry, Your Grace, we will ensure his safety and health. If there is nothing else, then we are adjourned."

The earl began to object when the Lord Chamberlain stabbed his rod into the stone floor, announcing the session was over.

CHAPTER 55

WOMEN

"Where have you been?" an overly curious Beth asked Oolada as she returned to her rooms. Beth was coiled up on the sofa in front of the fireplace. Kat sat in an overstuffed chair with a cup of tea in hand.

"I went to talk with the king. He is still concerned about the attack. The king is particularly worried about you, Kat. He wants to be sure you are safe. Also, he asked if all of us could join him for lunch. There is to be a hearing, or a trial, of Rogger Weirshem and Sir Timothy. The king wants to understand the details. I think Chancellor Goldblatt will join us." Oolada moved to the front of the fireplace and shivered. "It is cold today."

"Where did you find the king?" Beth asked.

"On the top of a tower, doing his daily exercises."

"That sounds cold without even going." Kat said.

Oolada turned. "I need to get to Queen Amanda. We are working on preparations for the Winter Ball."

"Please tell the queen we would be willing to help," Beth said.

"I will. See you at lunch."

The door closed behind Oolada. "Clever to offer to help," Kat said. "That would give you more time in the castle, near the king."

"I do not know what you mean," Beth giggled.

"You also know, I cannot help because I will be a half day's ride away at the manor."

"Oh, most unfortunate," Beth said with false concern.

Kat looked at her cousin. "I like Oolada. She has become a dear friend. Be sure whatever you do does not hurt her."

"Oolada is a warrior. She can take care of herself."

"Good morning, Your Majesty."

"Good morning, Oolada. I understand you have had a harrowing adventure," Queen Amanda said. The queen sat at her dining table, reviewing her notes for the ball.

"Not really. Two drunks broke into Katalynn's manor with havoc on their mind. Unfortunately for them, I was not amused. Neither is King Merryk. His first response was to hang them. I told him that if he hung every man who was drunk and stupid, he would not have any male subjects."

"So true," Queen Amanda said with a chuckle. "But Lady Katalynn would not have been spared without your presence. She is lucky you were there."

Oolada ignored the compliment. "Merryk intends to make it clear Katalynn is under his personal protection. He believes this will give her safety."

"It will, and it will also elevate Lady Katalynn as a potential Inland Queen. The court will now have someone else besides Lady Crescent and you for their gossip."

"Speaking of Lady Crescent, she stayed with Katalynn and me last night to be sure we were all right. She also said to let you know if you needed any additional help with the ball, she and Katalynn would be glad to assist."

"Of course she did," Queen Amanda replied. The queen took a sip of her tea. "Do you think the king will release the earl's son?"

"I do not think so, at least not today. The king seems furious. Also, there is potential horse theft. There will be a hearing to discuss both."

"The issue of the horse thieves is more important than the assault. I worry Merryk is focused on the offense to you and Katalynn, when the world expects him to focus on the horses."

"How can you say such a thing?" Oolada snapped. Then she caught herself. "I am sorry, Your Majesty, but the assault is more important than the theft."

"No offense taken, but the world does not afford women the respect or protection of horses. It is unjust, but it is a reality."

"Merryk will change this," Oolada said with confidence.

"I am sure he will try, but I worry about the cost to the power of the throne."

Queen Amanda's mind flashed. *Again, Oolada counsels Merryk to do the right thing. The right thing for everyone, except the king.*

CHAPTER 56

ROGGER

Chancellor Goldblatt entered the anteroom to greet the king. "The crowd has been growing rapidly. Nothing packs a throne room better than a conflict between the king and a noble," Goldblatt said.

"This is not a conflict between me and Weirshem. This is about civil order, respect for women, and preventing theft."

"You can tell yourself that, Your Majesty, but every eye and ear will view this as you versus the earl. How you treat nobles and particularly outland nobles. It is also about how you support the women. Both noble, one the daughter of a traitor, the other from a not quite noble clan, both prospective Inland Queens. Will you show favor?"

"Goldblatt, I've never known you to be so theatrical. This is about assault and theft, nothing more."

"Certainly, Your Majesty. Now, if you are ready?" Goldblatt's smile grew.

The Lord Chamberlain dropped his heavy staff to the stone floor. "His Majesty, King Merryk Raymouth," he pronounced in his over-sized voice.

Merryk entered and moved to his throne. Two tables were placed in front, one for the Chancellor and the other for the Earl of Weirshem, his son, and Sir Timothy. The prisoners looked clean and well fed, but both still showed the marks of their encounter with Lady Zoo. Sir Timothy's cast arm hung in a sling. Rogger's face was dark blue and green, his nose taped to allow for healing. The earl was clothed in his finest attire and irritation.

Merryk motioned with his head for Goldblatt to begin.

The Chancellor rose. "Your Majesty, there are two separate issues. The first is an attempted assault on the Duchess of Ressett and Lady Zoo. The second is the potential theft of horses from the Ressett's stable."

"I bought those horses," the earl declared.

"Your Grace, I will give you an opportunity to speak, but please, do not interrupt the Chancellor." Merryk's voice was firm. "Please proceed, Chancellor."

"Approximately ten days ago, Rogger Weirshem and Sir Timothy broke into Ressett Manor in the middle of the night. The best way to describe the events is through those who were present. Swenson, please come forward."

A stately looking, gray-haired man dressed in his formal attire as a butler stepped up to face the king. "Swenson, please introduce yourself."

"I am Swenson, the head butler for the Ressett Manor." Although accustomed to greeting and serving nobility, being called in front of the king left Swenson shaking.

Merryk saw the man's fear. Merryk asked in a gentle voice. "Swenson, how long have you been in the service of the Ressetts?"

"For most of my life, Your Majesty."

"Excellent. Now just tell me what happened."

Swenson began. "Lady Zoo and her guard arrived in the early afternoon. We had presented an excellent dinner, and the ladies had retired for the evening. Lady Zoo's guards had taken vacant servants' rooms for the evening. Near an hour before midnight, there was a commotion at the stables. Lady Zoo's guards went immediately to investigate. Then, there was a banging on the main doors. As is my duty, I went to see who was there. I opened the peephole door and two men stood outside."

Chancellor Goldblatt interrupted. "Do you see the men who were outside the door here today?"

"Yes." Swenson pointed. "Lord Weirshem and Sir Timothy. They had come to the manor to meet with the duke before."

"Did you let them in?" Goldblatt asked.

"I tried. I unlocked the door and started to open it, when Sir Timothy kicked the door into my face, knocking me to the ground."

"Is that how you got the bruises on your face?"

"Yes."

"What happened next?"

"Lord Weirshem stepped on my arm. He said, 'Stay down, old man, unless you want a beating.' My Lord, I am not as young as I once was. I knew I could not stop them. I am sorry. Then they began saying the most inappropriate things. They called for Lady Katalynn to come out to play. No need to get dressed. It will come off anyway. They said terrible things. I would prefer not to say more."

"Hearing these comments, do you believe that Lady Katalynn was afraid?" Goldblatt asked.

"She had to be. I know I was."

Goldblatt moved to look directly at the two charged men. "Please, continue. What happened next?"

"The first person down the stairs was Lady Zoo. The men did not expect her. They started making comments to her, like, 'Now we will not have to share.' She told them they were drunk, and they needed to leave. They laughed. In all my years, I have seen nothing like what happened next. Lord Weirshem reached to grab her. Lady Zoo stepped into Rogger, hitting him with the full force of her elbow in his nose. You could hear it snap across the room and blood squirted to cover his face. Sir Timothy pulled his sword. Again, Lady Zoo stepped forward, grabbed his sword, twisted his arm, and threw her weight to drive him to the ground. She yelled 'Yield!' He said, 'Never.' Lady Zoo stood over him, with his arm and sword twisted back. When he refused to drop his sword, she drove her knee into the back of his arm. There was a loud pop, followed by Sir Timothy's scream. He dropped the sword, then."

"Was that everything? Goldblatt asked.

"Soon Lady Zoo's guards came and dragged both men out of the manor. I do not know what would have happened if Lady Zoo had not been present."

Goldblatt looked at the earl. "Do you have questions for Swenson?"

"So, you saw Lady Zoo attack my son and Sir Timothy?"

"Yes, after she asked them to leave, and they refused. Your Grace would have been embarrassed by your son's language," Swenson added.

Shaking his head, the earl cast his eyes down in embarrassment and shame.

Chancellor Goldblatt looked at the earl. "Do you want me to ask both the Lady Zoo and the duchess to give their statements?"

"That will not be necessary, but my son would like to describe his actions, which he believes were misinterpreted."

Rogger Weirshem started to speak from his chair.

"Stand and come forward." Merryk commanded sharply.

Rogger moved to stand directly in front of the king. "The statement of the butler is essentially correct, with a few exceptions. First, we did not intend to knock him down at the door. It was an accident. Our words were meant in jest, not to frighten. They may have been more lewd than we intended, but we were both drunk. This did not justify Lady Zoo's unprovoked attack."

Merryk looked sternly at Rogger. "Two drunken men break into the manor, knock down the butler, yell lewd remarks, promise attacks and fail to leave upon request. This, in your opinion, does not constitute provocation?"

"When you say it like that, it seems worse than it was. Besides, that bitch broke my nose and Sir Timothy's arm with no warning."

King Merryk leaned forward in his chair. "I estimate the distance between where I sit and where you stand is about seven feet, and it would take me less than a second for my hand to grasp your throat. If you say another disrespectful word about Lady Zoo or Lady Katalynn, I will test my hypothesis. Is that unclear in any way?"

Rogger's eyes sprang wide open in fear. No one ever threatened him, much less the king. "Very clear, Your Majesty." Rogger's voice was soft and unsure.

"You didn't have any trouble the other night speaking loudly, so speak loudly now."

"Very clear, Your Majesty." This time, his voice was loud and clear.

"Sir Timothy, come join Lord Weirshem. Do you wish to say anything in your own defense?"

"No, Your Majesty." Sir Timothy's voice was strained, but loud.

"Lady Zoo, what punishment would you request?"

Lady Zoo stepped forward. "They have paid already, but if I were not a lady, I would afford them an opportunity for another encounter."

Merryk chuckled. "Lady Zoo, the outcome would be worse. Neither their male egos nor their reputations would survive."

A wave of laughter spread through the room.

"Duchess, as to the attempted assault, what punishment would you choose?"

"Your Majesty, my father was a traitor. I am not. It is not punishment I would like, but I want back the respect I had as a noblewoman before my father's acts." Kat's voice was thick with emotion.

"You shall have it." Merryk's voice increased in intensity. "Let all know, Lady Katalynn, the Duchess of Ressett, has my personal protection. Any man who harms her will not receive the measured indignation of a king, but the righteous wrath of a father or a husband. All women will be treated with respect in this kingdom. I will tolerate nothing else."

Merryk returned his gaze to the two men who stood before him. "The two of you are a disgrace as nobles and men. I sentence you to ten days in the dungeon with credit for the time already served. In addition, you will immediately and sincerely apologize to both Lady Zoo and the Duchess of Ressett."

Both men turned to face the two ladies. Lord Weirshem began.

"Stop. On your knees." The king commanded.

Rogger started. "I wish to give you my sincere apology for our actions at your manor. Although I was drunk, I know it is not a sufficient justification for our actions. We were crude and did not reflect the standards of nobles. I sincerely hope that you can forgive me."

Sir Timothy looked at the two women. "I also humbly apologize to you for my actions."

"Very well. Return to the table with the earl. Now Chancellor, let us proceed with the second matter, the duchess's horses."

CHAPTER 57

DUCHESS'S HORSES

"I bought the horses," the earl said emphatically.

"Then you will have no difficulty in answering a few questions about the sale." Chancellor Goldblatt said sharply. "Simple things. Like, if you bought the horses, why did you come to pick them up in the middle of the night and break into the stables rather than announcing yourself in the daylight and asking for help?"

"Gentlemen, we will proceed in an orderly manner," King Merryk said to calm the clash between the two. "Your Grace may begin. Please tell me the details of the sale."

"Very well, Your Majesty," the Earl of Weirshem replied. "I met with the Duke of Ressett at the Pint and Pipe one afternoon about a week before his act of treason. The duke asked if I was interested in some breeding stock. I told him it would depend on what kind of stock and the price. He said I could pick any six horses from his stable for six thousand. I asked why he would sell horses in this manner. He told me, confidentially, he needed the money. As to why in the nighttime, that was the decision of my son and Sir Timothy. Their judgment has already been fully explained." Satisfied with his statement, the earl sat down.

Chancellor Goldblatt rose and moved in front of his table. "Initially, did you receive any written memorandum of the agreement?"

"No, the word of the duke was sufficient," the earl replied.

"Did anyone else overhear the discussion?"

"No, the duke wanted it kept confidential."

"Very well. Your Majesty, I would like to call Jasper, the breeding master of the Ressett herds."

A sandy-haired man with a bushy beard came forward. Holding his tweed hat tightly in his hands, he stood before the king.

"Jasper, please tell the king about your position and about the horses taken from the stables."

"Your Majesty, I am the breeding master for the Duke—." Catching himself, then continuing, "the Duchess of Ressett. I have been in this position since the death of my father, who held it before me. The duke and I worked together on the breeding within the herd. The men who broke into the stables knew exactly what to take. All were very significant animals. The older stallion was a direct descendant of the original line of Ressett stock. The entire current herd is based upon him. The four mares are from diverse stock, gathered over the past four years. Each represents an effort to strengthen the herd. The final stallion is the son of the legendary Raj. The duke had traded for him last year with King Natas. He was to be the next great sire in our herd."

The Chancellor looked at the earl, then to Jasper. "Did the duke tell you he was selling the horses?"

"No, My Lord, not a word. His Grace always told me about his plans. We worked together on the herd for years, even through difficult times. He always shared information with me." Clutching his hat even tighter, he continued. "The claim the duke would sell all the horses for six thousand is, respectfully, Your Majesty, preposterous."

The earl snapped back at Jasper. "This man knows nothing about the value of horses. Six thousand was more than generous."

"The earl may be right," Goldblatt said. "Jasper may not be the best to identify the value of the horses. However, none in this room would deny

Monsieur Masterroff is the expert in horse valuation. Monsieur Masterroff, if you would come forward."

Masterroff moved through the edge of the crowd to stand in front of the king.

Goldblatt continued. "Sir, based upon your expertise and the review of the information about the horses, have you come to a conclusion about their current market value?"

"Yes," Masterroff answered in a clear voice. "The mares are reasonably easy to value. Each would be worth two to five thousand for a total of twelve to fifteen thousand for the group. The older stallion is the sire of a very established bloodline. Under normal circumstances, no one would consider selling him. The Ressett herd depends on him. If such a horse came on the market, it would be sold at an auction, where I would expect no less than twenty-five to thirty thousand. However, the real value is the young stallion. If his papers confirmed he was the son of the legendary Raj, the value would be at least fifty, more likely seventy-five thousand. The offspring of Raj are never sold in an open market or auction. They are always sold in select offerings and only to particular customers. Having a descendant of Raj is considered an honor and a privilege. In fairness, the value of the six horses would be one hundred-fifty to two hundred thousand.

A wave of whispers ran through the crowd.

"That is unreasonable!" the earl exclaimed.

"You have not purchased horses in a long time, Your Grace," Masterroff replied. "Prices have escalated, and the son of Raj is unique."

The earl puffed out his chest. "Raj is a myth about a horse with his own family of men to support him. This is a story for children and drunkards."

Merryk spoke from the throne. "Your Grace, I have seen Raj with my own eyes. He and his family are very real."

The earl was taken aback by the statements of the king. "In any event, it does not matter. The duke said he needed the money and wanted to keep it confidential. He agreed on the amount."

"Your Majesty, if I may continue?" Goldblatt asked.

Merryk nodded.

"I would like to ask Master Reynolds to come forward."

A well-dressed man stepped into the opening in front of the king. His composure and demeanor indicated he was more suited to an office than to a barnyard.

"Please identify yourself and your duties."

The man spoke. "I am Master Reynolds and I do accounting for the Duke of Ressett. I guess, for the duchess now."

"With your duties, do you have access to the total financial and cash positions of the late duke?"

"Yes. At the time of his death, the duke had cash positions greater than three hundred thousand and lines of credit for many thousands more."

"Did he need six thousand quickly in cash?" Goldblatt asked.

"Not at all," Reynolds answered firmly.

"One final question. Did you record receipt of funds from the sale of horses, and if so, did you record any receipts from the Earl of Weirshem or anyone else in the amount of six thousand in the week before the duke's death?"

Without hesitation, Reynolds responded, "None."

"I had not paid him yet," the earl declared from his seat, but with some hesitancy in his voice.

"I have nothing further," the Chancellor said.

Merryk looked at the earl. "Do you have anything else, Your Grace?"

The earl shifted in his chair and stood. "On my word as a noble, the duke and I had agreed, and it should be honored. The horses are mine."

Again, a murmur filtered through the crowd as everyone's eyes shifted their attention to King Merryk.

Merryk sat for a moment looking at the earl and then began. "The Earl of Weirshem is correct. He is a noble. The fact he has no written memorandum or witnesses to the transaction, or that his fool of a son and friend attempted to take possession in the middle of the night cannot distract from the strength of his word. The duke and the earl had agreed." Again, whispers filled the throne room. "Unfortunately, treason affects more than just the traitor. It affects the family, as we have seen with Lady Katalynn and those who are innocently doing business with them, like the earl. Without the duke to confirm his agreement or an actual payment, the agreement remained unfulfilled. The fact you had not paid the duke means he still could have refused the deal."

Merryk shifted his eyes to the crowd. "Lady Katalynn, do you wish to honor your father's agreement and accept six thousand for the horses?"

Lady Katalynn replied in a clear voice, "No, Your Majesty. I do not."

Merryk looked back to the earl. "The lady is the ultimate heir and has rejected an incomplete agreement. You will return the horses immediately, unharmed. Your Grace, although your word as a noble is to be respected, the next time you buy horses, get it in writing. Also, seek to enforce your claim in the light of day as a man befitting your station. You are entitled to the benefit of the doubt. Please, do not make a habit of requiring it."

King Merryk motioned with his head to the Lord Chamberlin, who immediately dropped his staff to the floor. "All rise for the king."

As Merryk moved toward the exit, he stopped. Turning to the earl, he said, "Your Grace, please join the Chancellor and I in the anteroom."

CHAPTER 58

BRIEF MEETINGS

The Earl of Weirshem followed the king and Chancellor into the small room, which connected the throne to the rest of the castle. Merryk waited until the door closed behind him.

"Your Grace, I believe it is important we understand each other. There is no question in my mind you intended to steal the horses. You asked your son and Sir Timothy to go at night with the specific purpose of abusing and humiliating Lady Katalynn. As a lady, her reputation and prospects for a husband would be destroyed if she acknowledged an assault by your son. The fear of being shamed would prevent her from telling anyone about the theft of the horses."

"That is not true," the earl began in protest.

"Do not speak until I tell you!" Merryk's voice filled with controlled rage. "Lady Zoo saved the lives of you and your son—twice. First, by stopping your son, and then by arguing on your behalf. When I first heard of this incident, my intent was to hang you both. Lady Zoo convinced me to wait for the evidence. I have heard the evidence. My first choice is still to hang you, but you are supposed to be a noble. There are others in this kingdom who are nobles, and they deserve the true *benefit of the doubt*. Your actions demean the image of all nobles. You walk from here a lucky man. You will not be lucky again. Do you understand me?"

"Yes," the earl said weakly.

"Yes, Your Majesty!" Merryk replied sharply.

"Yes, Your Majesty," the earl answered, this time in a full voice.

"One last thing. My range master has advised me that approximately one hundred horses are missing from my herds in the eastern pastures next to your lands. The land and animals came to me because of the duke's treason. I will not tolerate any horse thieves. Tomorrow morning, I am sending the wranglers and a company of soldiers to find the horses. If they locate them in the hands of others, my instructions are explicit. The offenders, regardless of status or title, will be hung."

The earl's face lost all color. In a shaky voice, he replied, "If the animals wander onto my lands, I will see they are returned at once."

"Thank you. You're excused."

The earl bowed awkwardly and hurried to the door.

"Our friend could not wait to get out of here," Goldblatt said as a broad smile covered his face.

"There is a certain advantage in having people believe you're ruthless. I hope my mother will approve." Now it was Merryk who was smiling.

"I am certain you did this just to gain her approval."

"Probably not, but a little fear is good for the soul."

"Who said that?" Goldblatt asked.

"Me."

Goldblatt smirked. "I am afraid the earl may find himself in a bind. Masterroff, as you instructed, has purchased and paid for his one hundred horses. If they are your horses, the earl will have to buy replacements on the market and quickly."

"Advise Masterroff to make the price a little over market," Merryk said with a chuckle. "The earl needs to learn the actual cost of horses, particularly those not belonging to him."

———— ❈ ————

Oolada, Kat, and Beth stood together near the door to the anteroom as the king, earl, and Chancellor passed.

"I wish we could hear the discussion in that room," Kat said.

"What do you think the king will tell him?" Beth asked.

"My guess is, the king is telling the earl he is lucky not to be on his way to the gallows," Oolada answered.

"Really? I cannot imagine anyone would really care about me. It must be because of the horses."

"No. The king does not care about horses. He cares about people; particularly women and children," Oolada said. "When he said he would protect you, he meant it."

"You certainly seem to have insights into our king," Beth said. "I sometimes wonder how you gain them."

"Nothing special, we just talk," Oolada said.

"When he has an Inland Queen, I am not sure she will appreciate your private discussions," Beth added.

"Unless Oolada is the Inland Queen," Kat replied.

"Oh no, I am not suited to be his queen," Oolada answered. "We are just friends."

"It is refreshing to know you understand your position so clearly," Beth said.

Kat looked at Beth with a stern glance of disapproval. "I would not count yourself out so quickly, Oolada."

Beth's face reflected her dislike of Kat's comment. "When do you need to go back to the manor?"

"I guess tomorrow, if I can stay one more night with you, Oolada?"

"Yes, of course, which reminds me. Kat, did your father have a winter place in the city?"

"Yes, we had a set of apartments near the main gate. Father did not want a house like the Duke of Crescent. My guess is, though, without my mother, they would have often gone unused."

"What has happened to them?" Oolada asked.

"They became the property of the king. My only holdings are at the manor."

"It is too bad you are so far away," Beth said. Her eyes were now locked on Kat with fake sincerity.

"Kat, I am going to ask the king to allow you to use the apartments so you will not be alone again at the manor. At least, until he can provide proper protection."

"Would you do that for me?"

"Absolutely," Oolada said.

Bowen interrupted the ladies' discussion. "Excuse me. His Majesty would like the three of you to join him for lunch, if you are available."

Oolada followed Bowen with Kat and Beth behind. Bowen led them to the king's new council chamber. Bowen stopped to open the door. Beth stepped in front and slightly bumped Oolada, allowing her to be the first to enter. When they entered the room, they saw a table set for four. One setting was to the right of the king, nearest the door, and the others were to the left by the windows.

"Your Majesty, your actions at the hearing were remarkable. I thought for a moment you were going to let the earl get away with the horses," Beth gushed. Her comments were accompanied by grabbing the king's arm to direct him toward the table. She stopped behind the chair to the right of the king and waited for Merryk to pull it out. This forced Oolada and Kat to the other side.

Merryk did not pull out the chair for Beth, but left her standing. Turning to the other women, Merryk said, "Lady Katalynn, how are you doing? I hope reliving the events of that evening did not cause you anxiety."

"Not at all, Your Majesty," Kat said as she bowed slightly. "Oolada was the one who was brave today and that evening."

"I can always count on Oolada not only for bravery but also for compassion." Merryk's eyes lingered on Oolada as he spoke. "But where are my manners? Please sit."

The attendants appeared to pull the chairs out for all to be seated.

Before anyone else could speak, Beth inserted, "Your Majesty, I fear for Lady Katalynn's safety being alone in the manor. Her father had apartments near the castle which became yours upon his death. Perhaps you could allow her to use them until she can acquire security."

"Absolutely, they are yours," Merryk replied. "Lady Katalynn, instruct your butler, Swenson, to prepare them at once. Beth, what a good idea. How very kind of you to think of it."

Kat turned to look at Oolada, shaking her head in disgust.

Later in the afternoon, Chancellor Goldblatt knocked on the door of Queen Amanda's suites.

"Enter," Queen Amanda said. "Good afternoon, Chancellor."

"Good afternoon, Your Majesty." Goldblatt nodded his head.

"If you would leave us for a few moments." the queen instructed her ladies. When they had departed the room, the queen began. "I understand my son acquitted himself well this morning."

"I thought so. How did you hear?"

"The Duchess of Crescent stopped by after the hearing. She and Lady Elizabeth were in attendance to provide support for Lady Katalynn. She was waiting while her daughter, Katalynn, and Oolada had lunch with the king."

"What was her impression of the king?"

"She thought he had done a masterful job of convincing everyone the earl and his son intended harm to Katalynn and were intent on stealing the horses. Their reputation will sink lower—even though I do not know how. Also, she was quite impressed by the way the king reprimanded the earl but held up the rights of other nobles. A fine line which my son appears to have negotiated perfectly. Did you assist him in his decision?"

"No, this was all Merryk. As I told you, he has excellent intuition and a practical understanding of complex situations. You will also be proud of the way he handled the earl in private. After the hearing, he took the earl into the anteroom and told him Oolada had spared his life twice; once by stopping his son, and later by arguing for leniency for their actions. Merryk told him that his first inclination was to hang him, and he was lucky to be walking out of the castle with his life. He added the earl would not be so lucky again."

"I do not know which part of that story pleases me the most. My son acting like the king he is, or Oolada showing compassion even though she is a warrior."

"Speaking of Oolada, how has your instruction gone?" Goldblatt asked.

"She has a unique ability to deal with details. Once we agreed on the outline for the ball, she has effectively directed others to complete them. The only shortcoming is she has never been to a ball and does not understand the need for much of the elegance. However, the bigger issue is she does not think she is worthy to attend, much less to direct the event. It is hard for me to envision her as queen when she does not feel worthy. How can she support the king, particularly if Merryk does not want to act like a king?"

"Maybe by tempering his wrath with compassion," Goldblatt offered.

"Yes, Merryk hanging the earl would have been a disaster."

CHAPTER 59

FRIENDS — FAR & NEAR

T he deep blue sky was a stark contrast to the pillows of snow which surrounded Crag d'Zoo. The valley of Zoo was completely immersed in a sea of snow which splashed up against the mountains and trees. Only the trails for the messengers and hunters marred the pristine blanket of white. Helga stood in her fur coat, staring at the scenery. She did not have it tightly wrapped around her. The sunlight made things seem warmer than the actual air. At least, it felt that way until the wind blew.

Winter is always so beautiful. Oolada loves this time of year. Her thoughts of Oolada triggered a flash of insight. Instantly, Helga was far to the south; in the Capital City within Merryk's castle. *Oolada and Merryk are both physically safe, but conflict surrounds them. Much is changing.*

"Gaspar," Helga called as she entered the council chamber. Gaspar was in his big chair in front of the fire. As he often did in the afternoon, he had drifted off. "Sleeping again," Helga said with fake mockery.

"Just resting my eyes. Besides, there is not much to do but wait for spring," Gaspar replied.

"Perhaps I should make a list of projects for you. You know, all the things you put off when the weather was warm, because you were too busy."

Gaspar just shook his head. This was an argument he would not win. "What made you interrupt my thoughts?"

"Things are in motion in the south."

"Are Oolada and Merryk all right?"

"Yes. Physically, they are fine, but there is much confusion and conflict around them. Oolada was involved in an attack. She was not the target, but fate placed her in its path."

"Where was Merryk?" Gasper asked with concern.

"I think Oolada had traveled without him. When he heard of the attack, he was furious. Oolada kept him from doing something rash. The way I do for you."

"Taking a nap is not rash," Gaspar said.

Now it was Helga's turn to ignore Gaspar. "There are new people: some for Merryk and others for Oolada. The challenges are political and emotional."

"I expected one or more of the nobles would attempt to challenge Merryk, to see if he was strong enough to be king. But I had not thought it would come so soon."

"Merryk has successfully managed that challenge. Now he faces an onslaught of women. The contest for his heart and the Inland Queen is in full force. I worry Oolada still does not understand the nature of the competition. People pretending to be her friend pose the greatest threat. Tara and Yvette are the only women Oolada had as models, but they were both genuine friends."

"I should have asked you to stay with her," Gaspar said.

"You know I could not stay. But she is not alone. I feel Queen Amanda and another woman are genuine friends. In any event, Oolada must find the way to her destiny alone. All we can do is watch."

———— ❈ ————

In little more than a day, Swenson had prepared the apartments for Lady Katalynn.

"These are beautiful rooms," Oolada said as the two entered the apartment.

"Thank you. My mother decorated them before her death. Keeping them up was the only concession my father ever gave to her memory. Everything in the manor which reminded him of her was removed. Even then, he made every excuse not to use the apartments. I do not know why he did not get rid of them. Now, however, I am glad he did not. Thank you again for thinking to ask the king to allow me to use them."

Oolada just shrugged. "But it was Beth who asked the king, not me."

Kat sat on the sofa. "I wanted to talk to you about Beth. She is my cousin and I love her dearly, but she can be very selfish. We both know the only reason she asked was because you said the king would agree. She knew the request was of low risk and potentially high reward. She got what she wanted: the king's compliment and attention."

"That is all right," Oolada said.

"No, it is not. Oolada, the king must have an Inland Queen. He literally cannot be king without one. The law says he must have a queen within the year, or the throne passes to someone else. Beth knows this. She wants to be the queen and will do whatever she can to make this happen. Taking your idea as her own is nothing to her. Do you not want to be queen?"

"Merryk will have to do what is necessary for him to remain king. I am not a suitable choice for queen."

"Are you willing to let Beth become the queen, and then make sure you never see him again? Because that is what she will do. She could never allow you to be near him. She sees, even if you do not, how the king looks at you;

how he defends you. His love is the only thing you need to be a suitable queen."

"But he does not love me," Oolada said as she felt her eyes welling with tears.

"Are you so sure? I know you love him."

"He is my friend, my best friend." Oolada protested.

Kat shook her head in frustration. "You have spent so much time with men, as a warrior, you do not recognize your own feelings."

Oolada slumped into the chair and began to cry in earnest. "He must be king, but I could not bear to go without seeing him again."

"Then you need to fight to stay next to him. We can begin by making you look like a queen. Tomorrow, we call in the dressmaker. You need something special for your first ball."

CHAPTER 60

DRESSES

"Oolada, I believe you have everything in good order for the ball," Queen Amanda said. "I am proud of the work you have done. You should be very proud of yourself."

"Thank you, Your Majesty. I had a lot of help. The staff was amazing," Oolada said.

"How is your dress coming?"

"Katalynn and I are going to the dressmaker this afternoon for the final fittings. She is so busy; she could not come to us."

"Excellent." Queen Amanda took a sip of tea. "Oolada, you have been spending a lot of time with Lady Ressett and Lady Crescent. Although I do not share the opinion of others, you need to be aware, as the daughter of a traitor, Lady Ressett's position in the court has been greatly reduced. Be careful that you do not have her stigma attached to you."

"She has been a good friend to me, more so than Lady Crescent, who I am sure is well liked by all."

"Why do you say that about Lady Crescent?"

"Beth is sometimes friendly and other times acts as if she is better than Katalynn and me."

"What do you mean?" the queen asked.

"After the trial, King Merryk asked the three of us to join him for lunch. When Bowen opened the door, I had the distinct impression Beth bumped into me so she could enter the room first. Then she took credit for my idea of getting Kat a place to stay in the city. She also makes comments, small but hurtful, about my understanding of my place. In contrast, Kat has encouraged me. Perhaps it is just that Kat and I are both without parents."

Queen Amanda reached across the table to grasp Oolada's hand. "First and most important, I hope you know you can always come to me. No matter what my son ultimately does, I consider you family."

"Thank you. You have been so nice to me. I can never thank you enough." Oolada's eyes were moist with emotion.

"Second, your judgment of Lady Crescent is not wrong. She wants to be queen. She will do anything to improve her chances. You must not let her take credit for your ideas." The queen's tone was insistent. "You have as good a chance to be queen as she does—better, actually."

"My response has always been to reject the idea, but Kat told me an Inland Queen, like Lady Crescent, would not allow me near Merryk. I could not bear not seeing him."

"Does this mean you would like to be the next queen?"

"No, I still do not want to be queen. But I want less to be denied contact with Merryk."

Queen Amanda rocked back in her chair with a slight chuckle. "You have yourself in an interesting position. The only way to stay near Merryk is to become what you do not want—queen. You would like to be his wife, true?"

"He needs more than just a wife. He needs someone who understands this environment. I do not."

Queen Amanda's voice became measured and soft. "Did you ever consider he has Chancellor Goldblatt, Lord Commander Bellows, and me to help him with this environment? What he does not have is someone to help him with his heart."

With only a week to go before the Winter Ball, the dressmaker's shop filled with patrons coming and going. All the noble families recognized *Omorfo Forema*. For almost one hundred years, the same family—mother to daughter—had designed and delivered gowns for critical events: balls, weddings, and coronations. The sudden decision to hold the Winter Ball had thrown their orderly processes into disarray. Under normal circumstances, the dressmakers went to the patron, but in this year's rush, the patrons came to them.

Omorfo Forema had a sitting area, multiple small dressing rooms, and a large area in the rear for the actual dressmaking. Sophia Weirshem, daughter of the Earl of Weirshem and Anna Tallon, daughter of Lord Tallon, entered the outside sitting area, chattering about their fittings.

"I hear the king went riding with Lady Zoo, again," Sophia said. Sophia, the oldest daughter of the earl, was a pretty, dark-haired woman in her late teens.

"Lady Crescent said Lady Zoo only rides with the king as an extra bodyguard, not as a potential wife. She also said Lady Zoo is as hard as a rock and never smiles."

"No man would want a woman for a wife who is as hard as a rock and just as cold," Sophia said.

"Father said all the Blue-and-White Mountain Clans are barbarians and the only reason we have this king is because of their military support," Anna added.

"Well, this king needs a wife and a queen. I really do not care if my father likes him. I am going to be sure the king knows I am very soft and very warm."

"I think I could get used to a broad chest and deep blue eyes," Anna added with a giggle. "I also would not mind being queen."

"The only problem is every woman in the kingdom feels the same way," Sophia said. "But it is good to know that 'the rock from the north' does not have a chance."

The curtains of one of the dressing rooms slid open. The woman inside stepped out. She was wearing a magnificent red dress which hung gently on her shoulders then flowed to the floor in a graceful sweep.

"What a beautiful dress. The king will notice you for sure," Anna said.

"Thank you, I do like it."

A second woman pushed her curtain back. She also wore a new dress. This one was a deep green.

"Kat, your dress is beautiful," the first lady said.

"Thank you," Kat answered. "But you are the one that has been transformed. I am sure you agree?" Kat said as she turned to Anna and Sophia. "Lady Zoo looks nothing like the cold, stone-hard barbarian you described. And I agree with you. The king will notice her."

Chapter 61

WINTER BALL

"Jamas," King Merryk yelled. "Do I really have to wear this crown?"

The head butler had become accustomed to the seeming anger of the king. He knew it was frustration, not rage. In a calm voice, he replied, "Yes, Your Majesty. It is expected for events like this. The good news is this is the light one."

"Oh, good news. It could have been worse."

Jamas simply smiled at the king.

"Are you sure you have never met Smallfolks? The two of you are like peas in a pod."

"Now, Your Majesty, you are simply nervous about all the attention you will receive this evening. You can make it subside if you just pick an Inland Queen."

"I was wrong about you. You are more like Goldblatt."

"Both, I take as a compliment," Jamas replied in his usual unflappable voice.

"Jamas, it's just all the focus on the Inland Queen is keeping me from my proper duties. People don't want to talk about schools or roads, just queens."

"Your Majesty must remember, the Inland Queen represents the stability of the kingdom, the prospects for an heir, the continuation of the throne. All are of critical importance to the people."

"Intellectually I understand. It's just..." Merryk's voice trailed off.

Now Jamas' voice softened. "It is just that you remember your Outland Queen."

"Yes," Merryk said. "This is just the sort of evening she would have loved. One year ago, she held a fete at the Teardrop on Christmas Eve to brighten everyone's spirits. I don't know how this will ever compare."

"It is not intended to be a comparison. It is a separate event, in a new place and time. I know she would want you to enjoy it. She would also want you to keep open eyes and, perhaps, an open heart for someone special."

Merryk waited outside the ballroom for Queen Amanda to arrive. "You certainly look lovely this evening," Merryk said to the queen.

"Thank you. I see Jamas convinced you to wear the crown," Queen Amanda said with a smile.

"He told me it was the light one."

"It is, and I must say, you wear it well. Shall we?"

The two turned to enter the ballroom. They specifically designed the ballroom for events like this. The walls were covered with polished metal to reflect the light from the multitude of candles. Large chandeliers hung from the ceiling, equally spaced down the length of the room. Separate chandeliers on the individual tables which lined the walls of the room added sparkle. All the seating was assigned, with careful attention to status and title of those present.

Dark green garlands of holly and bright red berries circled the columns along the sides of the room. Small white birch trees without leaves stood in groups as a hint of the winter which lay outside. The orchestra played gentle music to add to the mood.

As the king and queen stepped through the door, the Lord Chamberlain struck his staff and announced their entrance. "Their Majesties King Merryk Raymouth and Queen Mother Amanda Raymouth. The entire entourage stood and bowed as they passed through the room to their table at the far end.

"Everything is beautiful," Merryk said to Queen Amanda.

"We have Lady Zoo to thank," the queen replied.

The king and queen mother had barely found their seats when a bold Lady Elizabeth stepped forward. "Excuse me, Your Majesty. The ball cannot begin until you start the first dance."

"I understand, Lady Elizabeth, but the first dance should go to my mother. But I would be honored if you would accept the second."

"Thank you, Your Majesty," Lady Elizabeth smiled with obvious pride.

"Mother, I am told the ball will not begin until we dance. Shall we?" Merryk asked.

"Actually, I would prefer to watch this evening. But I would suggest, as thanks for her efforts in arranging all of this, you give the first dance to Lady Zoo." The queen's voice was loud enough to be heard by most.

"Excellent idea. Where is Lady Zoo?" the king asked.

One side of the room parted to allow a beautiful, dark-haired woman in a sweeping red dress to pass. "I am here, Your Majesty," Oolada answered in a firm voice which hid her internal shaking.

"May I have the honor of the first dance?" Merryk's eyes had not left Oolada since she stepped forward.

Oolada nodded.

The orchestra began a simple waltz. Merryk took Oolada's hand and led her to the center of the room. She bowed and extended her arms to Merryk.

"You are absolutely breathtaking," Merryk said to Oolada as he swept her across the floor.

"You look handsome yourself," Oolada answered with confidence from being close to Merryk. "Your mother loaned me her tiara. I must admit, it feels a little excessive."

"You wear the tiara beautifully. However, I understand what you mean. This crown is not particularly comfortable."

"Perhaps it would have been better without it," Oolada said.

"No. I would change nothing about you. You are perfect." Merryk locked his gaze on Oolada as though he were seeing her for the first time.

———

Across the room, a steely eyed Lady Elizabeth forced a smile as she waited for her dance with the king. *What just happened? This was supposed to be my dance. Where did she get that dress? She was a big enough problem dressed in deerskins and a tunic, but now dressed as a lady, Merryk cannot keep his eyes off her. If I let him choose, she will be the next Inland Queen. No, I must find a way to get her to remove herself from his choice.*

———

As the evening wore on, the guests divided themselves into groups. This sorting process left Oolada and Katalynn standing alone.

"You should go to Beth," Kat said. "Everyone is avoiding me. I am sure there are men who would ask you to dance."

"I am all right staying with you. Besides, they would only ask because I am close to the king."

"Or they would ask because you are *beautiful*," Kat's voice emphasized the last word.

"It must be because of the queen's tiara."

"Yes, that is it. Men choose women to dance because of their hair ornaments."

"Stop it! I have already danced with the only man I wanted," Oolada said.

"Speaking of men, who is the young officer talking with the king?"

"That is just Captain Johnny Bellows. He is the captain of the RS *Broadsword*. We met in the Teardrop after the attack by the Council of Justice."

"Just Johnny Bellows! He is Jonathan Bellows, the son of Lord Commander Bellows, nephew to Lord Bellows and the only grandson of the Grand Duke. After the king, he is the most eligible bachelor in the kingdom. He has been at sea for most of his adult life and, as a result, seldom comes to events like this. I am not sure I have seen him since we were children."

"He is really nice. Would you like to meet him?" Oolada offered.

"Oh, no. I could not. I am not suitable for a man such as he."

"Suitable? You have been listening to me too much or not listening to what you have been telling me. He will not care about your father's crime. If he likes you, it will be enough. Now come on." Oolada grabbed Kat's hand and virtually drug her across the room.

"Johnny."

"Oolada, you look fantastic," Johnny said as he gave her a kiss on the cheek. "It is good to see you again. My father has kept me at sea the last month. Please forgive me for not being here. I was so sorry to hear about Queen Tara. I know how close the two of you were."

"Thank you, I do miss her. But where are my manners? Johnny, I would like to introduce Lady Ressett."

Johnny turned to look at Kat as his face broke into a soft smile. "Lady Ressett, I am pleased to meet you. Your dress is beautiful. It reminds me of the deep green of the sea, as do your eyes."

"Why do I think you might say that to every lady you meet?" Kat replied. She also had a broad smile on her face. "I have heard stories about sailors."

"Stories? I cannot imagine what you mean. Perhaps if you allowed me a dance, we could discuss them." Without waiting for a reply, Johnny took Kat's hand, and the two disappeared onto the dance floor for the rest of the evening.

"Oolada, join me," Queen Amanda said from her table. "Why are you not dancing?"

"I have danced with the man I wanted."

"I understand," the queen said. "Your dress is as beautiful as you are."

"Thank you, Your Majesty. I think even Merryk liked it, even though he did ask me where I hid my knife."

"He did not!" the queen said in mock surprise. "What did you tell him?"

"I told him he would have to use his imagination."

"Perfect."

The evening wore on. Merryk had sat out only a couple of dances to have some water and a small snack. Then he was pulled again to the floor by the daughter of another nobleman. Finally, it looked like everyone was becoming tired.

Lady Elizabeth appeared again. "Your Majesty, the evening is about to end. It is time for the last dance."

"What an excellent idea. Thank you, Lady Elizabeth." Merryk immediately turned his back on Lady Elizabeth and moved into the room, searching for someone special.

"Oolada, I have been looking for you. It's time for the last dance of the evening and I wanted it to be with the most beautiful woman at the ball."

CHAPTER 62

JOY & ANGER

Oolada and Kat made their way back to Oolada's apartments in the castle. After the maids had helped with their dresses, they returned to the fire burning in the sitting room.

"I think I might get used to balls," Oolada said with a broad smile on her face.

"I have been to many," Kat replied. "But never one as magnificent as this one."

"Thank you for staying the night. I know I should be tired, but I have so many thoughts swimming in my head." Oolada said. "I am sorry that Beth could not join us."

"I am not. Beth would not have been any fun this evening."

"Why do you say that?"

"The evening did not go as she had planned. She wanted the first dance with the king, but you got it. I know she also wanted the last dance, but you got it. She wanted the evening to solidify her position as most likely to be the next queen. Now you hold that position," Kat explained.

"It was just two dances. They cannot be that meaningful."

"The two most important dances of the evening. My guess is Beth is furious," Kat said.

"In that case, I am glad she did not come, because I do not want this feeling to end. I feel like I am floating. I probably drank too much wine."

"The only thing you are filled with is love for the king."

Oolada sank further into the sofa. "I know. I just cannot stop."

"Why would you ever want to? He is perfect; not only as a man, but perfect for you. The only one who has not seen this is you."

"Oh, I have seen it, but I did not want to recognize it. I still do not know how he could choose me. But enough about me. Tell me everything about Captain Johnny Bellows."

Now it was Kat's turn to glow. "We danced and danced; near the end, we walked to the balcony and looked at the moon reflected on the water. It was beautiful, although cold; so, he gave me his coat. We talked about everything—the sea, horses, even the attack. He told me if I was bothered again, I could come to him, and he would take care of it. I believe him. His arms are amazingly strong. We came back in time for the last dance. I did not want the evening to end. I did not want to say good night."

"I think neither of us wanted the ball to end."

Beth sat in silence as she rode with her father and mother back to their winter house. After she settled the duke, Lady Crescent went to see her daughter.

Her gentle knock on Beth's door was immediately answered. "Come in."

The room was in disarray, pillows had been tossed from the sofas and a footstool was turned over. "I thought you would still be awake."

"I could not sleep," Beth said. "There are too many things running through my head. What a terrible evening."

"All caused by watching the king slip away from you?" Lady Crescent asked.

"Yes, things did not go well. I had mustered my courage to ask for the first dance, but when the king thought he should ask Queen Amanda, I understood. When the queen shifted the privilege to Oolada, I understood. But when I reminded him of the last dance and he turned his back on me to go find Oolada, it just seemed like a rejection."

"I told you they were just allies, but now I have seen the way he looks at her. I think I was wrong. I must say, however, she was exquisite this evening."

Beth sighed. "Unfortunately, I agree. She was beautiful. The problem is in deerskin pants and tunics, she is equally beautiful, particularly to him. When she is around the king, it is almost impossible to get his attention. The only thing which gives me hope is she has said many times she does not want to be queen."

"Is it possible she is just trying to hide her desires from others?"

"I do not think so. The one thing about Oolada is she is extremely honest. I believe she truly does not want to be queen, but I also believe she is completely in love with the king."

"So, we have a quandary. She is in love with the king and does not want to be queen, you want to be queen and do not love the king."

"I am sure we would grow fond of each other over time," Beth said. "I just need to move Oolada aside and make the king see the advantages for the throne in selecting me."

"Perhaps you should focus not on changing the king's mind, but on changing Oolada's. Find a way to use her love of the king against her."

Beth nodded.

Lady Crescent wrapped her arms around her daughter. "But let me caution you, do not go to an extreme which will alienate the king. The Raymouths have supported our family for over four hundred years. Your father's position must not be endangered.

"In the end, I want you to find someone to love, not just to be fond of. As a family, we have all we could want and more. Sacrificing your happiness is not worth the title *queen*. So be very cautious in how you treat Lady Zoo and remember, she could end up being the queen."

CHAPTER 63

NOBLE

The Pipe and Pint was scarcely populated. Only a few patrons were spread around the oversized salon. Lord Tallon sat in a large leather chair sipping a glass of sherry, staring out the window at the gray of an unremarkable January day.

The maître d' opened the large doors to allow a clearly frustrated Earl of Weirshem to enter. The earl continued to brush droplets of rain from his jacket as he moved toward Tallon.

"You look like you were caught in the rain," Tallon said. "You need a drink of sherry."

"Make it wine," Weirshem answered. "I have been caught in more than the rain. Our devil of a king is bent on destroying me."

"I am sure you are exaggerating. We both know if he wanted you dead, you would be."

"They said he was ruthless, but now I see he is as cruel as his brother and uncle."

"What can you possibly mean?" Tallon asked.

"As I told you late last year, stray horses wandered onto my lands. I gathered them and sought to sell them quickly to avoid having to feed them. I sold them in small lots to what I thought were multiple purchasers at a discounted price."

"Yes," a now curious Tallon answered.

"Well, all the purchasers were, in fact, *one*—Masterroff acting as the agent for the king.

Tallon laughed out loud. "You sold him his own horses. How sweet!"

"No. The king somehow found out I had his horses. He sent his range master and a squad of military to locate them. At the hearing, the king told me if the horses were found in the hands of another, whoever it was, regardless of title, they would be hung."

"Oh, my. What did you do?"

"I had to purchase one hundred horses on the open market."

"Which means from Masterroff," Tallon said.

"Yes, and because of the number and the immediate need, the price was at a premium. When all was done, it cost an extra one hundred a horse over market, just not to be hung. In addition, Masterroff refused to extend credit, which required me to sell grain at an additional loss."

"My dear earl, you need something more than wine," Tallon said in sympathy. "How about whiskey and lunch?"

After the meal, Tallon returned to his chair with another sherry. "You know, we may have underestimated our young king. He intended his purchase not only to make money but also to send a very distinct message—he knew exactly what you had done. It was sent in a way you felt the pain, but others would not see it inflicted. But it did not destroy you. Why I wonder?"

"He was trying to tell me he has no respect for nobility. At the hearing, he claimed to give me the benefit of the doubt. Then he had Lady Katalynn be the one not to honor her father's word. What else could I expect from the daughter of a traitor?" Weirshem was again agitated.

"You need to remember, the Duke of Ressett was our friend, and we agreed with him in his efforts to rid us of the inland bastard. Attacking the girl for a few horses, regardless of how much they were worth, was foolish. I cannot support you in that."

"It was without risk until the clan woman appeared with her guard."

Tallon shook his head from side to side. "You must admit Lady Zoo is quite remarkable. I know it was not my son that was beaten, but from all reports, he was lucky she did not kill him. Those on the wall, the day that Merryk fought his brother, say she fought the redheaded assassin standing back-to-back with the king. Her combat was as intense as any they had ever seen. In addition, they credited her with planning the Winter Ball, which was a great success. I guess the nobility of the ZooWalt runs through her."

"She may have the blood of her grandfather, but she is still a barbarian. One which, if my women are to be believed, has an excellent opportunity of being our next queen."

Lord Tallon sipped his drink. "Having a queen who does not understand our structure of nobility could be a significant problem. I would prefer someone like Lady Crescent or even Lady Katalynn. Both would understand respect for the nobles. Of course, it would be best if it was one of our daughters."

"Do you really think they would even get a reasonable chance?"

"They or someone like them if pressure came from more than just us. We need to get other members of the nobility to express their concerns about Lady Zoo. But who?"

"It will need to be more than Crescent. He will not listen to us and would not consider pressuring the king."

Tallon took another sip of his sherry. "Not Crescent or Bellweather, they are both too close to the throne." Tallon looked out the window for a moment in thought. "It needs to be someone with power, but who seldom uses it—like Blountsmyth."

"Blountsmyth certainly has the clout, with his lands and a son who is the Master of Revenue. However, the duke has never been political."

"But he has always been noble," Tallon said with a nod of his head. "Distinctively noble, and he is the oldest of the outland houses. A threat to his way of life by introducing the clans might make him act. He does not need to agree with us. He only needs to question her ability to be queen. It will cloud what might seem a simple selection. Goldblatt will understand the political implications. It could create an opportunity for others."

"Yes, but how would we approach him?" Weirshem asked.

"My father is from the same generation as Blountsmyth. He could talk to him about how things are changing too fast, the way King Merryk is turning his back on our traditions. He could suggest the selection of the clan woman would be a blow to nobility. Another queen might not be better, but if she were noble, we would at least have a place for appeal," Tallon said.

"Both of our daughters need to be part of the selection process," Weirshem said. "I will ask my wife to go directly to Queen Amanda. The king may not want a wife, but the queen will know he needs one. The queen will see the wisdom in her being from a noble house."

CHAPTER 64

UPDATE

A month had passed since the winter ball. The slow monotony of normal life had replaced the frenzied activity of preparation. Chancellor Goldblatt took the opportunity of a quiet afternoon to visit Queen Amanda. He found her in her sitting room in front of a warm fire.

"Good afternoon, Your Majesty."

"Good afternoon, Chancellor. I assume you want an update on our efforts since the ball. Our winter event had two objectives: first to introduce Merryk to as many young ladies as possible, and second to introduce Lady Zoo to the court. One went extremely well. The other has had mixed results." The queen paused, waiting for Goldblatt's response.

"I have the distinct feeling you enjoy letting me hang before you release critical information."

"I must admit a small joy in making you wait," Queen Amanda said with a soft chuckle. "The quick answer is Lady Zoo did a fantastic job, not only in organizing the ball but also in presenting herself. She received compliments from many, even from a few who had no reason to do so. I am sure you will agree she looked every bit a queen."

"Yes, Oolada was beautiful. I think it surprised many how gracious and poised she was." Goldblatt said in concurrence. "Although I am not sure all appreciated her beauty and skills. Lady Elizabeth did not gain the attention she had hoped."

"Lady Elizabeth found herself in the position of being just another of the group, not a position she relishes. I expect her to become more aggressive in seeking Merryk's attention."

"Which brings us to Merryk. Do your comments mean we failed?" Goldblatt asked.

"Not at all. We succeeded, but not as we intended. Merryk's attentions to Oolada has everyone believing he has made the selection."

"I wish it was. This process is taking up an unbelievable amount of time."

"And it will take more," the queen inserted. "I am receiving requests to see if I can get Merryk to invite others to go on rides or to dinner. The Duchess of Blountsmyth has politely asked if I might introduce her granddaughter to the king. She and the duke never get involved in the politics of court."

"I did not know Blountsmyth had a granddaughter."

"Lady Jane. She is just fifteen."

"We both know Merryk will consider her a child."

"Child or not, he needs to reach out with some kind of invitation." Queen Amanda rose from her chair and moved to the fireplace. "There is a bigger issue growing. The Earl of Weirshem and Lord Tallon have been rallying concerns about Merryk. What they are saying is he has a lack of respect for the nobles. They were pointing to Merryk not having a wife and his attentions to Oolada as proof of their fears. The lack of progress in seeking a wife is a rejection of our laws. In addition, they would deem his selection of Oolada a rejection of their nobility."

"Merryk is meeting with other women, and Lady Zoo is every bit as noble as others," Goldblatt snapped.

"I agree with you," Amanda said calmly. "But they do not want to give him time to make his decision. To them, it is just a wife. What could be so hard?"

"You and I know they will not push Merryk into a marriage just to please the nobles," Goldblatt said.

"Perhaps they know Merryk would abandon his throne rather than be forced to marry someone he does not love."

Goldblatt's hand moved to rub the bridge between his eyes as to appease an oncoming headache. "I think I liked it better when all we needed to worry about were matters of state and not matters of the heart."

"You know full well Geoffrey, when it comes to the king, everything is a matter of state."

"With enemies and nation states, I do not have to worry about emotion." Goldblatt said, shaking his head. "How am I going to tell him he needs to spend more time with other women and not so much with Oolada?"

CHAPTER 65

LADY JANE

Having finished his morning exercises, Merryk turned a corner to the corridor leading to the stables. A small-framed girl with light blonde hair in riding attire approached from the opposite direction. A look of relief crossed her face as she saw Merryk.

"Sir, I am glad to see you. I am so lost! I am supposed to be going to the stables for a ride, but somehow, I got turned around. Can you help me?"

"Certainly, I'm headed that way myself."

"Thank you. I am Jane, granddaughter of the Duke of Blountsmyth."

"Nice to meet you, Lady Jane. I am Merryk."

"Just Jane, please, the whole 'Lady' thing reminds me of my mother and grandmother, and we do not always get along. I was supposed to go for a ride with the king. I am so nervous. I do not even like horses. Do you know the king?"

"Yes," Merryk concealed his smile.

"They say the king is really tall. You are tall. Is the king taller than you?"

"No, about the same."

"Good, I do not know what I would do if he were taller than you. Not that I dislike tall people, but when you are short like me, it is hard to see their faces. They say he is good looking for a king. Mother and grandmother said I need to make a good impression. Grandfather said, 'just be yourself.' Mother said under no circumstances am I supposed to 'be myself.' She thinks I am too outspoken. I told her if we came to the Capital City more often, maybe I would learn to throttle my tongue. In any event, I am supposed to make a good impression."

"So, you want to be the queen?"

Jane shook her head violently. "Heavens, no! I just turned fifteen. I have hundreds of things I want to do before I marry. Mother said it is a matter of family honor I be considered. 'We have just as good a chance as any,' she said. Ha, that is a joke. The king would be daft to choose me. My grandfather said to look at this as an experience. Secretly, he told me there was plenty of time to marry. But I am not supposed to tell mother or grandmother. My grandfather is the best."

"Your grandfather sounds like a wise man. Perhaps I will get to meet him sometime."

"I hope so. I know you would like him. Everybody does."

"Well, we are in the stables. Where were you to meet the king?"

"Something about there would be a group."

"Are you sure you were supposed to be here today and not Wednesday?"

"Originally it was Wednesday, but we got a note changing it to today. I now wonder if the note was a mistake. That would explain why no one else is here. It is just as well. I really dislike horses, but I will probably be required to come back again tomorrow."

"While you are here, I want you to meet my horse, Maverick," Merryk said as he pointed toward a black stallion. "Maverick, this is Lady Jane, granddaughter of the Duke of Blountsmyth. Bella, this is Lady Jane." Maverick and Bella had both poked their heads over their stable walls as the two approached. Maverick nodded his head in acknowledgement.

"Just Jane, please," she replied to the horses.

"You should pat him on the neck," Merryk said.

"The truth is, I am afraid of horses," Lady Jane admitted.

"If you are afraid of horses, why did you agree to go on a ride with the king?"

"I did not, but my mother did. So here I am."

"I have an idea." Merryk turned and walked over to the stable hand. Returning, he said, "Why don't we use this time for you to get a little more comfortable with horses?" Merryk opened the stall doors to both Maverick and Bella. "We're going to the arena."

With no further directions, the two horses moved out of their stalls and down the aisle toward the open arena.

"Will they run away?" Jane asked.

"Not a chance," Merryk replied. "Come with me."

The arena was a large, covered area at the end of the stable, which allowed for exercise without having to brave the outdoor weather. The stable hand Merryk had spoken to was waiting with a small mare saddled and ready to ride.

"Jane, this is Sally. She's a little older and quite gentle. I want you to ride her." Both Maverick and Bella stood by Merryk as he pointed towards Sally.

"I really am afraid of horses, even gentle ones," Jane said.

"But I insist you be brave," Merryk said. Maverick bobbed his head in agreement.

"What if she runs away with me on her back?"

"Maverick and Bella will not allow that to happen." Again, Maverick bobbed his head in agreement.

Merryk gave Jane a boost into the saddle. Sally barely moved. "Now take the reins and go in a little circle. Nothing bad will happen."

Jane gave Sally a little push with her legs and the horse walked in the slow circle around the arena. Maverick and Bella followed.

"Look at you, you're riding a horse," Merryk said, his face covered with a broad smile.

"Yes, I am," Jane replied with pride.

"I think you need a little more experience with horses before you go on a ride with the king. I also think you need a horse of your own; one as gentle as Sally."

"We have horses, but only the men ride them," Jane said. "But I will ask."

Now Jane's face scrunched up. "What am I going to tell my mother and grandmother? We came on the wrong day. I will have to come back tomorrow."

"Why don't you allow me to speak with your mother and grandmother? Perhaps they could have lunch with us. Where are they now?"

"They are waiting in the throne room. It was empty. We do not come to the Capital City often, so we did not know where we were supposed to wait," Jane answered.

A blue-cloaked Royal Guard stepped into the arena. "Your Majesty, I have been looking for you."

"Bowen, may I introduce Lady Jane Blountsmyth? She has been with me this morning. Please locate her mother and grandmother, who are in the throne room, and ask them if they would like to join Lady Jane and I for lunch."

"Yes, Your Majesty," Bowen replied.

Jane's eyes grew enormous. "You are the king."

"Yes, I am sorry for the deception, but people don't speak openly if they know that I'm the king. I appreciated your candor."

"Oh, great. I cannot remember what I said. I know it was bad. Please, do not think badly of my family. Please, do not tell my mother."

Merryk gently grabbed Jane by her shoulders. "You spoke as one friend to another. You spoke your heart and the truth. There is no greater honor that can be shared. You were every bit noble and represented your family with dignity. I am pleased to say you, Lady Jane, are my friend."

Queen Amanda, with her guards in tow, made their way to the throne room. Two people sat in one row of the otherwise empty room.

"Duchess and Lady Blountsmyth, why are you two sitting in here? You should have had the guards notify me immediately upon your arrival."

"We did not want to bother you, Your Majesty," the duchess answered.

"Bother me. You seldom come to the Capital City, and you could never bother me. Jocelyn, we have known each other most of our lives. I came right away when I received word from my son. You are to join Merryk, Jane, and I for lunch. Now gather your things." Queen Amanda's last statement was more a command than a request.

"When did you come to the city?"

"We came two days ago," Duchess Jocelyn answered.

"We needed to do some shopping," Lady Blountsmyth added.

"Lady Blountsmyth, you are looking well. I heard you had a bad bought with a fever last fall."

"Yes, I did, but I am much better. Thank you for asking, Your Majesty."

"It is my understanding your daughter, Lady Jane, has been on a ride with the king. I struggle to believe she has grown so quickly. How old is she?"

"My granddaughter is fifteen. Although there are days when she seems to be a child and then the next, she seems all grown."

"I think at that age they are all caught between being a child one moment and an adult the next."

Queen Amanda led the ladies down several halls to a small dining room, one with a table that seated twelve. "I have asked to have lunch in this room. It has a view of the gardens. They are not yet in bloom, but they are leafing out. And I love the light. Shall we have tea while we wait?"

They filled the next hour with light conversation. The duke was fine, although getting older and slowing down. All of Jocelyn's sons were doing well. The duchess made a point of thanking the queen for the appointment of her second son as the Master of Revenue. The queen assured the duchess her son was doing an excellent job and was greatly respected by the king.

The sound of laughter and lively discussion between the king and Lady Jane interrupted the conversation. Lady Jane flowed into the room with a joyful exuberance. "Mother, I have had the most amazing morning." Only after her outburst did she see the queen. Catching herself, she bowed politely. "Excuse me, Your Majesty, I did not see you."

"It is perfectly all right. Please tell us about your morning," the queen inquired.

"Before I do, grandmother and mother, I would like to introduce King Merryk," Jane said with a smile. Both ladies bowed appropriately.

"It is my pleasure to meet the two of you. Jane has told me much about you. I trust the duke is well?"

"He is, Your Majesty. Thank you for asking."

Lady Jane then began. "I met King Merryk, or more correctly, King Merryk found me on the way to the stables. He introduced me to his horse, Maverick, and a beautiful white mare, named Bella. These are two of the most intelligent horses I have ever seen. Rather than a long ride, we went to the indoor arena. The king found a gentle horse for me to ride. It was the first time in my life I have been comfortable on a horse."

"I allowed her to ride Sally. I hope you don't mind," Merryk said to the queen.

"Of course not. I am sure she was happy to have someone ride her. I seldom get to do so."

"Sally is your horse?" Jane asking in amazement.

"Yes, and I am glad you were comfortable riding her."

"Thank you so very much," Jane said, her voice filled with excitement.

The balance of the lunch was uneventful. As the Blountsmyth ladies rose to leave, Jane moved to speak privately to Merryk. "Thank you for allowing my grandmother and mother to join us for lunch. The presence of the queen with you means a great deal. Also, thank you for not divulging the mistake, my being lost, and hating horses."

"Friends would never divulge such secrets," Merryk said confidentially, forcing his face not to burst into a smile.

"Now Jocelyn, you must bring your ladies back to the castle more frequently. You are always welcome, but please let me know when you are here," Queen Amanda said.

"That was a most successful lunch," Queen Amanda said. "The Blountsmyths have been supportive of the throne longer than most can remember."

"Jane is a delightful child. She just turned fifteen, has no interest in marrying anyone, but was pressured by her family to make an impression. Being considered for the Inland Queen was a matter of family honor. I am not sure who I pick is as important as just allowing people to be considered."

"Who you pick is important. The Blountsmyths have deep roots. Offending them would have been costly."

"You know, they were supposed to be here tomorrow. Jane said they received a note under their door this morning. Jane has a fear of horses. Having her attempt a ride would have been an embarrassment to the family," Merryk said.

"Someone gave the Blountsmyths the wrong date? It could have been a disaster, embarrassing for the family and us. Instead, a personal riding lesson and a small lunch with just them has turned into a major victory. They will tell everyone how they were singled out by the king and queen and were treated special, just like the Crescents."

"Thank you for your help, mother. I can't keep meeting all these young women. I can never move forward on more meaningful things until this is behind me. How many more I wonder?"

Queen Amanda reached out and touched Merryk on the arm. "You will know when you have seen enough."

CHAPTER 66

REQUEST

The Duke and Duchess of Crescent sat with Lady Elizabeth around their dining room table. The day had begun its normal rhythm. Servants collected the breakfast dishes and moved to their ordinary duties.

The duchess began to plan her day. "Beth, you and I should go into the city shopping today. I need to look at the new spring fabrics. You will also need some new dresses, particularly since you are going to the castle so frequently. When are you going again?"

"Kat, Oolada and I are riding with the king the day after tomorrow," Beth replied. "I just wish it was only me. I need alone time with the king."

"Excuse me, Your Grace, but this just came from the castle." The head butler handed a note to the duke. "The courier said he would wait for your verbal reply."

The Duke of Crescent read the note. "Tell the courier I would be pleased to join the king tomorrow mid-morning."

"What did it say?" the duchess asked.

"Just that the king wanted me to join him tomorrow morning."

"What do you think it is about?" a very curious Beth asked. "Do you think it might be about a wedding contract?"

"Well, it certainly might be," the duchess said. "You may have all the alone time you want with the king sooner than you think."

"Or it can be the king wants my opinion or help on some matter. The two of you need to lower your expectations. The king will decide on an Inland Queen when he is ready. Right now, I am pleased he would want my opinion on anything. Remember, we are first loyal supporters to the throne, regardless of who he selects as queen."

The next morning, the duke arrived at the castle mid-morning. Two Royal Guardsmen immediately greeted him. "Your Grace, we have been waiting for you. The king sent us to guide you to your meeting."

The men led the duke toward the throne room, but then turned to go down a long corridor to a room which overlooked a garden. Four others were already there when he entered.

"Your Grace, thank you for coming," the king said. "You know the Chancellor and the Lord Commander, but have you met Monsieur Masterroff?"

"No, Your Majesty, we have never met. Although everyone knows Monsieur Masterroff by reputation," the duke said as he extended his hand.

"I am not sure my reputation is the best," Masterroff replied.

"On the contrary. You are known as an excellent businessman who is firm, but fair."

"Thank you, Your Grace, I could not ask for more."

The king motioned for everyone to find a seat at the conference table. "Your Grace, the three men who have joined us are members of my inner circle of advisors: Goldblatt for the political, Bellows for military, and Masterroff for commercial. We meet about once a month to assess the conditions of the kingdom, and to decide where the throne should place its attention and its resources.

"I have asked you to join us today because we have a need for a diplomatic mission. You are aware I struck a peace treaty with Queen Stephanie before she returned home. With the help of Admiral Burat, they have been able to stabilize the queen's throne. However, there are those within her kingdom who question whether it was a mutual peace agreement or a surrender by Queen Stephanie. We need to show support for Queen Stephanie, and open trade relations between our two nations. We have three commercial ships with products ready to deliver our goods and then return with theirs."

"Our support needs to be seen as more than commercial," Bellows added. "We want to send King Michael's flagship, rather than one we seized from Natas or the Council, as an escort for the merchantmen. One of our warships coming into their harbor will show our support, militarily, for the queen."

"My guess is the mission will also require several presentations to explain our support and request for trade," Goldblatt said.

"In addition, the Lord Commander, Masterroff and I have been working on a document to define the rules of the sea," Merryk said. "We have an agreement with Admiral Burat to cooperate on making the seas safer, but there are other rules for things like the payment for freight."

"The commercial rules are as important to trade as the safety of the ships in open waters," Masterroff added.

Merryk continued. "Our aim is to make international trade safe and predictable."

"A most laudable and ambitious goal, Your Majesty," the duke replied. "How can I help?"

"There is more," Merryk added. "The destruction of the Army of Justice effectively stopped all work on the Great Cathedral. I would like to help finish the building. However, I don't know if the Council of Justice or the new Provost will accept my help. I am not willing to just send money, but I have contracted with the engineers who were on the project to pay for them and furnish the materials necessary to finish. If the Council does not want our assistance, I will understand. We will divert the engineers to projects within the High Kingdom.

"In addition, I would like to ask the Council to act as the tribunal for the disputes under the new rules of the sea. I believe their position of neutrality will strengthen the rules and offer consistency in their application. This would encourage other nations to join. But they would be hearing this request for the first time, and I don't know how they will react.

"In short, I need an ambassador to represent the High Kingdom in the court of Queen Stephanie and to the Council of Justice."

"We all believe you are the best man for the job," Chancellor Goldblatt said. "But you are under no obligation to agree."

"I appreciate you have duties with your own estates and may not be able to assist. This is beyond any normal request," Merryk said.

"Are you sure there is not someone younger or better suited for this position?" the duke asked.

"My ambassador needs to have the gray hair of experience to add weight to our proposals. You, my duke, are the embodiment of stability and integrity. A young king with grand plans and a young ambassador would not engender the same confidence as you will. No, you are perfect," Merryk said.

"If you are sure, then I am honored to accept your position. Now, when do I leave?"

CHAPTER 67

A HORSE

Chancellor Goldblatt knocked on Queen Amanda's drawing-room door.

"Please come in, Chancellor. I had hoped you would get my note," Queen Amanda said.

"You said as soon as possible, How can I be of assistance?"

"Two days ago, we almost had a disaster. Luck intervened, and the entire incident turned into a major victory, mostly because of Merryk's nature. The king found a young girl lost on her way to the stables. As he guided her, he discovered she was Lady Jane Blountsmyth on her way for a ride with him. Someone had slipped a note under her door telling her the ride with the king was on Tuesday rather than on Wednesday. We were not expecting the Duchess and Lady Blountsmyth. They were left to wait in an empty throne room while their granddaughter got lost. Earlier, the duchess had sent me a note asking for an opportunity for her granddaughter to meet the king, but there was no specific date. I do not need to tell you what embarrassment would have occurred if Merryk had not found the girl."

"A note under the door. We would never have communicated in such a manner," Goldblatt said.

"Merryk quickly understood the situation and sent word to me. We arranged a tea and a private lunch for the duchess and her daughter. Merryk seemed to take a liking to the girl. He gave her a private riding lesson. She is afraid of horses. Lady Jane was totally struck by him."

"That explains the note to Masterroff. King Merryk has purchased a horse for Lady Jane, one which is particularly gentle. He has asked Masterroff to find and deliver it to the girl. I objected, but Merryk said the only way the girl would ever get over her fear of horses was to have one of her own."

"My son surprises me again. This is a very thoughtful and generous gift. Rather than being irritated by the child, Merryk sought to protect her. He has completely covered any insult the Blountsmyths might have felt."

"Who would benefit from having the king insult the duke?"

"Who indeed?" the queen replied. "The two ladies who were to ride with Lady Jane the next day were Lady Sophia Weirshem and Lady Anna Tallon."

"Both from outland noble families," Goldblatt said. "My sources indicate that the Earl of Weirshem's father visited the Duke of Blountsmyth about ten days ago."

"Which was just before I received a note from the duchess."

"Yes, this appears to be an attempt to drive a wedge between the throne and the House of Blountsmyth. Weirshem is still stinging from the cost of his attempt to sell the king's horses."

"I heard about that incident. Again, Merryk handled it perfectly. The earl felt the pain, but everyone else thought it ended with the hearing."

"I tried to tell the king others would consider the gift of a horse to Lady Jane an early engagement gift. He just laughed. 'She's only fifteen,' was all he said."

"I think it will be fine. The girl will see it as a gift only. Everyone else will have a new front runner and the honor of the Blountsmyths will definitely be enhanced," the queen said.

"The bigger question is, how do we control any future notes under the door?" Goldblatt asked.

"I have instructed the guards to let me know of any noble visitors imme-diately. This will let us react to any who are here. However, getting Merryk to choose a wife would be the easiest and best solution."

"I do not think that will happen anytime soon. The king has learned of flooding in the east, particularly on the lands of Ott and Weirshem. He is organizing a group of engineers to join him on a visit to see the problem 'firsthand.' This is exactly what he did before he built the dams around the Teardrop. The king likes to find ways to 'tame wild rivers' as he says."

"Weirshem will love the king suddenly showing up on his doorstep. Be sure Merryk takes sufficient members of the military. I am not sure all will welcome him."

"The Lord Commander was organizing the forces before Merryk had finished telling us what he intended to do."

"It is too bad the distance is so great. I would love to see the borderline traitor receive a king who has actually come to help him," Queen Amanda said with a chuckle.

"King Merryk also has recruited the Duke of Crescent to act as his ambassador to the court of Queen Stephanie and the Council of Justice," Goldblatt said.

"I understand sending the ambassador to Queen Stephanie, but why to the Council?"

"The king has two purposes. The first is to offer to pay for the comple-tion of the Great Cathedral, and second, to ask the Council to act as the tribunal for his new rules of the sea."

"Is this what he, the Lord Commander, and Masterroff have been work-ing on? The staff has told me there have been several late nights working on a document."

"Yes, I have reviewed it. Merryk's hand is all over it: rules for safety and rules for international commerce."

"Chancellor, is this too ambitious for one as young and unproven as he?"

"I would never consider the king unproven. Queen Stephanie will most certainly agree to the document. It is written in an even-handed manner, and I believe the duke can convince the Council. We all need to stop judging the king by his age. He is going to do amazing things and he will not wait until he is older."

"From a political point of view, asking the Duke of Crescent to act as the throne's ambassador is a great honor. If Merryk does not select Lady Elizabeth, he still has shown great respect for an old noble house. But I think you should advise him to select a wife before he starts any grand projects," Queen Amanda said.

"You are his mother. I will let you do that," Goldblatt said, with no shortage of irony.

CHAPTER 68

GIRLS

Merryk appreciated the earlier rising of the sun, but more light didn't immediately transfer into being warmer. The air still had a nip as he made his way to the top of the tower. The morning clouds rolled in neat lines from the sea to the land. The open space between each line cast the tower in bright light one minute and two minutes later to a light gray. Merryk used this natural timer to increase the speed of his exercise with the sun and to slow it with the gray.

"The sunshine is magnificent," Oolada said as she stepped onto the top of the tower.

"I do like it best," Merryk said as he grabbed a towel to mop his brow. "I was thinking you had forgotten how to get here."

"I remember how to get here. It is just getting away from other people to do so that seems harder every day."

"I had hoped my mother would no longer need your help."

"I think she is transferring more to me each day, rather than less. Do you think she is intentionally trying to keep us apart?"

"She is the queen and I'm not really sure I fully understand how she thinks," Merryk said honestly.

"I would be here every morning if I could," Oolada said. "Today, at least, we get to go for a ride."

"Yes, you and others. In truth, I dread my morning rides. All the idle talk is becoming tiresome."

"Other than you are the king and they are looking for a husband," Oolada said, her tone mocking Merryk.

"You can laugh, but do you really like others being with us today?"

"You know the answer to that question. We can ride, say nothing, and have a marvelous time. Others always want attention. I broke away this morning so I could talk with you before Lady Elizabeth tried to monopolize the discussion."

"She is bad, but you would not have believed Lady Sophia Weirshem. She would have crawled on the saddle with me if I would have allowed it."

"Perhaps you should take your walking stick to beat the women away." This time, Oolada could not mask her huge smile.

"You're funny," Merryk said. "Perhaps I need my walking stick to beat you."

"The king needs to be careful in choosing his opponents." Oolada said. "I understand you gave a pre-engagement gift to Lady Blountsmyth."

"I gave a young girl a horse of her own so she could learn not to be afraid. She has just turned fifteen. She told me she had to go on the ride as a matter of family honor, even though she was afraid of horses. I think Lady Weirshem sent her a note changing the date to insult her and her family."

"Well, everyone is now worried you have chosen. Lady Elizabeth was beside herself. You can expect to be questioned today."

"Thank you for the warning. I think I will describe Lady Jane as a fascinating young woman," Merryk said.

"Delete the word 'young.' It will drive Beth crazy."

"I'm glad you're on my side," Merryk said. "Have dinner with me. We won't invite anyone else. I'm considering a trip to the east and may be gone for a couple of weeks."

"Very well. I will see you in the stables later."

—— ❈ ——

Riding with Oolada, Kat and Beth is at least a ride. Merryk thought to himself. *All of them are excellent riders. We often discuss wide-ranging things, at least when Beth isn't trying to steer the conversation to herself.*

The four were just returning and approaching the eastern gate to the castle. Merryk noticed several young girls near the guard's door. "I wonder why they are here?" he asked, pointing to the girls.

"Probably just beggars looking for a handout," Beth replied quickly.

"Not at all," Kat answered. "They are girls older than twelve forced out of the church's orphanages. When a girl turns twelve, the church tries to find jobs for them in the community. They place many as servants in big houses or, if they are not so lucky, in small inns as attendants to clean the tables or be scullery maids. The intent is to help them learn a skill. In any event, they must leave the orphanage. Some who take the girls have other things in mind. Often, the girls run away in order to be safe. They often come to this guard station seeking protection. Sometimes they find it and sometimes they do not."

"How do you know so much about them?" King Merryk asked.

"My current attendant, Jana, was an orphan. She came to us from the church when she turned twelve. She has been with us for the last six years and is a loyal member of our staff. Unfortunately, her younger sister was not so lucky. When she turned twelve, Jana asked if we would take her into our service. Mother was in favor, but father said we had enough urchins and refused to allow it. Jana's sister was given to an inn, which was, in fact, more like a brothel. Her sister ran away to here. Jana visited her whenever she could. After a while, she said she did not recognize her little sister. Six months later, the girl just disappeared completely."

"That is a terrible story," Oolada said.

"I am afraid it is only one of many. I just wish there was something that could be done," Kat said.

"Kat, you need to stop being so involved in the lives of others," Beth said. "The church did the best with what they had. It is to be expected some will slip through the process and be lost. We have done all we can."

"Lady Elizabeth, we have a duty to find ways to do better," King Merryk's voice was quick and harsh.

"I did not mean any offense, Your Majesty," Beth said, clearly surprised by the king's response. "There are just so many. No one would know where to start."

"We start small and see what works, then we expand," Merryk said. "Please go ahead without me. I want to speak with the Master of the Watch."

The three women continued to the stable.

"What do you think the king is going to do?" Beth asked.

"I do not know. But I know, in the Teardrop, he took in a dozen children as his personal wards to protect them," Oolada said.

"Oolada, tell the king I will do whatever I can to help him," Kat said. "I feel like it is the least I can do to make up for Jana's sister."

"I am sure the king has better things to do than worry about a few lost girls," Beth said.

"You clearly do not know our king," Oolada replied.

CHAPTER 69

DINNER WITH OOLADA

Merryk rose as Oolada entered the room. "You look lovely this evening."

"Thank you, Your Majesty."

"I had them put us away from the regular dining rooms. I thought of the roof of the tower but decided against it because it might be too cold."

"That was a good choice," Oolada replied with a smile.

"I hope this is all right?" Merryk asked.

Oolada surveyed the room. It was higher in the building than the normal dining rooms and afforded a glimpse of the setting sun through its windows. The light from the fireplace illuminated a small table prepared for two. Candles twinkled throughout the room. "This is perfect. I see you only expect the two of us."

"This morning you said it was hard for us to get time alone. I wanted to be sure that we had some tonight."

"Thank you, but I should not complain. So much happens every day. I do not know how you manage."

"I have Goldblatt, the Lord Commander, my mother, Masterroff, and you to help me."

"If you are relying on me, then the throne is in trouble."

"Absolutely not," Merryk said. "You are, after all, my best inspiration. This morning, I saw how you reacted to the abandoned children. Well, I have spoken to the Master of the Watch. The guards will now always give shelter to any girl that asks. Then I talked with Goldblatt. Evidently, I own many abandoned buildings throughout the city; some of which might be suitable housing for the girls. I have selected one just inside the walls and near the east gate. We will see if we can make it work."

"Merryk, this is fantastic news. Kat will be excited when she hears. After you left, she told me she would like to help in any way possible. May I suggest you let her take the lead? I will help, but I think she needs a purpose."

"Won't she be going back to her estates?"

"Yes, but not as frequently as you might think. She has been seeing Captain Johnny Bellows. The two met at the winter ball and she tries to be in the city whenever he is not at sea."

"I would have thought this would have come up on one of our rides, but not a word," Merryk said.

"The two have kept it very confidential. Kat mentioned it once to Beth, who immediately pointed out Captain Bellows is the second most desirable bachelor in the kingdom, after you. Then she reminded Kat she was the daughter of a traitor and would never be accepted by his family. Kat now thinks she is unworthy of him."

"Not again. I just went through this for a year with Commander Yonn, not thinking he was worthy of the contessa."

"Yes, I remember. It is very much the same. In any event, she will be in the city and would love to help."

"All right, the two of you should contact Goldblatt. You can review the property and prepare a list of what you need."

"Thank you. This means a great deal to Kat and to me."

"This is what a king should do."

"You mentioned you were going east. Why, may I ask?"

"I have learned the Ott River floods every year over large swaths of land owned by both Ott and Weirshem. This year it is particularly bad. I want to see if we can do something to prevent it from happening. In many ways, it's like the problem of the Teardrop and we found a solution there."

"*You* found a solution," Oolada said, correcting Merryk. "When will you leave?"

"Tomorrow morning. I have the engineers who built Newport going with me, along with a larger than needed group of soldiers. I will stay with the Otts. They are the grandparents of both Kat and Beth. I will then visit the Weirshem property."

"Weirshem will not be pleased to see you, even though your purpose is to help."

"I know, but this may give me an opportunity to change his opinion of me. Flooding is something I understand."

"I am not sure changing his mind is going to happen. I asked Kat and Beth about the possibility Weirshem was behind the changing of the schedule for Lady Jane. They both agreed it was an almost absolute certainty. Beth said the ire of Weirshem goes beyond just schedule changes, to direct attacks on your right to be king. He is a single-handed storm of criticism of both you and me."

"You! What can they possibly say about you?" Merryk asked.

"Just that I am not truly noble, and I am a barbarian."

Merryk reached across the table to Oolada's hand. "You are the most noble woman I know, and being strong doesn't make you a barbarian. If anything, it makes you more of a lady and a strong, confident woman."

"What they say about me is not important. Their attacks on your right to be king are growing louder each day. I know over time everyone will see how qualified you are to be king, but right now, your association with me is causing them to question your judgement and your support of the nobles."

"If they don't want me to be king, then so be it. I still am not fully convinced I should be here."

"Stop it! You are the only person who should be the king. You have earned it by merit, not by treason, as your brother attempted. Petty nobles, like Weirshem, do not understand your greatness."

Merryk's eyes softened. "You might be a little prejudiced. Don't worry, I have no intentions of giving up the throne."

"Good! So do not mention it again, because I cannot imagine a world where you were not king."

Chapter 70

BETH

Spring sunlight filtered through the thin curtains to fill the sitting room. The Duchess of Crescent sat in her favorite chair reading a book of poems and sipping her tea. The quiet of the room and the warmth of the sun tugged on her eyes. Her daughter's entering the room disrupted her personal solitude.

"Beth, I thought you were going to spend the day at the castle with Kat and Oolada."

"I had hoped also to see the king. However, he left yesterday to go east to see the flooding on the Ott river. Kat and Oolada went on an excursion to review dusty old buildings as potential sites for a new halfway house for older orphan girls. I just came home."

"When did this project arise?" the duchess asked.

"Three days ago. As we came through the East gate, the king saw several young girls loitering about the guard station, looking for handouts. He asked about them and Kat told her sad story about what happened to her attendant's sister. Evidently, Oolada asked the king if there was anything that could be done and just like that, they have buildings and support."

"This sounds like an excellent project," the duchess replied.

"The project is fine, but what is irritating is how it arose. Oolada asks for it and the king makes it happen."

Beth walked over to the sofa and plopped down. "It is so frustrating. Oolada gets alone time with the king whenever she wants. I cannot even get on his schedule. Oolada asked for something, and the king gives it to her without question. Mother, as long as Oolada is here, the king will never see me. I have no chance with her around."

"The roads to the north are opening. Do you think she will return home?"

"Not without some push. I have tried to tell her she is unqualified to be queen, then she plans the ball and receives compliments from everyone. I was hoping she would stay in buckskins and tunics, but the queen and Kat took her to the dressmaker and, just like that, she looks like a lady. I had hoped the king's meeting with other women would reduce her influence, but if anything, it strengthened their connection. I just do not know what else to do."

"From my discussions with Queen Amanda, I believe Lady Zoo and the king have a special friendship borne out of conflict. If one is challenged, the other comes to their aid. The queen believes this arises from them fighting together. They are used to protecting the other. As long as they are near one another, the tie will be unbreakable. But the king will be gone for at least two weeks. Lady Zoo will not have him to run to with any insecurities."

"Mother, I know if I could have time with Merryk, without Oolada, he would come to love me. I will never have a chance while she is here."

"Do you think that the king loves her?"

"I am not sure. I know he talks with her constantly and listens to her advice. He is extremely protective of her. She told me he wanted to hang Rogger Weirshem because he had attacked her. She is, at the very least, an extremely close friend."

"Men do not marry their friends," the duchess said.

"Unless he feels pressured, then she is the easiest solution."

"Do you think Oolada loves the king?"

"She claims she does not and is emphatic about not wanting to be queen. What do you think I should do?"

The duchess thought for a moment. "My instincts are saying Oolada loves the king, and he may love her. Love is a powerful emotion. It can bring people together, but it can also force them apart. If you could convince Oolada that her presence was endangering his throne, then she would leave to save him."

"I think you are right. The desire to protect him would be driven by her love. She would do anything to save him, including leaving," Beth said. "What could I tell her? Everybody, including Oolada, knows about Weirshem's attempt to discredit the king. Tallon has supported him with his backhanded comments about Lady Zoo. None of this is new."

"It is good everybody knows the facts. You should expect she will attempt to verify whatever you tell her. Oolada has connections with both Queen Amanda and Chancellor Goldblatt. If you focus on threats to the throne, you may direct her to talk with the Chancellor. It is his job to watch for challenges. When the information you give her is validated, you can help her with the conclusion by telling her the Chancellor will not tell her the truth: she is the cause of the threat. The Chancellor would discount the threat and not want to hurt her feelings. If she loves the king, this would push her to leave," the duchess said. "But you must do this before the king returns. If she speaks with him, he will assure her everything is fine."

Beth thought for a moment. "Do you think this will work?"

"If you focus on what the Chancellor will not tell her. She needs to know he would not say how bad it is, nor would he say she is responsible. He will not want to alarm her or hurt her feelings."

"The truth is the complaints are minor, and they mention her, but she is certainly not the cause," Beth said.

"You and I know this, but Lady Zoo does not," the duchess said. "You need to amplify the size of the issues and focus them on her. We both know how important this could be. Not only would you become the

Inland Queen, but in the absence of an Outland Queen, my grandson is guaranteed to be the next king. It would forever change our position in the kingdom. We would no longer be just noble; we would be royal. Your great-grandfather, on my side, used to say with great risk comes great reward. Beth, clearly understand, this carries great risk. If the king finds out you pressured Lady Zoo to leave, you will have no chance to be queen and you may significantly hurt the position of our house. Your father always believes we have enough. The king just gave him a very prestigious appointment as his ambassador to the kingdom's two most important international relationships. I know he would tell you to step back, let the king decide, and be ready to be gracious if you are not the king's choice. This would be best for him."

"Mother, I do not think I can just let the king marry someone else," Beth said tearfully.

"I understand, but remember, you are playing a dangerous game."

CHAPTER 71

OOLADA'S CHOICE

Oolada opened the door to the top of the tower and was greeted by bright sunshine. *I know Merryk will not be here, but something about the tower makes me feel close to him. He would love today's sunrise. He just left. How can I miss him so much?*

Returning to her room, she found Beth waiting outside the door. "Beth, what a pleasant surprise."

"I hope you do not mind the intrusion. I needed to talk with you, and it could not wait," Beth said.

"Of course. Come in and tell me what is bothering you."

Oolada led Beth to the sofa in front of the fire.

Beth hesitated for a moment, then began. "There is no easy way to tell you. King Merryk is under a great deal of pressure. Some say his position on the throne is in jeopardy. You are aware of the efforts of Weirshem and Tallon to destabilize the king. Well, it is more serious than we have been told. In addition, some noble houses are pointing to you as the reason he is not their king. They are saying, as long as you are here, you are directing his actions and steering him away from the best interests of the kingdom. I am telling you because Chancellor Goldblatt and Kat will not tell you the truth; neither wants to hurt your feelings. But your presence has put Merryk's throne at risk. As your friend, I knew you would want to know the truth."

———✦———

There was a gentle tap on Goldblatt's door as Oolada entered. "Chancellor Goldblatt, do you have a minute?"

"For you, of course," the Chancellor replied.

"Chancellor, I will be direct. Is the king in trouble?"

"Trouble? No, not really. There are always a few issues, but no real trouble. Why do you ask?"

"I have heard the swell of discord over King Merryk has grown throughout the kingdom. Many noble houses are questioning his right to rule."

"Yes, there are a few houses, like Weirshem and Tallon, who are spreading rumors. Their reputations do not add credence to their claims. You know how people view the Weirshems. Tallon's reputation is better, but his association with the earl hurts it. I watch all the houses and I would know if there was any real threat."

"Are people blaming me for the king's actions? Am I perceived as leading him astray?" Oolada asked.

"Who planted these thoughts?" Goldblatt asked.

"Who is not important. It is just I could not bear to be the cause of Merryk's throne being threatened." Oolada's eyes were now welled with tears.

"You are not the cause in any way," Goldblatt said, as he reached across the table to console Oolada. "Anyone who says otherwise is just jealous of your relationship with the king. You know how many want to be the Inland Queen."

"He would have less resistance if he selected any of them. I fear he will not do so while I am here."

"What are you saying?"

"I think I should leave so he can focus on getting an Inland Queen and silence all the rumors."

Goldblatt's hand moved to his beard. "You know what the king would say, 'do not go.' You are not the source of his problems. He would want you to stay."

"Exactly. He would want me to stay even if it threatened his throne, which is why I cannot."

"At least stay until he returns. You need to talk with him personally," Goldblatt pleaded.

"You know he would convince me to stay. There is no real choice. I need to leave before he returns. I will go in the morning. Some of the clan's guards will ride with me. Chancellor, thank you for all you have done. I will miss you."

———————⚙———————

The rap on Queen Amanda's parlor door was sharp and filled with urgency. "Yes," the queen answered.

An agitated Goldblatt entered.

"Chancellor, what has you so upset?"

"Oolada is leaving!"

"Why on earth would she do that?"

"Someone has convinced Oolada her presence is causing a severe threat to the king's throne," the Chancellor answered. "I do not know who."

"That is simple. Just ask who has the most to gain," the queen replied.

"Lady Elizabeth," Goldblatt answered, immediately.

"Yes, but this has a depth to it beyond the lady herself. I perceive she is receiving help." The queen's face was pensive.

"What should we do? I could order her to stay. But if she refused, she would force me to arrest her. King Merryk would put me in irons if I arrest her."

"I think we should let her go. Be sure she has guards. Instruct them to protect her with their lives. Tell them the truth. She is precious to the king, even if he has not recognized the truth."

"The king will be furious," Goldblatt said.

"Yes, and then he will be forced to make hard choices," the queen said.

A bright blue sky hung over the meadow in front of Crag'd Zoo. Helga carried a wicker basket to collect some of the early spring flowers, which had forced their way through the thinning snow. The deep snows of winter had retreated to the shadows of the trees, and even there it was losing its fight with the warm air. Small forest creatures scurried about, having awakened from their winter burrows.

Helga thought. *It will not be long before the entire valley is free of snow. I will not miss the gray of winter. Everyone is ready for spring.* A slap of cold air from the south disrupted Helga's thoughts. Her inner eyes immediately searched south. "Oh no!" she said out loud.

CHAPTER 72

OTT

It was a three-and-a-half-day journey from the Capital City to the estate of Ott. Although there were inns along the way, Merryk had insisted on staying with the engineers and soldiers in tents. Each night, he had circled through the campfires to speak with the men.

All did not appreciate Merryk's choice of tents over inns. The Lord Commander, who had insisted on coming, was not a fan of sleeping in tents. "I prefer a warm berth and the snap of wind filling the canvas over my head."

Nevertheless, he was a good sport and by the third evening seemed to enjoy the camaraderie of the men and the fires.

The engineers, headed by Mack, were the ones who had worked the year before in Newport. Merryk knew they were serious and efficient men. At first, the engineers didn't seem to blend with the soldiers, but by the third night, they too were engaged.

Merryk's personal guard, headed by Bowen, continued their careful watch. "Although we are in our own country, we should set sentries and rotating watches," Bowen said to the Lord Commander.

"I have placed two circles of sentries, and scouts are reviewing the road ahead by at least half a day. This many armed men will make even peaceful men nervous. We need to be cautious."

At midday on the fourth day, the entourage broached a knoll and saw Castle Ott. Merryk's first impression was one of surprise. *This is not what I expected. The manor houses of other noble families I have seen are more manors and less castle. Castle Ott is all castle surrounded by a strong wall with turrets on each corner and a real moat. It is also well maintained. Fill it with men and it could withstand a prolonged assault. Goldblatt said the Duke of Ott was a little eccentric. This castle reflects a man who might be more cautious than eccentric.*

The sound of a horn rang across the pastures in front of the castle. At the same time, the royal blue flag of the king unfurled over the castle, joining the flag of the Duke of Ott.

"They are acknowledging your arrival," the Lord Commander said. "Your flag says the king is in residence. It also is a sign of honor."

"Goldblatt said the family of Ott had been involved at every major event in the last four hundred years and was always on the side of the throne," Merryk replied.

The Duke and the Duchess of Ott, together with their Bannerman and the household staff, lined up to greet the king. Everyone bowed as Merryk dismounted. "Your Majesty, welcome to our home," the duke said in a clear voice. The duke was impeccably dressed and well-groomed. His eyes had a bright sparkle indicative of a keen intellect. "May I introduce you to my wife," the duke said, pointing to his wife, who was a perfect match for the duke.

"Your Grace," Merryk said politely. "Thank you for allowing us to stay in your home. Duchess, I have met your daughter and two granddaughters: Elizabeth and Katalynn. I now know where they got their beauty."

"Your Majesty is too gracious," the duchess replied, her cheeks reflecting a slight blush.

"Forgive me, Your Majesty," the duke said. "I was told that you resembled your grandfather—Great King Mikael. But they were wrong. You look exactly like him. When I first saw you, I thought I was seeing the man at whose side I fought many years ago."

"That's a story I very much want to hear. Your Grace, have you met Lord Commander Bellows?"

"Oh, yes. I met young Bellows many years ago. How is your father?"

"He is well, Your Grace," the Lord Commander replied, extending his hand.

"And I hear you have a son who you named after your older brother."

"Yes, he is now a captain in his own right."

The duke returned his attention to the king. "Excuse my manners, Your Majesty, please come inside. We thought you might like something light to eat before you get settled."

"That would be very nice," Merryk answered. "However, I would like a tour of the castle and gardens, if possible."

"We can do that after you have something to eat, and still have time for you to freshen up before dinner," the duke answered.

"If you could have someone show our men where you want us?" the Lord Commander asked.

"Certainly. My steward will take care of them."

After lunch, the duke and king went to survey the castle. Bowen and two Royal Guards followed at a discreet distance.

"Your castle and grounds are truly magnificent. I do not believe I have seen their equal anywhere in the kingdom. When I first arrived at the Teardrop Castle, I noticed how the walls had fallen into disrepair. Fortunately, the Teardrop had an old stone mason—a master craftsman. I found a couple of strong young men who became his apprentices. With their help, he soon made the repairs. But their efforts still look like repairs. Your castle looks new."

"My great-great-grandfather built the castle as the first line of defense to the invasions from the east. I am sure you know the history of how the barbarians swept from the east and pushed everyone almost to the Capital City. Your ancestors organized the other families to push them back. This is when the houses of Ressett and Crescent, along with mine, were saved by your family. They built this castle after the first war. We have seen several incursions by the barbarians and the most unfortunate treason by the Duke of Ressett against your grandfather—Great King Mikael. It was in the revolt's suppression that I rode at your grandfather's side. Throughout all these challenges, the Otts and this castle have stood to serve the king."

"Your loyalty to the throne is beyond question. Chancellor Goldblatt was not sure, but he thought I may be the first of my family to stay at the castle."

"Great King Mikael visited for a morning, but you are the first king to stay," the duke replied. "Your visit is indeed an honor."

"The honor is mine. Now tell me about the stonework."

"After they built the castle, my great-great-grandfather determined it must be maintained. In those days, we were at the edge of the kingdom. Not much traffic came this way. So, he hired a master stone mason and made a place for him and his family within the walls. Since then, we have had our own master mason. Our current stonemason is third generation. Our philosophy is not to repair, but to replace, as new, anything in need. As a result, our castle looks new because it is."

"Maintaining the skills locked in masters is very important. Not only did I have apprentices for the stonemason but also for several blacksmith and armor makers. Most recently, I sent young men to a master shipwright. Saving their knowledge is critical," Merryk said.

"Your Majesty, while we are alone, I wanted to talk with you. The duchess and I do not know how to thank you for your protection for our granddaughter, Katalynn. You can imagine our angst at learning her father, the Duke of Ressett, had followed his father into treason. Your grandfather's mercy should have been enough to earn the loyalty of the young duke. After the death of Katalynn's mother, we tried to spend more time with the child. But the duke made it known he did not want our involvement. I greatly appreciated your generosity in allowing her to keep her title and the manor as a dowry. When we heard of the last attack, we were beside ourselves. I do not know how Rogger Weirshem could behave so badly." The duke shook his head. "If I were a younger man—"

Merryk interrupted. "You do not need to worry. Lady Katalynn and I are friends. She rides with me frequently. In addition, I know other noble houses also protect her. After the last hearing, I do not believe the Weirshems or anyone else will try to take advantage of her. But rest assured, I will do all in my power to see she is protected."

"Thank you, Your Majesty. I do not know what to say."

"Nothing is required," the king said. "Now tomorrow, we need to take the engineers to see the river; then the next day, I will follow the river south to the Weirshems."

Chapter 73

Home

Helga found Gaspar looking out toward the southern road. "This is a reversal. It is usually me searching for answers in the sky, but today it is you."

"I was just looking for any sign of her arrival."

"She is safe and will be here before sunset." Helga's reassurance did not move Gaspar from his gaze.

"I have been a fool. I was so certain she would fulfill the prophecy. It blinded me to the realities of our world. We are from the north and will never be considered the equal of the southern noble houses."

"When did you become such a skeptic? How many times do I have to tell you, nothing is over until destiny chooses?"

"Oolada has chosen to leave. There is nothing left."

Helga moved forward to place her hand on Gaspar's shoulder. "What are you going to say to her?"

"Everything I want to say, I know I cannot. She is my granddaughter. I know she did not leave without good reason. I just cannot believe the king let her go. Even I saw the connection between them."

"Did it ever occur to you, the king may not know she is gone?" Helga said. "We need to let her tell the story, her way. I sense she is in great pain. If it is any consolation, she is questioning her choice constantly. This has not been easy. It was a difficult choice."

"Well, it will help to have her home. I have missed her. Do not worry, I will be gentle. I will not ask; how could you be so foolish?"

Helga reached out to strike Gaspar's shoulder. "You better not, or your tea will be cold for a month."

The further from the Capital City Oolada rode, the more the sky opened. *I had forgotten how clear and bright the sky could be at dawn. I had become accustomed to the gray morning clouds of the sea. But it is not the openness of the sky which occupies my mind. I already miss Merryk. I know he would have said stay. I could not bear causing him being challenged. He is the only one who deserves to be king.*

Four full days on the road finally brought Oolada, and the six clansmen who came with her, to the crest of the road revealing the front of Crag'd Zoo. The early days of spring had pushed the snows from the open area in front of the crag.

I am always amazed by the sight of the fortress carved from the face of the mountain. But I am worried about what I must tell grandfather and Helga. Helga will already know what has happened, but grandfather will have questions. Questions I do not know if I can answer, or at least answer in a way which will make sense to him. I am not sure any of my answers even make sense to me. How can I miss Merryk so much? I am filled with a deep ache. My heart cries for me to turn around and return to the Capital City, but my head says I cannot without placing Merryk in peril. My life in the capital is over. At least, I am home. Soon I can go to the hot springs, but I already do not want to stay.

The sound of the signal horn broke Oolada's internal debate. The lookouts had spotted their group. Everyone now knew they were coming.

Chapter 74

Earl of Weirshem

M erryk, Lord Commander Bellows and the Duke of Ott rode out of the castle toward the Manor House of Weirshem. Yesterday they had surveyed the Ott river. Unlike the river that surrounded the Teardrop Castle, this river moved onto a broad plain.

This river is much more like the Mississippi than the Columbia. "Mack, I think this river will be better guided than blocked, as we did in the Teardrop. Levies carefully placed can channel the excess waters of the spring," Merryk said.

"I agree, Your Majesty. Even though in some ways, it is easier to build dams," Mack replied.

"This entire area is more soil than rock. My guess is the very thing which makes this great farmland—the deep soil—also makes it susceptible to flooding," Merryk said.

"We will need stone if we are to make decent levies."

"I agree. Perhaps we can bring in the materials by barge."

"Interesting idea, Your Majesty."

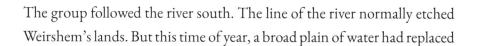

The group followed the river south. The line of the river normally etched Weirshem's lands. But this time of year, a broad plain of water had replaced the discreet line. As expected, the speed of the river had slowed as it moved south.

Three hours after leaving the castle, the Earl of Weirshem, Rogger Weirshem, Sir Timothy and a dozen armed men greeted the king and his group.

I can feel Bowen and the Lord Commander getting tense. Caution is never a fault. Merryk confirmed the location of his walking stick and his grandfather's sword.

"Good morning, earl," the king said, in his best lighthearted voice.

"Good morning, Your Majesty. We did not expect you until later in the day," the earl replied.

"We came early to allow more time to survey the water issues. You know the Lord Commander and the Duke of Ott. This is Mack, the head engineer."

Weirshem nodded perfunctorily to all. "You are really here to look at the river?" a skeptical Weirshem replied.

"Absolutely. Why else would we come?" *Weirshem is almost spoiling for a fight.* "The river appears to be moving nicely through this section. Where is the area of flooding?"

"It has left its banks closer to the manor. In fact, it has created a new channel which is threatening a small village of my workers."

"I would like to see it," Merryk said.

It was a brief ride from where Weirshem had greeted the king to the village. Before the flooding, the village sat near the river, but now the swollen waters were pushing up against the outlying structures. "A few more feet and the entire village will be underwater," Merryk said. "Where does the river divert into this channel?"

"It is up the river about a quarter mile," Rogger replied. "I can show you."

"There is the problem," Mack said, pointing to a slide which had moved dirt and a large tree into the primary channel.

"Yes, it backed up the water to create another channel. I think if we could remove the blockage, the river would go back to the original path," Merryk said as he dismounted Maverick.

"Getting to the obstruction is going to be tricky," Mack said as he joined Merryk on the ground.

"We need to be careful not to get too close to the edges. I fear they are being undercut by the water."

The Earl of Weirshem dismounted and moved toward the edge of the bank, disregarding the king's warning.

"Earl, be careful. I don't think the bank is solid," Merryk said.

"It will be fine," the earl replied.

"No, do not go closer," the king shouted.

Weirshem ignored the king and took two more steps. It turned out to be two steps too many. Without a sound, the bank gave way, tumbling the earl and dirt into the swiftly flowing water.

"We need a rope!" Merryk yelled.

One engineer grabbed a coil from the wagon and handed it to King Merryk, who was following the bobbing Weirshem down the river.

"He does not know how to swim," a panicked Rogger yelled.

"Great," Merryk said as he stripped off his coat, outer tunic, and belt.

"What are you doing, Your Majesty?" the Lord Commander asked, his face filled with anxiety.

"Trying to save a drowning man." Merryk continued down the riverbank until the swift waters hit a flat spot. Merryk tied the rope around his waist. With no notice, he tossed the rope to the nearest soldier. "Pull when I yell."

Bowen could not believe his eyes. The king dived into the water and disappeared. Seconds later, he broke the surface with a swimming motion Bowen had never seen. Merryk arrived as the earl slipped beneath the murky waters for the third time. King Merryk followed, and when he reappeared, he held the limp form of the earl in his arm and yelled, "Pull!"

The soldier and several engineers dragged the two men to the shore.

"Get the earl first," Merryk ordered.

Rogger pulled his father to the shore. "He is not breathing! He is dead!" the panicked son exclaimed.

Merryk rose from the water and went to the earl's side. "Not breathing and dead are different. Move out of the way."

Merryk turned the earl on his back, turned his head to one side to allow some water to come out. Then he reached into the earl's mouth and pulled his tongue forward to open the air passage. Merryk turned the earl's head back to the center and grasped his nose to hold it shut and blew four powerful breaths into Weirshem's mouth. Merryk waited for a couple of seconds and then repeated the process. Four times he blew into Weirshem's mouth.

"He is dead!" a tearful Rogger proclaimed.

Just then, the earl coughed, and water flowed from his lips.

"Help me turn him on his side," the king commanded.

Again, the earl coughed and spewed water. This time, a gasp of air and more coughing followed it.

"Not breathing is not the same thing as dead," Merryk said as he stepped away from the prone figure and allowed Rogger to attend to his father.

"My Lord, are you all right?" a very concerned Bowen asked.

"What were you thinking?" a gruff Lord Commander asked. "You could have been lost."

"Now neither of us is lost. I am wet and a little cold. Does anyone have blankets and a dry shirt?"

Maverick's response was less subtle than the Lord Commander or Bowen. He walked up to Merryk and used his head to push aggressively directly into Merryk's chest.

"I'm all right," Merryk said as he wrapped his arms around the horse's neck.

One engineer had an extra tunic. "I am afraid it will be too small."

"It will be fine, thank you," the king replied.

They found blankets for both the wet men.

"Rogger, your father is breathing, but he is not out of danger. The next two days are critical. You need to take him back home and put him in a very warm room. You are trying to dry the water out of his lungs. Do not let him lie down for too long at a time. He will need to stand, walk, and move his arms from side to side at least once an hour to help him pump the water out. Expect he will cough a great deal and perhaps throw up. This is to be expected. Do not stop him from coughing. Oh yes, don't let him drink too much brandy. Also, he may be grumpier than normal, if you can tell." Merryk could not help but smile.

"Thank you, Your Majesty. I do not know what to say. You literally blew life into his body."

"It was just air. Now get him warmed up," the king said.

Rogger and his men quickly gathered around the earl and moved south to the manor.

"We need to get you someplace warm," the Duke of Ott said. "My castle is four hours away. You should be warm before we start our return."

"How about a fire?" the Lord Commander said. Within minutes, a raging blaze filled the air with smoke and warmth.

"This feels great," Merryk said.

The Lord Commander, with his sternest expression, spoke to the king. "You cannot do things like that. One man is not worth the loss of you as king. He almost died anyway."

"But he did not, and I am fine. Remind me to command the earl to learn to swim."

"You can joke, but Chancellor Goldblatt and Queen Amanda will put me on a ship and sink it. I cannot believe you sought to save a man who despises you." The Lord Commander shook his head in disbelief.

"No one is going to sink today," King Merryk said.

CHAPTER 75

DUKE OF WEIRSHEM

King Merryk, the Duke of Ott, Lord Commander Bellows and Mack stood around the end of the dining room table in Castle Ott. A collection of maps and rough sketches were positioned on the tabletop to show the river and the surrounding areas.

"I never thought of my river in this way," the duke said. "It has always been just a line on my map."

"I like to think of the river as a living thing," Merryk said. "It grows in the spring, then shrinks in the summer; changes size for the fall, and even seems to stop in the winter. The river never thinks of its banks as boundaries, just part-time obstacles. It is ever intent on getting to the sea, no matter what."

"That is a poetic way of seeing a river," Bellows said. "In some ways, it is exactly how I view the sea. She has her moods. Sometimes she is angry beyond belief and then can be as gentle as a mountain lake."

A black cloaked butler with white gloves entered the room. "Excuse me, Your Grace. The king has visitors outside the front door."

"Ask them to enter," the duke said.

"I had suggested that, but they prefer to meet the king outside," the butler replied.

"Very well," King Merryk said. "Show me the way."

The Lord Commander looked at the king with a narrow eye, grabbed his sword, and followed him to the door. Bowen and the Royal Guard had already gone outside.

Standing outside in a row were three men. Merryk recognized Rogger Weirshem and Sir Timothy. The third man was quite elderly, with a shaggy beard and long gray hair. Only his clothing gave any indication of high rank. Upon seeing the king, all three dropped to a knee.

"Please stand," Merryk said, a little confused by the formality. "What can I do for you?"

Rogger stood quickly, then reached to help the older man stand. At first, he accepted the help, but once standing pushed Rogger away.

"Your Majesty, I am the Duke of Weirshem. You know my grandson, Rogger, and our Bannerman, Sir Timothy. Also, you know my son, the earl."

Merryk nodded in acknowledgement.

"I have come to apologize to you and to the throne for the actions of my family. I want to assure you, we were not always so objectionable. In fact, like my friend the Duke of Ott, I fought on the side of the Great King Mikael in the rebellion. I listened to the ramblings of my son, when I should have known the grandson of the great king would be himself, a man of honor."

"Your Grace, this is most kind, but your son and I have resolved whatever difficulties we had. I am confident that is all behind us. Now please come in and join us. We are reviewing our findings about the river."

"Not until I thank you for saving my son. He can be difficult, but he is my son. Everyone says you risked your life to pull him from the waters and literally breathed life into his body. For this, my family is deeply and eternally thankful. You can trust there shall be no further difficulty arising from the House of Weirshem."

The Duke of Weirshem looked at his grandson and Sir Timothy. Both men pulled their swords, laid them on the ground, and dropped to their knee again. "We pledge our undying allegiance to you, King Michael Merryk Raymouth. Call and we shall come."

Merryk looked at the Lord Commander, who seemed to be as surprised as he.

"I accept your vow of allegiance. I will hold you to your pledge. Rise," King Merryk proclaimed.

As the men rose, Merryk swept his arm toward the door. "Now, Your Grace, please come inside and join our discussion. I also want to know how the earl is doing today. Has he stopped coughing?"

Chapter 76

RETURN

Maverick smelled the smoke of the Capital City before Merryk spotted it on the horizon. The many fires of the city pushed the stream of gray into the afternoon sky. Maverick became fidgety and wanted to increase his pace. "I know, my friend. We all want to be back."

When I was a boy, it always seemed like it took longer to get somewhere than to come home. On this journey, it seemed to take longer to get home. I guess it takes longer to get where you want to be the most. I am so looking forward to seeing Oolada.

Merryk patted Maverick on the neck. "I know you want to see Bella too."

Maverick bobbed his head.

⁂

The group returning to the Capital City was smaller than the one that had departed. The engineers stayed behind to do more survey work. Mack had promised to shift the stream away from the Weirshem village. "We will fix the immediate problem and develop some alternatives for a long-term solution," he had proclaimed.

After passing through the East gate, the soldiers and the bulk of the guards broke off to go to their barracks. The Lord Commander and Merryk went to the king's stables.

"I will catch up with you later," Merryk said to Bellows. "I'm sure Goldblatt will want a complete report, but we can do that tomorrow."

"Thank you, Your Majesty. I am looking forward to a proper bed," the Lord Commander replied.

As Maverick moved down the row of stalls, Bella extended her neck as far as possible. Maverick had given a whinny upon entering the building, and Bella had answered immediately.

"There you go," Merryk said as he brought the two together.

Oolada's stall is empty. I wonder where she is this afternoon. Merryk caught the attention of the stable hands. "How long ago did Lady Zoo leave and when do you expect her back?"

"My Lord, Lady Zoo left with several clansmen about three days after you did. I do not know when she will return," the man replied.

"Did she say where she was going?"

"She said she was going home."

The distance from the stables to Chancellor Goldblatt's study was much longer than Merryk remembered. Merryk knocked and entered almost simultaneously.

"Welcome back, Your Majesty," Goldblatt said as he rose from his desk to greet the king. "I trust you had a productive journey."

"Where is Oolada?"

"That is a complex issue. Perhaps you would like to get cleaned up and get something to eat before we talk?"

"Where is Oolada?" Merryk demanded.

"The short answer is she went to Crag'd Zoo. The reason is more com-plicated and will take some time to explain."

Merryk moved to the chair in front of Goldblatt's desk. "You might as well start. Neither of us is going anywhere until I have an answer."

Goldblatt moved to his side table to retrieve two glasses and the entire bottle of sherry. "I am going to need a drink and you may as well."

Goldblatt spent the next half hour trying to explain the circumstances of the departure. Merryk listened in silence.

When he finished, Merryk spoke. "That is all rubbish. Why did my chancellor not stop her? Why didn't you tell her to wait? Why didn't she wait to talk to me? Surely you could have delayed her."

"I spoke with the queen to seek her advice. She recommended Lady Zoo be allowed to leave. She said I could not just restrain her. If I locked her in a room, she was certain you would have had me in irons."

Merryk had not touched his sherry. "You're probably right. Neither of us can make someone do something they don't want to. And even if we could, we shouldn't. I just don't know why she didn't wait."

"Lady Zoo said if she waited, you would convince her to stay."

"Of course, I would have," Merryk said with a deep sigh. Merryk shook his head. "I think you're right. I need a bath and a good meal."

Merryk rose from his chair, grabbed the glass of sherry, and drank it in a single gulp. "We have much to tell you about our trip. I've asked the Lord Commander to come tomorrow. Good evening."

Stepping outside the door, Merryk turned to his guard. "Have a message sent to Lady Katalynn, the Duchess of Ressett. Ask her to come to the castle as soon as possible, if not tonight, then the first thing in the morning. I will be in my rooms."

"Yes, Your Majesty."

The Chancellor made his way to the rooms of Queen Amanda.

"Enter. Chancellor Goldblatt, your expression says a thousand things. What is going on?"

"The king has returned."

"How was his journey?"

"I do not know. I assume fine. He discovered Lady Zoo is gone and wanted answers."

"What did you tell him?"

"Everything I knew, but it was not enough. I have never seen him this way."

"How is that?" the queen asked.

"Defeated."

The queen broke into a smile. "Good. He will now be required to make hard choices. He can no longer delay decisions. He will be required to act, or he will lose Oolada forever."

"Certainly, he would have decided without this event. He looked so devastated."

"My son had found a comfortable place. He was pretending to be looking for a wife, but with Oolada here, he had what he needed without having to choose. I believe he has known all along, Oolada is his queen. He just found a way not to decide. It was unfair to her and to him."

"You wanted Lady Zoo to leave so Merryk would recognize how he truly felt?"

"Yes. Now he must decide. Will he choose politics or love?"

Merryk had taken a bath to remove the silt from the road. Jamas had dinner sent to the sitting room. The head butler had stoked the fire to reduce the chill from the room, but somehow Merryk still feel cold.

"Thank you for the fire and the food, Jamas."

"Of course, Your Majesty. If I may say, I do not believe I can get the room warm enough to remove the chill which surrounds you."

"You know about Lady Zoo?"

"Everybody knows about Lady Zoo. If I may speak openly, everyone is surprised. We always thought she would be here forever. Her leaving has raised many questions."

"Well, I do not know what questions they have, but I assure you, I have more. No matter how old you are, I still don't understand women."

Jamas smiled. "Even the oldest men have the same thought."

"I just don't know why she left without talking to me," Merryk said.

There was a knock on the door and Jamas went to answer. "Your Majesty, Lady Katalynn has asked to see you. Shall I send her away?"

"No, I sent for her. Please let her in and leave us."

"Kat, thank you for coming on such short notice," Merryk said, as he rose to greet the duchess. "I know it's late, but I have some questions that I hope you can answer."

"I was expecting you would want to talk. I want you to know, I begged her to wait for your return. The two of you need to talk, but she was afraid you would convince her to stay."

"She was right. I would have convinced her. But why would she leave at all?"

Kat reached out and grasped the king's hand. "She left because she loves you. I do not know if you realized, but she is completely in love with you. When people told her she was endangering your throne, she panicked. She could not bear to cause your kingship being questioned. Oolada loves you so much; she would leave you rather than to cause you harm. She could not think of a world where you were not the king. She believes with all her heart; this is your destiny. Her love would not allow her to threaten it."

Merryk shifted in his chair. "My throne is not at risk. If it were, there would be no one else that I would want at my side to fight for it. Oolada does not make me weaker. She strengthens me."

"Have you ever told her?"

"No, I just assumed she understood."

"Understood. You want her as an ally, a battle companion?"

"Yes, and much more than just an ally."

"Did you tell her?"

"No," Merryk rose to move to the fireplace. "Kat, even if I had, Oolada gets to choose for herself. I am a king, but I cannot compel her to do something she does not want. Leaving was her choice. I need to respect her decision."

Now Kat rose and grabbed her coat. "Then with all respect, Your Majesty, the two of you deserve what you get. She left because she loves you and you refuse to fight for her because you accept her decision. The question you need to answer is, what is your choice? You get to choose too. Do you love her enough to fight to change her decision? I cannot help you any further."

Merryk nodded his head. "I will have the guards escort you home. Thank you for coming."

"There is no need. Captain Bellows is waiting to escort me home." Kat stopped before she reached the door. "You are both dear to me. You deserve to be together. Remember, you are not only the king; you are also a man. You deserve to be happy, too.

It was near midnight when Merryk made his way to the stables. The lights were low. All the stable hands were asleep. The horses were quiet.

Maverick heard Merryk as he approached. "I'm sorry to be here so late." Merryk said. "I just needed to talk to someone."

Maverick nuzzled Merryk's shoulder.

"I'm sure Bella told you. Oolada left."

Maverick nodded.

"She left without talking to me. You know I didn't want her to go, but if she feels so strongly, I have no choice but to honor her decision."

The stallion shook his head. "No."

"I can't compel her to do something she doesn't want."

Maverick whinnied.

"I know she didn't want to stay because she thought her presence would cost me the throne. I don't want the throne if she is not with me. But I am the king. I can't just ride north, like an ordinary man, and challenge her to combat to let her know how I feel."

This time, Maverick bobbed his head vigorously.

"Are you suggesting after I defeat her, if I defeat her, I could let her choose? At least she would know I was willing to fight for her."

Maverick nodded his head in agreement. "Yes."

CHAPTER 77

NORTH

"Enter," Chancellor Goldblatt said, in response to a knock on his study door.

Beth entered the room with a hesitancy of a schoolgirl going before the headmaster.

"Lady Elizabeth, how can I help you?" Goldblatt said, looking up from his desk.

"I heard the king had returned from his journey to the east the day before yesterday. I was hoping to speak with him, but no one knows where he is."

"I am afraid you have missed him. He left early this morning."

"When do you expect him to return?"

Goldblatt thought for a moment. "My guess is he and Lady Zoo will be back within a fortnight."

"Lady Zoo?"

"Yes, the king has gone to get her. Was there anything I could do in his absence?"

"No, I just wanted to see how he was doing."

"Well, he was in excellent spirits this morning when he left," Goldblatt said. "I am sure he is fine."

Not all of Helga's visions were triggered by flashes of lightning or slaps of cold air. Sometimes ordinary events brought them to her attention. Today, a goldfinch landed on the railing of the terrace overlooking the Valley of Zoo. It made a sharp, crisp chirp to herald the sun breaking through a cloud bank, flooding the valley with bright sunlight. Helga flashed an enormous smile, lighting up her eyes. "I must find Gaspar," she said to no one but herself.

Oolada returned to the kitchen and collapsed into a chair. "What is going on with grandfather? I do not remember him ever being so intent on spring cleaning. He has everybody cleaning and organizing everything in sight. I swear the floor of the Great Square is clean enough to eat from. This week has been impossible. No one can sit down for even a minute."

"Gaspar gets like this now and then," Helga replied, her face covered in a perpetual smile. "I am sure he will return to his old ways in a day or two, at the most."

"I hope your opinion is prophecy. I am exhausted, and so is everyone else."

"I have an idea. You and I should disappear tomorrow afternoon and go to the hot springs. We could use a break. And you never know when we will have an opportunity again."

"That sounds great, but how are we going to escape grandfather?"

"Leave your grandfather to me."

The next day, after the mid-day meal, Helga motioned for Oolada to follow her. Each crag sat on an internal hot spring which provided warmth in the winter and a place of quiet solitude. Midafternoon was not a popular time to visit the spring. Helga and Oolada were alone when they eased into the warm waters.

"I love the springs," Helga said. "It is one of the many blessings of our home."

"I did not know how much I love this until I got to the Capital City. The staff did their very best to match the experience with hot baths, but it was not the same as a pool where you can swim in the warmth," Oolada said.

"This is the first time you have spoken about the Capital City since you arrived."

"I guess I was hoping if I did not speak of the capital, it would slip from my memory."

"You mean *he* would go away from your memory."

"Yes, I know you warned me I might love a man who could not love me back. I could accept this if I could just be near. However, the politics of the throne meant I could not be near without putting him at risk. This peril was more than I could bear. I had to leave."

"Has your avoidance driven him from your mind?"

"You do not have to be a seer to know the answer. Everything reminds me of him. The truth is I miss him more every day. I wake in the middle of the night wishing I had not left; wishing for another way."

The sound of the signal horns interrupted the quiet of the spring.

"What in the world is going on?" Oolada asked.

"I do not know, but we need to get dressed," Helga said. "I brought fresh clothes for both of us and your sword."

"Why would you bring my sword?"

"We need to hurry," was Helga's only reply.

It took several minutes for the two to dress and return to the Great Square.

"What is going on?" Oolada asked a passing clansman.

"Armed warriors are coming up the south road. Gaspar is marshaling everyone."

"Marshaling everyone?" Oolada asked with a look of perplexity. "Helga, I must go to Jamal and grandfather."

"Go!" Helga said, her face still covered with a smile.

Fully armed warriors moved up the road and across the plain to the front of the stone gate. The group did not show any markings or colors as a sign of their affiliation. They stopped outside the gate. One man rode forward on a large black stallion. In a loud and clear voice, he proclaimed, "I challenge the one called 'Oolada Zoo.' If I am victorious, I will ask permission to marry her, as is the custom of the clans."

Oolada stopped in her tracks. Being in the stairwell meant she could hear, but not see, the challenger. *I do not believe what I just heard.*

Gaspar came down the stairs to meet Oolada. "You have a challenger. Why are you going up the stairs? You need to go out to meet your challenger."

"Grandfather, this is a mistake. Who would be so foolish as to challenge me? You know I will not lose."

"Then go out and make our clan proud. Everyone is watching."

Gaspar was right. Absolutely everyone in the clan was gathered to watch her meet the challenger. The crowd parted as she moved forward through the Great Square until she was standing at the front gate. A tall man with extremely broad shoulders and deep blue eyes stood before her. The only weapon he held was a walking stick.

Before she could speak, the man said, "So this is the one called Oolada Zoo. They say you are a warrior. Is that true?"

"We shall see," Oolada said as she removed the sheath from her sword and allowed it to fall to the ground.

———❦———

Helga moved to Gaspar's side. "This will be interesting."

Gaspar reached down and tightly grasped Helga's hand. "She does know she is supposed to lose?"

"We shall see," Helga replied.

CHAPTER 78

CHALLENGER

Oolada moved forward. The challenger never let his eyes stray from her. Oolada's first attack was smooth and predictable. "Why are you here?"

The challenger easily countered the strikes. "I have come to get my Inland Queen."

Now the attack was quicker, including a final slash toward the middle of the challenger. "I can never be the Inland Queen. The peril is too great for the throne."

She forced the challenger to jump backwards to avoid the middle stroke. The entire clan gasped at its closeness. "I can have anyone I want as my queen. I want you. If there is a threat, I accept it. But I want you at my side."

Oolada's eyes were watering, making it more difficult to see. She stopped for a moment to wipe them off and then attacked again. "You need someone who understands how to be a queen. Someone more qualified than me."

The challenger's response to the attack was more aggressive, driving Oolada back. "My mother told me the only requirement needed for my queen is my love, and you have it. I will give up my throne if I must have another."

Now Oolada was frustrated. Her attack was less organized. "You cannot give up your throne. That is the reason I left, so that your throne would be safe."

For the first time, the challenger advanced with strong sweeps of his walking stick. "If my throne is threatened, you are the only one I want at my side to defend it."

Gasper's grip on Helga's hand tightened. "What are they doing?"

"Talking," Helga answered.

Oolada moved forward quickly, hoping to gain an opening to the challenger's defenses. "I can never be defeated," she said with as much confidence as she could muster.

The challenger moved his hand to the center of his walking stick.

Oolada, thinking she had the advantage, extended her sword.

The challenger rotated the stick in the middle, not to strike Oolada's hand from the top, but an unexpected blow from beneath. "I would never want you defeated, only disarmed."

The strike from below broke the grip on her sword, which flew upward, then crashed to the ground. "You are disarmed. Do you yield?"

Oolada's face became a mixture of tears and smiles. "Yes, I yield."

Merryk dropped his walking stick to open his arms to Oolada. She crushed herself against him. "I have missed you so much."

Merryk released Oolada from his arms. Grabbing one hand, he pulled her to where Gaspar and Jamaal stood. "Unless someone in your clan objects, I claim this woman to be my wife, as is your custom."

Jamaal spoke first. "No one in the Zoo clan will object. She has been a burden for years. I just hope you know what you are getting."

Merryk smiled. "I believe I do, and I am proud to have her."

Next, Gaspar spoke. "As Walt of the Council of Walters, no one in the clans will object. As her grandfather, I give you my permission to marry her."

"Thank you," Merryk answered. "Now there is just one more thing."

Merryk turned to Oolada and dropped to one knee. "Oolada, I have chosen you. The clan has accepted my claim. Your grandfather has consented. Now you must decide if you want to marry me. The final choice is yours."

Oolada pulled Merryk to his feet. "You really are a foolish man. Why do you think I brought a sword, rather than my knives? I wanted you to have a chance. Yes! Yes!" Oolada locked her arms tightly around Merryk's neck and kissed him.

A cheer rose from the clan. Jamaal came forward to shake Merryk's hand. Helga reached out and gave Merryk a hug. Instantly, her eyes shifted, and she tightened her grip. She pushed away to look up into Merryk's eyes. In a voice only the two could hear, Helga said, "I see a mirror split into two parts. The man reflected in the mirror is also split—one old and one young, brown eyes and blue eyes. This explains much. We must talk before you leave."

"Agreed," Merryk replied. "I knew we would."

Helga turned to give Oolada a hug.

"Helga, why did you not tell me?"

"So you could run away? No, this was the way it had to happen. You needed to be unprepared so you could choose with your heart."

Oolada looked at her grandfather. "Now I know why you had everybody cleaning the crag."

Gaspar simply shrugged.

Oolada felt a push to the center of her back. She turned to see Maverick, who had forced his way through the crowd and now demanded her attention. "Thank you for bringing him safely to me," she said as she stroked his neck.

Maverick nodded his head and made a low, small snort.

"Really," Oolada replied.

"Merryk, Maverick says I have him to thank for convincing you to come north."

"Don't believe everything he says," Merryk replied. "I already knew what to do before I asked him."

Maverick just shook his head. "No."

Chapter 79

PLANS

Goldblatt's guess of a fortnight had been correct. After staying at the crag for a few days, the entire group began the journey back to the Capital City. The full force of spring returned with King Merryk and Lady Zoo. Spring flowers bordered the road along the way. The weather was as fair as the spirits of the travelers.

"We have a great deal to plan," Merryk said to Oolada as they rode south. "We need to have a wedding and a coronation. We will need time to deliver the invitations and time for the guests to arrive. I'm thinking at least two months."

"Are you always thinking?" Oolada asked as she reached over to clasp Merryk's hand.

"I think I am," Merryk replied in jest.

"I am glad we convinced Gaspar to send Helga with us."

"Yes, I agree. I know Queen Amanda will help you, but there is something special about having Helga with you."

"Thank you, again. Now, who are you thinking about asking?"

Merryk did not need to think for long. "I will let the Chancellor take care of the list of dignitaries and nobles and Council of Walters for the coronation. Also, I was thinking about asking the new Provost to come to officiate the coronation."

"A very good idea," Oolada said. "It will help mend the relationship with the Council of Justice."

"If you don't mind, I was also going to ask Father Bernard to come from the Teardrop to perform the wedding ceremony."

"Absolutely, and you must also send for Yonn and Yvette."

"My list from the Teardrop is longer. I will send a ship. I want Smallfolks. He has never left the Teardrop. Also, Nelly, the swordmaster, and Maizie. I would also like Father Xavier to accompany Father Bernard. There are many others, but we can go to the Teardrop in the fall to see everyone else."

"For the wedding, it will be my grandfather, Jamaal, his wife, and my nephews. Helga will already be with us."

Merryk turned to Oolada. "I want you and Kat to take Helga dress shopping."

"Oh, do not worry about dress shopping. My guess is your mother is going to take care of all our needs."

Oolada turned serious for a moment. "Merryk, are you ready for the complaints from the Weirshems?"

"We will not have any problems with the Weirshems. My guess is the earl, and his family, will be the first to arrive and they will want to sit in the front."

"What has changed?"

"He and I went swimming."

"Swimming?"

"A story for another time. I don't want you upset with me until after we're married."

Oolada wrinkled her brow with disapproval. "You just told me you did something stupid."

"It seemed like a good idea at the time."

CHAPTER 80

SPECIAL GUESTS

The RS *Broadsword* lowered its sails as it rounded the bend to enter the harbor of the Capital City. Within a short time, men in rowboats attached lines to help guide the ship to its slip.

Captain Johnny Bellows shouted commands to his crew in preparation to dock. Immediately next to him, a small girl had taken the position of his shadow.

"Maizie, come now. We need to gather our things to leave the ship," Yvette called to the child.

"Captain Bellows, I will see you later," Maizie said, in her most adult voice, and then bounced her way across the deck to where Yvette waited.

Nelly and Smallfolks stood toward the bow, watching the Capital City grow with each passing moment. "This is even bigger than I thought," Smallfolks said. "I will get lost, and no one will ever find me."

"King Merryk is waiting for us. He will not allow you to get lost," Nelly said, in assurance. "Although I agree, it is bigger than I expected."

"The two of you stay close to me. I have been here before and I know how to get around," the solid voice of the swordmaster said.

"Well, if you've been here before. But remember, do not to walk too fast," Smallfolks said.

It was only a few more minutes until the gangplanks of the *Broadsword* dropped to the dock. The berth was near the end of the pier. Commander

Yonn and Yvette, holding tightly to Maizie's hand, walked down the plank, immediately followed by Father Bernard and Father Xavier. The swordmaster, Smallfolks and Nelly were last.

"Where is Merryk? Where is Merryk?" an impatient Maizie asked.

"I am sure we will see him soon. Also, you need to call him King Merryk, not just Merryk. He may be busy and may send someone to gather us rather than coming himself. We just need to wait and see," Yvette said.

"No! He will come himself. I am certain," Maizie asserted. "There he is!" she exclaimed. Squirming from Yvette's grip, she charged down the finger of the pier. Bowen and the Royal Guards circled the king, as was their practice anytime the king was out of the castle. Their task was to stop anyone from directly approaching him. Despite their years of experience, it did not prepare them for the swerving dervish which weaved and shifted past their positions to dive headlong into the arms of the king. When she had lessened her grip on Merryk's neck, she began, "I told them you would come yourself. So much has happened. Smallfolks is still a handful. The ship was amazing. The sea is so big."

"Speaking of big, how much have you grown, two feet?" Merryk asked.

"Some, but not that much. JoJo and John are like little trees."

"I am sorry, Your Majesty," Commander Yonn said, as he finally caught up with the girl. "She has not changed, as you can see."

Merryk set Maizie down and reached out to give Yonn a hug. "I have missed you, my friend."

Yvette joined the group and received enormous hugs from Merryk and Oolada. After everyone had been welcomed, Merryk said, "I have carriages waiting to take us back to the castle. I want everyone to settle in and this evening, Chancellor Goldblatt will join us for dinner. We have so much to catch up on.

"Maizie, after you are settled and if it's all right with Yonn and Yvette, I have something special to show you. Yonn, I would like for you to come as well. I have something I want to tell you."

"Very well, Your Majesty," Yonn answered.

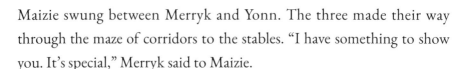

Maizie swung between Merryk and Yonn. The three made their way through the maze of corridors to the stables. "I have something to show you. It's special," Merryk said to Maizie.

"Maverick!" Maizie exclaimed, as she saw the stallion's head reaching out across the top of his stall. "I have missed you." Maizie climbed the fence and grasped Maverick tightly around the neck.

"Yes, seeing Maverick is special, but that's not the surprise." Merryk moved to Bella's stall and pointed to a recently born foal. "This guy was born yesterday, and he's still a little wobbly. The gray foal stood next to Bella for support.

Maizie's eyes grew large. "What is his name?"

"Well, I would like your opinion. He's very gray, so perhaps Shadow. I was also thinking as the son of Maverick, Mischief might be a choice. What do you think?"

Maizie did not answer immediately, as both men expected. Instead, she scrunched up her nose and stared at the young foal. "What do Bella and Maverick think? Have you talked to him? What would he like? This is not a simple thing. I will need some time."

Yonn shook his head. "I think she spends too much time with Yvette. I need to warn you, a wife can make what seems obvious anything but."

"While she is deciding, you and I can talk," Merryk said. "I have reviewed your request. Have you spoken with her?"

"No. We wanted to know your opinion first."

CHAPTER 81

DINNER

"I believe Your Majesty is more nervous about dinner this evening than the coming wedding and coronation," Jamas said as he helped Merryk with his coat.

"These are the people I have known the best. They were there when I was recovering from my injuries. As I fought the Army of Justice, they were the ones who believed in me. For all intents and purposes, they are my family. I just want tonight to be special."

"I understand, My Lord. You have been blessed to have so many to support you. Your steward, Smallfolks, is an interesting man. He told me a great deal about your years in the Teardrop and about the Teardrop itself. He truly loves his home."

"I was concerned he wouldn't come to the Capital City at all. This is his first trek away from home."

"I was a young man when your grandfather became king. Although I served him for many years, I never heard the stories of his younger years in the Teardrop. Spending time there seems to have affected both you and your grandfather significantly."

"Well, don't believe everything Smallfolks says. It is always mostly true, but we have known him to distort things a bit."

"Have not we all?" Jamas replied. "It is time to go."

Merryk selected the smaller dining room overlooking the garden. Summer had fulfilled the promise of spring with flowers and bright bushes. The area outside the large windows was alive with colors and smells.

Merryk and Oolada stood by the door to welcome each person as they arrived.

"Father Bernard, thank you for agreeing to do our wedding ceremony," Oolada said.

"It is my pleasure and honor. I feel like I have known the two of you forever. I must admit, I have been looking forward to this service ever since I received your request."

"Father Xavier, how nice it is to see you again," Merryk said as the older priest entered. "Destiny seems to have woven us together. You always seem to appear at critical times. Having you here, now, seems most appropriate."

Father Xavier had grown slower with age, but his face still sparkled with an inner joy. "Yes, you and I have been bound together. I am sure neither of us knew my work on a wedding contract would end up here at the wedding of the king."

The swordmaster escorted Nelly and Smallfolks into the dining room. Merryk looked at the swordmaster and joked, "I see you haven't lost Smallfolks, yet."

"Lose me! Lose me! Was he supposed to lose me?" Smallfolks replied with a start.

"Of course not, Smallfolks, I knew he would keep an eye on you. Now, I want all three of you to find your places at the table," the king responded to assure Smallfolks.

"Thank you, Your Majesty," the swordmaster said as he guided the others toward the table.

Before they got very far, Oolada captured Nelly to give her a hug. "This evening, you are the guest," she said to Nelly. "Others will serve you. Merryk has vowed to send you to the dungeon if you dare try to help."

Merryk placed his arm around Nelly. "I can't tell you how good it is to see you. I understand Yonn had to threaten you to get you to allow Jane to take over in your absence."

"Jane is more than capable. I guess I worry she will do too good a job and they will no longer need me."

"Never fear. You will always be needed," Merryk said as he gave her a hug.

Yonn, Yvette, and Maizie were the next to arrive. Maizie had a new dress that stood out when she spun around. Finally, Chancellor Goldblatt joined the group.

The group chattered, sharing bits of news about the Teardrop. Yvette and Oolada were setting the schedule for shopping the next day.

After a few moments, everyone found their seats, and Merryk asked Father Xavier to give the blessing. The meal was one fitting for a king and a queen with multiple courses and additional conversation.

Before they served the dessert, Merryk rose from his seat. "If you will all indulge me. I can honestly say my life as Merryk began when I woke up in the Teardrop Castle. The people in this room have been my guardians, teachers, mentors, and most of all, my friends. I believe you are the ones who have made me what I am today. You are and forever will be my family.

"Tara is not with us this evening. I know how the news of her loss must have affected all of you. Destiny moved me forward, and an unbelievable act of evil took Tara away. But she would not want us to be sad. The Chancellor told me she had already selected Oolada as the Inland Queen. This was before anyone knew I was going to be king. But I guess she knew and was prepared, even if I wasn't. I know she will be with us as we go forward and would want us to celebrate this occasion."

Oolada reached out to clasp Merryk's hand. Merryk looked across the table. "Tonight is about celebration. I cannot express how pleased I am that everyone could come.

"I have several announcements. Bowen, please bring my sword. Oolada, if you and the Chancellor will assist me. Yonn and Yvette, please come forward. Yonn, take a knee." As Yonn dropped to one knee before the king, Merryk withdrew his grandfather's sword and placed the blade on Yonn's shoulder. "Yonn Gryson, I hereby bestow upon you the title of Count of the Teardrop Kingdom. You are a man born of the Teardrop. No one could love it more. You have fought at my side and even swore to follow me over a cliff. Your loyalty is without question, but more than anything else, you are my friend. There is no one more noble than you. Now you have the title which matches your heart."

Goldblatt stepped forward and opened a flat wooden box. Oolada withdrew a large medallion attached to a gold chain. "It is my honor to give you the badge of position. I know you and your children will wear it with honor," Oolada said.

"Arise, Count Yonn Gryson," Merryk said.

The rest of the room clapped their hands. Yvette gave Yonn a kiss. "What do you think of my sheepherder now?" Yvette asked with a smile in her voice.

Oolada hugged both Yonn and Yvette.

"Thank you, Your Majesty. I do not know what to say."

"Nothing is required. But I wonder if this would be an appropriate time to ask Maizie your question," Merryk suggested.

Yonn and Yvette nodded. Yonn began, "Maizie, please come here. We were wondering if it would be all right with you if we adopted you as our daughter. What would you think about that?"

Maizie's face was covered with a huge smile as she hugged Yvette tightly. "You would be my mother and father?"

"Yes, and when you are older, you could be a *Tessa*."

Maizie stopped for a moment, glanced at the king, then asked. "Would it be all right for me to continue to love Prince Merryk?"

"Absolutely," Yonn answered.

"Then, yes!" Maizie exclaimed.

When things calmed down a bit, Merryk said, "Maizie, have you decided on a name for the new foal?"

"I spoke with everyone, and it seems Maverick and Bella prefer Mischief. The little one does not talk much, but he is already getting into trouble, so Mischief is my choice."

"Very well. When Mischief is old enough to be away from Bella and Maverick, I will send him to you. He is now your horse."

"Really, I got a mother and father and a horse all on the same day. No one is going to believe this!" Maizie said, shaking her head from side to side.

Count Yonn turned to the swordmaster. "It seems my new position has deprived the Teardrop Guards of a commander. How does Commander Hugo sound to you?"

"Commander will be sufficient," the swordmaster said in his normal gruff voice.

"Nelly and Smallfolks, the Teardrop Castle is your home and will be so forever. In addition, I have granted you an annual stipend to spend as you will. Perhaps you will want to visit the Capital City from time-to-time," the king said.

"No offense, Your Majesty, but once is enough for Smallfolks. It is too big," the diminutive man replied.

"Thank you," was Nelly's only response, other than the tears streaming down her face.

CHAPTER 82

BIG DAY

Merryk's memory of the next two weeks was a blur of activity. Oolada and Kat first took Yvette, Nelly, and Maizie shopping. Later, they took Helga and Jamaal's wife on a similar excursion.

"For someone who liked to roam freely in the mountains, you certainly have taken to shopping in the city," Merryk teased Oolada.

She simply shrugged. "Just think of it as a different wilderness. Both filled with exciting opportunities."

Maizie insisted on visiting Mischief at least twice a day. So much so that Nelly memorized the route to the stable in order to free Yonn and Yvette to take part in the preparations.

Smallfolks and Jamas seemed to have a special connection. "We both have served Great King Mikael and you. There is much that we can share," Smallfolks said.

Being gone had stacked up a long list of official duties for Merryk. Chancellor Goldblatt had kept most under control, but some required Merryk's personal attention.

"Ambassador Crescent made exceptionally good progress on his trip. He returned with three full merchant ships from Queen Stephanie. The new Provost and the Council of Justice appreciated your offer to complete the Great Cathedral. They also are very interested in the proposal to act as the maritime tribunal. You should expect the Provost will want to discuss the proposal when he comes to officiate the coronation," Goldblatt said.

"I knew the duke would be the right man. Please arrange for me to talk with him before the Provost arrives," Merryk said. "I need him to know how much we appreciate his efforts."

"Oh, yes. Chancellor, did you have the chance to get my personal invitation to Monsieur Masterroff? I want him to join us. His years of being an outsider are over."

"Absolutely, Your Majesty. I delivered it to him personally. He also said he would love to have another evening with food and wine."

"It took three days before I was hungry after the last visit. But yes, I would like that as well."

As the date for the wedding and coronation drew near, the number of official tasks increased. *Today Queen Stephanie and Admiral Burat will arrive. I want to see them, but they will also stir memories. Oolada said I should embrace the memories. They are part of the story which brought us to this point. 'Tara would want you to remember the good.' Oolada always brings me back to the center.*

As the women moved through the city on one shopping adventure after another, Merryk found as much time as possible to spend with the men. First it was Yonn and the swordmaster. Later, Gaspar and Jamaal joined. *I wish I had more time with just this group.*

Unfortunately, the list of dignitaries grew by the day, preventing him from the time he wanted. Soon the rest of the Council of Walters arrived. Merryk and Oolada held a dinner in their honor. The same as they had done for Queen Stephanie and Admiral Burat, and for the new Provost and his entourage. *I remembered Jamas saying my father and mother enjoyed breakfast because every other meal was a matter of state. I now know what he meant.*

When the big day arrived, a warm breeze off the ocean escorted in the rising sun. The sky was a pure blue, not even a high wisp of clouds marred its luster.

"What a beautiful day," Queen Amanda said as she looked out the windows overlooking the inner court. "You could not have commanded it to be any better. Are you ready?"

"Ready for what—to be married, or to be crowned?" Merryk replied.

"Both, of course. Although it is hard to determine which is the most significant. For you, it is the marriage. For the kingdom, it is the coronation. And for our family, it is both."

"I'm glad the wedding is a smaller event with just the immediate family," Merryk said.

"It also makes the coronation possible. An Inland Queen removes all objections. You will have complied with the law."

"Right now, I don't much care about the niceties of the law of succession. I just want to marry Oolada," Merryk said emphatically.

The queen moved forward to give Merryk one last hug. "I hope you know how proud I am of you." Releasing her son. "Now it is time to go."

At the end of a long day, Merryk sank into the sofa in front of a warm fire. Oolada joined him. Merryk pulled her close and wrapped his arms around her. The two sat quietly for a moment, staring at the fire.

Oolada broke the silence. "Important days are filled with so many memories. It is hard to break them apart."

"I remember only the most important parts; like how beautiful you were in your wedding dress. You looked nothing like a warrior, and yet I saw the sparkle in your eyes. Later, when I put the crown on your head, in a flash, you were the queen—my warrior queen."

"Are you sure you are not remembering the endless reception line, or are you still lightheaded from lack of food?" Oolada's tone was mocking.

"I remember thinking we would never have a moment alone."

"But here we are, and it is just the first of many."

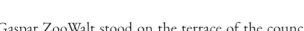

Gaspar ZooWalt stood on the terrace of the council chamber in Crag'd Zoo looking out toward the rising of the full moon. Helga located him and followed him out. "Here you are, searching the night sky. I am beginning to think you want to be the seer."

"Not hardly," Gaspar replied. "I was just thinking about how far we have come; not in distance, but how the status of the clans has changed."

Helga moved to wrap her arms around him. "Did you see the Walters sitting among the other noble houses at the coronation? The Duchess of Crescent and Jamaal's wife were chatting incessantly. And Aaron Gorg-Walter seemed to strike a friendship with Lord Bellows. We are no longer viewed as lesser houses. Destiny has fulfilled your wish."

"And do not forget, our Oolada is the queen," Gaspar said, barely able to suppress his joy.

Helga squeezed him tightly. "I told you it is not over until destiny chooses, and now, destiny has chosen."

"Certaninly, you must agree, King Merryk has shown himself to be the man of prophecy."

"I still believe he is a man of destiny and will do many great things. But only time will tell if he is the man of prophecy."

EPILOGUE

Doctor James Jamal ZooWalter walked up the stone stairs leading to the main doors of *The King Merryk and Queen Oolada Museum of History*. His eyes scanned the front of the great building. Although many additions had been added over the building's 2000-year history, the façade, columns, and the steps were the same as when they were built. King Merryk had insisted the museum have its own master stonemason, whose function he considered as important as the curators. Today, the stonemason held advanced degrees in structural engineering and architectural history, a far cry from a man with a chisel and hammer. The records indicated King Merryk said if the building had its own mason, it would always be new, not just repaired. *Well, you were certainly right.* James thought as he progressed up the stairs.

"Good morning, Dr. ZooWalter," a cheerful guard said, as he held the door open to the museum's head curator. "Are you excited about this evening?"

"I understand my excitement. I'm a historian," James said. "I would have thought the opening of a new permanent exhibit would have had a little less fanfare, but everyone seems to be looking forward to the event."

"The PR department has been running ads and blogs for the last six months," the guard replied. "Both the King and the Prime Minister will be here, and all the major networks will cover the entire opening. Yes, doctor, this is exciting for everyone."

"Well, I guess. Thanks Robert." Dr. ZooWalter walked across the massive foyer to the two fifteen-foot doors to the new exhibit. Over the opening, a banner hung:

The Golden Age of King Merryk and the High Kingdom
1000 Years of Glory

ABOUT THE AUTHOR

J R Clemons is a retired business executive and life-long resident of the Pacific Northwest. His family consists of his wife, their four daughters and nine grandchildren. All live within a fifteen minute drive of his home. J R grew up on classic science fiction, Dune and Foundation, although nothing impacted his view of storytelling more than Tolkien.

Books in **The Raymouth Saga**:
The Shell – *Book 1*
God's Tears – *Book 2*
Destiny's Choice – *Book 3*

Made in the USA
Middletown, DE
25 September 2023

39185124R00236